THE WIFE APP

CAROLYN MACKLER

SIMON & SCHUSTER

NEW YORK   LONDON   TORONTO   SYDNEY   NEW DELHI

Simon & Schuster
1230 Avenue of the Americas
New York, NY 10020

First Simon & Schuster hardcover edition June 2023

SIMON & SCHUSTER and colophon are registered trademarks of Simon & Schuster, Inc.

For information about special discounts for bulk purchases, please contact Simon & Schuster Special Sales at 1-866-506-1949 or business@simonandschuster.com.

The Simon & Schuster Speakers Bureau can bring authors to your live event. For more information or to book an event, contact the Simon & Schuster Speakers Bureau at 1-866-248-3049 or visit our website at www.simonspeakers.com.

Interior design by Erika R. Genova

Manufactured in the United States of America

10 9 8 7 6 5 4 3 2 1

Library of Congress Cataloging-in-Publication Data has been applied for.

ISBN 978-1-9821-5879-8
ISBN 978-1-9821-5883-5 (ebook)

For Jonas

Wages for housework is only the beginning, but its message is clear: from now on they have to pay us because as females we do not guarantee anything any longer. We want to call work what is work so that eventually we might rediscover what is love and create what will be our sexuality which we have never known. And from the viewpoint of work we can ask not one wage but many wages, because we have been forced into many jobs at once. We are housemaids, prostitutes, nurses, shrinks; this is the essence of the "heroic" spouse who is celebrated on "Mother's Day."

—SILVIA FEDERICI

THE
WIFE
APP

lauren

LAUREN ZUCKERMAN WAS GOING TO kill it as a Wife. She had her reservations, but the voice telling her *go for it* was louder than the internal warning that this would be a stress-filled slog that no person in their right mind should agree to. But the money was good and the app was growing and this was not the moment to turn anything down.

And so, on a Wednesday evening in January, she met up with Claudia Von Pelt, a cosmetics executive and mom to six-year-old Matthias. For this particular Wife gig, Claudia wanted Lauren to fly Matthias from New York City to Seattle. Then, eight days later, Lauren would fly back to Seattle and retrieve the child.

"My husband is working there this year and he doesn't like to go a month without seeing Matthias," Claudia explained as she gestured to a slight boy with a halo of blond curls. He sat cross-legged on the floor, staring at an iPad in a blue protective case. "I've been flying him out since September. My nanny is afraid of flying and my husband says he's too busy to make the trip here himself."

"I completely get it," Lauren said, even though she did *not* get it, or maybe she was done letting husbands hide behind "too busy." She ran her palm across Claudia's white leather couch. Who actually has a white couch? Definitely not someone with little kids. Lauren often witnessed her twin daughters, who at twelve couldn't be considered little, wipe their hands on furniture when they thought no one was looking.

Lauren studied Claudia's face as she told her the flight details and then they agreed on a price. Claudia had close-set eyes and collagen-puffed lips. She wore so much makeup it was hard to tell if she was thirty-five or fifty.

"I'll add a bonus if you can get Matthias to finish his homework on the plane. His teachers always send a packet when he misses a few days, and my husband blows them off." Claudia rolled her eyes. "First-grade homework is not in his wheelhouse."

Lauren glanced at Matthias, who other than a hasty hello hadn't looked up since she walked into the swank Upper East Side apartment. "Just put it in his backpack. I have daughters in middle school. I'm no stranger to homework."

Claudia reached for her phone, which was buzzing on the coffee table. As she did, Lauren pushed her wavy brown hair back from her face. Lauren's eyes were her most striking feature. On a cloudy day, they flashed steely gray. In the summer, her eyes were practically turquoise. The rest of Lauren was more ordinary. She had a square British chin, an olive complexion, and a straight nose with a slight bump at the bridge.

"It's all set," Claudia said as she rested her phone on her thigh. "I'll have Matthias ready in our lobby."

"I'll order a car with a booster seat," Lauren said. "We're going to have so much fun, right, Matthias?"

Matthias scowled at Lauren and stuck out his tongue.

"Sorry." Claudia laughed uncomfortably. "Boys will be boys."

Are we still making that excuse? Lauren wanted to say. *Shouldn't we aim higher with the next generation?*

Instead, she smiled and told her, "See you Saturday morning."

So here they were, Saturday morning, thirty thousand feet above the earth. Lauren had packed a Mary Poppins bag for the trip—cereal bars, gummy candy, activity books, Magic Tree House books, markers, construction paper. They would finish Matthias's homework! She would read to him! They would draw a picture to give to his dad when they landed!

Except there was a big glitch: Matthias refused to let go of his iPad. He played *Minecraft* in the car, watched *Captain Underpants* at the gate, and had to be bribed with candy to put down the screen during takeoff.

"Want a snack?" Lauren asked as the plane flew over Western New York, her childhood stomping grounds. Not that she could see much from this altitude.

"No," he grumbled. He was back to *Minecraft*.

"How about I read you a book?"

"No! I'm busy."

Lauren's cheeks flushed with annoyance, and she felt hot. She wriggled out of her blazer and folded it onto the aisle seat.

In the air above Ohio, Lauren suggested they do a word search from one of the activity books.

"I told you I'm busy!" Matthias said.

Lauren sighed. He was a certifiable little shit, but he wasn't her shit. And he was a shit she was getting paid to spend time with, so really, what could she do? Her best college friend, Sophie, had recommended a collection of short stories that Lauren downloaded a few weeks ago. Turning away from Matthias, she sipped her sparkling water, nibbled an apple-cinnamon cereal bar, and began to read.

An hour later, Matthias jammed his bony finger into her arm. "Wife Lady! I need to charge my iPad."

"It's Lauren," she said. She was grateful that the aisle seat was empty. The last thing she wanted, especially after this past year, was to have anyone witness her being degraded by a first grader. "Do you have a charger? We can plug it in."

"I dunno. My mom always does it for me."

Lauren glanced out the oval window at the Rockies—phew, more than halfway to Seattle—and then lifted up Matthias's backpack. She dug her hand around until she found a charger. As she plugged in the iPad, Matthias kicked his Velcro sneakers back and forth.

"Is it charging?" she asked him.

"I dunno. That's your job."

Lauren glanced at his screen. The battery life was a precarious three percent, but she didn't see the charging bolt. She briefly thought about letting it slide—let his iPad die!—but if he was this awful *with* the stupid screen, she couldn't imagine him without it. Lauren's other best friend, Madeline, had recently compared technology's effect on children's brains to the pharmaceutical industry's mishandling of opioids.

"It's not charging at this outlet," she said. "If you give me the iPad for a few minutes, I'll try the outlet next to me."

"But I'm in an important part of my build! You can't take it."

"Just for a second." Lauren clenched her teeth. She felt a longing for her own daughters. Cady and Amelia could be sassy, but they also knew when to tone it down. "If it charges at my outlet, we'll just trade seats."

Matthias passed over the iPad. As she leaned down to plug it in, her T-shirt slid up. Lauren reached behind her with one hand and pulled it back down.

"No." Lauren glanced at the screen. It was now at one percent.

"What do you mean? That never happens."

The screen went black.

"Noooo!" Matthias wailed. He unbuckled his seat belt, climbed onto his chair, and stabbed his finger into the button to summon the flight attendant.

"What are you doing?" Lauren asked, her voice rising. "Get down from there."

"If you can't fix this, Wife Lady, I'll find someone who can."

Passengers across the aisle were starting to stare. They had no idea about the app. They had no idea what she'd been through, what led her to this. All they knew was that her Veruca Salt knockoff was poised to ruin their flight.

Lauren unbuckled her seat belt, stood up, and turned off the button. With the reflexes of a snapping crocodile, Matthias snatched the iPad, still connected to the charging cable, and scrambled into the aisle.

"Does anyone have an outlet that works?" he shouted as he dashed toward the rear of the plane. "I need an outlet and I'm willing to pay for it."

Lauren lurched into the aisle. Back near the bathrooms, a flight attendant with a shiny bald head spotted Matthias. His eyes popped in surprise. Gripping the backs of chairs, Lauren started after Matthias.

"Lauren?"

Lauren froze, startled by the sound of her name. And then, an instant later, exponentially more startled by the person who'd said it.

"Wow, it *is* you." Gideon smiled at her from his aisle seat. "My god."

Lauren's heart pounded in her chest. Gideon Crane had been her boyfriend her senior year in high school. He played varsity tennis and had killer legs, mild acne across his temples, a thin scar under his left eye. They took AP chemistry together because Gideon wanted to go premed and Lauren was determined not to be the girl who dropped out of science. Lauren and Gideon were each other's firsts—first sex, first "I love you," first heartbreak. He broke up with her before they left for college on opposite coasts. She was headed to Vassar and he was going to Berkeley. He was trying to be practical but it shattered Lauren. *You will always be my Princess Bride*, Gideon wrote in her yearbook, referring to the movie they could quote by heart. When Lauren read his inscription, she sobbed so hard it felt like her insides were splitting.

"Gideon," Lauren managed to say. He had the early etchings of crow's feet and his hair was sprinkled with gray. But he still had those broad shoulders, those expressive eyebrows, those toasty brown eyes.

She had googled him over the years, of course. Point to someone who says they don't google exes, and that person is a liar. Just a few months ago, Lauren had told her friends that her Gideon searches never yielded results, and Sophie said that thing about how Doctors Without Borders guys are egotistical cowboys, then Madeline said, *Speaking of cowboys*. . . .

"When was the last time we saw each other?" he asked. "Like, almost twenty years?"

"It was right after I got married," Lauren said. It was an awkward lunch two months after she and Eric tied the knot. Should she tell Gideon that it had ended with Eric, that on a January morning almost a year ago, she discovered her marriage was a sham? Lauren glanced toward the rear of the plane. Matthias was whining to the flight attendant, his little face scrunched, his fingers gripping his iPad.

"That would have been fifteen years ago," Lauren added. She touched her hands to her hair, then slid her fingers down to the hips of her jeans. There were flakes of apple-cinnamon cereal bar on her left thigh.

"Oh . . . yeah . . . that seems about right."

"You were flying somewhere and on a layover in New York City." Lauren wished she had something to tie back her hair. She reached into her pocket but all she pulled out was a single faded Advil. "Was it India?"

"Probably. I was outside of Mumbai for two years. I'm always flying somewhere." Gideon gestured around the cabin of the plane. "This is my life."

"So you're still doing Doctors Without Borders . . . or I guess you call it MSF?" Lauren looked again at Matthias, whose high-pitched voice was getting louder. When she'd seen Gideon at that lunch years ago, she'd been struck by how far his rugged world seemed from her newly married Manhattan life where she and Eric spent weekends at open houses for two-bedroom co-ops on the Upper West Side.

"Yeah, still with MSF." Gideon rotated the phone in his hand. "I'm only in Seattle for a few days to deal with some business. Then I'm headed back to Uzbekistan. This might be my last field gig for a while. Long story."

Back in high school, Gideon had never been out of the country, not even across the border to Canada. He used to peer at the world map mounted on the wall in Lauren's house and say, *Let's close our eyes and touch the map. Wherever our fingers land, we'll go there together someday.* It was crazy to imagine he now lived in Central Asia.

"How's your sister?" Lauren asked. Gideon's little sister was two years younger—outgoing and smart—and she had often tagged along with them. In fact, when Lauren was a sophomore at Vassar, Katie Crane took the train to Poughkeepsie and slept over in Lauren's dorm room to check out the campus. She ended up going to Smith and they'd since lost touch.

"Katie's good," he said. "She's a high school teacher in Virginia. She's married, and they have a daughter."

There was a yelp from the back of the plane. Matthias had begun to stomp his feet. The flight attendant gestured to the iPad and shrugged as if to say, *You're out of luck, little brat.*

Gideon followed Lauren's look to the back of the plane. "Seems like your son is having a tough flight?"

"Oh no!" Lauren shook her head. "He's not my son. I mean, I have children. Twin daughters. Cady and Amelia. But definitely not that boy. I'm just . . . uh . . . flying him cross-country." Lauren coughed as she realized how bizarre her life had become these past few months. "It's a long story too."

"Congrats on having kids," Gideon said. "I hadn't realized that. I mean, I assumed but—"

"What about you?"

"No . . . uh . . . we . . ."

We. So Gideon was half of a *we.* Lauren had heard rumblings about his marriage through high school friends, maybe ten years ago. In the rear of the plane, Matthias cried louder. The flight attendant looked around desperately.

"I better go," Lauren said.

Gideon nodded. "I get it. Hey, are you staying in Seattle? It would be fun to catch up."

"I'm hopping on the next flight back to New York. Otherwise . . ." Lauren trailed off. She didn't have the emotional fortitude right now for interpersonal drama, especially if Gideon was nestled into a happy *we.*

"It really was good to see you," Lauren told Gideon.

"You too."

Gideon smiled at her, and Lauren's stomach ached with longing. She quickly waved goodbye and hurried to the back of the plane.

"You can have my phone," she said to Matthias after apologizing to the flight attendant. "It's at ninety percent. And a bag of Swedish Fish."

He wrinkled his upturned nose. "Do you have *Minecraft*?"

Lauren tried to remember what games her daughters had installed before they had phones of their own. "Maybe. I definitely have some games."

"*Minecraft* isn't just some *game.* And it's not like you'll have my world. But fine."

Two hours later, they landed in Seattle. Lauren was attempting to reclaim her phone when Gideon passed their row.

"My number," he said as he gave her a folded piece of paper. "Stay in touch."

"Thanks." Lauren pinched the paper between her finger and thumb and slid it into her pocket.

"It works internationally," Gideon offered. Then he wheeled his silver suitcase down the aisle and off the plane.

Lauren escorted Matthias to the baggage claim and handed him off to his father, a barrel-chested man who never jumped off his call—not to greet his son, not even to thank Lauren. *Ugh.* But not her problem. She stuffed a few Magic Tree House books in the boy's backpack, tousled his blond curls, and then circled around and got in the security lane. Her flight to Kennedy was in one hour.

As the eastbound plane steered toward the runway, Lauren sent a few rapid-fire texts to Claudia.

> **Lauren:** Matthias is with his dad. Regarding his pickup . . . I'm sorry but you're going to have to find someone else to do it. I'll cancel my flights and reimburse you for those expenses.

> **Lauren:** If you want to find a new Wife for the School Concierge Package, I understand.

> **Lauren:** Even a Wife has her limits.

Claudia didn't respond so Lauren tapped over to her text chain with her best friends, Madeline and Sophie.

> **Lauren:** You were right. I was wrong. Effective immediately, the Wife App no longer has direct contact with children. My flight to Seattle was every single nail in that coffin.

Lauren: Also, guess who was on my plane?

Lauren: Think high school boyfriend. Think first love.
Think cowboy.

Lauren texted them an emoji face with gritted teeth. Then she powered down her phone, ordered a glass of white wine, finished a short story, and slept the rest of the way to New York City.

ONE YEAR BEFORE

lauren

LAUREN ZUCKERMAN'S WIFE ALARM BELLS sounded and so, at 6:57 a.m. on January 20, she slid her husband's phone across the bedside table to have a snoop. Eric had left it there on his way into the bathroom. He often dropped his phone on the bedside table, along with Lauren's coffee, which he delivered to her every morning before he headed into the shower. If Lauren had to grade their marriage of fourteen years, she would give them low Bs and high Cs. They had a hectic life on the Upper West Side of Manhattan. They juggled their careers, their twin eleven-year-old daughters, the occasional date night in Tribeca or the West Village when Lauren got her act together to score a dinner reservation. Then factor in Eric's work travel, Lauren's less frequent work travel, and the nonstop demands from the girls' school as if none of the other obligations in their life existed. Sometimes the only way Lauren and Eric connected was a functional fuck before they fell asleep. But the daily wake-up coffee from Eric? That scored a solid A.

Lauren's pulsed raced as she cupped Eric's phone in her hand. But she didn't have time to lose. He wasn't a marathon shower guy. She only had three to four minutes to see if there was any validity to her hunch that her husband was up to no good.

Maybe Lauren was being paranoid. But it was hard to forget five years ago, right after her mom died of ovarian cancer, when Eric had that affair. Lauren was a disaster during the entire time her mom was sick— six months from diagnosis to death—and she'd lost interest in sex. She squirmed away if Eric cupped her breasts as she undressed. She didn't want him to spoon her in bed. When Eric got back from the annual Consumer Electronics Show in Vegas three months after they cremated her mom, he confessed that he'd had stupid, drunken conference sex.

Lauren considered demanding a divorce. Everyone thinks infidelity is their line in the sand until it happens to them. But they went to couples counseling and took up hiking and did the work to save their relationship. She told herself it was worth saving. Lauren loved her family of four. She didn't want to throw it away because Eric messed up once, and neither did he.

But every now and then the bells went off.

Last night, Eric went out drinking with other lawyers from his investment firm. He'd gotten in after midnight. Usually when Eric came home high on wine, he prodded her awake with his erection. But all she remembered from her melatonin-induced coma was the chill of him tugging away more than his share of the comforter.

It was a relief not to have to stir awake for sex. Lauren had a big freelance deadline this week. To add to her stress, she'd volunteered until 9:00 p.m. on the silent auction committee for the girls' new middle school. But the fact that Eric *wasn't* horny last night was odd. Lauren's best friends, Sophie and Madeline, didn't believe that Eric Turner— geeky lawyer and middle-aged dad—had developed an insatiable libido over the past few years. But he had. Lauren told herself it was better than the married moms she gossiped with on playground benches who confessed to months-long dry spells. Sometimes the sex with Eric was good, especially if she was ovulating and her body craved it. Other times Lauren went through the motions in the same way she tackled a sink of dishes or filled out those endless back-to-school forms.

Lauren rarely turned Eric down. If she did, she worried he'd look elsewhere. His company, Equity Investors, had recently hired a few young, female data analysts—slim, stylish women straight out of business school. They were librarian-hot, totally Eric's type. Lauren used to be slim, stylish, and librarian-hot, but try being pregnant with twins. Try seeing what forty does to your metabolism. Lauren had turned forty last summer. Not over the hill, but she could no longer eat cheese fries with reckless abandon.

The other thing that triggered Lauren's Wife Alarm Bells was a random text from Eric at 9:47 p.m. She'd just gotten home from the school auction, paid the sitter, and checked to make sure the girls were asleep. She was unclipping the leash from their goldendoodle when her phone chirped with a text from her husband.

Eric: Hey.

That's all he wrote.

Why would a husband text *hey* to his wife while he's drinking with colleagues? That's what a frat bro texts to a girl he's lining up for a booty call. Lauren waited a minute and then texted him back.

Lauren: What's up with hey?

Eric didn't respond, so Lauren called him. No answer. That wasn't a surprise. Eric rarely picked up her calls. When Cady was nine and broke her arm on the monkey bars, Lauren couldn't get through to Eric until their daughter was already casted and home from the emergency room. If Lauren were generous, she'd say that Eric ignored her texts and calls because he had the uniquely male ability to hyper-focus on work. After another minute, Lauren tapped open Life360 and located Eric. He seemed to be at a bar in midtown, so she turned her phone to silent, swallowed 3 mg of melatonin, and brushed her teeth.

Lauren took another sip of coffee, wiggled her toes under the sheets, and tapped in Eric's password. It was comically easy—the month and year he graduated from Columbia Law. As her finger hovered over his text app, she felt a stab of guilt. Maybe she shouldn't check. It had been five years since that conference. Then again, what's the worst that could happen if she dug around? At the least, she could get a heads-up if her mother-in-law had invited them to Brookline for Presidents' Day weekend. Or she could see if Eric had a work trip he'd forgotten to mention. It wouldn't be the first time.

Feeling a fresh surge of annoyance at her husband, Lauren twisted her wavy brown hair into a loose knot and opened his texts. His last message was a receipt from Uber at 12:14 a.m. Fine. Innocent. She glanced at the previous text.

"Oh my god!" Lauren gasped.

Don't look. She shook her head rapidly from side to side. *Don't read more. You don't want to know.*

But she'd seen enough to know that she had to keep reading.

Eric: Hey.

646-555-7613: Oh, Eric! Our favorite client.

Eric: Does Molly have time tonight? Around 10:30?

646-555-7613: Yes! Is 11pm okay? Same as last week?

Eric: Perfect.

646-555-7613: We look forward to seeing you again. We've moved to a new suite. We're still at the same address but now on the 3rd floor.

As Lauren heard Eric's shower shut off, the coffee bounced in her gut. Where the fuck was her husband a "favorite client"? And who was *Molly*?

Carolyn Mackler

16

The bathroom faucet turned on. Lauren heard the tap of Eric's razor on the edge of the sink. Her fingers were shaking so hard it took three attempts, but she finally copied and pasted last night's address into a search bar. Nothing. Next she googled the 646 phone number.

We offer discreet sexual services to discerning male clientele.

Lauren wanted to collapse into her pillow in tears. *Eric? Hon? Did you really go to some woman named Molly and pay for sexual services?* Her throat tightened. There was no denying that her husband really did this, that in this exact moment on her bed she was hovering between a before and an after.

Before Lauren could descend into nine million circles of hell, she needed to get proof. She quickly took a screen grab of the site and the texts and sent them from Eric's phone to hers. Lauren had the tech prowess to know that despite common assumptions it would be hard to fully hide that she'd been on Eric's phone. But she didn't care at this point.

She also wanted to loop in Sophie and Madeline, get her friends on board for her impending major fucking meltdown. Except that her phone was docked in the kitchen where Cady and Amelia were likely hunched over bowls of Honey Nut Cheerios. If Lauren ventured out there she'd get snared in their morning BS and she couldn't deal right now.

Hang on!

Eric had Sophie and Madeline as contacts in his phone. Back when Sophie was married to Joshua and Madeline was married to Colin, the six of them hung out as couple friends. Lauren and Eric were the last marriage standing. Not for long.

Lauren's teeth chattered as she wrote a group text to Sophie and Madeline.

Eric: It's Lauren not Eric. Check out these screenshots.

THIS is what I just discovered on Eric's phone. Turns out

what happened in Vegas didn't stay in Vegas. Guys, I
think my marriage is over. Don't write back to me here.

As soon as she sent the text and the screenshots, Lauren deleted her tracks from Eric's phone as best she could. Then she ran to the bathroom, shoved past her naked husband, and vomited her coffee into the toilet.

NINE MONTHS LATER

lauren

LAUREN WAS NO LONGER A wife. Three minutes ago, she signed the final page of her divorce agreement. Her lawyer offered her a sweaty handshake, a travel pack of tissues, and a shiny pen with his name embossed in gold letters. As Lauren rode down in the elevator she wondered if she was a moron for doing this.

Not for getting divorced, but for agreeing to meet her newly minted ex-husband for coffee. Eric's office was five blocks from her lawyer. They still had their daughters together and nearly two decades of shared history. Even though Lauren wanted to kill Eric more days than not, she was committed to the idea of conscious uncoupling. Also, their divorce process had been extraordinarily smooth. Lauren was grateful enough to Eric for this that, sure, she could do coffee.

As she crossed the lobby of the office building, she chucked the lawyer's pen in the security guard's trash bin and examined herself in the tall mirror. There were mascara smudges under her gray-blue eyes. She desperately needed a haircut. Self-care had been exiled to the bottom of her to-do list ever since that awful January morning when she found out that her husband had a hankering for two-hundred-dollar hand jobs.

Lauren gave herself one more hard look in the mirror. At least she wasn't wearing her ratty fleece and yoga pants. She had on a new polka-dot dress, tall boots, and her knee-length fall coat that she was pleasantly surprised to discover still fit.

Later this evening, Lauren, Sophie, and Madeline had a dinner reservation at Lincoln Ristorante. They'd exchanged more than thirty texts to choose the right place for Lauren's post-divorce celebration dinner. Should it be uptown, downtown, Michelin-starred, classy, hipster? They'd finally settled on The Lincoln, as Madeline called it. Madeline said it was elegant but not a party scene. That was a must for Lauren. While she was relieved the legal headache was over, she was also deeply sad.

As Lauren waited for the light to change, she texted the sitter to confirm she'd be at the apartment when Cady and Amelia got home after school. It was a new babysitter. They'd used Trish for the past few years, until recently when she stopped returning Lauren's texts. No major loss. Trish was a twenty-three-year-old aspiring fashion designer with massive breasts and zero initiative to help the girls with their homework or do anything that required her to set down her phone. Trish used to linger after Lauren and Eric got home from date nights, asking where they ate and what movie they saw. Then she'd make a big display of sliding her phone into her bra. After Trish left, Lauren would alternately seethe to Eric about sitters who overstay or would worry aloud that the next generation of women will wind up with rectangular tumors in their breasts.

It was frigid for early October. Lauren breathed in the chilly air and then pushed through the door of the café. Eric was at a table by the window, looking down at his phone. He didn't notice her, so she watched him for a moment. He'd grown a beard. His hair was strawberry blond, like Cady's, and his beard had come in with flecks of orange. The only other time she'd seen Eric with a beard was the summer before they married. They'd borrowed his parents' spare car, a maroon Toyota, and zigzagged around the country, camping and having sex in countless national parks. On their eastern swoop toward home, he went down on her in their steamy tent in Shenandoah National Park. Even now, fifteen years later, she could feel the pebbles jabbing into her spine and the bristle of his facial hair as he thrust his tongue inside her.

Remembering that, Lauren leaned against the wall of the café to steady herself. Just as she did, Eric looked up from his phone and pushed back his chair. She latched her arms protectively across her chest. She could feel it in the space between them—the palpable sorrow. Yes, he'd paid for those hand jobs, but that was just part of their story. They'd also eaten thousands of meals together, laughed at movies, and binge-watched shows. They'd held hands when airplanes took off and during her mom's memorial and his dad's funeral. He'd held her hand when the obstetrician sliced open her abdomen and pulled out their two daughters.

Lauren's knees were watery as she walked toward his table. She hoped he wouldn't hug her because she already felt like crying.

"Thanks for meeting me," he said. He widened his arms to bring her in.

Lauren shot her palms out like a traffic guard halting an oncoming truck.

"Don't!" she said, probably too loudly. She slid out the chair on the other side of the table and tumbled into it.

"Are you okay?" he asked.

"Of course I'm not okay. I'm awful, Eric. What do you think?"

Lauren examined her chapped hands and willed herself not to cry. To fight off the tears, she conjured up a mental image of Eric with his erection out. Sandy pubic hair coated his groin. A sex worker slathered lube on while Eric grimaced and groaned and made those pre-ejaculation faces that she knew so well. Most days, Lauren didn't dwell on this imagery. But when the pain of no longer being married felt unbearable, it helped to remind herself *exactly* why their marriage was over.

"I love that red coat on you," he said as he drummed his fingers from pinky to pointer on the tabletop. "I remember when you ordered it. You look great."

Eric was making her work hard not to cry. Of course he was. He seemed to enjoy making her work.

"Thanks," Lauren said even though Eric was full of shit. In her twenties and well into her thirties, she'd coasted on her natural good looks. She rarely wore makeup, just a little mascara and gloss. Men loved the solo dimple in her right cheek. These days, though, Lauren felt pale and flabby and exhausted. There was no way it didn't show.

"I mean it." Eric ran his hand over his beard. "It's good to see you. I'm glad you were able to meet. I wanted to find a few minutes to check in after we signed everything."

Lauren stretched her neck from side to side. "You grew a beard," she said.

"I was ready to try something new."

Their waiter showed up. Eric ordered a coffee and Lauren asked for an Americano with almond milk. They talked about the girls—Cady and Amelia had just started seventh grade, and were both petitioning for upgraded iPhones for Christmas.

"Do you think we should do it?" Eric asked. "They just got new phones a year and a half ago."

Lauren swallowed hard. She wanted to inform him that, as of this afternoon or maybe as of nine months ago, *they* were not a *we* anymore. Instead she said, "You'll have them for presents in the afternoon. I'm not going to do phones so that gift idea is all yours."

"It's going to be sad not having Christmas morning all four of us," Eric said now. He pushed his lower lip out. "Maybe we should do it together, for old times' sake."

Lauren stared at him. Eric had never done crap for Christmas. Every December, she picked up the stocking stuffers. She interfaced with the grandparents about whatever was on the girls' letters to Santa.

She frosted sugar cookies and played Christmas carols and wrapped embarrassing mounds of presents and signed them "Love, Mom and Dad" as if Eric had any part of it except that he'd helped pay. *Helped.* Through their entire marriage, Lauren always worked, always contributed to the family pot.

Lauren paid her dues to get Christmas morning and she wasn't sharing it, even as he blinked at her with sad eyes that made her stomach twist. Luckily, the waiter came over with their drinks. The light was silvery outside the café, with early evening shadows around the edges. A guy nearby took a selfie with a croissant. A woman giggled into a video call.

Lauren pressed her thumbs into her temples. "Let's keep the holidays where they are. It's less complicated that way. Plus, we've already told the girls. Is this what you wanted to talk about?"

"Right." Eric coughed into his fist. He lifted his water glass to his mouth and took a long drink. When he set it down, he cleared his throat. "There's actually something I need to tell you. I'm in a relationship with a woman. The girls don't know yet. I wanted to tell you first."

Lauren stared at Eric. She tried to process what he just said . . . *I'm in a relationship with a woman* . . . but she was having a hard time registering the words. This was her husband. *Ex-husband.* They had been together and now he was with someone else and she had to sit across from him and figure out how to react.

"Does she know?" Lauren said before she even knew the words were in her brain.

"Know what?"

"About the sex workers. The hand jobs."

Eric jerked backward as if Lauren had slapped him. "Do you really want to go there?"

"Yes." Lauren gripped her mug. "I do, actually. Since you dragged me here to tell me this, I want to know if you told your new girlfriend why our marriage ended."

Eric looked around the café the way you search for emergency exits in crowded theaters.

"So?" Lauren pressed.

"I didn't see any good reason to tell her."

"Well, I think she deserves to know. That you were a *favorite client*, for fuck's sake. She should know what she's getting herself into."

Eric set down his coffee. "I messed up, Lauren. I'm sorry. Jesus. Is that what you want to hear? But I also think it's obvious that what I did was a symptom of my unhappiness in our marriage. I wanted out."

Lauren did *not* see that coming. For nine months, she'd waited for him to say he was sorry. She wanted begging. Groveling. And here was this watered-down apology chucked at her like a regifted birthday present.

"What are you even talking about?" Lauren's fists tingled with anger. "When did you start wanting out? Why didn't you mention that in our marriage counseling?"

All those forty-five-minute sessions with their couple's therapist on West End Avenue. The counselor, with her pillowy chins and flowing Eileen Fisher tunics, talked to them about recovery after sexual infidelity and how you can have many marriages within the same marriage. What a waste of time! Lauren could have taken a ceramics class. An investment class. She could have learned how to make goddamn mozzarella cheese.

"Hang on," Eric said. "I didn't come to fight about our marriage. We're divorced now. We can move on. I wanted to tell you so you don't hear it from someone else. The person I'm with . . . It's someone you know."

Lauren inhaled sharply, her lungs tight. She scanned her mental database for who Eric could possibly be fucking. Cute teachers from elementary school? Random single women in their building? One of her friends behind her back? No. Sophie and Madeline would never.

"It's Trish," Eric said. "Trish and I are together."

"Trish the *babysitter*?" Lauren shrieked, and then she laughed in astonishment. "I thought you said you were in a relationship with a *woman*."

"That's not fair. Trish turned twenty-four in September."

"Don't talk to me about fair." Lauren coughed dryly. "So Trish can vote. Trish can buy beer. But she's closer in age to Cady and Amelia than to us. How long has this been going on? Months? Eric, were you cheating on me with *Trish*?"

Eric's temples were dotted with perspiration. It was like he just realized it was a terrible idea to invite his brand-new ex-wife to a café to tell her he was having sex with the babysitter.

"I asked Trish to babysit in August when the girls were with me," he said. "It started then. The girls don't know yet. I'm not sure when I'm going to tell them."

Tell Cady and Amelia? They'd been through so much with the divorce and the stress of middle school. Also, of all the women in this city of available women, Eric was sticking it in *Trish*? At best, she seemed dull. At worst? Slightly dumb. Lauren imagined Eric's beard bristling Trish as he ate her out while she lay there . . . watching TikToks?

"I realize Trish has been over to help you since then." Eric squirmed in his seat. "It made her uncomfortable. That's why she stopped returning your texts."

"Do you understand the irony of this?" Lauren asked. She hated to think of Eric and Trish talking about her behind her back. "I paid the person you're having sex with to watch *your* children but when you and I were together I watched them for free?" Lauren reached for her bag and her coat and stood up. "Don't *ever* tell the girls about this."

"Hang on," Eric called after her, but she didn't turn around.

Lauren didn't know if she wanted to laugh or cry as she walked to Columbus Circle. She eventually went with tears. She wasn't so innocent to imagine that Eric would wait until after the divorce. But *the babysitter*? And what was that bullshit about wanting out of their marriage? The summer before last, when the girls were at camp, they'd taken a four-day hiking trip in Vermont. When they weren't focused on the rocky footing or making it up a mountain, they laughed together and talked about how solid their relationship felt. He even said he won the wife lottery. *His words.*

As Lauren started down the stairs to the subway platform, she wiped her eyes with the sleeve of her coat. She desperately needed to burrow under her covers and sleep this shitty day off. Maybe she could grant the girls unlimited screen time, order them burritos, and beg them not to bicker.

But then she remembered—she had dinner with Sophie and Madeline in an hour and a half! She *had* to cancel. She was in no mood to celebrate. She definitely wasn't ready to tell them about Trish, to analyze it from various angles, to find the humor in Eric's latest transgression. Then again, Sophie had hired a sitter for her children tonight as well. And Madeline had gone overboard with the restaurant selection. Not to mention that if Lauren bailed on her own sitter she'd be marooned at home like every other evening.

No, it would be good to be out. Lauren could use a laugh with her best friends and a few drinks to calm her nerves. In the meantime, she was across the street from the Shops at Columbus Circle. She could kill time browsing the pricey boutiques, maybe treat herself to something extravagant that she couldn't afford now that she was no longer married.

madeline

MADELINE WALLACE HAD HER SHARE of first-world problems, and some meatier problems too. But right now, on this Thursday evening in October, her life felt perfect. Screw the judgers. She donated to charities. She volunteered for the homeless. She chaired committees at her daughter's school. Bottom line, she paid her karmic dues.

As Madeline puttered around her spacious kitchen in a red-striped Williams-Sonoma apron, her fourteen-year-old daughter, Arabella, practiced cello in her bedroom. Madeline was meeting her friends at a restaurant tonight for Lauren's post-divorce celebration. Arabella could easily order dinner, but Madeline loved to cook for her. Call it a passion. She definitely wasn't passionate about the procurement of groceries. Thankfully her housekeeper, Willow, took care of all that. Every week, Madeline texted Willow a grocery list and, like domestic magic, ingredients appeared in her fridge on the days she needed them.

Recently Arabella told her mom that she wanted to go more vegetarian-slash-pescatarian, so Madeline was test-driving a recipe she found on Epicurious. Quinoa with roasted butternut squash and feta, hold the pomegranate seeds because those made Arabella's lips swell.

Madeline was such a kick-ass chef that sometimes she wondered if she should start a catering business. She'd completed a year of B-school at Stern before dropping out because she got pregnant with Arabella. But, truth be told, she didn't need the money, so why take on the stress of catering? Madeline had inherited a lot of money at fourteen, when her dad died, and even more when her trust fund matured. Of course, Madeline would give anything to have her father instead of the money, but the millions he left behind made it possible for her to devote her life to raising her daughter. Madeline jokingly referred to herself as the CEO of Arabella's Life. But Madeline could afford to do it, all while cooking lavish meals, and volunteering, and hitting the gym, and having sex with men from meet-up apps when she had the apartment to herself.

Screw the judgers!

She and Colin had been divorced for a decade. She was thirty-nine years old and had yet to experience a libidinal dip. If the tables were turned and a single man worked the hookup apps the way Madeline did, he would be celebrated.

Madeline opened the oven and pushed around the cubes of butternut squash that burbled deep orange in the ceramic roasting pan. They smelled sweetly fragrant, like apple orchards and fall in New England. She set the timer for six more minutes, then checked the quinoa. Across the apartment, Arabella's cello had stopped. She studied cello at the prestigious Juilliard Pre-College program, the most rigorous music school in the country. It required one hundred percent dedication from the child, and total support from the parents, which Arabella had, at least from Madeline. Colin lived in London so he wasn't part of the cello scene, other than to fly over for concerts a few times a year. But, truly, Madeline had no beef with Colin. When Arabella visited her dad, Colin made sure she showed up for virtual lessons with her cello teacher. Which Madeline set up, of course. Because she was the CEO of Arabella's Life. But all joking aside, the commitment to cello was driven by her daughter.

Which was why it was surprising to hear silence from Arabella's bedroom. Usually when she practiced—an hour in the morning and two hours at night—she rarely took a break, except to dash out to the kitchen for water.

"Everything okay, sweetie?" Madeline paused her podcast and called across their apartment. It was just the two of them in this large penthouse on Central Park West. Maybe it was extravagant, but Madeline could afford it. Let people talk. She had long since stopped caring what people thought of her.

There was a brief pause and then Arabella said, "No, it's fine. Sorry. I just got distracted."

"Ah . . . got it."

Madeline rinsed the cutting board and a few knives. Arabella resumed playing the Bach Cello Suite No. 2 in D Minor. As music filled the apartment, Madeline dried her hands on the dish towel, then took her long dark hair out of its clip and shook it around her shoulders. Madeline was tall, nearly five ten, and people often called her stunning. It was hard to assess her own beauty but Madeline saw her looks reflected in her daughter. Madeline and Arabella had tilted brown eyes with full lashes, broad smiles, willowy frames. More than once, especially in her twenties, Madeline had been approached by modeling scouts. Any day now, her daughter would get asked about modeling too. That happened when you lived in New York City, and Madeline was already prepared with her answer: It's your choice if you want to model as long as you can manage cello and school. If and when this came up, Madeline was confident that Arabella would follow her advice. They were an airtight team.

In the bedroom, the cello stopped again. Madeline wiped her hands on her apron, crossed the apartment, and peeked into her daughter's open door. Arabella sat with her cello between her thighs, the sheet music propped on the stand in front of her, as she typed away on her phone. Her long hair was pulled into a messy bun. As soon as she noticed her mom, her mouth dropped open.

"Oh . . . Mom," Arabella said. She set her phone facedown on the floor, picked up her bow, and played a quick scale. Her fingers trembled with vibrato as they danced over the strings. "Sorry, I got distracted."

"You know what Mei says," Madeline told her. Mei Chien was Arabella's cello teacher.

"She says don't practice with my phone in the room. Or turn it to 'do not disturb.' She says it's impossible not to get distracted."

"Exactly." Madeline glanced around her daughter's room. The walls were painted lavender with a plum trim, Arabella's favorite colors in middle school. Now that she was in ninth grade, she'd recently asked her mom if they could change the color to off-white. Madeline already had a call in to the painter.

Arabella hugged the neck of her cello and wrinkled her nose. Her nose was narrow like Madeline's, with a lift at the tip. It was the same nose that Madeline's mom, Bianca, had endured two nose jobs to achieve. "There's just a lot going on right now," she said.

"Like what?" Madeline crooked her head to one side. She hadn't heard any rumbles of school or friend drama. "Anything you want to talk about?"

Arabella's cheek twitched nervously. "Did you get Dad's email?"

Across the apartment, the alarm for the butternut squash beeped once, twice, then three times before going silent.

"Is Dad okay?" Madeline asked. She and her ex-husband had a decent rapport, meaning she didn't hate Colin the way Lauren and Sophie hated their exes. There hadn't been cheating, or financial woes, or even any knock-down, drag-out fights. Colin Smith had been a finance guy, obsessed with work, eager to return to his native England. Madeline had just finished her first year at NYU's Stern Business School when she found out she was pregnant. She was a star student and hotly pursued by investment firms. Much to everyone's surprise, she dropped out to marry Colin and raise her daughter. The sexual chemistry was there but the baby demanded so much attention that she never had the mental space to consider what it meant to leave a career, to marry young. They spent five years going through the motions of husband and wife. When Colin got the opportunity to manage a hedge fund in London, she was relieved to call the marriage quits. The few times a year that they saw each other, they ate in restaurants and walked through Central Park like old friends.

"Dad's fine," Arabella said. She loosened her bow and then tightened it again. "It's just . . . there's something he needs to tell you. Dad does. He emailed you. That's what he just texted me about. About what he needs to tell you."

Madeline reached into her back pocket for her phone. There was something about the stilted way that Arabella was talking that put her nerves on high alert.

"I haven't gotten an email," Madeline said. "Let me look. . . ."

As Madeline tapped her phone awake, Arabella squinted at her sheet music. She shuffled one page to the side and replaced it with another.

"Oh," Madeline said quietly. There it was. An email from Colin. Subject line, *Arabella*. Madeline could feel her daughter's eyes looking at her, then away, then on her again. She tried to keep her mouth steady as she read her ex-husband's email but her chin began to wobble.

"Mom?" Arabella slid her hand up and down the neck of her cello. It was a stunning Italian cello that she and Arabella picked out in August. They flew to Boston to make this massive purchase after a six-month nationwide search. Madeline and Arabella, the airtight duo.

The timer beeped in the kitchen again.

"Mom?" Arabella asked. "You look pale."

This was the moment that Madeline was supposed to say something wise, but her mind was blank.

"I should turn the timer off," she said.

She tucked her phone into the pocket of her apron and walked slowly toward the kitchen. As she passed through the living room, she felt the wood floor tilt under her and she suddenly pictured their penthouse crashing down to the marble lobby, through the damp basement, deep into the bedrock that propped up Manhattan.

sophie

"Mommy, do you have to go out tonight?"

"Yes," Sophie told her younger son, Charlie, for the third time. He was seven and had separation issues.

"Why?" he asked. He stood in the living room, swinging a yo-yo from his fingers, which were covered in Band-Aids.

"Because we're meeting Lauren." Sophie tucked her bobbed blond hair behind one ear. She could feel sticky sweat under her arms and weighed whether she should escape the apartment or duck back into the bathroom for another layer of deodorant. "Madeline and I are taking her out."

"But why can't you do it next week?" Charlie peeled off a Band-Aid and dug at his finger. He had Sophie's thick blond hair and her small stature but her ex-husband Joshua's dark eyes that flashed inky black when he got upset. "I don't understand why you can't do it next week when we're at Daddy and Beatrice's?"

As always, Sophie flinched at the mention of her ex-husband's new wife, Beatrice. Sophie was over the divorce anger. In fact, she felt relieved to have that behind her. But Joshua's beautiful Family 2.0 had definitely set her back a few degrees on the coping scale. She reached into the hall closet for her tan jacket.

Charlie whimpered as Sophie slid her arms into the sleeves. Her older son, Noah, tapped away at his laptop on the couch. He said it was homework but if Sophie rotated the screen around she was almost certain he was checking soccer scores. *Whatever.* All she could focus on was getting out the door without Charlie having a meltdown. She didn't have to meet her friends for over an hour, but she was paying a babysitter—a rare luxury in Sophie's broke existence—so she wanted to take advantage of every child-free moment.

Speaking of, where was Kristen? Sophie had dispatched her to the tiny alcove kitchen to put in the frozen pizza and slice a few carrots. But how long did that take? Sophie's entire apartment was eight hundred square feet so Kristen could no doubt hear Charlie right now. Weren't sitters paid to peel worried children from their parents? Kristen came recommended from a mom of one of Sophie's students; it was time for her to step up.

Charlie's mouth puckered. "If I miss you and I want to say good night, can I use Noah's phone and call you?"

Noah shook his spiky brown hair in annoyance. At twelve, Noah was already tall and handsome like Joshua. He didn't know it yet, but his looks were going to get him far—perhaps too far.

"You don't need to call me," Sophie said. She touched her face with one hand. She had a peaches and cream complexion but when she got worked up her cheeks turned apple-red. "I'll only be gone for a few hours. I'll be here when you wake up tomorrow morning."

"Can I call Daddy then?" Charlie asked.

"Quit it," Noah said. "You know Dad has some famous client tonight. He told you that when you called him a few hours ago."

"But—"

Sophie craned her head toward the kitchen. *Where is Kristen?* Also, what famous client did Joshua have? He ran a recording studio in Tribeca, mostly recorded books, but sometimes VIPs came at night. She got all this from her sons. Back when they were together, Joshua was still with the band and mostly freeloaded off her slim salary as a literacy teacher.

"What about Beatrice?" Charlie asked. "Can I call her?"

Beatrice Allen, their stepmom, Joshua's wife, mother to the boys' baby half sister Clementine. Sophie wanted to hate Beatrice because Joshua was such a narcissistic jerk and he didn't deserve good in his life. But Beatrice made it hard. A successful estate lawyer, Beatrice had a warm smile, long black hair, and golden eyes. Every time Sophie met her, she was nothing but lovely.

As Charlie awaited her response, Sophie zipped her purse, then arranged her mouth in a neutral smile. "Of course you can call Beatrice if you want to say good night," she said. "I'm sure she'd like that."

Thankfully Kristen emerged from the kitchen.

"Hey, Charlie!" Kristen said. "Want to play a game? Or I can show you pictures of my dog on my phone!"

Charlie eyed the babysitter suspiciously, but Sophie took advantage of the brief distraction. She waved goodbye, dashed through the front door, and hurried down the four flights of stairs. She stepped over a crack in the sidewalk and a spilled bag of trash, then glanced up at her five-story building with the rusty fire escape clinging to the faded bricks. The lights in her living room glowed bright. Hopefully all was calm. She'd have to trust Kristen to deal.

As Sophie walked toward Columbus, she quickly scrolled through Instagram to keep tabs on who she should be jealous of tonight. There was the usual bevy of happy couples, well-adjusted kids, expensive meals, and home renovations. With a sigh, Sophie closed social media and slid her phone back in her purse. It was a blustery evening, but she needed the walk to clear her head. If she had a few extra minutes, she'd pop into her favorite indie bookstore on the way downtown.

In a perfect world, Sophie had money to buy every novel her heart desired, but it was not a perfect world. As things stood, she took pictures of hardcovers in the bookstore and ordered them from the library. It was what it was. What Sophie's life lacked in extravagance, she made up for in fiction. When she read, she could tune out her dumpy apartment, her jerk ex, and her kids' bottomless pit of needs. And if one novel didn't provide the right escape, well, she could close the cover and simply open a new one.

lauren

It was time to meet Sophie and Madeline. Even though her shopping expedition yielded only a pair of socks for Amelia, a sports bra for Cady, and nothing for herself, she had to wrap it up. As Lauren hurried past the fountain at Lincoln Center, she looked up to admire the massive, swirling Chagall murals in the window of the Metropolitan Opera. Marc Chagall had been her mom's favorite painter. Lauren couldn't believe her mom had been dead for over six years. She couldn't believe Eric was sleeping with the babysitter. At least the Chagalls remained extraordinary.

Lincoln Ristorante boasted an elegant exterior with walls of glass overlooking Lincoln Center and a sloped roof covered in grass. It was all very beautiful, and Lauren was grateful she hadn't canceled. And there was Sophie Smart! A minute before six and she was right in front. No surprise. Lauren had known Sophie since their first year at Vassar and she'd always been punctual.

"Hey." Lauren leaned in for a kiss. As she did, her hair toppled messily over her eyes.

Sophie, in contrast, looked as put together as always. She wore her tan belted jacket, black tights, and ankle-high boots. Her blond hair was cut into a blunt bob. Sophie was petite, barely five one, with narrow shoulders and delicate hands. Other than the vertical lines that creased between her eyebrows, Sophie was nearly identical to the diminutive eighteen-year-old from Indiana that Lauren befriended more than two decades ago. Sophie had always been self-deprecating about her looks. Back in college, she cheekily described herself to Lauren as "dental-hygienist pretty." Lauren didn't agree that she was pretty with a caveat, but Sophie wouldn't hear otherwise.

"You did it?" Sophie asked now. "The divorce is final?"

"Yep." Lauren dropped her head. She hadn't had bridesmaids at her wedding because she and Eric eschewed the traditional ceremony but Sophie had been an honored guest. She'd made a toast about friendship and enduring love. Funny how the friendship endured beyond the marriage.

"I'm impressed you were able to come out tonight," Sophie said. "Do you remember what a wreck I was after my divorce? I was the one who asked for it, but it hit me so hard. As you know."

Oh, Lauren knew. She'd had a front-row seat to the entire shitshow. Sophie's ex-husband, Joshua, used to be a guitarist in a marginally successful indie band called Friend of the Sun. His passion for weed came way before his devotion to family. Sophie, who poured her heart and soul into being a mom to their two boys, had given him an ultimatum four years ago: clean up your act or we get a divorce. Joshua devastated her by choosing divorce. Then, two years ago, he married Beatrice, ditched Friend of the Sun, and took out a loan to open a recording studio. They purchased a spacious condo around the corner from Sophie's tiny rental apartment. Joshua and his new wife had Baby Clementine, the bane of Sophie's existence, especially since Beatrice flooded social media with images of *Clementine and Daddy strumming a guitar* or *Clementine snuggling on the sofa with her big brothers.*

There were many times in the months after Sophie's divorce when Lauren pressed her breasts into Eric's chest and felt relieved she wasn't Sophie. Is this what she got for being smug? Lauren had a mental image of Eric's frenzied ass as he pumped into Trish the Babysitter.

An icy blast blew east from the Hudson River. Lauren shivered and hugged her arms against her coat. "Have you heard from Madeline?"

"Not yet," Sophie said. "It's really freezing, though. Want to go inside? Charlie gave me hell about getting a sitter, so I slipped out early and walked all the way here."

They pushed through the revolving door and stepped into the warm dining room. Soft jazz played and candles flickered. Waiters in white shirts and burgundy ties glided around with squares of focaccia nestled on silver trays.

"We have a reservation for three," Lauren told the hostess. "Under Madeline Wallace?"

"Yes," the hostess said. "Ms. Wallace reserved a booth. Would you like to wait for her at the bar or do you want me to take you there?"

"I'd love to go to the booth," Lauren said. She needed a buffer from the world right now.

Sophie wiped her nose with a folded tissue and nodded in agreement.

The hostess reached for the cocktail list, scarlet red with gold trim, and escorted them to a dimly lit circular booth. It was private and tranquil and just right for a divorce celebration.

"Madeline just texted us," Sophie said, handing her tan coat to the hostess. "She's running late."

As Sophie tapped at her phone, Lauren noticed her sucking in her lower lip. It was a habit Lauren had observed since their Vassar days, when they'd pull all-nighters in the Davison common room, binging on microwave popcorn and Diet Snapple Peach Tea. That was twenty-three years ago. They met in September of their freshman year of college—Sophie Smart the bookworm, Lauren Zuckerman the techie nerd. This was back when they were both small-town girls, back when Lauren's heart was shattered over her breakup with Gideon, and Sophie hadn't had actual sex yet. Sophie admitted one night in the hush of Lauren's dorm room that she'd gone to third base with a girl on her high school soccer team. That's when they still talked about sex in terms of bases, and when anything but straight felt like a confession.

"So how are the boys?" Lauren asked as Sophie set her phone on the table.

Sophie smiled. Her sons were the light of her life. "Charlie was a pain in the butt when I was leaving, but it's okay. He just lost his front teeth, and he looks adorable. I love how at seven they still let you read to them. Noah made the travel soccer team so he's flying high on ego."

"What are you and Charlie reading?"

"We're on a Roald Dahl kick. We just finished *James and the Giant Peach*. What about Cady and Amelia? Are they still reading?"

Lauren considered her daughters for a moment. Cady was the younger twin by three minutes. She was four inches shorter than her sister, with a chubby frame and a more outgoing personality. On quick glance, she looked older despite the height deficit. Amelia, on the other hand, was often sullen, a loner, a deep thinker. She was tall and bony, built like Lauren's late mom, with brown hair and a pointy chin. Thank goodness Amelia played Ultimate Frisbee, otherwise Lauren would have worried about her withdrawing from the world.

"Cady says she likes YA but, truly, she's obsessed with TikTok. She posts TikToks of herself putting on fashion shows or cooking a recipe with me. It's a losing battle whenever I tell her to get off her phone."

"What about Amelia?" Sophie asked.

"Amelia's on her phone a lot too," Lauren said. "She's currently making her way through every season of *The Office*. Whenever I fight them about screens, they pull the whole 'maybe it was different for your generation' thing. Are we that old, Soph? Because I didn't get *that* memo."

"Speaking of growing up," Sophie said, "want to hear something funny? Noah asked me to buy him Old Spice deodorant. He told me he wants to smell like a man!"

Lauren howled and slapped her thigh with one hand. "What does a *man* smell like?"

A server appeared at the booth. "I'll get you started with water," he said. "Would you like sparkling? Still? Tap?"

"Tap water is fine," Sophie said quickly. As soon as he was gone, she pressed her palms to the table and leaned toward Lauren. "Did you look up the menu? It's prix fixe. And really extravagant prices."

Lauren needed to tell Sophie not to stress. Sophie was a public-school literacy teacher and a single mom. She routinely got dicked around by Joshua, who debated every additional expense for the boys that went above his court-mandated child support. But in situations like these, when their other best friend was a multimillionaire and had picked the restaurant, it was implied that Madeline would treat. But before Lauren could respond, their waiter arrived.

"Can I get you ladies a drink while you wait for the rest of your party?" he asked. This waiter was a hunk—tall and muscular with a surfer's crest of blond hair and a chill twang to his accent. Was he the one they dispatched for divorce celebration dinners? "How about a round of cocktails? Cosmopolitans?"

Sophie scratched her hand. "Just water is fine for me."

Lauren squinted at the drinks list. Eric was a wine snob, so he always ordered for them. He would sniff into his glass and rave about grapes from Sicily or New Zealand. "May I please have a martini? Vodka with olives."

"No worries," the waiter said.

"I bet *he* smells like a man!" Lauren whispered to Sophie as the waiter strode toward the bar. "No worries for sure."

Sophie nodded in agreement. "It's all good."

Lauren looked over at the hunky waiter again. Imagine having no worries! Lauren had seen Sophie panic about money. Would that be her life now too? In the divorce agreement, Eric committed to eighty percent of Cady and Amelia's future college tuition, but Lauren's portion could still topple her. Damn her decision to go from full time to freelance. The summer before the twins started kindergarten, both she and Eric worked full time and paid their nanny a whopping salary to cart the girls from preschool to the playground.

Back then, Lauren was a product manager for a tech company in midtown. She earned good money. About the same as Eric. They both put in the hours to grow their careers. But she was exhausted from balancing nonstop work demands and even more nonstop parenting demands. She had frequent sinus infections and guzzled Emergen-C like it was juice. When they crunched the numbers that summer before kindergarten, Lauren knew something had to give. From a financial perspective it would be ridiculous to keep their nanny on payroll while the girls were in school. But the good nannies insisted on forty hours a week. Finally, they decided that Lauren would leave her job, take on freelance product management work, and pick up the girls from school every afternoon.

Lauren was the natural choice to quit full time. They earned around the same salary, true, but since the twins were born she handled the pediatrician appointments, made the mommy friends, arranged the music and dance classes, and bought the presents for the birthday parties. Eric didn't have the kids' pediatrician's number programmed in his phone. He probably didn't even know the man's name! Plus, he despised sitting on the sidelines of kiddie soccer games while Lauren found it hilarious. Also, how could Eric fall off the lawyer track before he'd paid off his law-school debt?

And yet. And yet. And yet.

Lauren had majored in computer science and graduated from a top college. She'd been sharp. She'd earned praise in a male-dominated field. In the eight years since Lauren left full-time work, she managed the development of several apps but her career hadn't grown in the ways that her full-time colleagues' did. Her earning potential plummeted. Meanwhile, Eric got promoted. His salary flourished. Eventually the disparity was so big that it actually *seemed* like income was the reason that Eric was the natural choice to remain in the workforce.

Nine months ago, when Lauren discovered that her husband was a chronic cheater, this carefully constructed world collapsed. These past nine months, Lauren would toss in bed with terrible realizations like, *Holy shit, Eric could have just programmed the number for the pediatrician into his phone! Holy shit, some parents like kiddie soccer games and some parents hate kiddie soccer games but should that really determine the fate of professional lives?* But the worst of the midnight *holy shits* was that Lauren had taken on the traditional female role under the pretense that it was an empowering, do-this-with-my-eyes-wide-open choice. But it wasn't a choice. It was an assumption.

As Lauren swallowed the tightness in her throat, she spotted Madeline coming into the restaurant. Madeline towered over the hostess, who led her through the dining room toward their booth. With her lustrous dark hair, cream-colored cropped jacket, and designer pants, Madeline's presence garnered stares from several guests in the restaurant. *Is that woman a celebrity? Haven't we seen her somewhere?* Early in their friendship, Lauren asked Madeline what it was like to be so beautiful. Lauren liked that she and Madeline could be blunt with each other.

"My take on beauty," Madeline said, "is that people are attractive because an attractive man and an attractive woman fuck. Unless there are ugly recessive genes tucked away, they'll produce a beautiful baby. If that baby is a girl who grows up with money for a trainer, a skin-care routine, and a hair stylist, she'll be beautiful for decades."

Madeline could be an odd bird. Sometimes she was too much for Sophie, but she always made Lauren laugh. And Lauren definitely needed to laugh tonight.

"Hi, mamas!" Madeline arrived at their table. "Sorry I'm late. Minor drama with Arabella as I was leaving."

"Everything okay?" Lauren raised her eyebrows in surprise. Most moms expressed frequent annoyance at their children, or at the monotony of motherhood, but not Madeline. She lived to be Arabella's mom. She transformed parenting her daughter into her career.

"It'll be fine," Madeline said. She kissed Lauren and Sophie on their cheeks and then slid into the booth. As she ordered a cosmo, Lauren sipped her martini and thought how strange it was that they were all divorced now. When they met Madeline at an infant-toddler CPR class, Arabella was almost two, Lauren's twins were six weeks old, and Sophie was eight months pregnant with Noah. At first, Madeline seemed too gorgeous to be approachable. But it was a long day in a stuffy room with crash-test babies. Lauren leaked double pools of breast milk on her shirt. Sophie was so pregnant she couldn't stop farting. And Madeline admitted that her husband was a workaholic who hadn't been home for their daughter's bedtime in four months. Not a friendship made in heaven but a certain kind of mommy-hell that can bond women for life.

"So how are you?" Madeline asked Lauren. "I love your dress. Polka dots are the best when you feel like ass."

"Thanks." Lauren dabbed her eyes with her napkin. "Well . . . I'm officially divorced. The paperwork is signed."

"Welcome to the club," Madeline said. "I'm impressed you were able to push it through so quickly."

"I'll drink to that." Lauren raised her glass even though, deep in her gut, she felt a stab of pain that she and Eric had dismantled their entire life in less than a year.

"Oh!" Sophie said. "I've been meaning to tell you, Laur, that one of my students loves your app."

"Which one?" Lauren asked, relieved for the subject change.

"The one where the star shoots through the words and you collect meteor points for getting things correct."

"Ah, Reading Starz."

"She was blown away when I told her that my friend built it. She looked at me like I was famous by association."

"I didn't exactly build it. I oversaw one tiny part."

Madeline's cosmopolitan arrived. She lifted her drink and tapped glasses with Lauren. Sophie raised her water and clinked as well.

"Not drinking?" Madeline asked.

"I have to wake up early," Sophie said apologetically.

"If it's about price," Madeline said, "I'm treating and don't argue. I know it's not cheap. So let's order a ton of food and too many drinks and celebrate the grand finale to Handjobgate."

Lauren smiled stiffly. By this point, Handjobgate had become a running joke. When Madeline first coined the term, Lauren was appalled. There is *nothing* humorous about discovering that your husband pays to get jerked off. But by this point, Lauren could roll with it. Tragedy plus time equals laughing at your ex. That said, Lauren *definitely* wasn't ready for Madeline to have a go at Babysittergate.

"Thanks for treating," Sophie said to Madeline. "I have to admit to you guys that I'm freaking out about money. Charlie is struggling and needs therapy. And not the bargain-basement therapist that comes with my insurance plan. He needs cognitive behavioral therapy. I've found this place that's perfect but it's insanely expensive."

"What's going on with Charlie?" Lauren asked.

"He's a deep thinker," Sophie said. "Which seems to go hand in hand with anxiety. You know how he's anxious, right?"

They both nodded.

"He's become a picker. He picks at the skin around his fingernails until they bleed. And guess what he told me this morning? He said his dad promised if he doesn't pick he'll buy him the four-hundred-dollar LEGO Death Star set. But when I told Joshua that Charlie should go to CBT, he said that's too expensive. But Joshua knows I can't afford it alone. I'm sorry to rant. I'm trying not to be mad at Joshua, but he's making it hard."

Lauren reached across the table and squeezed Sophie's slender hand. Joshua Greene was a self-absorbed prick. He was handsome in a chiseled indie-rocker way. Throughout his twenties, he had female groupies swooning over him. As a result, he treated women as disposable as paper towels.

"Did I mention they're going to Hawaii next week?" Sophie pressed her thumbnail into the webbing of her opposite hand. "And Southern California for Thanksgiving? Beatrice has been posting about the Hawaii trip. Tiny swim outfits for Clementine and matching green Crocs for all of them. I'm sure Beatrice is paying for these trips but Joshua is more than happy to let her."

"Sophie," Lauren said. "Following your ex-husband's new wife is not good for your mental health. You know that."

Sophie nodded. "Let's stop talking about Joshua, okay? He doesn't deserve it."

"Agreed," Lauren said, relieved to be off the topic of exes. She did not want to spill about her afternoon coffee with Eric, about the Trish bombshell. "Tonight is about us."

Madeline smiled at Sophie. "When our sexy waiter comes over, I'm having him bring back a cosmo for you."

"Thanks, mama." Sophie blew a kiss across the table. "So enough about me. What's up with you guys?"

Lauren glanced toward the glass wall of the restaurant that faced Lincoln Center. "I was thinking as I walked here that I want to see some Chagall paintings. My mom loved Chagall. Where can you see them in this city, anyway?"

"The Guggenheim," Madeline said. "They have a collection of Chagalls. The Jewish Museum might too."

"I'm in," Lauren said. "Anyone want to come with?"

"Sure," Sophie said. "On a weekend that the boys are with their dad."

"There's an amazing Italian restaurant around the corner from the Guggenheim," Madeline said. "Arabella will kill me if I don't bring home their penne alla vodka for her. But back to you, Lauren. Let's order and then you have to tell us everything you won't miss about Eric."

Lauren glanced wearily at her menu. She'd been a vegetarian since she was thirteen. In times like these, when she was so drained that making a decision felt insurmountable, she appreciated that there was only one vegetarian appetizer on the menu and one entrée.

Their server arrived, and Madeline ordered several sides in addition to their selections. Within minutes, another server appeared offering risotto balls with sun-dried tomatoes, compliments of the chef. It was all so sublime, so far from the million mundane evenings in Lauren's life. Madeline definitely knew how to celebrate.

Lauren tucked into her fennel salad. "Here's something I won't miss. When Eric washed the dishes he would leave greasy pans to soak in the sink overnight, as if elves would magically appear and finish the job. Elves being me, of course."

"Joshua did that too!" Sophie said, nodding. "Also, if he cooked dinner he wanted applause like 'How amazing . . . you heated up pasta!' Can you imagine if a mom needed someone to clap every time she fed her children?"

"At least Joshua fed your kids," Madeline said. "By the time Colin and I divorced, I don't think he'd ever made Arabella a box of mac and cheese! He found the baby stuff tedious. And the kid stuff. It's only now that she's able to carry a conversation that he's even—" Madeline paused abruptly, folded her cloth napkin, and ran her finger along the crease.

"Madeline?" Lauren leaned closer to her friend, who seemed to be having a brain freeze. "Hello?"

Madeline shivered. "Sorry . . . I was just thinking . . . never mind."

A busboy cleared the salad plates and they ordered another round of drinks. Lauren could feel the alcohol buzzing in her brain. Exactly what she needed.

"Another thing I won't miss," she said as she touched her hand to her cheek. "Eric would bring his phone into the bathroom for thirty minutes. Is any mom allowed to take a crap for that long? Oh, and he wore socks and Crocs, like, to buy bagels or walk the dog."

Madeline fanned her long hair over her shoulders. "Socks and Crocs are the worst. You could have told your divorce lawyer and he'd be like, 'Socks and Crocs, Ms. Zuckerman? Immediate grounds for divorce.'"

They were still laughing when three servers swooped in with their entrées. Madeline and Sophie sighed over the platters of bloody steak. Lauren didn't get the red-meat thing. Nothing revved Eric up more than cooking meat over an open fire. Whenever she rented a vacation house for the family, she would sift through listings until she found one with a charcoal grill. To prepare for the trip, she'd buy steaks and burgers and pack them on ice. As a vegetarian, she saw it as testament to her superior wife skills. And he complimented her for it. He said he won the wife lottery!

"The truth is . . . I miss being a wife." Lauren poked her fork into her pasta in brown-butter sauce. "I always bitched about the health-insurance invoices and thank-you notes and greasy pans and camp forms and doctors' appointments. But I miss being mad at Eric for not helping. I miss folding his laundry. I actually like folding boxers."

Sophie sliced a sliver of steak. "I used to love painting pottery with the boys at Little Shop of Crafts for Father's Day. We'd make Joshua a *Best Dad* mug or a *Best Dad* plate. It's not even like he was the best dad!"

"They can't all be best dad," Madeline said quietly.

Lauren dug into her pasta, a delectable blend of sweet and savory. "I was good at being a wife. I planned family vacations. I remembered when everyone needed to go to the dentist. I went back and forth with the in-laws on visits and gifts and holiday plans. Think about all the wife stuff. The kid stuff but also the mental load."

"Joshua didn't believe in mental load," Sophie said, chewing thoughtfully. "He told me it's a concept invented by bitter wives. He said that women whine about mental load to justify staying home."

"That's awful!" Lauren shrieked. "You've been a teacher the entire time you've been a mom. When you were married and Joshua toured with the band, did he ask you to cover the kids or did you just do it?"

"You have to ask?" Sophie laughed. "The one time I went to a literacy conference, I left pages of instructions for Joshua. Food. Wrapped birthday presents for whatever party was happening that weekend."

"Mental *fucking* load," Lauren said. "Wouldn't it be nice to have gotten paid for what we did as wives? Personal assistants get paid. Dog walkers get paid. Housekeepers get paid."

"I'm paying Kristen twenty-five an hour so I can be here tonight," Sophie said.

"Sex workers get paid," Madeline said. "Did you ever figure out what Eric paid for his little . . . sessions?"

Lauren smiled and, at the same time, gulped back tears. When her mom died, it was solid grief. But since she and Eric split up, she fluctuated from crying to giddiness in the same exhale.

"From what I can tell," Lauren said, "two hundred bucks. I went through our bank records with the divorce lawyer."

"For a *hand job*?" Madeline said. "I can't even imagine what sex would cost."

Lauren pressed her palms against her tired eye sockets. "To think he got it all for free. Fourteen years of marriage, sixteen years together . . ."

"Between the sex and the mental load," Sophie said, "husbands save hundreds of thousands in free labor with their wives."

Madeline drained her cosmopolitan and set it down hard. "You should build an app, Lauren. You should build a wife app."

"A wife app?" Lauren asked.

"There's an app for everything these days," Madeline said. "There's an app for dog walkers. There's an app for cello teachers. There are a million apps for drivers. Why not an app for wives?"

"Oh . . . god!" Sophie said. "You're joking, right?"

"That is completely batshit crazy," Lauren said.

"Thank you." Madeline raised her chin defiantly.

Everyone laughed and sipped their drinks.

After a moment, Madeline added, "But it's also kind of an awesome idea, right?"

"No!" Sophie wrinkled her nose. "Even though I can't stand Joshua's new family, I still think marriage is sacred. You can't pay for certain aspects of it."

"Tell that to Eric," Lauren said, groaning. "Anyway, in this so-called *wife app*, who would be the wives?"

"We would," Madeline said. "Professional wives. Finally charging for what women have always done for free. Health insurance forms, a hundred bucks. Sort the summer and winter clothes, drag the kids to the sneaker store, even book annual checkups!" Madeline ate a forkful of roasted mushrooms while her eyes twinkled mischievously, and then said, "Can't you see the drop-down menu? Want your cock tugged through your boxers while you watch *Monday Night Football*? For a premium, your wife will let you fuck her while she organizes the class potluck on her phone!"

After the day that Lauren had, she needed a laugh. But all of a sudden, the tears started. She slid out of the booth and bolted down the stairs. She dodged into a bathroom, locked the door, and collapsed onto the toilet.

A few minutes later, she heard Sophie's voice. "Lauren? You okay? Want me to come in?"

"Sorry, I'm okay." Lauren blew her nose with toilet paper. "It's been a long day. I just need to pull myself together."

"Madeline was joking about that wife app," Sophie said through the door. "You know she can be crass."

"No . . . it's okay," Lauren said. "Madeline was being funny. I'm just tired. I'll be up in a minute."

When Lauren got upstairs, there were three desserts on the table and a carafe of French press coffee.

"I'm sorry if I went too far about a wife app," Madeline said. "I didn't mean a man would pay for a rub-and-tug during *Monday Night Football*." She took a spoonful of chocolate mousse and licked her lips. "Maybe just during the Super Bowl."

Lauren smiled weakly. "No, it's not anything you said. I'm a little emotional right now. I'd been doing better these past few months but today has been a ten-car pileup."

"It's a big deal to sign your divorce papers," Sophie said. "I warned you it would hit hard."

Lauren sighed. "There's that."

Madeline and Sophie stared expectantly at her. Lauren looked back at them. Madeline's eyes, which were long-lashed and espresso brown, had an ache in them that Lauren had never seen before. Sophie's eyes looked exhausted, as if she hadn't had a full night's sleep in a decade.

"Well . . . what?" Sophie finally said. "You can't keep us hanging!"

Lauren exhaled slowly. "I met Eric for coffee this afternoon after I left the lawyer. Don't kill me, okay? I thought he wanted to talk about Cady and Amelia. Maybe I'm an idiot to have agreed. Or maybe I'm still used to being a good wife. Anyway . . . holy shit."

"Holy shit is not good," Madeline said.

"Holy shit is very bad," Lauren said. "Remember our old babysitter? Trish? Eric is sleeping with her. No . . . it's not just sex. Eric told me they're together."

"Why didn't you tell us before?" Madeline's voice rose. "You've kept this inside all evening? Oh, Lauren. Fuck Eric! How could he?"

Lauren shook her head. "Honestly I was too upset to talk about it. It's almost comical. I mean, Trish is twenty-four."

"Remember she babysat for my boys once last year?" Sophie asked. She tapped her temple with one finger. "No offense but there's not a lot going on upstairs."

"Hang on!" Madeline shrieked. "Trish with the big tits and the phone stuffed in her bra?"

"Yep," Lauren said. "*That* Trish."

"Oh, Lauren," Madeline said. "I'm so sorry."

Lauren rubbed her eyelids. But instead of crying, she felt angry. She was sick of Eric making her feel like the last sixteen years were a waste.

"This is the husband that I had sex with thousands of times," she said. "I made sure he wore sunblock at the beach and got weird moles checked out and I even booked the appointments. I'm the one who reminded him to call his parents on their birthdays. I waited in those long lines at Trader Joe's because he likes their stupid maple cookies. No two ways about it, I was a good wife."

"And then he went and paid for what you gave him for free," Sophie said.

"Now he's fucking someone you paid to watch your kids," Madeline said, "which is completely messed up."

"It *is* messed up," Sophie said. "We need to find a way to stick it to Eric. We need to make him hurt."

Lauren stared in wonder at Sophie. Her old friend was not the vengeful type. She was more of a turn-the-other-cheek person. Or, if Lauren was being honest, a roll-over-and-take-it type.

"Not just Eric," Sophie said. "Joshua too. Because damn him promising my son a LEGO set but denying him therapy. Or quitting weed for Beatrice but not for me. We need to see these guys hurt the way they've made us hurt. We need the last laugh!"

"Sophie!" Lauren squealed. "I have no idea where this is coming from, but I love it."

Madeline, who'd been uncharacteristically quiet, raised her coffee cup as if she wanted to make a toast but then set it down again.

"You okay?" Lauren asked.

"Actually . . . not really." Madeline pinched her necklace between her forefinger and thumb. It was a gold and diamond *Arabella* pendant from Tiffany. "I hadn't wanted to talk about this because I didn't want it to be real, but I got an email from Colin this afternoon. It sounds like he and Arabella have been talking about her spending the next school year in London. He said that Arabella told him, quote, 'It sounds like a dream come true.' Except this is the first I've heard about it. Arabella never *once* told me. And she tells me *everything*."

"Can Colin even take her for a year?" Lauren asked. Madeline and Arabella had been inseparable for as long as Lauren had known them. "Is that in your custody agreement?"

"I called my former matrimonial lawyer on the ride down here. She's reviewing our custody arrangements. I have residential custody, but we share joint legal custody. So technically Colin is allowed equal consult on all major decisions. Not that he has ever taken advantage of that." Madeline laughed but it came out like a seal's bark.

"Maybe this is all something out of nothing," Lauren said.

"Right," Sophie added. "Maybe Colin and Arabella had one brief conversation and she didn't want to hurt his feelings so she said it was a good idea?"

Madeline shook her head. "Arabella is the one who told me about Colin's email. As I was leaving she said, 'London might be cool, right? I could get a legit British accent.'" Madeline looked like she wanted to wilt into her chair. "Arabella is my entire life. I knew someday she'd go to college. But I didn't think she'd go away from me so soon. I just can't believe Colin would do this."

Sophie perked up. "Okay . . . so now we need to stick it to Colin too. A major, across-the-Atlantic-Ocean sticking."

Madeline sighed. "I wouldn't even know how to *begin* to stick it to Colin. He's some guy I had sex with and briefly married fifteen years ago. But I do want to stick it to Eric and Joshua because they are certifiable assholes."

Lauren took a bite of lemon tart. "Guys," she said. Her lips spread into a slow smile. "Maybe the idea isn't so crazy. Maybe I should build it—maybe I should build a wife app."

"Yes!" Sophie shrieked.

"Really?" Madeline asked.

"Fuck Eric for lying to me and not valuing what I did as a wife," Lauren said. "Fuck Joshua for denying that mental load is real. Fuck Colin for only wanting Arabella once you've done the hard work of raising her. Do I want revenge? Maybe. Or maybe it's because I was a good wife and Eric didn't deserve it. But I deserve the recognition and some wages too. I'm ready to collect."

Lauren flashed a triumphant smile. She was inspired. Or maybe she was drunk. Probably both. "I've been wanting to get back into tech on a more hardcore level. This idea is batshit crazy but it's also brilliant."

"I'm not sure I'm wife material," Madeline said. "But if we can stick it to every husband or ex-husband who undervalues women's labor, I'm in. My ladies will get the last laugh." She raised her coffee to the center of the table. "To a wife app!"

"To a wife app!" Lauren and Sophie responded.

Lauren took a heaping spoonful of chocolate mousse. Even saying *wife app* tasted delicious on her tongue. Lauren suddenly felt better than she had in a long time.

madeline

MADELINE FUCKED MEN SHE MET on apps the way some women got pedicures. And not the ladies with chipped polish and crud under their toenails. Madeline's was the sex of the women with year-round, gleaming, sandal-ready toes. Indulgent: yes. Need to schedule into your busy day: yes. Part of a necessary maintenance routine: yes.

She'd tried them all—Hinge, Bumble, Tinder—and she always returned to Bumble. She liked it because women were in charge of making first contact. Swipe right to any man you wanted to fuck. If he's a match, you message him. *My place?* Hopefully. She preferred to do it on her turf. Her housekeeper, Willow, was there on Monday, Wednesday, and Friday so Madeline had sex on Tuesdays or Thursdays when Arabella was at school. Not always. She had volunteer work, yoga, cooking, self-care appointments, fundraising for the PTA, and managing Arabella's life. That alone was a full-time job!

Madeline never let her daughter discover what went on between her Sferra sheets. Sure, she'd talked to her about sex since she was little. She answered her questions and bought her human-sexuality books and always maintained an age-appropriate dialogue. When Arabella was younger she used to ask her mom if she was going to get a

boyfriend. Madeline would say, "I go on dates. If it's someone important, you'll be the first to know." *Conversation over.*

Boyfriends? No interest. Madeline loved making multicourse dinners for Arabella, chatting and lingering over their food. She loved
eating out with friends. Hell, she loved a delicious meal alone. She
liked *her* shows at *her* volume. She was not a hand-holder—it made
her fingers sweaty. She had all the money in the world to pay for her
own vacations. So why on earth did she need a boyfriend? She'd been
down the husband road with Colin, and that hadn't worked out. The
best byproduct of her marriage was Arabella, and for that Madeline
was deeply grateful.

But then last week happened.

A week ago yesterday, Colin had detonated a bomb when he told
her that he'd invited Arabella to live with him for a year. It wouldn't
have been such a bomb if her daughter had responded with, *No thanks.
Mom and I have a good life here. I barely know you, dude.*

The hardest part was that Madeline couldn't say a single thing
about it to Arabella. Strict advice from her matrimonial lawyer. Serena
Kilgannon had proven herself a highly skilled lawyer during Madeline's
divorce. Madeline brought her back on immediately upon hearing from
Colin about this London business.

And this was Serena's mandate to Madeline: *Keep calm, carry on,
do nothing.*

"Keep calm and carry on?" Madeline asked into the phone eight
days ago. She'd forwarded Colin's email to the lawyer and also texted
her to say *Check your email ASAP.* Serena called back as Madeline
was in the Uber on her way to meet her friends for Lauren's divorce
celebration dinner.

"Sorry for the British reference," Serena said. "I've found that, when
in the eye of a custody storm, it's best to do nothing until we have more
information."

"But how can I do nothing?" Madeline pressed. "I want to kill Colin and maybe wring Arabella's neck while I'm at it. Arabella belongs with me, in New York. This is her home. This is our life."

"Just do nothing for now. I'm in court all week. I need a few days to finish up and then I'll review your custody paperwork and call you back. Middle of next week. But in the meantime, Madeline, promise you won't send angry texts to Colin, and you won't threaten to keep Arabella in Manhattan for winter break. He has Christmas, if I remember correctly?"

How had she read her mind? A few pointedly pissed-off texts to her ex was *exactly* what Madeline had been planning. Also, Arabella was supposed to go to London on December twentieth. Madeline was tempted to whisk her to the Caribbean instead. If Colin thought he could blow off their custody arrangements, then she could too!

"But—" Madeline said.

"It won't help. Trust me. This is what I do. Just keep calm and carry on for now. And don't beg Arabella to stay with you next year. That will make things worse. She'll feel torn. Or she'll be tempted to rebel against you and that'll push her further away. Teenagers are unpredictable."

Madeline wanted to say, *Not my girl. Not Arabella.* Up until an hour before, she thought she knew every molecule of her beautiful, loyal daughter. Instead, Madeline thanked her lawyer and then cried for four blocks in the back seat. She asked the driver to let her out early and she slipped into a Starbucks bathroom to fix her makeup before meeting Lauren and Sophie.

For the past week, Madeline had practiced restraint like never before. Restraint was not her strong suit. She preferred to do what she wanted when she wanted. She'd inherited this from her late father, Timon Wallace. He'd been an investment banker at Morgan Stanley, larger than life, every bit as impulsive as his only child. It all came crashing down when he had a heart attack at forty-nine. Madeline was fourteen, brushing her teeth before school. She was the one who heard the thud when his body smacked the living room floor. Her mom had been at water aerobics, so Madeline was the one who called 911. She was the one who watched in horror as EMTs flooded their Upper East Side apartment and tried without success to bring life back to her dad.

Restraint.

That's exactly what Madeline repeated in her head, like a mantra, when Arabella took a break from cello so they could eat homemade sushi on Monday night. Madeline had been working on sushi-making since last year when she took a class with a star Japanese chef.

As they ate the spicy tuna rolls, Arabella described how a girl at school had killer knee-high boots with silver buckles. Arabella asked where she got them, and the girl told her about a punk-inspired shop in London.

"I looked it up and I even mapped it from Dad's place," Arabella said as she raked her roll through soy sauce. "Isn't that wild? That I could actually shop at places like that? If I lived there next year?"

Madeline's stomach spasmed. *No! It wouldn't be wild. It would be awful. Because you would be across an ocean and I would be—*

Keep calm. Carry on.

"The boots sound cool." Madeline clenched her teeth in restraint. "You should get back to your Bach cello suites. I'll pop in to listen when I'm done with the dishes."

On Tuesday morning, when Arabella was in the shower, Madeline glanced at her daughter's phone while it charged on the counter. The texts that flooded in! Her best school friend, Ria. A few girls from Juilliard. Group chats up the wazoo. When she bought Arabella her first phone, the deal was that Madeline had the password and was allowed to do random checks. Her daughter was only fourteen, but she looked like a college student. Madeline was determined to protect Arabella from online creeps.

This morning her daughter was mid–text exchange with Colin. He'd written an hour ago, around noon in London.

Dad: Have a great day at school. Send more suggestions of shows we can watch together. I loved the last few!

Colin and Arabella had been watching shows together? What shows? Why hadn't her daughter told her? Madeline rubbed her free hand across her forehead.

Arabella: Thanks! Okay. I will.

Dad: Should we go for K-drama? Comedy?

Dad: I guess you're busy. Talk later.

Once Arabella left for school, Madeline's fingers tingled to write her ex-husband and tell him that he was a kid-snatcher. Where was Colin when she sat with Arabella and watched all the *Sofia the First* bullshit? Or when she took her to chamber music rehearsals in blizzards? Or when she hugged her as she cried after a tough lesson?

Restraint.

Later that morning, Madeline hit the gym, showered, and then went in for her monthly highlights. Head full of foil, she nervously checked her phone. She wasn't sure what she wanted to see. Maybe something from Colin that he changed his mind? Or Arabella? No, she was at school. Let her be.

As she left the salon, she tapped Bumble to check who was horny and hot and nearby.

A chef from an upscale Italian restaurant in Hell's Kitchen.

He said he could be at her place in ninety minutes.

That gave Madeline time to dash home, have a quick bite, and brush her teeth.

An hour and a half later, the chef walked into her apartment.

"Wow," he said appraisingly.

Madeline showed him where he could hang up his jacket. She wore snug jeans and a low-cut blouse. She imagined how he was counting the seconds until he could pull her shirt over her head, unzip her jeans, and cup his hand around her smooth cunt. *Desire*. That was what Madeline loved. To desire a man. But more than that, *to be* desired.

"An Italian restaurant?" Madeline asked as they stood in her kitchen, making small talk and sipping seltzer. "Do you have any specialties?"

"Parmesan gnocchi," he said. "People come from all over the city for my gnocchi."

"I'd love to get the recipe," Madeline said. "I've made gnocchi a few times and it's always turned out . . ." She tilted her right hand from side to side, like *comme çi, comme ça*.

"The key is russet potatoes," he said. "I would never use any other potato."

"I'll have to remember that," Madeline said.

They set their glasses in the sink and made their way to the bedroom, where they kissed and then quickly stripped down. His hands smelled like garlic and his teeth were stained with coffee, but his cock was rock solid as he rolled on a condom, gripped her thighs, and pushed inside her. She opened her legs wider and they moved their torsos together until they found a rhythm.

"Did you come too?" he asked a few minutes later.

"Not yet," she said. She appreciated that he asked. A lot of men didn't.

He pinned her hips down with his thigh and rolled her clit between his finger and thumb. She wondered, briefly, if her cunt now smelled like garlic.

After the chef left, Madeline tossed her sheets in the wash, took a shower, ordered soap on Amazon, and congratulated herself on an entire day of restraint.

Wednesday, Madeline went to Vinyasa yoga and then met Lauren at a café on Amsterdam. When Lauren texted and asked if they could meet to discuss "wife app business," Madeline was shocked. Sure,

Lauren had said she was going to build that app at dinner and they'd toasted the shit out of her. But they'd been fired up on cocktails and wine and ex-husband rage. By the light of day, an app that pawned wife jobs sounded ludicrous.

"I love your highlights," Lauren said as she raised her coffee mug to her mouth.

"Oh . . . thanks." Madeline patted her long hair. "I just got it done."

Lauren paused. "Are you okay?"

"Yeah . . . why?"

"You seem a little down. Don't get me wrong. You look great. Just . . ."

Madeline nodded as brightly as she could muster. She'd already decided she wasn't going to talk more about the Arabella-Colin drama with Lauren. Why make it real until it was?

"No, I'm fine. A lot going on at Arabella's school. I'm on the fund-raising committee and it gobbles up so much time. Plus, I just finished a pastry-making class that ran late in the evenings. I'm exhausted."

Madeline hoped Lauren wouldn't call her bluff. She had no idea how to elaborate on what was happening with Arabella. It was a bottomless pit of sadness.

Thankfully, Lauren shifted gears.

"I know it seems crazy," Lauren said, her pale-blue eyes flashing, "but it feels like there's something unique with this app idea. I realize there are dozens of marketplace apps out there but there's nothing specific that tackles the unpaid labor in marriage."

Madeline bobbed the green-tea bag in and out of the hot water. "I'm confused. You're saying if this app happens you want to sell people as wives?"

Lauren raised her eyebrows. "Not sex, of course. We'll leave that underworld to Eric."

"Damn!" Madeline snapped her fingers. "Who would be the wives?"

"Like you said at dinner, you and me and Sophie. At least at first.

Obviously if there's demand, we'll scale up."

The hairs prickled on the back of Madeline's neck. She wanted to encourage her friend, but she hadn't realized she was *actually* going to be called on to be a wife. "What kinds of jobs?"

"We'll do narrowly focused verticals," Lauren said. "Like, health-care paperwork. Specific childcare tasks that usually fall to a mom. All the school crap wives take care of. Booking vacations. Decluttering apartments. I'm not being sexist. I'm being realistic. Think about anything a wife might do and we could list it on the app."

"I'm not scrubbing toilets," Madeline said.

Lauren laughed. "You don't even clean your own toilets."

Madeline inhaled slowly through her nose until her chest and stomach were expanded. Truly, this sounded awful. But the path between a crazy idea and Madeline working as a wife was long and likely impossible. The least she could do was be a friend. Lauren had always been there for her in ways that other people hadn't. Women were intimidated by Madeline's wealth and looks. Men wanted to sleep with her. Her mom wanted to change her. Her dad, well, he died on her. Lauren just wanted to spend time with her, no strings attached.

"So what's next?" Madeline blotted her lips with a paper napkin. "How can I help?"

Lauren shrugged. "I'm in the planning stages. The app would start small. I'd build it out for Apple and see how that goes before we expand into Android. I know some good designers I've worked with before, and I have a few mobile app developers in mind. I'm going to reach out to people with a proposal and see what they would charge."

Money! Madeline could call her financial advisor immediately and transfer a chunk to Lauren. Name the amount, girlfriend! Oh, and maybe spare me some of those wife jobs. "Want me to pay for the designers . . . or whatever you need to hire?"

"No," Lauren said quickly. "I mean . . . thank you. That means a lot, really. Once my funds get tight I'll probably kick myself for turning you down. But this feels like a risk I need to take." She sipped her coffee. "I have money from the divorce settlement. I'm going to dip into that."

Madeline shrugged. "That sounds cosmically right."

"I need help with one thing, though," Lauren said. "I want to hire a lawyer to review the legalese and draft the contracts that we put on the app. Can you recommend anyone good?"

Madeline shivered at the mention of lawyers. She was waiting for a call back from Serena Kilgannon with word on how they could put an end to Colin's London scheme.

"I can help you find the right lawyer," she said after a moment. "I'll ask my financial advisor for recommendations. He knows everyone. Will you let me pay for that at least? It'll add up fast."

Lauren pressed her hands together in gratitude. "That I'll accept. Thank you."

They finished their drinks and stepped outside. After they air-kissed on the sidewalk, Madeline texted her financial advisor. Then she dropped by her favorite salon for a pedicure. As she dipped her feet into the steaming soak, she decided to splurge and add a facial to the appointment. Two hours later, as she walked home, she congratulated herself on another day of stunning restraint.

sophie

Sophie Smart had a major case of FOMO. It was a problem similar to the eczema she suffered as kid where she scratched her hands raw until the skin oozed even though the dermatologist told her *Don't itch, use prescription cream.* Sophie continued to scratch her way through social media, to ogle the lives she wasn't living, and to arrive at the miserable conclusion that her forty-one years had not amounted to nearly enough.

It was another cold October day in New York City, and her ex-husband, his new wife, and their baby were at a luxury resort in Hawaii. "The Jewel of Waikiki," according to Google. They'd landed yesterday and Beatrice had lit up Instagram with images of Joshua and Clementine—fat cheeks, tight brown curls—bobbing in the turquoise pool. There was Joshua as he sipped rounds of drinks under a tilting palm tree, a flowery lei lassoed around his neck. The three of them in front of the ocean at dusk, with the sky and water streaked in exquisite pink. Beatrice topped it off with hashtags like *#aloha* and *#Icouldgetusedto Hawaii.*

Sophie had woken early—six-fifteen, New York time—made a mug of English Breakfast tea, and fed her cranky old tabby, Edna, named after the poet and fellow Vassar alum, Edna St. Vincent Mallay. With tea in hand, she settled at the small table that overlooked her street. If she craned her neck, she could glimpse a patch of Central Park. Sophie planned to review a stack of student assessments before her sons got up at seven. But one sip of tea, one peek on Instagram, one sunset shot that Beatrice hadn't posted before Sophie went to bed last night, and Sophie was sucked down the FOMO rabbit hole.

It wasn't just her ex-husband's Family 2.0 that messed with her brain. It was old friends from Vassar who posted about trips to Scotland, high-end kitchen renovations, rambling tributes to their perfect partners. And don't even get Sophie started on her sister! Eva and her husband, Matt, and their daughters lived in Indiana, two suburbs away from Sophie's parents. Matt made a killing as a marketing exec and Eva spammed social media with images from their Midwestern McMansion. Sophie did not want Eva's life. But to see it so shiny and happy on Instagram was to be thirteen again, with Eva fifteen—bigger boobs, better clothes, and more popular friends than Sophie.

Sophie closed Instagram with a huff, glanced out her window to where the trash collectors flung garbage bags, and googled how to get rid of FOMO. She scanned several results before her eyes landed on one: *In order to get over the Fear of Missing Out, you have to acknowledge that FOMO starts with sadness. Social media makes it worse. Instagram isn't evil but relying on it for happiness is the root of your problem. Focus on the good. Gratitude is essential.*

Maybe Sophie would be more grateful if she could post about a lavish vacation. The only place she'd been recently were the Indiana Dunes. Her sister's family rented a house there in August. A week of getting sunburned on the shores of Lake Michigan. A week of her sons and Eva's daughters tumbling down the dunes. Endless tick checks. Dinners out and pricey boat rentals, always with Eva's husband, Matt, footing the bill. This would invariably lead to her mom's favorite topic:

It's time to do online dating, Soph. It's been four years since your divorce. Time to meet a new man. A man like Matt!

The Indiana Dunes had been nice—well, parts of it—but it was definitely no Jewel of Waikiki.

"Good morning, Mommy."

Charlie lingered in the doorway, already digging at his thumb. Sophie turned her phone facedown and pretended to mark up assessments.

"I've thought about it and I can't go to school today," Charlie announced as he scooped up Edna and squeezed her in his arms. There was a window in his mouth where his front teeth had been, and his streaky-blond hair clumped on top of his head like a nest.

"Why not?" Sophie slid her phone into her sweatshirt pocket, walked into the tiny alcove kitchen, and poured a cup and a half of oats into a saucepan to make oatmeal. Then she began running the tap to wash a few dishes left over from last night. In this old building, she had to run the water for several minutes until it got warm. Her older son, Noah, reported that at Joshua and Beatrice's condo, the water flowed hot whenever they needed it.

Charlie rattled off his usual litany of complaints—*stomachache, tired, feel like I might throw up.* His fingers were a ragged mess. He used to be a nail-biter, but this past year he'd started to peel bits of skin like he was ripping at string cheese. Sophie knew the real reason he didn't want to go to school. His second-grade class had their weekly field trip to the farmers market and Sophie couldn't be one of the parent chaperones. But Sophie wasn't a leisure mommy. She had to work! Not that she was bitter. Seriously, if she could, she would.

"Sorry, little man," Sophie said. "You have to go."

Charlie dropped a scowling Edna onto the ground and burst into tears, which left Sophie no choice but to break her No Screens in the Morning rule. She hugged Charlie, and then grabbed the iPad, located *Phineas and Ferb*, and stuck it under his damp face. As he robotically spooned oatmeal into his mouth, Sophie spun from counter to fridge to lunch boxes to sink. She packed salami and cheese sandwiches for all three of them and filled water bottles and downed her own oatmeal and drained the dregs of her now-cold tea.

"Hey, why does Charlie get to watch a show on a school morning? I don't even get my phone until I'm at the door!"

Noah had wandered out of the bedroom and he was fuming. Recently, he'd accused Sophie of being stricter than *every* mom of *every* kid.

"I don't feel well," Charlie told Noah.

"Yeah right," Noah said, rolling his eyes.

Sophie grabbed her older son's elbow and guided him into her room. She hurriedly explained that Charlie was trying to dodge his farmers market field trip so the iPad was a necessary distraction. Maybe it was too much to dump on a seventh grader but she needed solidarity. She even offered him his phone forty-five minutes early. But instead of taking the olive branch he slapped his forehead.

"Oh man!" Noah said. "I can't believe I keep forgetting this. I need you to sign my field trip permission form for Chinatown. Like, right now. Or I can't go. And I need twenty dollars cash. If I don't bring the permission form and the cash, I'll have to wait in the library and get points off my grade in social studies this semester."

Sophie gripped her fingers around Noah's phone. This was the first she'd heard of a Chinatown field trip.

"When is it?" Sophie asked.

"Today," Noah said. "*Shit.* I can't remember where I put the permission form. Ms. Ahmed gave me another copy on Friday after I lost the one last week."

"Don't swear. You lost the one last week? When you were at Dad's?"

"I gave him the permission form," Noah said. "He told me he'd sign it. Then they left for Hawaii. I'm the only kid in class who hasn't turned mine in. That's what Ms. Ahmed announced on Friday. It was so embarrassing."

"So get your backpack and look for your new form," Sophie said calmly. "If you can't find it, I'll write a note to Ms. Ahmed and explain that you have my permission to go."

Noah's expression softened. *His mom would bail him out.* As he left to get his bag, Sophie seethed. Of course Joshua dropped the ball! He probably didn't deem permission slips important enough to take up his precious mental space.

"What is this field trip anyway?" Sophie asked when Noah returned.

Noah hunched on his knees as he dug through his backpack. "It's part of the immigration unit. Hopefully Ms. Ahmed won't be too mad at me. She told me she's a fan of Friend of the Sun. Isn't that crazy that she knows Dad's old band? That'll buy me a few points."

Sophie ignored that comment. "You said you needed twenty dollars?"

"Yeah," Noah grunted. His massive backpack was a clutter of bent folders, raggedy notebooks, and cereal-bar wrappers. Every now and then, Sophie purged the bag so her son didn't tote trash back and forth to school. Is this how it all starts? Your mom cleans your disgusting backpack, your wife schedules your dental cleanings? What if she left her son's bag to fester? What if she let him get stranded for the field trip? It was a novel thought to raise a man who didn't rely on a woman to manage his mess.

"We're going to a museum in Chinatown and then a dim sum place for lunch. You don't need to pack my lunch today."

"But I already made your sandwich," Sophie said, her voice rising. She hated how she sounded right now, like a whiner, like the worst of what Joshua used to call her.

"They said we can bring along extra money for a candy store. Most kids are bringing thirty or forty. Bare minimum we need twenty." Noah narrowed his eyes at his mom. "Dad said he would send me with forty bucks."

Sophie wrinkled her nose. Did Noah have any idea what he was saying when he tossed out *Bare minimum . . . we need twenty?* Noah knew that his mom didn't swim in cash, but she tried to spare him the details about how much she had to sacrifice not to carry debt from month to month.

"Let's do thirty," she said as Noah produced a crumpled permission form from his backpack. Sophie smoothed it across her bedside table, signed it, and printed her cell on the required line. "Grab a little candy for Charlie too."

"Thanks, Mom," he said. "I'm sorry I didn't bug Dad more about it."

Sophie opened her wallet and handed her son a twenty, a five, and five ones. She'd wanted to dash out after school and get her eyebrows shaped but there went that money. Sophie's mom and sister visited a spa in Indiana every other Friday to get something waxed off. Eva dished to Sophie on a recent call that their mom had braved it and let them wax her a landing strip.

Is that brave? Sophie asked her sister. *For a woman in her late sixties to get a decent portion of her pubic hair waxed off?*

You're so weird, Eva said to her. *Like . . . even that you said that word. It makes me cringe.*

Sophie didn't tell her sister that *pubic hair* is two words. There was so much she didn't tell her sister or her mom. They were happy Stepford Wives and Sophie was the Other. Of course, they had no idea about the extent of her Otherness. They didn't know she hooked up with girls in high school. They didn't know about her dabbles in college and they definitely didn't know about Cara. They considered it rebellious that she moved to New York City and married a Jewish indie rocker. *That* was what Sophie was working with.

Once Noah left her room, Sophie sank back on her bed, slid her phone out of her sweatshirt pocket, and opened Instagram again. She did that when she felt like crying but the tears wouldn't come. And they hadn't come for years.

Sophie waded through more of this morning's posts. Her sister was hosting a Halloween party next week. She'd put up photos of decorations and costumes. Madeline's beautiful daughter, Arabella, documented a recent shopping spree. And then there was Beatrice, with her shockingly golden eyes. Sophie folded a pillow under her head and glanced again at Beatrice's eyes.

When Sophie first met the boys' stepmom, Beatrice had hugged her tight, their breasts mashed together.

"I don't know what it is," Beatrice said, "but I feel like I know you."

Sophie wriggled out of Beatrice's grip and ducked her chin away. It was weird, meeting the person that your former husband has sex with. There should be a special allowance for rudeness in these situations.

After an awkward moment Sophie said, "Thanks for being sweet to Noah and Charlie."

"No problem." Beatrice batted the comment away with her hand. She wore a simple wedding band with a row of inset diamonds. "They make it easy."

Sophie stared at Beatrice's post from last night. #LavaFlow. That was the name of Joshua's drink. She popped over to the Jewel of Waikiki site. One of Joshua's drinks cost fourteen bucks. Two were twenty-eight. That covered Noah's field trip today, plus candy.

She tossed down her phone, called to the kids to rinse their breakfast dishes, and then went into the bathroom to start the shower. She didn't have extra minutes to wait for the water to heat up. She'd have to make do with a cold rinse.

lauren

LAUREN STROLLED THROUGH THE UNION Square Farmers Market, bought a honeycrisp apple, and wiped it shiny on her jeans. She had five minutes until her meeting, and she didn't want to go in hungry because she was nervous enough already. She was about to have coffee with a team of savvy young app developers. She'd had two similar meetings earlier in the week. Both disasters. For the first, they met at a brewery in Brooklyn. After Lauren described the wife app idea, they quoted a price so high she nearly spewed her local beer. The second agency told Lauren they were booked solid through next August.

This meeting was at a Starbucks near Union Square. Before they gathered, Lauren emailed a few questions to the CEO, a twentysomething guy named Brick. He responded that they had availability. He said they could discuss the fee in person. Even so, she had the jitters as she pushed open the heavy glass door at Starbucks.

"So you're envisioning a marketplace model," Brick said as he sipped his oat-milk chai a few minutes later. He had curly red hair, a pointy nose, and an arrogant tilt to his chin. He, along with his friend Magnus, started Mega Agency right out of MIT three years ago. They'd built several notable apps and came highly recommended. For today's meeting, they brought along a female colleague, Chloe, yet they hadn't given her a second to talk since they all sat down. If Lauren were being snarky, she'd say that Chloe was their token woman and their token person of color. Brick and Magnus gave off the vibe of caring more about how things looked than how they treated people.

"Exactly," Lauren said. She explained how the wife app would itemize and market the unpaid, behind-the-scenes work that a wife traditionally does.

"Hmmm." Magnus stroked his goatee and glanced sideways at Brick. His eyes were hooded with a purple tint to the skin underneath.

"Imagine all the things a wife complains about," Lauren said. "Or a wife does without complaining because she feels she has no choice. Kids' camp forms. Thank-you notes. Staying in touch with in-laws. Overseeing home maintenance, school applications, clothing donation, everyone's medical appointments. With this app, we would change the rules. Women could choose whether to do the work, or hire it out, or get their spouse to hire it out. As soon as the jobs become a choice, it relieves so much of the burden."

"Let me spitball this for a second," said Chloe. She touched her hijab and then looked to Brick and Magnus like *Please don't interrupt this time*. "There's the problem of privacy since you're offering windows into people's homes and marriages. Then again, task apps have been so successful. And this one has a fresh angle. I definitely think there could be something here."

Magnus continued to rub at his goatee. "But how would you monetize it?"

"We would discuss that," Lauren said. She had to resist the urge to knock Magnus's hand off his facial hair. "Obviously with the App Store you lose that percentage, so I was thinking—"

"What would be the screening process for bringing a wife on board?" Magnus pressed. "What kind of cut would you take? Would it be membership only?"

Lauren bunched her napkin in her fist. "I was thinking we would start with—"

"Sorry to cut this off," Brick said. "I'm all for women . . . for people of all genders . . . being empowered. That's obvious, right? Of course they should. But is compulsory domestic work really even a *thing* anymore?" Brick shook his head. "I'm just not feeling it. I mean, my girlfriend—" He gestured at Chloe and then said, "Chloe and Lila are good friends. Lila doesn't complain about me the way you're talking about. I think this whole gender-inequity thing is dated. Boomer stuff."

Lauren glared at him. What was he, twenty-five? When she was studying computer science at Vassar, this guy was still peeing in a diaper. "I beg to differ but—"

Brick nodded curtly. He was done here. "We have to think about our brand at Mega. We can't take on a wife app, Ms. Zuckerman. We would become a punch line."

Lauren jumped to her feet, thanked them for their time, and walked to the bathroom. *Ms. Zuckerman?* She wasn't even a boomer! Not that there was anything wrong with boomers. But he acted like she was ancient. Lauren washed her hands and then glanced at her phone. She still had a few hours before the girls got home. Maybe time for a nap, or a glass of wine on the couch. There was only so much rejection she could take in a week.

"Hey."

Chloe was waiting outside the bathroom door, glancing nervously toward the exit.

"Oh . . . hi," Lauren said, surprised. "I thought you all left."

"They're waiting outside. I said I had to run to the restroom." Chloe paused. "I just wanted to tell you that Lila complains about Brick a lot. I thought you should know. Like, he'll finish food and leave the empty package in the cupboard. And she has to tell him to drop off his laundry like she's his mom. Oh, and he never returns Amazon packages. He clicks to return them but then everything sits in a pile in their bedroom until she nags him about it. That drives her crazy."

"But doesn't he . . . ?" Lauren tried to gather her thoughts. "Does Brick know that Lila complains?"

"He's *heard*. I'm just not sure he's listened. Also, they were total douchebags back there. Don't tell them I said that because I need this job. Good luck, okay? Take care."

Chloe disappeared into the bathroom. As Lauren walked across Starbucks, she found herself smiling. Fuck them. Those guys dismissed her idea when all along they were *exactly* the sort of people who made a wife app necessary. Lauren sat at an empty table, entered the password on her phone, and composed an email to another round of developers.

"Hey, van Gogh!" Lauren exclaimed. She gave Sophie a hug as her friend walked into Paint and Sip on a Friday night in late October. Norah Jones played on the speakers. The air smelled of acrylic paint and wet brushes. Bottles of red and white wine sat on a table next to clear plastic cups and two bags of tortilla chips.

"More like Kahlo," Sophie said. "Or O'Keeffe. I'm here to represent overlooked female painters."

"I hardly think Frida Kahlo and Georgia O'Keeffe were overlooked," Lauren said.

"Sure, okay." Sophie squirted a puddle of blue onto a paper plate and studied her blank canvas. "But name three or four other famous female painters. Like, as quickly as we rattle off Picasso and Monet and Rembrandt and—"

"Got it, got it," Lauren said, laughing. "So you'll be Frida and I'll be Georgia."

"Are you ready to see some really bad art?" Madeline said as she walked in a few minutes later and hung her coat on a hook. "I have zero artistic talent, but it was hard to resist an evening out with my ladies."

"You can't be that bad," Lauren said.

Madeline grinned. "Oh yes I can."

Way back in January, when Lauren had bid for the Paint and Sip date night at the girls' school auction, she'd imagined a silly outing with Eric. She pretty much forgot about her painting voucher until recently, when she cleaned out her inbox and realized it would expire soon. Once her friends agreed to come, Lauren called Paint and Sip and booked the Paint Your Pet–themed evening, complete with cheap wine.

Sophie cinched a black apron behind her back. "Well, maybe some wine will help your art. Who's in?"

They both raised their hands and Sophie wandered across the studio to fill some plastic cups.

"What animal did you bring to paint?" Lauren asked as she clipped a photo of her goldendoodle, Coco, next to her palette. It was taken last fall, in Central Park. On the other side of the room, the instructor began to make the rounds, helping people outline their animals' eyes, snouts, body proportions. "I realize Paint Your Pet is a bit of a stretch for you."

Madeline reached into her purse and produced a printout of a generic orange goldfish in a round bowl.

"Since when do you have a fish?" Lauren asked.

"As you know, we're not a pet family," Madeline said. "I had to dredge up a goldfish to represent my childhood pet."

"You had a fish?"

Madeline soaked her paper plate in orange paint. "It wasn't a long-term thing. Maybe five or six months before the fish went belly-up. After that, Bianca said we were done. My mom isn't a pet person either."

"Wow," Lauren said. "That's the first time in our twelve years of friendship that I've heard you compare yourself to your mom."

Madeline rolled her eyes. "Oh god . . . please don't."

Lauren arranged her brushes in a row. Madeline peered at her photo of the goldfish. Sophie came back a moment later balancing three cups of wine in her hands.

"The drinks have arrived!" she sang.

"Let's paint some pets," Lauren said.

Madeline groaned from the back of her throat.

An hour later, the instructor suggested a break to clean brushes, refresh waters, and prepare new palettes. By this point, their canvases were in various stages—Coco was starting to look like a dog, albeit with lopsided ears and a crooked nose. Sophie's cat, Edna, definitely resembled a cat. And Madeline's goldfish . . . well . . . no comment there.

"I have a quick project for us," Lauren said after they tidied their painting areas. "Remember that wife app idea?"

"Where we wreak vengeance on our thankless exes?" Sophie said. "How could I forget?"

Madeline sipped her wine. "Are you still working on it?"

"Still?" Sophie asked.

Lauren nodded. She hadn't told Sophie yet that she'd asked Madeline about lawyers. Not that she was hiding anything. She just hadn't had the chance.

"I've had a few meetings with developers," Lauren said. "Most of them have been awful. I'm still searching."

"Hang on!" Sophie's voice rose. "You're actually building this thing?"

Lauren shrugged. "I'm trying. I don't know. I'll start simple, like, I don't think I'll do both iOS and Android. Android is a more open ecosystem, and I wouldn't have to submit it to the App Store. But if we want a high-value audience, then—"

"English, please," Sophie said.

"I'm saying it would be for iPhone," Lauren said quickly. "I'll do the initial build just for Apple. And it would be a limited audience, three or four zip codes. We can't have that many MAUs to start out."

"English," Sophie said again.

"Monthly Active Users. But that's light-years away. I still need to find developers. Since I come from the world of product management, I have a lot of names in mind."

"So what's the project?" Madeline asked. "For tonight. You said you had a quick project for us."

"Right." Lauren tapped on her phone. "I've just shared a link with you guys. It's a questionnaire about your strengths and weaknesses. I'm going to create an algorithm that will match wives, based on their abilities, with potential customers, based on their needs."

"What kinds of abilities?" Sophie asked.

"Open the link," Lauren said. "I think the questionnaire will speak for itself."

As her friends studied their phones, Lauren thought back to the past few weeks. Developers had either mocked or dismissed the idea. Madeline's lawyer warned her that a wife app concept was rife with privacy and trust concerns. Despite these setbacks, Lauren wasn't ready to give up. Once she assembled her team, she could picture the whiteboarding sessions, the brainstorming. . . .

"Am I good at domestic paperwork?" Sophie asked. "Heck yeah. I'm a demon at tracking down medical invoices and getting reimbursements from heartless health insurance companies."

Madeline nodded. "Oh my god, the school stuff! Yes. And I have no patience for pets. Can I click no to that?"

"Can I click no on ski rentals and lift passes?" Sophie said. "Rich-person sport. Sorry, Madeline."

"Be as honest as possible," Lauren said. She loved watching her friends tackle the questionnaire. It made her feel like a wife app was an entity that might actually become something.

"Kid stuff," Sophie said. "I'm great at anything from tutoring to school-related questions to direct childcare. But do we really want to interact with children? That seems dicey."

"I can arrange for housekeepers," Madeline said. "I have a PhD in setting up domestic help. This seems like a dating profile, Laur. Just without the sex."

"Imagine getting paid for all these things," Lauren said as she twirled a wet paintbrush between her fingers. "That's when the fun begins."

madeline

As ARABELLA BLOW-DRIED HER HAIR in her bedroom, Madeline glanced at her daughter's phone and sucked in her breath. Colin had texted Arabella a photo of a stone school building with a black wrought iron gate.

> **Dad:** Check this out! This is the school you'd likely go to next year. I'll set up a tour and interview for you over the Christmas holiday.

Arabella hadn't seen Colin's text yet. Madeline was tempted to delete it except that was the opposite of Serena Kilgannon's dictate to do nothing. But a school tour? *Keep calm and carry on, my ass!* Colin did NOT have Madeline's permission to move her to England!

Madeline grabbed her own phone, snapped a photo of this text, and forwarded it to the lawyer.

> **Madeline:** Look what Colin just sent to Arabella.

> **Madeline:** Please call as soon as you can.

> **Madeline:** I'm having a very hard time doing nothing

"Mom?" Arabella shouted from her bedroom. "Where's my pale pink top? I can't find it! I literally have nothing to wear."

Madeline jerked upright, her heart racing. Knots pinched at the base of her skull. She needed to get a massage soon or she could wind up with a migraine.

"Your shirt's probably in the laundry," Madeline said. "Willow is going to do the wash today. We want everything ready so we can pack for Florida."

Ugh. Florida. Madeline dreaded Thanksgiving with her mom and stepdad. That likely contributed to her tightening neck.

"What should I wear, then?" Arabella asked.

"Want my help?" Madeline asked. "You can borrow my clothes if you want."

"Nah, I'll find something."

Madeline glanced out the picture window onto Central Park. It was a sunny November morning. She could see runners and bikers, tiny as mice, as they whizzed south on the park loop.

"Okay, I'm off," Arabella called from the foyer a few minutes later. She had on tight jeans and a black tank that revealed her midriff, and she shoved sections of tangerine into her mouth. In her other hand, she gripped her phone and a leather jacket. Clearly Arabella had read her texts by this point, yet not a word about it to her mom.

Madeline forced herself to smile. "Have a great day, sweetie. Good luck on your bio test."

Arabella rubbed her hand on the thigh of her jeans, then slung on her boxy Swedish backpack. "Mom, are you okay? You have a strange look on your face."

Her daughter knew her too well.

"No, I'm okay," Madeline said. "Just a little headache."

As soon as Arabella left, Madeline lowered the blinds in her bedroom and curled onto her California king bed. She stared at her phone, waiting for Serena to respond. She clicked on Bumble and then closed it. Today was not a sex day. Willow would arrive soon to do the breakfast dishes, the laundry, help them get organized for their trip.

A minute or two later, her phone rang.

Serena Kilgannon Lawyer!

Madeline shimmied up so her hips were against the stack of pillows and swept her hair back from her forehead.

"Hi, Serena." Madeline tried to sound composed, not like someone who had just been in the fetal position.

"I saw your text," Serena said.

"Thank you for calling. Can you believe Colin sent Arabella a picture of a school?"

"Of course I can. I've seen it all. My initial reaction is that they can tour every school to the moon and back but it doesn't make a difference because you have primary residential custody."

Madeline sighed. "Can you review with me again exactly what that means in this circumstance?"

"As we've discussed," Serena told her, "it's not in Colin's rights to take Arabella to London even for a year. If he wants to go through with this plan, he would have to start by hiring counsel. I imagine he would retain counsel in New York. Then there would be back-and-forths between his counsel and me to see if we can strike an agreement. If we can't, Colin would have to file a motion and we'd all go to court for a hearing."

"Court." Madeline moaned. Serena had mentioned this before, when they first spoke in October. She hated the idea of putting Arabella through court, making her pick sides.

"And if, with all the motions and lawyers and litigations, a compelling enough case is presented to the judge that Arabella would benefit from *one year* with her dad in London, then we would put that in writing, mutually signed. *One year.* Not all of high school. Not forever."

Madeline whimpered from the back of her throat. "That could actually happen? But she goes to school here. She goes to Juilliard Pre-College and has a cello teacher, one of the best in the country."

"I'm presenting scenarios so nothing catches you off guard," Serena said. "Colin's counsel would have to make a compelling case to take Arabella away from her home and school and mom. He would have to arrange for a cello teacher at the same level as the one in New York."

Madeline wiped tears away with her sheet. She loved being the CEO of Arabella's Life. It was a job that fulfilled her. Colin had chosen London. She had chosen Arabella.

"The law is on our side," Serena said. "Your side. But from what I gather, Colin hasn't even retained counsel. Keep doing nothing, Madeline. Call me whenever you get nervous. That's what I'm here for. And have a happy Thanksgiving."

After they hung up, Madeline pressed her fist into the base of her skull. The glare from the phone hurt her eyes. She had some calls today and an Urban Zen yoga class but maybe she should cancel and get some sleep. The front door opened and footsteps entered the foyer. Madeline flung her phone onto her bedspread. She generally liked to be up when Willow was over, doing her part to seem productive. But as soon as she stood, her brain exploded with a wave of pain that sent her flat onto her back.

"Hello?" Willow called out. "Madeline?"

"Hey," Madeline said quietly. "I'm in bed. A bit of a migraine."

"Oh . . . oh shit . . . poor you. It's been a while, right?"

Willow was in her late twenties, Irish, perennially cheerful despite also swearing like a sailor. A decade ago, Willow moved from Dublin to New York City to become an actor. She had a boyfriend she loved and a solid group of expat friends. There was a lack of angst in Willow that Madeline envied.

"Is there anything you need?" Willow asked from the other room.

"An ice pack? A strong cup of coffee? I've heard that helps."

"I think I'll just try to sleep," Madeline said.

"Okay, well . . . let me know."

Willow sounded so sympathetic, so kind. Madeline suddenly missed a mom's hug. Not that she'd ever had that kind of mom. Bianca didn't do coloring books on sick days or kisses on boo-boos. That was one of the reasons that Madeline was hands-on with her own daughter. She'd been lonely throughout her childhood, and she never wanted Arabella to feel that way.

Madeline's phone rang. *Arabella!*

"Hey . . . honey?" she asked. The pain surged in her head so intensely she thought she might vomit. "Are you okay? You're at school, right?"

"Yeah . . . but, Mom, you wouldn't believe what happened on my way here. I got pooped on by a bird! On my shirt! It was too warm out to wear my jacket so my only clean shirt got completely disgusting."

"Oh, gross." Madeline pushed her knuckles into her eye. "Want me to bring you a new shirt? I'm sure I can find something." Even with the migraine, Madeline would stumble to Fryer Prep so her daughter wouldn't have to walk around with shit on her clothes.

"It's okay," Arabella said. "I have an extra in my gym locker. I just wanted to tell you. Gotta go. I'm late to class!"

Madeline lay back on her pillow, whimpering in pain. It was all Colin's fault! She was done with keeping calm and doing nothing. She was done with restraint.

She picked up her phone and texted her ex-husband.

> **Madeline:** I can't believe you would do this.

> **Colin:** Hi to you too.

> **Colin:** Do what?

> **Madeline:** Invite Arabella to London for a year.

Madeline: Take her away from me.

Colin didn't respond immediately. Madeline stared at the ellipsis on the screen even though the glow made her stomach roil with nausea.

Colin: Madeline, I didn't invite her.

Madeline: What do you mean?

Colin: It was her idea. Arabella was the one who suggested it.

sophie

Sophie was working with a student at the small table in her office when Lauren texted.

> **Lauren:** Can you talk?

> **Sophie:** Not right now.

> **Sophie:** I'm with a student.

> **Lauren:** Let's talk ASAP. Exciting update with TWA!

Sophie turned her phone over. That night at Paint and Sip a few weeks ago, she was trying to be supportive of her friend. But the last thing she wanted to do was get hired out as a wife. It sounded awful.

Across the table, her student stared at the worksheet and shifted uncomfortably. It stunk to be the kid who could barely decipher picture books when your peers bonded over *Diary of a Wimpy Kid*. But with Sophie's help he was improving. That's why she liked her job. Usually. If only it paid more. If only her office wasn't a repurposed utility closet.

Sophie wanted to call Lauren back but, once this student was gone, she had to email his parents with an update. *Parents*. Who was she kidding? Sophie only ever corresponded with the boy's mom. Moms were the ones who emailed the literacy specialists and occupational therapists and swim teachers and doctors. Once, when Noah was tiny and Sophie brought him to the pediatrician, she apologized to the doctor for her long list of questions.

Dr. Thierry reassured Sophie with a smile. "You and every new mom I've ever had in my practice."

"Not dads?"

Dr. Thierry's laugh was so infectious that Sophie smiled. Dr. Thierry was a lesbian, probably in her early fifties then, with a cowboy vibe—tight jeans, tall boots, Western shirts. Sophie had only known her a few months at that point but she already had a crush.

"Do you want to hear what dads ask at infant checkups?" Dr. Thierry said to Sophie. "When new dads bring in their babies, which isn't a lot, they rarely have the long list. But they uniformly have urgent questions about their baby boys' penises. *Did the circumcision heal okay? Why is the penis so small? When will it grow?*" Dr. Thierry swiped rubbing alcohol across Noah's little thigh to prepare him for his vaccine. Sophie looked away. She hated to imagine her baby feeling a pinch of pain.

"Really? That's what they ask?"

"True," Dr. Thierry said. She injected the shot and then stabbed the used needle into the exam table. Moms on Yelp raved that Dr. Thierry was "the fastest shot on the Upper West Side."

As Sophie thought back on her now, nearly twelve years later, she missed Dr. Thierry. She and her wife retired early and moved to the Caribbean to sail and run an early childhood healthcare program.

Sophie hit "send" on her email and finally called Lauren.

"Hey, Soph!" Lauren said. "It's been too long."

"I know . . . but I only have a few minutes." Sophie tapped her screen to speakerphone and leaned back in her chair.

"Got it," Lauren said. "I'll dive right in. I'm done with the Wife App. That's what I'm calling it. Wife App."

Sophie lurched upright, her spine straight. "You didn't really build it, did you?"

"Of course I did. Remember your questionnaire? Did you think I wasn't going to do it? Well, I got a lot of help." Lauren paused. "I spent a fortune hiring a team of people."

Sophie didn't answer. She honestly didn't know what to say.

"The developers are working out the final bugs," Lauren said. "We've had about a million setbacks, of course, but I think we're almost there. I've asked the designer to do some final tweaks. I'm going to submit it to the App Store in the next day or so. If they approve it, we're good to go. Isn't that crazy?"

Sophie stared at a poster of a kitten on her wall. It was one thing to be mad at Eric and Joshua and Colin and plot *faux* revenge. It was another entirely to turn women into prostitutes for the mental load!

"Soph?" Lauren asked. "Are you following me?"

"I hadn't . . ." Sophie paused.

"I promise you it looks awesome. I've overseen dozens of apps so I'm unbiased when I say that it's fresh and new. Just wait until you see it. For a fee, the Wives—capital W—relieve people of their Mental Load. Capital M, capital L."

Sophie twisted a strand of her blond hair around her pinky.

"We'll bring on more Wives if it takes off," Lauren said. "They don't have to be cisgender women. Or even women! A Wife just has to be someone who can keep ten million balls in the air without having a nervous fucking breakdown. Imagine getting paid for it."

Sophie sipped her water. "Does Madeline know yet?"

"I just texted her."

"What if people don't use it? What if people think it's a big joke?"

Lauren cleared her throat. "Then we'll—"

"Hang on," Sophie said to Lauren. Someone had just knocked on her office door.

Charlie's second-grade teacher, Jessi Choi, peeked her head in. "Is this a bad time? I can come back."

"I've got to go," Sophie told Lauren. "I'll call you later."

Sophie beckoned Jessi to the low wooden table where she worked with students. She tried to smile but her mouth felt stiff.

"Sorry to bust in," Jessi said as Sophie joined her at the table. Everyone loved Jessi. She was the teacher who hatched ducklings and played piano, the one every mom requested for their child. "I just dropped my class off at art. Do you have a few minutes? I wanted to talk about Charlie and the farmers market field trip. We had another one today."

Sophie tried to get a deep breath but couldn't pull in enough air. "Right. Charlie always gets worried about those field trips."

"As you know, he's an amazing student. He's so bright and he always asks fascinating questions." Jessi pressed her lips together. "I know you said he struggles with anxiety."

At the parent-teacher conference, Sophie had explained to Jessi about Charlie's bloody fingers. It's not like it was a secret. She sent Band-Aids in his backpack every day and instructed him to put them on if he was peeling at his skin.

"Right," Jessi said. "So . . . the field trip."

Jessi adjusted her knees under the table. She was probably five six. Sophie was shorter at five one but her body still jammed awkwardly into this child's chair.

"It was a rough field trip for Charlie," Jessi explained. "He was in Penny's mom's group, but I had to switch him into my group."

"*Charlie* had to get switched?" Sophie asked. She wouldn't have been surprised to hear this about her older son but Charlie was always too timid to get himself in trouble.

"Yep," Jessi said. "He stopped every minute to check the bottom of his sneakers. Finally, Penny's mom asked what was going on and Charlie said he was worried he'd stepped on dog poop. She reassured him that he didn't. *But what if I did?* he asked. He wouldn't stop checking."

Sophie reached for a paper clip on the table and began to unbend it. This new sneaker-checking habit had started a few weeks ago, after Joshua took the boys to Central Park and Charlie stepped in dog poop. After that, he checked occasionally. Now it was several times a walk.

"Did he check that many times?" Sophie asked. "Was it actually disruptive?"

"We got to the farmers market ten minutes after the other second-grade classes. I'm not saying kids are going to make fun of him. They're not that aware yet. But I wanted to talk to you as soon as possible because it seems like a growing problem."

As Sophie's fingers worked at the paper clip, Jessi shook her head quickly.

"Charlie's young," she said. "Problems can be worked on. I'm not a clinician so I don't want to speak where I'm not qualified. But have you considered he might have OCD?"

"I have." Sophie swallowed some water but her mouth felt immediately dry again.

"You could take him in for a consultation," Jessi offered. "Maybe a few CBT sessions can nip it in the bud."

A few sessions. The good cognitive behavioral therapists were more than three hundred a session. And no one did just a few. More like six to twelve months of sessions. That kind of bud-nipping would sink her.

Once Jessi left, Sophie flicked the mangled paper clip across the table. Her neck was hot and her eyes stung. She snatched up her phone and opened Instagram. *Backyard tree houses. Happy couples. Perfect kids.* All the things she desperately wanted and could never have.

That afternoon, Charlie had martial arts in the school gym. Sophie hurried to Trader Joe's in the deluded hope that there wouldn't be a crowd and she could take care of her Thanksgiving grocery list. Unfortunately, the line stretched down the block. She'd come back later, once the boys were in bed.

Sophie walked over to Central Park, sat on a bench, and looked through Beatrice's Instagram. Joshua, Beatrice, and Clementine were visiting her parents in Los Angeles and had just driven out to Palm Springs for a sun-drenched overnight. Sophie had thought bearing witness to the Hawaii trip last month was bad enough. She couldn't stand to think what these trips cost. Ten sessions of CBT therapy for Charlie? Throw in the soccer camp in New Hampshire that Noah desperately wanted to go to, but Sophie couldn't afford.

Thinking about all this, Sophie tapped Joshua's number. She didn't care that he was on vacation! She was going to tell him that Charlie needed therapy and they would split the cost and that was that.

"Sophie." Joshua's voice was flat.

"It's about Charlie," she said. "He needs help."

"I'm in Palm Springs. We're about to order lunch."

When Sophie didn't say anything, Joshua sighed loudly. "I'll get back to you in five minutes."

"Good," Sophie said. She stood up and started walking toward the Reservoir.

Five minutes later, her phone was silent. Did Joshua even *ask* if Charlie was okay? Most parents would start with that. Is he sick? Injured? Not her ex.

After fifteen minutes, Sophie slowed her pace. Joshua still hadn't called back. Now she felt stupid. She imagined him complaining to Beatrice about his nagging ex-wife, and for some reason, that felt worse than anything. People celebrate divorce like it's a big milestone, but a bad marriage is never over. It's a grueling slog with no end in sight.

At four-thirty, Sophie picked up Charlie from afterschool. He gripped tight to a gourd from the farmers market. This was part of the food study that would culminate in a Harvest Festival next week.

Sophie had planned for them to walk home but after Charlie checked his sneakers twice in one block she steered him onto a bus, handed him her phone, and stared out the window for the next fifteen blocks.

At nine-thirty that night, as Sophie was walking out of Trader Joe's with a canvas bag on each shoulder, her phone rang in her pocket.

"So . . . what's up?" Joshua asked casually.

Not: *I'm sorry it took me six hours to return your call.*

Not: *Is this a good time?*

Sophie wanted to hang up on him. But then she thought of poor Charlie, and she knew she had to swallow her pride.

"Charlie had another farmers market field trip with his class today," she said.

Silence from Joshua.

"It didn't go well," Sophie added.

More silence.

She pictured Joshua scrolling through his phone. She never got his full attention, even when they were together.

Sophie crossed Broadway. "Jessi came to my office to talk to me. She said Charlie had to be switched to the teacher's group."

"What happened?" Joshua asked.

Sophie shifted both bags to one shoulder and explained about Penny's mom, the dog-poop checks, what the teacher said about cognitive behavioral therapy.

Joshua snorted. "Is Jessi offering to pay for CBT?"

Sophie froze mid-step. She did not see that coming, but of course she should have.

"Penny has a goddamn lisp," Joshua added. "Why doesn't her mom deal with her lisp and leave Charlie the fuck alone? His IQ is probably higher than the two of theirs combined."

Sophie began to walk again. The groceries were heavy on her left shoulder but she had forgotten her earbuds so she needed her right hand to hold the phone.

"I've found some CBT centers," she said. "They specialize in working with anxious children. The sooner we get him started, the better. And IQ doesn't have anything to do with this. A lot of intelligent people struggle with anxiety."

"We've talked about this," Joshua said. "You're pathologizing a seven-year-old. Also, I've read about how to handle it. He and I have a deal. If he stops doing these things, I'm going to buy him the Death Star. Admit that's not a more appropriate way to spend money on a child."

This is what burned Sophie to a crisp. Joshua did a twenty-minute Google search on "childhood anxiety" and deemed himself more qualified than a psychologist.

"Charlie needs therapy," Sophie said but her voice caught.

"What was that, Soph?"

Sophie shuddered. She hated when he called her *Soph*. He had lost that privilege. They weren't family anymore.

"Joshua, he couldn't stop erasing his homework tonight. His fingers are bloody. I'm just asking you to cover half."

"How are you going to come up with your half?" Joshua asked. "I know the budget you're working with. You don't have it."

True. Sophie didn't. But that wasn't his business. She could run up her credit card. She could borrow it from her sister and beg her not to tell their mom.

"I'm just asking you to cover half," Sophie said again.

Joshua groaned. "Dammit. I'm on vacation. I had a shitty day. And no matter how much guilt you heap on, you are not going to twist my arm into this."

Sophie's body felt both hot and cold, like she was spiking a fever. She wanted to scream but it wouldn't help to lose her cool right now. Anyway, that wasn't in her DNA. Someday, when Sophie was eighty, she planned to become a royal bitch. When she was eighty, she'd poke her umbrella at people on the bus who tried to steal her seat. She'd hold up grocery lines to count dimes from her wallet. She'd sample as many ice-cream flavors as she wanted. She'd scream at people who cycled the wrong direction in bike lanes. And she'd love every righteous minute of it. But she had forty years left to be the bigger person.

"Subject change," Joshua said suddenly. "Do you remember when I got my last tetanus shot?"

"Why?"

"I fell and gashed my hand on some metal today. It was stupid. I tripped in a parking lot. My doctor in New York doesn't have record of a tetanus shot, and said if I haven't had one in the last ten years I need to go to urgent care here."

Sophie hoisted her bags higher on her shoulder. Interesting how Joshua's new wife didn't mention this during all her *#palmsprings* and *#californialove* posts today.

"No," she said. "I don't remember."

"Are you sure? I feel like I got one at some point. You're always so good at remembering that stuff."

Of course Sophie remembered. Clear as the blue sky over Palm Springs. *That's what wives do,* she wanted to tell Joshua. *They store decades of information in their brains. They know who needs to be when, where, and why. Oh, right. You don't think mental load is real.*

Sophie made the instant decision not to remind Joshua about the August she dragged him to a mildewy rental on Fire Island to rekindle the dying embers of their marriage. That first afternoon, Joshua had sliced his foot on a rusty wagon wheel. They caught a ferry to the mainland, then a cab to urgent care for stitches and a tetanus shot. For the rest of the trip, Joshua smoked weed in the Airbnb while Sophie took long walks on the beach and worked up the nerve to issue him an ultimatum: clean up or get out. They separated four months later.

"No," she said. "I really don't."

"Shit . . . too bad," Joshua said now. Then he cleared his throat. "I have to meet Beatrice for dinner. I better jump off."

After they hung up, Sophie called Lauren. "Hey, is it too late?"

"Nah," Lauren said. "I'm organizing the girls for their Thanksgiving trip to their grandma's. Eric is taking them to Brookline. Everything okay?"

"I just wanted to ask—" Sophie paused. "With the Wife App, would it be possible to earn five or six thousand dollars?"

Lauren laughed. "Seriously?"

"It's either that or robbing a bank. Charlie needs expensive therapy and I'm sick of begging for handouts. Do you think there are big Wife jobs that aren't . . . you know . . . illegal?"

"Conceivably, yes," Lauren said. "I've designed the app to start modestly. But the big money could definitely happen. It all depends on people's Mental Loads."

Sophie shivered. The temperature had dropped. The forecast threatened a slushy mix tomorrow.

"I can drop by your place this weekend and walk you through the app if you want," Lauren offered.

"Not in front of the boys, okay? I have no idea how I would even begin to explain that their mom is becoming a wife-for-hire."

Lauren laughed. "Of course."

"How would we collect payments?" Sophie pictured crisp bills slid from a silver money clip.

"I can explain more in person. It would be a free app on the App Store. But if someone wants to join as a Spouse, they have to become a paid member. That entitles them to certain access to Wives. For more money, more Wifing. Do you think you want to give it a try?"

Sophie turned onto her block. "I'll be a Wife. Or I guess I should say . . ." She grinned and then tacked on the two words she never thought she'd utter again. "I do."

lauren

THANKSGIVING WEEKEND AND LAUREN'S DAUGHTERS were gone for four days. Four days of freedom! Four days to eat when she wanted, sleep when she wanted, stream whatever shows she wanted. She missed cuddling with the girls on the couch or being an audience at one of Cady's fashion shows, or kissing Amelia's forehead as she tucked her in at night. But between finalizing the divorce and building the app and keeping up with her regular freelance workload, it had been an intense fall. Some nights, Lauren was so spent from balancing it all that she had to limp into bed.

The first evening they were gone, Lauren changed into pajamas at six, ate microwave popcorn for dinner, fired up Netflix, and fluctuated between elation at the freedom from responsibility and guilt over how happy she was that her children were gone.

Back when she was married, she once asked Eric if he felt guilty missing parent-teacher conferences and classroom potlucks when he traveled for work. He laughed and said, "I expense five-star dinners with wine pairings in San Francisco and London. All while earning a living. Nah, I'm okay skipping those things. Especially since you represent so well." He didn't even say it in an asshole way. It rang as a compliment. Because she *did* represent well. Even if her one-star dinner was often pasta with the girls.

The thing was, Eric wasn't actually an asshole. A silver lining of the divorce was that Eric had stepped it up with Cady and Amelia. This Thanksgiving, instead of relying on Lauren to be the family cruise director, he had made plans! The three of them were staying with his mom in Brookline, Massachusetts. He set up a family brunch in Boston, and he'd gotten them all tickets to a *Wicked* matinee on Saturday.

Did it gnaw at her stomach that she wasn't there, like past holidays in Eric's childhood home, unfolding the pullout couch and creaking through back twinges and bad sleep? Of course it did. She missed the familiar smell of Eric's chest hair. She missed the mugs of morning coffee. But she was happy that Cady and Amelia got to celebrate Thanksgiving with their dad and grandma. Lauren briefly panicked that Trish would join them for the long weekend. But every time Eric talked about plans, he only mentioned their daughters and his mom, so Lauren forced herself to put this particular fear out of her mind. It was good for the girls that Eric—usually distracted with his long hours at Equity Investors—granted them four days of his undivided time.

If only Lauren could make the happy feeling last.

But, goddamn, she was stressed.

She was stressed because she had maybe, possibly fucked up big-time.

Unlike when you're married and there's a partner to bail you out, Lauren's impulsive decision was one hundred percent on her.

Lauren paused Netflix, carried her half-finished popcorn to the kitchen counter, and lowered her head into her hands.

Fuuuuuuuuck.

In her blind enthusiasm over the Wife App, she'd burned through almost all of her divorce settlement in six weeks. She tried to push this terrifying knowledge aside but sometimes, like at this very moment, the realization came hurtling back to her.

But it had also been so thrilling! How could she not do it? Over the past month and a half, Lauren had contacted everyone she'd ever known in tech and asked for recommendations of designers and developers. She queried people about who was between jobs, who was good, who could work at lightning speed. Quickly she assembled a dream team. She hired a designer from the Dominican Republic who knocked out a catchy Wife App logo that took her breath away. Lauren interviewed several developers and chose two Stanford grad students. Both women. Since they were still students, she was able to score a discount rate. Not dirt cheap but better than those initial quotes. Lauren paid a bit extra in exchange for them agreeing to relinquish equity.

None of it had been easy—software development never was—and whenever the Stanford women encountered a bump in the road that would cost yet more to smooth out or steer around, Lauren was overcome with anxiety about the money she was pouring into a gamble that may not amount to anything. At many points during the past month, Lauren's stress levels were through the roof—she had a sore throat for two solid weeks in early November—but it was also a relief to freak out about something other than her failed marriage. Despite struggles and setbacks, Lauren and the developers and the designer worked their asses off and, in record time, the first iteration was complete.

Yesterday afternoon, Lauren submitted the Wife App to the App Store. Now she awaited approval. The Apple review team generally took a day, maybe two. Lauren checked her account nonstop. Every time she saw that her build was "processing" her heart grew heavier. If the app got rejected—a large percentage did—she would appeal. But that would involve more coding, more testing, more money. Then again, what if the Wife App was approved and nobody downloaded it?

Lauren stretched upward from the counter, scooped a handful of popcorn, and tapped her password into App Store Connect.

Processing.

How could it *still* be processing? Okay, sure, it was the night before Thanksgiving. Lauren refreshed her account just in case.

Processing.

She refreshed again.

Processing.

She had to get outside.

Lauren stripped off her pajamas, pulled on jeans, a bra, a blouse. She tapped a playlist on her phone, zipped up her jacket, and walked to the elevator. There was a festive vibe on the sidewalk. Couples and families laughed together on this night before the holiday. Lauren bravely squared her shoulders and turned right in the direction of the Museum of Natural History, where they inflate the massive balloons for the Macy's parade. She used to bring the girls to see the balloon inflation when they were younger, usually with a brigade of other moms and kids. As they herded their children through the crowd, the moms would pass out snacks and then receive crumpled wrappers as if they were human trash cans. The kids would whine that they were cold, they had to pee, this was *boooor-ing.* The more deplorable the kids got, the more the moms ramped up their justification. *What a privilege that we're available in the afternoons,* they would murmur to each other. *It's a trade-off, but it's worth it.*

"Lauren?"

Lauren pushed her headphones around her neck and turned toward the sound of someone calling her name. It was busy on the sidewalk, a block from the museum.

"Hey, Lauren!" said a woman. She had earbuds in, and her hair was blown out, her toothy smile shiny with lipstick. "It is *so* good to see you. It's been way too long."

As the woman pinched out her earbuds and cupped them in one palm, Lauren struggled to remember her name. Oddly, she could picture the food this woman provided for potlucks in the girls' various classes. She always brought in freshly cut fruit with a sprig of mint and an air of smugness. Right. It was Ayala Grant. Mom of Daisy.

"I love your boots," Ayala said as she planted a light kiss on each cheek. At least she stopped at two. "I was eyeing the same pair on Zappos."

"Thanks." Lauren mustered a smile. "It's great to see you too."

Total lie. Lauren had never liked Ayala. It wasn't just the fresh fruit or how Ayala raised her hand at back-to-school nights and asked questions like, *What if the math isn't challenging enough for my child?* Rail thin and always with a dusting of makeup, Ayala was an oral surgeon but she also managed to fetch Daisy from school a few afternoons a week. On the other days, her hunky husband brought Daisy to violin lessons or modern dance. Ayala was perfect and Lauren—admittedly, guiltily—resented her for that.

"You're in town for Thanksgiving?" Ayala asked.

"No big plans this year. What about you?"

Back when their daughters went to school together, Ayala often mentioned a country house in the Hudson Valley. Or was it Connecticut?

Ayala nodded. "I'm on call. We'll do Thanksgiving here and then head to Connecticut on Saturday morning. We've leased a horse for Daisy up there and she can't stand being away from him."

Lauren forced herself to hold her smile in place. She hadn't even realized leasing a horse was a *thing*.

"Daisy begs us to enter her into shows," Ayala said as she rolled her eyes. "Nick and I tell her, 'Just enjoy riding . . . don't worry about competition,' but she keeps winning blue ribbons."

"Wow," Lauren said flatly.

Ayala cocked her head to one side. "So how *are* Cady and Amelia?"

Lauren knew what was coming next. She knew in the way you know it's going to rain or you sense your period is coming. "They're happy in school," she said. "Lots of homework."

Ayala released a long breath. "I guess, more importantly, how are *you*? Are you hanging in there?"

Lauren coughed into her fist. Ayala must have heard about Lauren's divorce through the mom network. Now she was offering her ear in exchange for a savory nugget that she could pass on to other mommies like bad-news currency in the market of playground-bench gossip. Lauren knew this because she'd partaken in it too. She wasn't proud of the fact, but it was true; she'd relished in other women's rocky marriages as their kids arched across monkey bars and dipped their grubby hands into bags of Pirate's Booty.

"I'm okay," she said. "It hasn't been the easiest year but we're figuring it out."

Ayala waited, red lips pressed together, eyes unblinking. Lauren was not in the mood for this.

"We'd been married for fourteen years," Lauren added. No way was she going to tell Ayala what really happened. "We'd grown apart."

Ayala shook her head. "I was shocked when I heard. You guys seemed like one of the solid couples. I loved talking to Eric at the school auctions. Nick thought he was great too."

"It happens." Lauren glanced toward the museum. "So I'm headed to see the balloons getting inflated. I should probably . . ."

"I'll walk you over. I'm going to grab Nick's favorite Oktoberfest beer. You can only get it at this special place on Columbus. He loves the beer and you know how it goes . . . got to keep him happy!"

As they walked together, Ayala warned her to watch for clenching her jaw at night. "I must do two extractions a week for recently divorced women. Hairline fractures in their molars. Implants aren't cheap."

"How much?" Lauren asked. With her recent Wife App spending spree, she didn't have a lot of spare money for, well, anything.

"Several thousand with the crown," Ayala said. "More if your insurance doesn't cover the extraction. I'm not trying to scare you. Clearly, there are a lot of people who go through a divorce and keep all their teeth. Just ask your dentist to fit you for a mouth guard. Nick and I have mouth guards."

They reached the end of the block. As Lauren watched Ayala go, she wondered if that's how she used to sound. Did she mention Eric in practically every sentence? Did she dash out to pick up his favorite beer because, you know, *got to keep him happy*? Yes. Probably.

Well, if the Wife App got approved, she wouldn't scurry around for a man unless she was getting paid. Lauren pulled out her phone and checked App Store Connect.

Processing.

She ran her tongue over her teeth and was relieved that, for now, everything was intact.

madeline

MADELINE HATED WIVES. No. NOT completely true. She hated wives who were married to men. Okay, still not totally true. Some hetero wives maintained a sense of individuality and didn't answer every invitation with "Let me check with my husband." But most women swapped their autonomy for a wedding band. Madeline wanted to line them all up and slap sense into them.

This violent reaction always happened after twenty-four hours with her mom. Bianca pampered Madeline's stepdad like he was a prince. She and Arabella had landed in Florida the day before. Madeline was already biting her tongue to keep from telling her mom to screw herself, her oppressive marriage, and her plastic mansion on the beach.

Madeline counted the seconds until they got on the plane back to New York City. This often happened when she left Manhattan—a panic crept in as if she'd lost her child in a crowded store. Her freshman year at Colby, after only a few months in rural Maine, she'd sprinted back to her palatial childhood apartment on the Upper East Side. Oh, the disappointment on her mom's face! That wasn't anything new. For as long as Madeline could remember, she'd been on the receiving end of her mom's frowns.

"What will I tell my friends?" Bianca had asked when Madeline announced over Christmas break that she wasn't going back to Colby. "Do I say you're dropping out of college?"

"I'm not *dropping out of college*," Madeline reassured her. "Tell your friends I'll transfer in the fall. I've already put in applications to Columbia and NYU and some of the CUNYs."

It wasn't until years later, once Madeline gave birth to Arabella, that she realized the ridiculousness of that whole argument. It was all about Bianca's peer group's reaction! Not: *Are you okay?* Not: *Did something bad happen at college?* Because she hadn't been okay that fall in Maine. When she was away from home, she felt more than ever that her dad was truly dead. She knew rationally that he'd been gone for four years. But when Madeline was in the city, she sensed her dad's presence in the chaotic sidewalks, the cabdrivers, the pedestrians who raged at each other just because they felt like raging. She had no memories of her dad in rural Maine.

Unlike Madeline's dad, her mom was all about conformity. She was petite and blond and reminded Madeline of a nervous bird—bony arms that fluttered and a bitty beak of a nose. Bianca and Ron, Madeline's stepfather, spent winters on Sanibel Island and summers in the Hamptons, a migration pattern nearly identical to Bianca's entire flock.

This Thanksgiving in Florida, Bianca was obsessed with Arabella. She listened, enraptured, as Arabella played Schumann's Cello Concerto in A Minor, op. 129. She took Arabella shopping and brought her to the country club for tennis lessons. Ron didn't say much—he'd always struck Madeline as bland. When he did talk, it was to comment that Arabella had turned out lovely, as if he were surprised Madeline did *something* right.

In her mom and stepdad's narrow worldview, she was a trust-fund dilettante who dropped out of school whenever she got bored. Which was why, for the month before Thanksgiving, Madeline had been worried that they would discover she was going to possibly lose residential custody of Arabella for a year. They'd crucify her for failing at that too.

It's not like it was a done deal. Serena reassured her that the law was on her side. But as Madeline was discovering, the law was one thing and emotions were another. When she first learned about London, she felt enraged at Colin for trying to steal her daughter. But then she found out it was Arabella who suggested it. *My daughter wants to be away from me? What have I done wrong? Is it too late to make things right?* These were such painful questions that Madeline could barely think them, much less voice them out loud. Which was why she hadn't talked about London with Arabella since Colin first emailed her about it. Well, not until yesterday.

On the flight to Fort Myers, up in the first-class cabin, Madeline decided to break the silence. Arabella sat across the aisle with her cello buckled in next to her.

"Honey." Madeline reached across the aisle, touched her daughter's knee, and gestured for her to slide off her headphones. "Honey, I need to talk to you."

"What?" Arabella hated when her mom interrupted her screen-time. She was currently watching *Breaking Bad* for the third time and nibbling a bar of Jacques Torres chocolate.

"I just wanted to say . . . don't tell Grandma about London next year." Madeline quickly added, "About how that's a possibility. Dad and I have been texting about it. Nothing is decided yet."

Madeline pressed her palms together and exhaled slowly into them. It was true that she and Colin had been texting back and forth. It hadn't gotten ugly, but Colin also wouldn't concede to Madeline's request to scrap the plan.

"Why not?" Arabella combed her fingers through her long hair.

"Grandma will have too many questions. She'll get nosy. She'll want *in* on every detail."

Arabella shimmied on her headphones again. Madeline closed her eyes and tried a few calming breaths.

"Is that it?" Arabella asked. She pinched up a triangle of chocolate, waiting to take a bite.

Madeline smiled tensely and nodded, *Yes, that was it*.

Unfortunately, that brief conversation on the plane created a wall of tension. Arabella closed the door to their shared bathroom at Bianca and Ron's house as she brushed her teeth. She practiced cello for hours and then went to bed without calling out her usual good night. And whenever Madeline came near her, Arabella pulled her phone tight to her chest like she was protecting state secrets.

As Madeline lay in her guest bed on Thursday night, her stomach rumbled hungrily. On the night of Thanksgiving, of all times! Bianca and Ron were extreme dieters, so dinner had been dry turkey and steamed veggie sides. This was how they'd rolled for years. When her first husband died, something in Bianca shifted. Madeline's dad had been a large man—booming voice, big personality, bushy eyebrows, ravenous appetite—and his heart attack came after he ignored warnings about high cholesterol. Madeline doubted that anyone could have gotten her father to tame his lifestyle. Regardless, Bianca saw it as a personal failure. She'd flunked at her wifely job of keeping her husband alive. Once she landed her next husband, Bianca consulted nutritionists about heart-friendly menus and scheduled Ron for stress tests and exercised with him. Madeline was sixteen when Ron showed up. She used to sneak croissants the way other kids got drunk. Well, Madeline got drunk too. But carbs and butter were just as forbidden.

Madeline turned on her bedside light, tapped the text chain with Lauren, and wrote *Arabella hates me all of a sudden*. Madeline stared at those terrible words and then quickly deleted them. She paused before writing a different text.

Madeline: How's the Wife App?

Lauren: Still waiting for approval.

Lauren: Hate this suspense.

Madeline: It'll be fine. I'm sure it will be approved. Off
to bed. Love you!

Madeline set down her phone and turned her light off again. She
told Lauren it would be fine but, truthfully, who the hell knows? Who
the hell knows if anything will ever be fine?

The next afternoon, Bianca took Arabella to a spa on Captiva Island.
Facials, manicures, foot massages. Ron drove the other BMW to the
Sanibel Island Golf Club, his home away from home. Madeline never
saw the point in golf—the endless whacking of balls into holes, scooping them out of the holes. But there were a lot of things she didn't
get that other people loved. Like cocktail parties. Amusement parks.
Fireworks.

With everyone gone, Madeline decided to walk on the beach.
Maybe that would ease the tightness in her neck and shoulders. It was
early afternoon, warm and breezy. She changed into her black one-
piece bathing suit and a gauzy tunic, and smeared sunblock on her
face, arms, and chest. Then she fitted on a broad hat, dropped her
phone into a small purse, and slid open the glass doors that faced the
ocean.

So many nearly naked beachcombers! Fat women with freckled
cleavage. Skinny girls with thongs up their asses. Old guys with faded
blue tattoos and swollen guts that sagged over their waistbands. And
then, of course, the younger guys. It didn't matter if they were chubby
or pumped or slender—they exuded so much fuckability they'd jam it
in a jellyfish if they could.

When Madeline got back to her mom's house, she entered the security code on the gate that surrounded the pool. Ron had recently

installed an extravagant security system after a golf buddy's Lexus was broken into three miles away.

"He takes care of me," Bianca purred as Ron showed Madeline the codes the first evening they arrived.

"Got to keep my lady safe from harm," Ron said. He slung an arm around Bianca, who nestled into his shoulder. He wore his lavender-striped golf shirt and green shorts. It was all Madeline could do not to roll her eyes.

Madeline flopped into a lounge chair, pulled out her phone, and opened Bumble.

She definitely wouldn't scout for a man on Sanibel Island. The population was five or six thousand and most people knew her mom or Ron. They either worked for them or they played with them. Captiva Island was a possibility, but she didn't want to bump into her mom and daughter on her way to get her fuck on.

Madeline entered the zip code for Cape Coral. That was twenty miles away, forty minutes in an Uber, almost two hundred thousand people. Definitely enough room to get lost and found. She'd never used a hookup app outside of New York City but she was excited about the novelty. It was good to try new things, right?

Madeline swiped through the men in the twenty-five to forty age range. Pickings were slim on the west coast of Florida. Macho dudes who leaned on cars and macho dudes on boats and macho dudes on motorcycles. Madeline tweaked her settings and increased the age range until she got to fifty-plus. They had Viagra in Florida. Hell, they probably hauled cargo shipments of erection pills over the state line. Madeline stretched her legs straight as she browsed the Cape Coral fifty-plus.

And then she saw him.

"Holy shit!" she shrieked.

The man in the profile said he was sixty-two, which subtracted eight actual years. He wore a pastel golf shirt, blue-green like toothpaste, and he leaned against a palm tree. He wrote that he wanted "discreet flings" and that he would "pay for classy hotel dates."

He called himself a fucking "gentleman."

Madeline dropped her phone on her lap. She considered calling the Sanibel Island Golf Club. She could play dumb and ask if her stepfather was on the green like he said he'd be. Maybe he wasn't such a big golfer after all. Maybe he ran around Lee County chasing other holes.

As she glanced toward the ocean, a seagull swooped across the pristine sky. There was a red kite in the distance, or maybe it was a person strapped into a parasail.

If she busted Ron for not being at the country club, or if she showed her mom his Bumble profile, what would it prove? Wasn't this the life that her mom wanted? Wasn't this the life she pushed on Madeline during practically every conversation?

Madeline opened the sliding door and stomped into the kitchen to grab a snack but, damn it, all she could find were almonds and golden raisins. Ron was a cheating asshole but her mom was going to keep his rotten heart beating . . . *because it's a wife's job!*

Fuck wife jobs!

Madeline smacked her fist against an empty cupboard. Maybe Lauren was onto something with the Wife App. Maybe this was the only way women were ever going to make things right.

sophie

BOTH BOYS HAD PLAYDATES, SO Sophie grabbed a rare afternoon to herself. She kicked off her free time by cleaning Edna's litter box. Once that was out of the way, she changed into workout clothes and went for a run in Central Park. Every time her sneakers hit the pavement, she tried to release her anger at Joshua. She hated being this angry at her ex-husband. But everything he did chafed at her.

After her run, Sophie still had a few hours, so she walked over to the Strand to browse. She wiped the sweat off her forehead and wandered around, snatching up all the books that caught her eye.

In a quiet corner, Sophie dug into *The Soul of a Woman* by Isabel Allende, an author Sophie had loved since she devoured *The House of the Spirits* in high school.

Around page thirty, Sophie sucked in her breath.

I learned that anger without purpose is useless and even harmful, Allende wrote. *I had to act if I wanted change.*

Oh my god, Sophie thought. *That's me.*

As Sophie turned the page, she was vaguely aware of people moving around the store, kids whining, phones chirping. But mostly she was in the zone of a good book, where life fades and the story takes over.

More energy is needed to sustain ill feelings than to forgive, Allende wrote on page eighty-six. *The key to contentment is forgiveness of others and of ourselves.*

Sophie closed the book, pulled out her phone, and tapped open Instagram. She wouldn't even look at Beatrice's latest post. She wouldn't let herself push that bruise.

Sophie hit "unfollow" on Beatrice's profile, and then found all the people on Instagram who filled her days with FOMO.

Unfollow. Unfollow. Unfollow.

Sophie was sick of anger. She was sick of the energy it took. Maybe an unfollowing binge wasn't a big action, but it felt like a solid first step.

lauren

On the Saturday after Thanksgiving, Lauren woke up and reached for her phone on the bedside table. No further updates from App Store Connect. Ugh! She tinkered with a few settings on the app, adjusted the shade of blue that the designer had chosen, and then opened the news. Too depressing for 7:00 a.m. She poked around online and looked up various men she'd slept with before she was married. Gideon, her high school boyfriend and first lover. A few guys at Vassar, though nothing serious. On an outdated Go Fund Me page, she discovered a boyfriend from the first year she lived in the city. He was collecting cash to support his battle with colon cancer. She cross-referenced him on social media and was relieved to see that he was in remission.

Just then, a phone call came in from Cady.

"Hey, hon," Lauren said. "You're up early."

"Moooooomm!" Cady shouted as she sobbed hysterically.

"What's going on?" Lauren's heart raced with panic. *Please let the girls be okay.* Broken arms, she could deal with. Even broken legs. But nothing worse. "Is someone hurt? Your sister? Dad? Grandma?"

Cady cried so hard she was unable to talk.

"No one's hurt," Amelia called from the background.

"Thanks, Amelia," Lauren called back.

"But you wouldn't believe what happened!" Cady wailed.

"Give your phone to Amelia," Lauren said as calmly as possible. "Give her your phone, lovie, and go lie down. You're in the guest bedroom, right?"

Lauren heard a stifled *"Okay,"* and then Amelia came on.

"Hey, Mom."

"Hey . . . So what happened?"

"I hate Dad!" Cady shouted.

"Cady. Stop." Lauren clenched her teeth and then, remembering Ayala Grant's warning, forced herself to loosen her jaw muscles. "Amelia? What's going on?"

Amelia sniffled and then described how Eric went out to dinner with a friend last night. The girls assumed he met an old friend from high school. Grandma watched a movie with them. When Eric wasn't home by ten-thirty, they all went to bed.

As Lauren listened, her annoyance at her ex-husband mounted. What about his Thanksgiving weekend with his daughters? Eric had had them for two days so far and he'd already foisted them onto another unpaid woman in his life.

"So I got up to pee a few minutes ago," Amelia explained. "I was coming out of the bathroom and . . . oh my god . . . I ran right into our old babysitter—"

Lauren's fingers went to her throat. After Eric's announcement last month, they'd exchanged frosty texts and he'd agreed not to tell the girls about Trish.

"Wearing Dad's boxers!" Cady interjected.

"Shut up!" Amelia said to her sister. "Mom doesn't need to hear that part."

"Mom, I don't want to be here," Cady said. "Can you come pick me up *right now*?"

Lauren's pulse thumped in her neck, her wrists, her temples.

"I'm sorry that happened to you," she finally said.

"When I heard Amelia scream," Cady said in the background, "I woke up and ran into the hallway. Then Dad and Grandma came out and Trish stood there like an idiot. But get this! Are you ready for this, Mom?"

What was Lauren supposed to say? Truthfully, she wasn't ready for any of it. She wasn't ready to discover that her husband was a cheater. That he made bad choices in rebound relationships. That he was a fuckup as a parent.

"Here's the worst part," Cady said. "Grandma smiled and said, 'Oh, hi, Trish . . . I thought you were coming this evening.' And Dad put his arm around Trish and explained that it got late last night so he brought her back here. Then Dad turned to us and went, 'Surprise!'"

No one said anything.

What was there to say?

Lauren wondered if this was the seminal moment where her daughters learned that the grown-ups in their life, the people they trusted to protect and guide them, are imposters who fake adulthood and hope no one notices.

"Where is everyone now?" Lauren asked.

"Grandma and Trish are downstairs," Amelia said. "Dad went for a run. We saw him out the window."

"*A run?*" In the nearly two decades that Lauren had known him, Eric had never gone for a run.

"I know." Cady snorted. "He's this middle-aged dude showing off to his underage girlfriend. He sprinted to the corner but I bet he started walking as soon as he was out of sight."

Lauren resisted the urge to laugh. She inhaled deep into her lungs and then slowly exhaled. "When Dad gets back, you need to start by talking to him alone."

"Did you know about Trish?" Cady asked.

"I knew a little something," Lauren said, sighing. *High road. High* road. "But Dad and I are divorced, lovie. He's allowed to make his own choices. Regardless, I don't want Dad's actions to define you. When he gets back, you use your strong voices and you tell him how you feel. If you feel hurt, tell him. If you feel betrayed, tell him. You won't gain anything by hiding in the bedroom."

Once they hung up, Lauren walked into the kitchen to make coffee. As she ground the beans, she logged in for a status update and—

Approved!

Her hands trembled as she stared at App Store Connect. She was furious at her ex-husband for lying to her—again. For catching her off guard—again. And this time, he ran a tractor-trailer over her girls' emotions. But now, in her hands, she held the Wife App. Eric couldn't take this moment from her.

This was her chance to prove that her value transcended the ways that Eric had taken her for granted. It was time to get that satisfaction. It was time to get that *revenge*.

As the scent of coffee filled the kitchen, she set the features so the Wife App would be available in select neighborhoods in Manhattan, and then she hit "go live." It would take a couple hours to appear in the App Store.

Holy shit.

In a few hours, the Wife App would be available to download to thousands of New Yorkers.

madeline

"I HAVE BIG NEWS," LAUREN said to Madeline and Sophie over breakfast at Le Pain Quotidien on Monday morning. It was way too early to be out in the world. But Lauren texted on Sunday that she needed to talk ASAP, and this was the only window that worked for all three of them.

"*Good* big news or *ex-husband* big news?" Madeline asked. Before Lauren's messy split, Eric hadn't seemed like a high-drama husband, but ever since Handjobgate, Madeline never knew what to expect.

Sophie took a bite of oatmeal and glanced between her two friends.

"Good big news, thank god." Lauren paused dramatically and crossed her arms over her chest. "I was tempted to text you both but I wanted to tell you in person. As of Saturday afternoon, the Wife App is live!"

"Now?" Sophie held her phone to the center of the table for the three of them to see as she opened the App Store.

"You can download it," Lauren explained. "You have to live in the zip codes I've specified because, as you know, we're going to start in a small market and scale up. We only have the three of us Wives so we can't manage an onslaught."

An onslaught. Madeline appreciated Lauren's optimism, her feeling of hopefulness about this project. That was why Madeline said yes to being a Wife in the first place, even though the idea of becoming a hired Wife *or* a true, legal wife made her skin crawl. "Has anyone downloaded it yet?"

"Nothing yet," Lauren said. "But this is a soft launch. Making sure credit card processing works, making sure all our privacy issues are addressed. But hopefully someone will—"

"There it is!" Sophie held up her screen so Madeline could peer at the deep blue square with a white W in the center and two gold circles that swirled together like interwoven wedding rings. "This blue is for *something borrowed, something blue*, right? I just downloaded it. So now you have one."

"*We* have one," Lauren said.

Madeline searched for it on her phone and hit "download."

"Two," she said. She wanted to help Lauren. Of course she did. That's why she set Lauren up with a lawyer. But what she hadn't been able to voice to her friend was that she still didn't understand what she was supposed to *do* as a Wife. Someone's chores? She had Willow to run errands for her. She certainly didn't want to do it for anyone else. Was she supposed to fill out camp forms and book doctors' appointments? Or take care of someone's bratty kids?

"I'll post on a few hyper-local sites to get the word out and eventually we'll hire other Wives," Lauren said. "But I want the three of us to iron out the kinks. Make sure the app is ready for a larger scale."

Madeline sprinkled granola over her Greek yogurt. She felt a growing sense of dread that pulled at her stomach.

"How much does membership cost?" Sophie asked.

"For now, we're saying a hundred dollars a month," Lauren said. "That's Basic Membership, the bare-bones entry point. That entitles a Spouse to three half-hour Wife sessions. If they want more, they can buy in at a higher membership level. Or people can always à la carte it. I'm hoping Spouses jump on the School Concierge Package. That's where a Wife interfaces with your kid's school, tracks down field trip forms, signs up for parent-teacher conferences, provides homemade baked goods for the class, and even populates the parents' calendars with all the school events. Isn't that brilliant?"

Sophie pushed her hair behind her ear. "I could use a School Concierge Package."

"Right?" Lauren glanced over the rim of her mug. "If that works, I'm thinking we can add a Healthcare Concierge Package. And an Everything Holiday Package. Can you imagine how much Mental Load we will take over with just that?"

Madeline tried to fill her lungs with air. She should have spoken up sooner. She shouldn't have played along for this long.

"I'm sorry," she finally said. "I'm just wondering . . . How long is the commitment? And how does a Spouse pick which Wife to—"

"Let me jump in," Lauren said. "A Spouse dumps their Mental Load into the Wife App. They can link to secure forms or doctors where they need follow-ups. I've worked out the preliminary HIPAA details because privacy and trust will be core to the Wife App community. Then the app matches them with a Wife. The Wife sorts the jobs into categories and time frames and names a price if it's beyond Basic Membership. It might be in the hundreds for a few add-ons. If the load is big, it could be in the thousands. When the Wife and the Spouse agree on a price, they sign a Marriage Contract. There are more details, of course. That's the bare bones."

Sophie wrinkled her nose. "What if the person who hires the Wife—"

"We call them the Spouse," Lauren said. "It can be a single person or a couple."

"What if they're married?" Sophie asked. "Doesn't that get sticky?"

"Boo to cheaters," Madeline said. She'd told her friends as they were walking into the café about how her stepfather was trolling for Bumble flings. "Cheaters are number one on my shit list right now."

Sophie stirred her tea and groaned in disgust. "Ugh. Some kind of gentleman. Can I google Ron's profile, like, even if I'm not on Bumble?"

"No, you need an account," Madeline said. "I'll send you a screenshot."

"Speaking of googling," Lauren said. "I recently looked up Gideon. Remember my high school boyfriend? I went on the requisite post-divorce ex googling spree."

"Find anything interesting?" Madeline asked.

"Not much. Gideon doesn't seem to have social media. The last I heard, he was with Doctors Without Borders . . . or Médecins Sans Frontières. Sorry, my French accent is terrible."

Sophie sniffed sharply. "I've heard that those MSF guys are total cowboys, like, with enormous—"

"Dicks," Madeline said, laughing. She couldn't help herself. Sophie asked for it!

"God!" Sophie shrieked. Madeline watched as her friend's cheeks turned pink. "Egos, Madeline. Enormous egos. Like, *Oh look at me, I'm going to hop on a plane to a war-torn region and save a life because if I don't do it, no one else will.*"

"Isn't that kind of true?" Lauren asked.

"But they're cowboys about it," Sophie said. "Tough guys who think they're tougher than everyone else."

"I don't know," Lauren said, frowning. "I guess I want to believe that Gideon is a good person. I need to hold on to that myth."

As Madeline listened to the hiss of milk getting frothed, she observed the ache in her friend's face. Was this need to believe in the good actually about Eric getting hand jobs for hire and now fucking the babysitter? It all made Eric such an undeniable douche that Madeline itched to protect Lauren by shifting the conversation.

"Speaking of cowboys," she said, forcing a grin. "One guy I slept with in college moved to Wyoming and actually became a cowboy. When I think back to all his *ride me hard* comments, I—"

"Okay!" Sophie said.

"What about you, Soph?" Lauren spun her fork in a semicircle on the table. "Any ex googling gold?"

Sophie's neck turned as red as a McIntosh apple. She shook her head dismissively and said, "I don't want to be a bummer but I have to leave in fifteen minutes. I have a student first period."

"Yikes." Lauren glanced at the time on her phone. "Back to the Wife App, then. You asked something before I started talking about Gideon. About marriage, right?" Lauren gestured to Madeline. "Thanks to that lawyer you set me up with, we drafted the Spouse Consent, aka the No Cheating Clause, aka the Eric Clause. If a person is married, they need to get the consent of their actual spouse before they hire a Wife."

"Maybe this is a stupid question," Madeline said, "but what if we don't want to do the jobs a person needs?"

Lauren shrugged. "Then don't Marry them. The programmers and I created a matching algorithm based on priority—which Wife's turn it is to get a Spouse, what Wives have documented in their skill sets. Like if a Wife is dyslexic, that person won't get matched with someone who primarily needs forms completed. Remember at Paint and Sip when you filled out the questionnaire? You'll get matched based on that, but if you pass on a job—which I'm hoping you don't at first—then the Spouse's request will bump to the next Wife."

Madeline nodded slowly. It made sense. She'd have to poke around the app for it to be crystal clear. But *really*? This was *actually* happening? When they filled out that questionnaire, she'd dashed off her answers and then got back to contemplating how to paint her childhood pet, which ended up looking like an oversized Pepperidge Farm Goldfish cracker.

Madeline cleared her throat. "I'm not sure about contact with children. I honestly find most kids total brats. Not yours, of course. But when Arabella was younger, I used to count the seconds until her playdates wrapped up and the snotty children were out of my space."

"I'm so glad you said that," Sophie said. "I love kids. But I don't like the idea of forming short-term attachments to them."

Lauren looked between her friends. "I hear you. I promise I do. And I'm not trying to snowplow you into this but if you have children, being a wife and a mom are deeply entwined. Both require major emotional labor. We'll be clear that the Wife App is not a nanny service. Wives on the app can hire nannies and get them set up. And they'll pinch-hit if childcare issues come up. Just like how a mom or wife does without hesitation, no matter what else she has going on."

Madeline nodded reluctantly. Lauren made a good point. But still . . .

Lauren glanced at the time again. "I do want to set some ground rules."

"Ground rules?" Madeline asked.

Lauren smiled, her dimple creasing her cheek. "We are the founders of the Wife App. I mean, the *cofounders*. We don't have to come up with all the rules now, but I want to brainstorm about our guidelines, our ethics, our operating principles."

"I've got one." Sophie bunched her napkin in her fist. "If a Spouse gets handsy, he—or she or they—are thrown off the app. No second chances."

"We'll call it the Vegas Divorce Clause," Lauren said, laughing. She grabbed her phone and began writing. "Also, I think honesty is important on all fronts. Honesty with the other Wives. Honesty with your Spouses."

"Communication too," Sophie said. "If we're upset, we say it. If we need something, we ask for it."

As Madeline watched them talk, she felt butterflies in her stomach. Could it be that . . . she was actually excited about this? No! She didn't want to be a wife, in real life or on an app. But what if marriage actually started this way, with frank conversations about division of labor instead of bullshit haggling over the font of the invitation or the flavor of the cake? Would Madeline's marriage to Colin have stood a chance? Imagine still being with Colin, growing up together, raising their daughter, fucking their brains out the way they used to. No! What was she thinking? Madeline and marriage were oil and vinegar. Maybe it was the espresso in her latte that was making her jittery. She'd ordered a double to compensate for meeting at dawn.

"Speaking of communication," Lauren said, "we need to talk about equity."

"Equity?" Sophie asked, her voice high. "But you built it, Lauren. You spent thousands. It's all yours."

"Tens of thousands," Lauren said, "since we are being honest. I am wiped out."

"I could have helped with all that," Madeline said.

Lauren drained the end of her coffee. "Thanks . . . but I needed to do it on my own, which is why it's important to have this conversation about equity. I've done a lot of reading about it and there's no exact road map, so here's how I see it. The Wife App was your original idea, Madeline, but it was borne of our conversation. I invested my savings to build it, and I also relied on my professional expertise. But to get the Wife App off the ground . . . to give it any shot at success . . . I couldn't do it without both of you."

Madeline was too floored for words. *Her idea? Had it really been?*

"I suggest the breakdown for equity should be fifty percent for me and twenty-five percent for each of you," Lauren said. She framed her hands over her gray-blue eyes and shot nervous looks at her friends.

Madeline was relieved when Sophie spoke first.

"We don't need equity!" she said. "This is your baby. We're happy to help without grabbing parts of it."

Lauren let out a whistle of air. "I am so glad you're not mad."

"Why would I be mad?" Sophie asked.

"Because . . ." Lauren stalled. "I'm getting more equity. I was worried you'd say we should divide it into thirds."

"I'm saying the opposite!" Sophie said. "We don't need to divide it at all. It's yours. You built it. Also . . . sorry . . . but the Wife App isn't even worth anything."

All of a sudden, classes from business school appeared in Madeline's brain as if rousing from a long nap. Madeline closed her eyes and tried to remember Professor DuChamps's exact words as she delivered them from her lectern at Stern. She'd spoken about sharing business ownership thoughtfully, and how it can be useful for start-up founders to see equity as a pie. There's only so much pie that can be divided and shared.

"It's not worth anything *yet*," Lauren said.

"Laur," Sophie said, "you have two downloads and they're us."

"Lauren's right," Madeline said. She surprised herself by the thrust in her voice. "Equity has to be negotiated from the outset . . . before the venture has value. The value of all the pieces of the company increase as the venture becomes more successful."

"Exactly," Lauren said. "I've read case studies where cofounders of start-ups don't launch with an equity agreement and then sell for millions and wind up in court battling it out."

"I don't think we'll sell for millions," Sophie said. Then she lowered her head. "I'm sorry. I'm being a downer."

Madeline wove her fingers through her hair and thought for a moment. "You've proposed a fair breakdown that takes into consideration all the important factors. But I don't need my shares, so I suggest a different split, two-thirds to you and a third to Sophie."

"No," Lauren said firmly.

"No?" Madeline asked.

"No," Lauren said again.

Sophie glanced at the time on her phone. "I don't mean to—"

"Madeline," Lauren said, interrupting, "I realize I built it, which is why I would have more equity, but it won't work without full support from both of you. If we do this and you throw yourself into it and it gets huge, it will be *yours*. Something you earned. I'm not going to let you give that up."

Madeline stared at Lauren as she let that sink in. "Okay." Her stomach twisted with nervous excitement. "I'm in."

Sophie nodded. "Me too."

"We did it!" Lauren said, smiling. "We survived our first awkward conversation as cofounders. I'll have the lawyer draft up the equity agreement."

Sophie cleared her throat. "I'm sorry to cut this off but I have to be at school in a few minutes. Charlie's classroom is having a Harvest Festival at lunch so I moved around a few students."

"Don't worry about it," Madeline said. "You run and I'll get the bill."

Lauren held up her hand. "I will this time. I called the meeting. I can write it off."

"No," Sophie said as she waved over the waiter. "Three cofounders. We'll split the bill three ways."

As they all signed their credit card receipts, Madeline glanced at Sophie, who carefully added her tip and swirled her neat signature.

"Hang on!" Madeline said to Sophie. "You never said if you've googled exes?"

Sophie puckered her lips sourly.

"No one?" Madeline asked.

"I hate those questions." Sophie slid her credit card in her wallet and then stood up. "Off to teach and harvest. Love you guys. Let's text!"

Then she waved and ran out the door.

After breakfast, Madeline swung by the salon for a dry blowout and then the aesthetician ushered her into a back room for an emergency bikini wax. When Madeline had seen herself in the bathroom mirror last night, she'd been shocked to discover a feral animal between her legs. She'd never let herself go this long. She'd been so distracted with Thanksgiving travel stress. Not to mention the possibility of Arabella moving to London.

After she left the salon, she walked four blocks up Columbus to Arabella's school for the weekly PTA meeting. Madeline had been PTA president for four years before she passed the torch to an aggressive first-grade mom who left corporate law to do the stay-at-home thing. Now Madeline headed up the fundraising committee.

She flashed her Fryer Prep parent ID to the guard and walked through the familiar halls. Did all schools smell like Elmer's glue and chicken soup? She admired the children's art on the walls, the inspiring quotes, the awards not just for athletics but for Model UN and robotics. Fryer was Arabella's home away from home since pre-K. In many ways, it was also Madeline's.

"*Mom*? What are you doing here?"

Madeline had just turned a corner and nearly smacked into Arabella. And her daughter looked pissed, with her shoulders hunched forward and a scowl on her delicate face.

"I have the PTA meeting at ten," Madeline told her.

"Can you please go there right now? It's so embarrassing to have my mom wandering around school."

As her daughter hurried away, Madeline's fingers touched the diamond *Arabella* pendant around her neck. She'd once been a teenage girl who wanted her mom nowhere in sight. But Bianca had been clueless and out of touch. Was that how Arabella saw her now?

If Madeline was dejected when she stepped into the parent lounge, her mood was lightened by a welcome surprise in the sea of PTA women: a man! And not only that: a hot man. A single hot man with a scruffy five-o'clock shadow and a libidinous swagger that Madeline could sniff a mile away.

Full disclosure: that swagger was exactly why she invited this man to the PTA meeting when she met him last week after she dropped off fundraising paperwork in the main office.

"Are you new to Fryer?" she'd asked him.

"My daughter goes to kindergarten here," he said as they walked out of the school. He had a tiny pink scooter hooked over his elbow. "It was the top school on my ex-wife's list."

Madeline offered him eye contact, a smile. Any man who hits you with *ex-wife* so early in the conversation wants you to know, loud and clear, that he is fuckable.

"Do you do drop-off a lot?" she asked.

"Most mornings," he said. "My ex has to be at the office early. I work in television so I have a more flexible schedule."

Another mention of ex. *Flexible schedule*. This hottie was begging to get laid. Madeline told him about the PTA meeting, not expecting he'd actually show up.

"We're always looking for new parents," she'd added. "Granted, you might be the only man there."

"Which wouldn't be the worst thing," he volleyed back.

This morning, he wore khakis and a gray *Vanderbilt Rugby* tee, his too-long legs bent in a too-small chair. When she made her financial presentation, she could feel his eyes undressing her body.

"For anyone new to the committee who might be interested in fundraising," Madeline said, "I'll give my cell in case you want to text with questions."

He had his phone out. Madeline touched her mane of silky hair. Maybe it was indulgent to get a blowout for a PTA meeting. Nah, it was worth it. Madeline gave it forty-eight hours until this single hottie dad was in her bed.

sophie

AT TWO MINUTES BEFORE NOON, Sophie walked up a flight of stairs to the Harvest Festival. She carried a plastic container of mini-muffins down the second-grade corridor and into Charlie's classroom. The room was packed. Sophie had come up early, but it looked like she was the last parent to arrive.

Sophie glanced around at the moms and dads—well, mostly moms—who sat with their children. A row of immaculately groomed women—the class parents, all moms—arranged the food on the pot-luck table. Sophie quickly deposited her muffins at the end of the long table before anyone noticed they were from Trader Joe's and not home-made. Not organic. Not gluten-free.

"Hey, Ms. Smart," Jessi said, approaching Sophie. Teachers were always more formal with each other when students were around. "Good to see you. Now Charlie's crew is complete."

Charlie's crew?

Sophie scanned the sea of parents and children and nearly doubled over. There was Beatrice Allen in a little wooden chair next to Charlie. Their heads touched as they reviewed his storybook together.

Sophie squeezed her hands into fists. What was she doing here?

Charlie had emailed his dad the class invitation over the weekend, when they were still in California, and Joshua texted that he couldn't make it. *Too busy, I'll have too much catch-up after the trip.* He didn't say anything about Beatrice.

"Mom!" Charlie waved at her. He had on his favorite Star Wars T-shirt and his sandy hair stuck up in the front.

Sophie sighed heavily as she weaved through the crowd. "Hey, guys," she said. "Happy Harvest Festival."

"I hope it's okay that I crashed this," Beatrice said. She wore a pin-stripe suit and low heels, and her hair was pulled back in a tight po-nytail. She looked every bit the high-powered estate lawyer. "I felt bad that Joshua couldn't make it. I jumped in an Uber between meetings."

"I've decided I don't want to speak during the welcome part," Char-lie said. "I only have the one line that's on this card. Ayan said he'd do it for me."

"No chance," Beatrice shot back. "You'll muscle through it. Your mom and I will be right here cheering for you."

"I have to?" Charlie asked.

"Think how awesome you'll feel after you've done it." Beatrice nod-ded up at Sophie. "Agreed?"

"Yep," Sophie said and, despite herself, she felt a burst of affection for her ex-husband's wife. "Charlie, go tell Ayan he's off the hook."

As Charlie glared down at his index card, Beatrice shrugged at Sophie.

Thanks, Sophie mouthed to her.

No problem, Beatrice mouthed back.

"You flew home from California yesterday afternoon?" Sophie asked Beatrice once Charlie was gone. "I'm impressed you're even walking today."

"I'm definitely feeling the jet lag. Also, it's hard to travel with a baby."

"Which one?" Sophie asked. It slipped out before she could stop herself.

For a second, Beatrice didn't say anything, and then she burst out laughing. "Good one!" Her golden eyes flashed. "Oh my god. Two, I guess."

Sophie grinned at her. As Beatrice met her smile, Sophie felt warmth in her stomach. But no! She didn't want to like Beatrice. So why was Beatrice so likeable? Sophie would have to mull on this later, maybe even come up with a few things she didn't like about her ex-husband's new wife. Not to be a bitch. Just so it wasn't painful every time she was in a room with her.

Charlie appeared next to Sophie. "What if I mess up when I get up there? What if I forget my words?"

"You can do it," Sophie told him.

"Your mom is right," Beatrice added. "You'll be great. The world deserves your awesomeness."

Once school let out, Sophie locked her office door, pulled her blouse over her head, and unhooked her bra. Since this was a former supply closet, there didn't used to be a lock from the inside. But then the nationwide school shootings increased and every door got retrofitted for soft lockdown drills. In a soft lockdown, teachers secured doors and windows while students mashed into closets or packed tight under tables, out of view of a potential shooter.

Where does a child even file that in their brain? No wonder Charlie bubbled over with anxiety! He'd barely held it together as he recited his line during the Harvest Festival today. On evenings and over weekends at home, Charlie picked his fingers bloody and held his sneakers to his nose to sniff for dog poop. If the Wife App didn't become a lucrative venture, Sophie would have to come up with a Plan B to pay for cognitive behavioral therapy.

Sophie wriggled out of her slacks and folded them neatly on her desk chair. It was getting to a point where Charlie's anxiety controlled her decisions. Truth be told, Sophie lied to Lauren and Madeline about why she could only meet early this morning and not yesterday evening. She blamed it on Joshua. In reality, Charlie had a tantrum yesterday and begged to stay at her place for a few more hours instead of transitioning to his dad's apartment.

Sophie scratched at the dry rash on her naked stomach, then pulled on her sports bra and Lycra top. She desperately needed a run to clear her head. If she didn't hit Central Park ASAP, her brain might explode.

It's not just Charlie, Sophie thought as she snaked her feet into her leggings. She'd been off-kilter since breakfast with her friends, since that talk about googling exes. Sophie did not have the best relationship track record. She and Joshua were solid at first. He was handsome and broody and funny, so different from her bland—and blond—dad and brother-in-law in Indiana. The sex was good, and the chemistry was definitely there. At least it *felt* like chemistry until everything soured, until Joshua got mean. Toward the end of her marriage, she hated intercourse with Joshua so much that her vagina stung every time he came near her. Sometimes, afterward, she would go into the bathroom, run the faucet, and cry. Often, during those dark months, she'd wonder if the ghost of Cara haunted them.

Cara wasn't dead, of course. But she was dead to Sophie.

"I'm not into the friends-after-relationship thing," Cara said when they broke up for good, after several dry runs, in their last year of grad school.

After that, when she saw Sophie around the Penn campus, Cara looked past her like she didn't exist. Like they hadn't pressed their naked bodies together for nearly a year, slept wrapped in each other's arms, tasted between each other's legs.

But there were fights. Awful fights that left Sophie gutted and raw. *Why won't you tell your parents or your sister about us? You've met my friends . . . how come I've never met yours?* Cara had been out since she was a teenager. She hated it when Sophie said she didn't identify as gay or bi. The thing was, Sophie didn't identify as straight either. She didn't know what she was! Cara made her feel like she was an affront to every gay person who fought and even died for the right to live out loud.

"It's the twenty-first century, Sophie," Cara said. "You live in goddamn Philadelphia. You're not going to be locked up because you like women."

Sophie hated herself for not being able to live out loud. She also hated Cara for making her feel terrible about it.

Sophie leaned over now and laced her sneakers.

If she ever had another relationship, she wouldn't let herself be with a bully. First Cara. Then Joshua. Bullies do not make for good partners. Twenty-twenty hindsight.

Have you ever googled your exes?

Of course Sophie had. Cara lived in the San Francisco Bay Area. No kids. She'd been in a relationship for about a decade, but she was single now.

Sophie slipped her ID and credit card into her fleece and unlocked her office door. She had just stepped into the hallway when she spotted one of her fourth-grade students, a tall Pakistani girl, walking with her mom.

The girl giggled and waved like Sophie was a celebrity. "Hi, Ms. Smart!"

"Hey, guys," Sophie said, smiling. She'd taught this girl since second grade; she was one of her favorites.

"Ms. Smart," the girl's mom said. "I'm so glad we saw you."

"Call me Sophie." She and the mom had exchanged so many emails, especially in the beginning when this girl could barely read a word. Sophie had worked with the mom to put together a collection of enticing books. Also, Sophie had leaned hard on the school to purchase more books that were written by or featured people of color.

"I wanted to tell you that you are our hero," her mom said. "My daughter reads constantly now. She wants to be a writer when she grows up. Either that, or she wants to be *you*."

Sophie spread her fingers across her chest. How could she reconcile this praise with the way Joshua treated her, the insults he slung at her? "I'm so glad. That means so much to me, truly." And it really did.

After they walked away, Sophie opened Instagram. She was going to check up on Cara but she instead searched for Katie Crane. The little sister of Gideon, Lauren's high school boyfriend. Throughout Sophie and Lauren's first year at Vassar, Lauren nursed a low-level heartbreak over Gideon Crane, who'd gone to school in California. Sophie had never met him but she'd seen pictures and overheard fragments of Lauren and Gideon's phone calls. In the fall of sophomore year, Lauren announced that Katie was coming to check out campus, and would it be okay if she crashed on the floor of their shared dorm room? *Sure, fine.* Sophie and Lauren often hosted perspective students, or friends visiting from other colleges. They gave Katie the grand tour of Vassar's gorgeous campus—Main Building, Shakespeare Garden, the London Plane Tree on the library lawn with the longest known horizontal branch. As they walked, Sophie and Katie laughed over jokes and exchanged long glances. That night, when Lauren went to study at the café, Katie said she was tired and would hang back. Sophie and Katie made out in the dorm room and rolled around on Sophie's single bed. In the end, Katie chose Smith over Vassar, and Sophie hadn't thought about her much until years later, when Katie sent her a *follow* request.

Katie Crane didn't have a lot of pictures now. It looked like she was married to a woman and they lived in Virginia. There were images of a garden from last summer. A drooling black dog. An adorable young daughter. Sophie searched backward through Katie's Instagram, looking for photos of Gideon that she could screenshot and share with Lauren. But nope. Nothing at all.

Sophie "liked" Katie's most recent post—a beautifully domestic shot with wife and daughter. For Sophie, it was hard to see the paths she didn't take, the paths she didn't allow herself to consider. Then again, she was working hard to keep FOMO at bay, so she slid her phone into her leggings, jogged down the stairs, and sprinted all the way to Central Park.

lauren

SOMETHING ABOUT THE WIFE APP nagged at Lauren, and she couldn't figure out what it was as she sat on the couch on Wednesday evening and watched Cady and Amelia produce their latest fashion show. Cady was the twin who walked the runway of the living room. Amelia didn't give a damn about fashion. Her idea of dressing up was putting on a clean T-shirt instead of scooping a wrinkled shirt off the floor. But Cady was all sparkles and pink boas and cute dresses. While Cady strutted out of the bedroom, shaking her hips and puckering her glossed lips, Amelia DJ-ed from her phone.

Lauren had been worried that her daughters would be miserable wrecks after Thanksgiving weekend, after finding out in the worst possible way that their dad was banging their old sitter. But so far, things seemed calm. As usual, Cady wanted to process it ad nauseam while Amelia closed herself in her bedroom for hours with the excuse of "homework."

Okay. So maybe Lauren worried about Amelia. She seemed to brood more than ever these days, and it had actually started even *before* Thanksgiving weekend in Brookline. The fashion show was a good sign, though. Amelia scrolled through her music and they all munched on the pecan-pie bars that Lauren had baked earlier. It was a recipe Cady found on TikTok and begged her mom to make. Generally, Lauren didn't love toiling in the kitchen, but the Wife App was in a holding pattern while the developers fixed a few bugs.

Cady peeked out of their room and flashed a thumbs-up to her sister. Amelia nodded. This was the fifth or sixth outfit combo.

Amelia lowered the music and called out, "Presenting . . . Cady Turner."

Cady sauntered out of her bedroom in a short black dress and a silver tiara. To Lauren's relief, Cady didn't seem self-conscious about her fleshy arms or rounded stomach. Yet. Hopefully she never would. Amelia, who was tall and rail skinny, seemed more at odds with her body than her sister. Lauren had brought her to a therapist last spring, after Eric moved out, but Amelia sat on her hands for three sessions and refused to talk.

"I love this one!" Lauren said as she clapped and whistled.

Cady strutted through the living room, and then scurried into her room to change.

"One more!" Lauren called after her. "Then it's time for bed."

Amelia stared down at her phone, searching for the next song.

"Are you sure you don't want to model an outfit?" Lauren asked.

Amelia shook her head but didn't look up. "If I had a tux, maybe I would do it."

Lauren smiled at her daughter. This was the first she'd heard about a longing for a tux, or any clothing, for that matter. "What color?"

"I don't know, Mom." Amelia sighed heavily to show her annoyance. "Maybe powder blue. Stop asking so many questions. I'm trying to find a song."

"Ready?" Cady called from her room.

"Ready," Amelia shouted back.

As Cady danced out in high-waisted tight jeans and a half-tank, Lauren applauded her daughter. *May she always be this confident. May the world treat her with respect. May she always get equal access to every-thing she needs.*

Oh.

That was it.

As soon as Cady finished, Lauren shooed them into the bathroom to brush their teeth, then quickly texted Madeline and Sophie.

> **Lauren:** Big Wife App realization. We have to add something ASAP. But I need your help figuring out how we do it. Can either of you meet to discuss? Like an evening walk?

> **Madeline:** Ahhh, I wish! Arabella and I are at the Philharmonic. Brahms and Bartók! We won't get home until close to 11pm.

> **Sophie:** I can meet for a walk. Boys are at J and B. When? Like 30 min?

> **Sophie:** What's up btw?

> **Lauren:** I'll tell you in person. 30 is perfect. Let's go to Broadway. You walk down and I'll walk up. East side of the street.

> **Madeline:** Keep me in the loop! Now I have to put away my phone bc Arabella is glaring at me for texting during Bartók.

> **Lauren:** Bad girl.

143

The Wife App

"Hey, lady," Sophie said when they met up. She wore corduroys, a puffy coat, and a matching pink scarf and hat.

"Thanks for meeting me," Lauren said. She tugged at Coco's leash as the dog spun in circles, begging for attention.

They walked north on Broadway. Back when they first moved to New York City, Lauren and Sophie used to meet for walk-and-talks a lot at night. But then they got husbands and had babies and slipping out like this became a rare luxury.

"So what's up?" Sophie asked. "It sounded important."

"I've been thinking about how the Wife App is going to charge people to relieve the Mental Loads of women . . . or men . . . or Spouses," Lauren said. "All in the name of equitable marriages."

"Yep," Sophie said. "That's the basic idea."

"So here's what's bugging me," Lauren said. "The Wife App is only accessible to people with money to burn. So as much as we want our app to change the nature of marriage, it's not going to alleviate the mental loads of less-wealthy spouses. In fact, the lower-income people may *become* Wives and double their load while still being exploited at home."

Sophie scrunched her nose, deep in thought. "What do you think we should do?"

"We want to find a way for non-wealthy people to have a shot at equity in their marriages," Lauren said. "For low-income women to say to their husbands, *Hire a Wife for that. I'm done doing it for free.* And for that husband, we don't want a high price to prevent him from giving his wife's mental load a break."

"Sliding scale? They did that at Charlie's camp last summer and I *so* needed it."

"That's exactly what I was thinking," Lauren said. "But how should we get people to show they need assistance?"

"I'm all about the sliding scale using the honor system. It's humiliating when I've applied for financial aid and I have to hand over all my tax returns and, like, a right to my unborn grandchild. Let's just have people check a box, and then we'll have questions about how much they're able to pay."

Lauren nodded. She'd have to work through this feature and create requirements for the programmers. It would be more money, of course. *Crap.* Lauren could barely think about how much she'd poured into this without her stomach clenching up.

They walked half a block in silence. As they waited at the next intersection, Lauren said, "Amelia told me tonight that she wants a blue tux."

"For what?" Sophie asked. "That's so cute, by the way. I can picture Amelia in a tux."

"Not for any particular event. She just said she wanted it."

"You think she might be working through some gender stuff? Or does she just like the look of a tuxedo?"

Lauren shook her head. "I'm not sure. Cady has she/her on her Tik-Tok, but Amelia doesn't do social media. I've tried to talk to her about some of this, but she's always evasive."

"Maybe ask again?" Sophie suggested. "Or, instead of putting her on the spot, you could just tell her that there are no closets in your home. That if she ever realizes anything about her identity, you will support it."

Lauren studied Sophie's pale face on the dark street. Early in their friendship, Sophie told her that she was attracted to women as well as men, but her conservative family would flip if they found out. Lauren had a hunch that Sophie had a girlfriend in grad school, down in Philly, but they weren't in close contact during those years.

Lauren tugged Coco away from a fire hydrant. "I feel like Amelia is holding so much inside. I wish I could get her to open up."

Sophie smiled. "Tell her, 'The world deserves your awesomeness.' I heard someone say that recently. Isn't it beautiful?"

"It is," Lauren said.

When they parted ways a few minutes later, Sophie still had a dreamy look on her face.

madeline

"SHOULD WE TAKE A HALFTIME?" Bryan, the dad from the PTA meeting, asked on Thursday.

"Sounds good," Madeline said. It was noon, maybe twelve-fifteen, and they were in Madeline's bed. They were naked, save for his athletic socks. Turned out Bryan was an aging jock. Whatever. He was six-foot-three and could keep an erection going for so long Madeline wondered if he'd popped a Viagra in her bathroom.

"Daytime sex with you kicks ass," Bryan said.

Madeline soaked that in like a bath. Yes to being wanted. Yes to being craved. At the Philharmonic last night, Arabella barely spoke to her. That's why she responded to Bryan's text and invited him over today.

"How did you know I was single?" she asked.

Bryan touched her left hand. His nails were chewed short, giving his fingertips a blunt sheen. "You didn't have a wedding ring."

"Not every married woman wears a ring," Madeline said. "Especially if she's headed to the gym, which is the primary destination for PTA moms."

"Even if you were married . . . What's a husband more or less?"

Bryan grinned as he squeezed her tits, then probed his cock against her thigh. He was already getting hard again. Not a shocker. Along with his relentless erection, he'd been a pumper. It wasn't Madeline's favorite style of fucking. Plus, the skin around her cunt was still tender from Monday's waxing.

Madeline's phone rumbled on the dresser. She'd turned off the volume but several texts had come in over the past thirty minutes. Now it rang. She'd alerted Lauren that PTA Dad was coming over so it likely wasn't her calling. Maybe it was Fryer Prep? Did Arabella get hurt? Or was it her matrimonial lawyer letting her know that Colin had taken the next step?

"I'm sorry," Madeline said. "I have to grab that call."

"That's cool," Bryan said.

Madeline reached for her robe. As she rushed across the room toward her now-silent phone, she could see Bryan grab his phone out of his jeans, which were in a heap on the floor.

It was a missed call from Lauren. *Huh*. Lauren knew she had this sex date. As Madeline stepped into the other room, she noticed with mounting alarm that Lauren had texted her and Sophie several times with missives that ranged from exclamation points to *CALL ME ASAP*.

"Lauren," Madeline said now. "Is everything okay?"

"Is PTA Dad still there?" Lauren asked. "If he's still there, you can call me back. I'm sorry. I should have waited. It's just—"

Madeline crossed her apartment into the kitchen. "No, it's okay. He's here but I came into the other room. What's going on?"

"It's happening. The Wife App."

"What do you mean?" Madeline took a glass from the cupboard and filled it with water.

"I mean . . . we've gotten downloads," Lauren said. "Nineteen today. And then, a half hour ago, our first Spouse signed up as a member. And not just Basic Membership! This person requested a bunch of à la cartes."

"Like what?" Madeline set the glass on the granite counter.

"I want the three of us to look over the Wife requests and we can hash it out," Lauren said. "Let's have a call this afternoon—you, me, and Sophie—and I'll share the details. But forget unpaid drudgery. This Wife shit is real, my friend, and people are willing to pay."

That night, around ten-thirty, Madeline was reading the news on her phone when Arabella walked into her room. She wore an oversized T-shirt, and her hair was long down her back.

"I can't fall asleep," she said, rubbing her heavy lids. "Can I sleep in your bed?"

"Of course, honey," Madeline said.

As Madeline pulled back the sheet, Arabella crawled in. Madeline checked to make sure the alarm was set on her phone, then turned out her light. It was strange to think that, less than twelve hours ago, Bryan had fucked her in this same bed. Different sheets. But still. Moms wear so many hats.

Arabella lay in silence next to her. Madeline was tempted to pull her daughter into a hug. Instead, she stroked her hair as it splayed across the pillow. Arabella smelled a little fruity, a little tangy, a touch of sour. Blindfolded, Madeline could pick her daughter out of a lineup by scent alone.

"Do you hate me?" Arabella asked all of a sudden.

"Oh, honey . . ." Madeline's heart squeezed like a fist clenching inside her chest. "Of course I don't hate you. Why would you think that?"

"Because I want to live with Dad next year," Arabella said quietly.

Madeline's hand was still on Arabella's hair. She reeled it back and rested her palm flat against the comforter. She was grateful she'd turned out the light because she wasn't sure what her face was doing. After Colin told her that Arabella was the one who initiated the conversation about London, Madeline didn't breathe a word about that to her daughter. But then, last week, she finally worked up the courage to ask about it. It didn't go well. Arabella had sighed and said, *It's complicated, Mom. It's not a simple answer*. Then she left to meet her friend Ria at Starbucks without saying goodbye.

"I love you so much," Madeline after a pause. "I love everything you do."

Arabella didn't answer. After a few minutes, her shallow breaths shifted to rhythmic sighs. Madeline lay awake beside her and thought about what she'd just said. Did she really love everything Arabella did? She didn't like the way her daughter had begun to pull away. And she *definitely* didn't like that Arabella wanted to live with her dad. Even if it was complicated, even if there was no simple answer, they could talk it through, make adjustments so Arabella was happier at home. But Madeline couldn't cling too tight. Kids hated clinging if they weren't the ones doing it.

In the morning, Madeline's alarm rang at six-thirty. As she opened her eyes, she glanced at the other side of the bed. Arabella was gone but her pillow was still warm.

sophie

During Sophie's first time as a Wife, in early December, she was so nervous she had to pee a half dozen times. This Wife job involved overseeing maintenance on a high-end apartment near Columbus Circle while the couple wintered in Boca Raton. Thankfully, no one was around to see how much Sophie used the bathroom.

"The window washing went well?" the woman, Diana, asked her over FaceTime. "I used a different place last time and they left streaks."

"All good," Sophie said. She'd begged this company to come on a weekend so she wouldn't have to take a personal day. "Done and gorgeous. No streaks."

Diana nodded through her screen. Sophie could see the husband stroll past in white shorts. "And the marble and granite have been cleaned?"

"In the kitchen and both bathrooms," Sophie said. "They look brand new. And I've arranged to be here all day tomorrow for the carpet cleaning."

"Excellent," Diana said. "Watch those guys closely. Watch them around my porcelain cabinet."

Sophie's second Wife job felt equally ridiculous. She was hired by a newly divorced guy who had no clue how to stock his kitchen, plan meals, or manage his laundry. No wonder his wife left him!

Sophie was relieved when her third Wife job came in and it finally seemed intriguing. It was a gay couple. The two men hired Sophie to fill out applications for private preschools for their two-and-a-half-year-old son. Competitive preschool admissions were an only-in-NYC hustle but Sophie knew this world well.

"We think Finnian walks on water," one of the dads said when Sophie arrived in their Riverside Drive apartment. His name was Dan. He was tall and slim with eyebrows so arched they verged on perennially surprised. He explained that his husband was a violinist for the Metropolitan Opera and worked most nights. "But as his dads, it's hard for us to write about him objectively. We want you to spend time with Finnian. Try to discern his strengths." He rubbed his eyes. "I hate distilling my kid on an application. I'm glad you're here to help."

Sophie smiled at the toddler playing with a trash truck on the rug. He had silky brown hair styled into a bowl cut, dark eyes, a tan complexion.

"I can definitely help you." Sophie pulled a notebook and a pen out of her bag. "I work in a school, so I do write-ups all the time."

Dan gestured to a sheet of paper on the coffee table. On it, there was a list of preschools, the most competitive on the Upper West and Upper East Side.

"Sorry," he said. "My husband says we need to apply to ten. We can look at the essay prompts online, but it seems like there's a lot of crossover in the questions."

"No problem," Sophie said. Ten preschool applications would be a ton of work. Then again, she would be getting paid for this. When her sons applied to preschool, she did it without *any* compensation.

"Really?" Dan's shoulders sagged in relief.

"We'll go over a bunch of details tonight and Friday, and then I'll dig into the applications this weekend. When are they due?"

"Some in December. A few in January."

Over the next hour, Sophie asked Dan questions about Finnian. She took notes and began formulating essay ideas. She posed a few questions directly to the boy but every time she tried to talk to him, he covered his eyes with his hands and turned away.

"Please don't write that he's shy," Dan said apologetically. "We'll work with him before the family interview, but I don't want to call attention to it."

"Of course not." Sophie smiled.

The next time Sophie went over, she brought a copy of *Trashy Town* as a gift. It was one of her favorite picture books for toddlers. As she and Dan opened their laptops and began to enter information into various applications, Finnian eyed the book. After several minutes, he snatched up *Trashy Town* and crawled onto the couch next to her.

"Read to me?" he asked.

"Finnian loves books," Dan said. "You can definitely put that down."

Dump it in, smash it down, drive around the Trashy Town. That refrain! It brought back so many memories of when her boys were this age.

"Read more?" Finnian asked when Sophie finished the book.

After the third round of *Trashy Town*, Dan told his son it was time for bed. Finnian clutched the book and snuggled closer to Sophie, his eyes welling with tears.

"I have to go too," Sophie said as she slid her laptop into her bag.

Finnian's face crumpled. "Coming back?"

"I don't think so, buddy," Sophie said. "I was just helping your dad with something."

As Finnian began to wail, Dan scooped him onto his hip. Sophie zipped her bag, grabbed her jacket, and hurried to the door. She could still hear the boy crying as she waited for the elevator.

> **Sophie:** Hey Laur. I'm leaving the preschool application job.

Lauren: Thanks for letting me know. How did it go?

Sophie: I don't think we should have direct contact with kids. Too emotional.

Lauren: I know. I get it. But isn't that what a wife does? That means Wives need to do it too.

The boys were with Joshua and Beatrice over the weekend, so Sophie hunkered down with Finnian's preschool applications. She even ordered dinner one night! She justified it by telling herself that she was making money with the Wife App. She could afford to splurge a little.

On Sunday afternoon, Sophie shared some of the applications with Dan. A few minutes later, he texted back.

Dan: They look amazing. We just Venmoed you the full amount. One question though . . .

Sophie: What's up?

Dan: I can submit the applications online over the next month except the one to Ridgemont Academy. You have to bring that one in person.

Sophie: Yep, I saw that.

Dan: Did you see that you have to line up on a January morning at 6am?

Sophie: Sounds cold!

Dan: And they're only going to process the first two hundred applications received.

Sophie: Ugh.

Dan: Problem is, we have a trip booked to Turks that same week. Do you think you could do it? I know you have kids too . . .

Sophie: Give me a few minutes.

Dan: We will pay. A lot.

Sophie glanced at her January custody calendar. She had the boys that week, and she had to make breakfast and herd them out the door. But if Dan paid a lot, then Sophie could hire a babysitter and still be ahead.

"Being a Wife pays," Sophie said to her cat, who lay belly up on the couch. "And we are going to collect."

Edna flicked the tip of her tail, licked her paw, and went back to sleep.

lauren

"WE NEED TO WIFE UP big-time," Lauren told Madeline and Sophie as they gathered at Madeline's long dining room table. Arabella was at a friend's for a sleepover so they could talk frankly. None of their kids knew about the app yet.

"What do you mean, *Wife up*?" Sophie asked.

Madeline placed a large bowl of shrimp paella in the middle of the table. "What do you mean, *big-time*?"

"Want help?" Lauren asked as Madeline returned to the kitchen for the vegetarian paella that she had prepared especially for Lauren.

"No, that's okay," Madeline said breezily. She always made cooking and hosting look easy. If Lauren had cooked two paellas and this gorgeous platter of tapas, she'd be in a cold sweat by now.

"I thought we'd be fine with the three of us as the only Wives for a while," Lauren said when Madeline slid into her chair. "That definitely worked for the soft launch, but the Wife App is growing faster than I thought. Pretty soon we won't be able to handle all the Mental Loads."

"That's a good problem," Sophie said as Madeline filled her wineglass. "Thanks, by the way. Cheers."

"Cheers." Lauren lifted her glass and clinked with her friends. "Of course it's good but it also forces our hand into hiring mode. In an ideal world, I would love to interview and hire and train every single Wife. But if we truly want to become something big, that will be impossible. I'll need to work with the developer to build out a self-hiring mode where potential Wives can submit to background checks and fill out the skill-set questionnaire that will set them up for appropriate matches."

"How big?" Madeline asked.

Lauren took a bite of paella. "This is amazing. Saffron?"

Madeline nodded but didn't say anything.

"Big like a successful marketplace app," Lauren said. "We're only in a few zip codes now, but let's say membership doubles. Let's say it triples. Let's say we get a thousand new Spouses in a day. We'd be so far out of our league the app would instantly fail. I want to meet demand before it happens."

Madeline and Sophie stared at her.

"I'm basing this on adoption so far, when we've done very little to promote the app," Lauren said. She glanced at Madeline's twelve-foot Christmas tree in the corner of the living room, decked out in white lights and ornaments. Lauren was woefully behind on Christmas shopping for Cady and Amelia. *If I had a Wife, I'd hire that out,* she thought, smiling to herself.

"We're not just going to hire female Wives, right?" Sophie asked.

"Of course not," Lauren said. "Like I said before, a Wife has to be someone who can juggle a million balls. Female, male, nonbinary. Anything goes."

"Have you guys gotten any crazy Wife requests?" Sophie dabbed her lips with her cloth napkin. "So far, in addition to those preschool applications, I took over a single guy's entire healthcare load. I booked his colonoscopy, a root canal, and some gross procedure to get pus out of an ingrown toenail. It's insane what people ask Wives to do."

"I hear you," Lauren said. "I just finished arranging a man's golf vacation in the Dominican Republic complete with tee times and dinner reservations. I even put together a packing list for him and ordered shirts and visors and sunblock."

"Tee times?" Sophie asked. "That's so bougie."

"You want to hear about bougie?" Lauren asked. "I'm currently on the hunt for a horse for another Spouse."

"You guys have gotten off easy," Madeline said. "I had to inventory a family's cluttered basement bike room, and then wheel a bunch of filthy bikes to the store for tune-ups. And the bike room had a ton of dead spiders and cockroaches. Then I had to make sure everyone had new helmets, and they wanted me to pick out stupid spandex bike clothes for them like they're about to ride the Tour de France."

"We are calling work what it is," Lauren said. "On the bright side, Madeline, at least those bugs were dead."

The next morning, Lauren was on her third cup of coffee and her fifteenth call about a horse. She'd called stables in Western Massachusetts and Connecticut to inquire about leasing a Morgan horse for a year. Ideally, it would be a gelding between fourteen and sixteen hands high. Oh, and it had to be a bay.

She felt slightly ridiculous as she toggled between the horse calls and her freelance job, where she was product-managing the latest version of the Amazing Animalz App. The senior executives wanted to launch Animalz before summer, which meant Lauren had to present design solutions and incorporate feedback into the product cycle. She kept way too many tabs open on her laptop—Amazing Animalz, the main hub for the Wife App, research for various Wife jobs. Not to mention that she'd been up half the night wireframing the "Become a Wife" flow for the developers. She hoped to get that added in the next few weeks.

The Spouse who wanted a horse was named Conrad. *Bougie*

Conrad. They hadn't met in person but they'd had a few Zooms so she could assess his needs. It started with Basic Membership jobs. She ordered his wines, arranged for someone to fix his laptop, rented him and his wife a convertible for a week in Miami Beach. Things shifted into high gear during one call when he reminisced longingly about how the last time he was truly happy was when he was a boy with his beloved bay horse.

Here we go, Lauren thought. *I have become Wife as Therapist. But it's okay because I'm getting paid for it.*

Lauren and Sophie laughed about how Conrad's real wife signed the Spouse Consent Form within seconds of Lauren sharing it with her. Clearly she was ready to off-load the emotional labor.

When Conrad mentioned his childhood horse, Lauren recalled Ayala Grant, dental surgeon and humblebragger. Ayala Grant dropped to Lauren, over Thanksgiving break, that she'd leased a horse for her daughter! When Lauren recounted this to Conrad, he was instantly intrigued. He said that he had a country house in Connecticut. They agreed on a fee, and the horse hunt began.

At the moment, Lauren was on hold with a stable outside of Lenox, Massachusetts. They had a twelve-year-old gelding bay who was up for lease in March. For a fee, they could transport him to a stable in Connecticut if Lauren lined it up. But Tommy was in high demand; decisions had to be made today. Lauren texted Conrad and told him to answer his phone.

"Hello?" he asked on the first ring. He had a New England prep-school accent, with an overlay of bro entitlement. *Born on third base and think you hit a triple* kind of stuff.

"I've found your horse," Lauren said. She filled him in on the details, the size, the color of the coat. "We're on hold. His name is Tommy."

"That's a coincidence," Conrad said. "My childhood horse's name was Timothy."

"I know," Lauren said.

As Conrad waxed nostalgic about Timothy, Lauren set up an Airbnb for one of her sliding-scale Spouses. It was a woman named Hillary, with three young children, and a husband in grad school. Finally, the stable people came on. They made the Tommy pitch and Conrad was on board. They said they'd send a contract today. As they talked, Lauren forwarded them Conrad's email address.

"This is just wonderful," Conrad said when it was just the two of them on the phone again. "I'm so happy it's worked out."

"It took a lot of research," Lauren said, "but this horse seems perfect."

"Can you help find a stable for Tommy? Near my country house?"

"Mmmmm," Lauren said vaguely. When he didn't say anything, she added, "I'll set a fee on the Wife App. If that works for you, I'm happy to find a stable."

"You're the best," Conrad offered lightly.

Lauren's fingers tightened around the phone. Eric used to toss out things like *I won the wife lottery* or *You're the best* whenever Lauren got shit done for the family. In her head, she had a ballpark fee for Conrad's stable search. His "you're the best" comment prompted her to double it.

madeline

Madeline hated being a Wife. She hated being a Wife as much as she hated being a wife. Maybe if she needed the money, she wouldn't feel resentment every time she reviewed a Spouse's Mental Load.

She resented the Spouse who hired her to run around gathering forms so he could renew his passport.

She resented the Spouse who needed her to track down landscape architects to plant fruit trees on her roof garden.

She resented all the Spouses who interrupted her day with panicky questions, sheer cluelessness. *How much should I tip the hair stylist you set up? You know that coveted Saturday night dinner reservation you scored for us? Do they have gluten-free pasta?*

One Spouse texted five times when she was in bed with PTA Dad. She heard the chime of alert after alert as he thrust his cock into her from behind.

"Do you need to deal with those?" Bryan grunted.

"Not . . . now," Madeline managed to say. Damn, it felt like he was going to stab her uterus.

"Wanna turn off your phone, then? It's distracting."

Madeline shook her long hair back and forth. She wanted to tell

Bryan that she never turned off her phone when Arabella was away. But before Madeline could explain, he was off to the races with his signature pumping, followed by a triumphant moan.

That was last week, before Christmas break, before Arabella flew to London to see her dad. Arabella's visits to Colin always made her heart ache. This time was even worse because it felt like a foreshadowing of next year. Not that anything was decided yet, and Madeline's lawyer told her multiple times that it was dead in the water until Colin filed a legal motion for a temporary residential custody change. He hadn't done that yet so maybe Madeline shouldn't worry. Then again, if Colin was taking Arabella on school tours then he must have confidence that this would work out. Maybe he had a lawyer building a case right now? This spiral of anxiety stressed Madeline out so much that she often woke at 4:00 a.m. and couldn't fall back asleep. Other days, she stood in the shower for so long that her fingers turned wrinkly.

That's why Madeline posted her availability on the Wife App despite her resentment at the shit work people expect wives to take on. Of course, she could have trolled Bumble, found someone to help her pass the lonely days and nights. Except now she and Bryan had their regular playdates. Even though the sex wasn't stellar, Madeline didn't feel like adding other men to the mix.

She should end things with Bryan. It wasn't her style to keep someone around like this. But whenever she thought about being proactive, her brain froze. Anyway, he was currently in California with his daughter, so she had a ten-day reprieve from figuring anything out.

Which meant a ten-day sex drought. And a daughter drought. And a friend drought as well.

Lauren and her twins were in North Carolina visiting her father. Sophie and her sons were doing an activity-filled staycation. And not that Madeline *wanted* to see her mom, but Bianca and Ron the Cheater had decided to spend the holidays in Venice.

On the Tuesday between Christmas and New Year's, as Madeline read over a new Spouse's Mental Load, she groaned out loud.

> *Hey, my name is Damian. I need you to take my Yorkie to the vet for a rabies shot, a nail trimming, and a butt shave. My wife usually does it but she's out of the country and I can't board him without this rabies shot. It's urgent.*

A butt shave? Was that a canine version of a bikini wax? Madeline was not supposed to get pet jobs! When Lauren returned to town, she'd have to let her know there was a bug in the Wife-matching algorithm.

Also, WTF, why couldn't this Damian guy take his own Yorkie for a butt shave?

Sure, Madeline wrote to Damian. *I'd love to take your dog to the vet. Name the time and place!*

"Luna usually throws up when she's here," the veterinary technician said the next day, as Madeline secured the Yorkie's front legs and he held the hind legs while the vet filled a syringe.

"She's trembling," the vet said as she approached the dog. "Please hold her a little tighter."

Madeline looked away while the needle sank into the dog's side.

"Now the butt?" the tech asked Madeline. "It's definitely poopy."

Madeline kept her grip on the dog as the tech handed an electric razor to the vet, who lifted Luna's tail. Curls of white fur dropped onto the metal examination table. Madeline looked away again. She was feeling a little nauseous.

Just then, there was a loud gurgling sound.

"Here she goes," the vet said.

Madeline glanced over in time to see the dog hurl soggy kibbles all over the table.

"Can you hand us some paper towels?" the tech asked.

Madeline covered her nose. The smell was awful. A few chunks had dropped onto the floor, right next to her black boots.

"Excuse me? Can you please hand us a few paper towels?"

Madeline grabbed a stack of paper towels from next to the sink. She counted from ten to one and prayed they wouldn't ask her to clean the puke.

sophie

SOPHIE WOKE UP AT FIVE, let the babysitter into her apartment at five-thirty, and then took a cab to West Eighty-Fifth Street. It was dark as she walked toward Ridgemont Academy, Finnian's application in a yellow envelope in her hand. Sophie had bundled in long underwear, a fleece over her work clothes, a long puffy white coat. It wasn't even that cold for early January. Maybe high thirties.

There were about two dozen people ahead of her in line. Sophie texted Dan the good news. Finnian's application would be in the first two hundred when the doors opened at seven! Sophie would be out of here by seven-thirty, at work by eight.

As she waited in line, she could hear the sounds of the city coming to life. Sophie glanced behind her. The line now stretched down the block and wrapped south on Amsterdam. Ridgemont was a top-tier preschool, a feeder to private schools like the one that Madeline's daughter attended. But don't even get Sophie started on that. She was a public school mom—out of necessity but also out of principle.

"Hey, Sophie!"

Sophie turned around to see Beatrice Allen about ten people back.

Beatrice smiled and waved. "What are you doing here?"

Sophie's heart pounded and her mouth felt dry. Since she had un-followed Beatrice's Instagram, she was no longer aware of her every move. She didn't know that her ex-husband's new daughter was apply-ing to Ridgemont.

Beatrice said something to the woman behind her and then strode up in line and kissed Sophie on the cheek.

"It's good to see you," Beatrice said. "A familiar face. I can't believe they make us line up in the dark. I hate New York City sometimes." Beatrice tipped her head to one side. "But what are *you* doing here? You're done with this nonsense."

"It's just . . . I'm doing this for friends. They're out of town."

"Must be a good friend. I totally didn't want to apply Clem to the toddler program, but Joshua insisted."

"He did?" Sophie asked. Back when they were making school choices for Noah and Charlie, Joshua couldn't be bothered.

"Between you and me, I think it's a status thing. Some VIP who came to his studio sends his daughter here. Blah, blah, blah."

Sophie laughed despite herself. Just then, the line began to move. It was five minutes to seven.

"I better get back," Beatrice said. "But quickly . . . remember that thing you said at Charlie's Harvest Festival?"

What did she say at the Harvest Festival? She'd been so rattled that Beatrice was there, and also worried about Charlie getting stage fright.

"You said that thing about how I have two babies," Beatrice re-minded her. "Clementine and . . . you know . . . Joshua?"

"Oh god. I'm sorry. I didn't mean—"

"No!" Beatrice said quickly. "What I wanted to say is that it's true. About Joshua." Her face dropped into a frown. "It's not easy."

Sophie looked at Beatrice's eyes, her shiny hair spilling out of her gray wool cap. She wanted to ask what wasn't easy, but her ex-husband's new marriage was a line she shouldn't cross.

"I should get back to my place." Beatrice gestured her thumb over her shoulder. "Want to grab a bagel after we hand in these applications? I don't have to be at work until nine."

Sophie was tempted to say yes. The school day didn't start until eight-twenty-five.

"Sorry but I can't," she said instead. "Thanks for asking. I have to get to work."

"Okay. Well. Good luck to your friend's kid."

"Good luck to Clementine."

As the line snaked forward, Sophie's legs shook so hard she hopped from foot to foot to settle them down.

lauren

L̲AUREN̲ ̲SANK̲ ̲THE̲ ̲EGGBEATERS̲ ̲INTO̲ a bowl of softened butter and sugar and glanced again at the chocolate-chip cookie recipe. It was her mom's recipe, in her mom's loopy handwriting, on a yellowed 3 x 5 card splattered with stains. When her mom died, Lauren grabbed the box of recipe cards from her childhood kitchen, lest she lose the ability to re-create her mom's lasagna or chocolate-chip cookies. She'd doubled the recipe today, enough for Matthias's first-grade bake sale, plus a pile to set aside for Cady and Amelia.

As she sifted the flour into the wet ingredients, her phone rang. The screen flashed *Claudia Spouse*.

"Almost done with the cookies?" Claudia asked breathlessly. In the weeks since Claudia Von Pelt hired Lauren as a Wife—including the pricey School Concierge Package—Lauren had rarely heard her *not* out of breath. Lauren had googled Claudia; she was the CEO of a high-end cosmetics company so she must be steady and competent, but Lauren could never get over the feeling that the woman needed some stiff hits of albuterol.

"I'm about to put the cookies in the oven. Then let's say about an hour to cool. Then I'll send them in an Uber to your place. I bought a few containers that are eco-friendly and BPA free."

"You are a lifesaver," Claudia said. "The other mommies would slaughter me if I brought cookies for the bake sale in toxic plastic containers. As it is, I'm going to be a pariah because the cookies aren't gluten-free. But Matthias hates that chickpea flour, and I want him to like what he brings in."

"Don't worry," Lauren said. "I reviewed the school list and only three kids in Matthias's class are gluten-free. You won't be a pariah."

"Oh my god, I don't know what I would do without you," Claudia panted. "Are you still good to come to my apartment on Wednesday to discuss flying Matthias to Seattle? And returning to pick him up? As I said in that text, I'm way too swamped, and my nanny is afraid to fly."

"Yep." Lauren opened the calendar on her phone. "I have it down for Wednesday at seven. And I was going to bring wrapped presents for those two birthday parties Matthias has at the end of the month. Did you like the remote-control car links I sent you?"

"Love them. Let's get two for those parties, and one for Matthias. He'll have a tantrum if he doesn't get one too." Claudia sucked in air and then said, "I really had no idea how much I needed a Wife."

"I'm happy to do it," Lauren said before she hung up.

Lauren was thrilled when Claudia signed on for the School Concierge Package. She was rich, yes, and a bit out of touch. But with her husband working in Seattle for the year, and with a company to run, Claudia was legit overwhelmed.

"Text me when you put the cookies in the Uber," Claudia said. "I'll send my nanny down to the street to grab them. And please post all the expenses in the app. My admin will reimburse you right away."

After Lauren set the timer, she checked the Wife App. It was growing so fast. New Spouses and Wives every few minutes! The developers had built the self-hiring software, and Lauren had created a training manual complete with ethics, resources, and a Welcome to Wifehood video. They had so many Wives on the app that Lauren no longer knew all their names. As for Spouses, they were about to pass one thousand. It wasn't all smooth, of course. There were bugs that cost money to fix, and Lauren had had to personally boot a few Wives after complaints were logged about their incompetency. Same for some Spouses who whined too much or paid too little or attempted to cross inappropriate lines.

In her slivers of spare time, Lauren researched start-ups that made it, angel investors, the path to seed funding. She'd heard these terms for her entire career but they never felt relevant. She'd always just been a cog in the wheel. In one research burst, Lauren discovered a Women in Tech conference in Manhattan in March. The conference promised sessions designed to promote inclusivity in a field that historically was anything but. There was programming to help women make valuable connections with other attendees and discuss innovative trends. High-level female executives from an array of tech industries signed up to lead breakout sessions.

All interesting . . . but Lauren only had eyes for the keynote speaker: the legendary tech giant Anika Kim.

Anika Kim had made her fortune at the helm of a massive software company in the early 2000s. She'd had to battle the likes of Apple and Amazon and later all the Googles and Facebooks of the world to stay on top. In her retirement, she invested millions in Uber and Twitter but also in promising new start-ups. Men in the industry called her a ballbuster—but of course they did. Now in her early sixties, Anika Kim was one of the richest self-made women in America and one of the most powerful people in tech.

Lauren couldn't wait to hear what she had to say.

And yes, admittedly, she had fantasies.

Lauren watched YouTube videos of Anika Kim's speeches and TED Talks until she felt like she *knew* this woman. She recognized the clipped cadence of her voice, the slope of her silver hair, the ironic raise of her lids that were heavy with charcoal eye shadow.

Lauren imagined she'd approach her after the keynote. The

audience would part like the Red Sea. Anika Kim would spot Lauren walking up. She'd extend an arm—Lauren had seen videos of the way Anika Kim thrust out her hand for a firm shake—and they would introduce themselves. Lauren would pay homage to her hero and then she'd launch into her Wife App pitch. Anika Kim would be impressed by the innovation, by the growth of the Wife App, by Lauren's passion. She would invite Lauren to lunch and tell her she wanted to invest.

Men fall asleep to porn. Okay, a lot of women do too. But this fantasy of sweeping Anika Kim off her feet at the conference? That was what got Lauren through these chilly winter nights.

madeline

"GODDAMN IT," MADELINE GRUMBLED AS she sat cross-legged on the couch, her laptop balanced on her thighs. Two male Spouses needed her to shop for lingerie for their real wives. A bevy of early Valentine's Day gifts, one had bragged to Madeline on the phone, as if getting your wife to dress in a bodice and a thong is truly a gift for her.

Just as Madeline scrolled through pages of camisoles and tiny panties, sorting by size and price, another Spouse texted her on the app. This one was a woman—married, two kids, worked for the WNBA. She'd joined the Wife App with the highest level of membership so, basically, Madeline was her bitch. In the past three weeks, Madeline got this woman's ten-year-old son an emergency orthodontic appointment on a Sunday night, and she scored her an impossible-to-get reservation for four at Raoul's. Last Monday, Madeline found a rehab facility outside of Baltimore for this woman's elderly mother-in-law, who was getting discharged after a hip replacement. She even set up a car service to take the old lady from the hospital to the rehab!

> **Spouse Female WNBA 2 Kids:** Hey Wife3! I have a quick
> job for you.

Madeline winced at the "Wife3" thing but, then again, this was her choice. She preferred her Wife jobs to be anonymous.

Wife3: Sure, what's up?

Spouse Female WNBA 2 Kids: This one may sound weird but, you know, handling a husband is a full-time job.

Madeline braced herself for whatever "weirdness" was to come. After the barfing Yorkie and his butt-shaving extravaganza, Madeline thought she'd crashed into rock bottom on the Wife front.

Wife3: Hit me up.

Spouse Female WNBA 2 Kids: I'll cut to the chase. I want you to teach my husband to clean his whiskers off the sink after he shaves. I've told him and I've told him and still . . . whiskers!

"Goddamn Wife stuff!" Madeline said, shaking her head in shock.

"What's that?" Willow asked. "*Wife* stuff?"

Madeline looked up. She hadn't realized that Willow was over by the window, watering the daylilies.

"You're going to think this is crazy." Madeline considered how to complain about domestic work to the person who did *her* domestic work. "You know my friend, Lauren? We've started an app. It's just . . ." Madeline paused. "It's sucking up a lot of my time."

Willow tilted the watering can and doused each flower. "What does the app do?"

Madeline exhaled. She didn't want to come across as a spoiled princess. Then again, she firmly believed in living out loud. Not hiding who she was.

"Here, I'll show you." Madeline gestured for Willow to sit next to her on the couch. She opened the Wife App and scrolled through various features.

"You're shitting me!" Willow exclaimed as her eyes moved over the screen. Willow had a boxy jawline, freckles, and puppy-dog eyes. She always smelled like lemons. Madeline liked that about her. "You're telling me that women get paid to do the stuff we do at home for free?"

"Men too," Madeline said. She clicked over to the list of Wives on the app. "We currently have forty-three women working as Wives, nineteen men, and five nonbinary people."

"So what's making you so pissed off?"

"I sound awful complaining," Madeline said. "But I don't need the additional income. I don't want to create a system so some dude remembers to wipe his whiskers off the sink."

Willow lifted her thin eyebrows. "Hold on . . . What?"

Madeline clicked over to the text from Spouse Female WNBA 2 Kids.

"I could do that in five seconds!" Willow laughed. "The first time my boyfriend left nail clippings on the sink I was like, *Get your bony ass in here and clean this up. I'm not your mum.*"

Madeline grinned.

Willow gestured at Madeline's phone. "What's her real name?"

"I don't know. She told me at some point. Meredith? Heather? I can look it up."

"Does she know your name?"

Madeline shook her head.

"I would love to get my hands on her husband," Willow said. "Whip him into shape."

"Do you want to give this one a try?" Madeline asked. "She doesn't know what I look like, but we've talked on the phone a lot. No video calls, though. I'm just *Wife3* to her. Can you do an American accent?"

Willow gave her a double thumbs-up. "Seven years of acting lessons, baby."

"You could take over this Mental Load. I would pay you, of course. I would pay you *more* than this Spouse offered me just so I never have to deal with her or her husband. Honestly, you can have my whole Wife account if you want."

"Fuck yeah!" Willow said.

Madeline exhaled. How long had she been holding her breath? Days? Weeks? Her shoulders sagged in relief.

"But you wouldn't have to pay me more," Willow added. "Just whatever you'd be getting. And I wouldn't let it interfere with my work here."

"I insist on paying extra," Madeline said. "You are saving me."

Willow produced her phone from a side pocket and downloaded the Wife App. After Madeline recited her login and password, Willow snorted.

"Which one?" Madeline asked.

"The guy paying for a Wife to reserve classes for him at the gym. He can't get off his ass to arrange for getting off his ass."

Willow leaned back on the coach and read over the other Mental Loads. As she did, Madeline texted Lauren and explained that there was a new Wife3 in town. Hopefully Lauren wouldn't be mad. Madeline had tried her best.

For the past few months, whenever Madeline and Colin texted about Arabella going to London, neither would budge. Madeline insisted that Arabella's friends and musical education and school were in Manhattan. Colin held firm that Arabella wanted this, and he wanted it too. He said he could find her a top cello teacher. Over Christmas break, when the two of them toured secondary schools, he even had Arabella sit for an entrance exam.

As soon as Arabella told her that, upon her return from the U.K., Madeline called Serena Kilgannon in a panic.

"It would have been nice if he asked for your thoughts about the entrance exam," her lawyer told her, "but Colin has joint legal custody. Not residential, of course, but with joint decision-making, it's in his rights to take her for that test."

"But what if that specific step has to do with a change in residential custody?"

"If you start coming down hard on him about his decision-making powers," Serena said, "he could just as easily turn it around and question your decisions. I don't know if Colin is vindictive—"

"He's not," Madeline said quickly. She was surprised by how fast she defended her ex-husband. Until now, he'd never given her reason to hate him.

"Good. It's better not to have a vindictive ex. So remember that until he or his counsel file that legal motion—or even try to negotiate with us out of court—it's empty talk. Arabella isn't going anywhere. Her home is in New York. With you."

That should have calmed Madeline's nerves, except it didn't. Her anxiety only got worse when, suddenly, Colin stopped texting her back. All through Arabella's childhood, Madeline and Colin had stayed in touch frequently over text.

"Is Dad okay?" she asked Arabella on Friday evening after her daughter finished her scales and came into the kitchen for orange juice.

"He's fine, why?"

"I haven't heard from him in a few days," Madeline explained.

Arabella flipped her hair to one side and frowned at her mom. "I've talked to him plenty. Anyway, it's not like you're married anymore."

Madeline stared at her daughter. When had Arabella become so salty?

"Can I get back to practicing?" Arabella wiped her hand over her lips. "I have to work on this orchestral piece for the seating audition. Also, can I sleep over at Ria's tomorrow? She asked me."

"Of course." Madeline glanced into the living room at her yoga mat. She should probably do some stretches, a little meditation, or she would descend into a panic attack. "Thanks for telling me about Dad."

sophie

Sophie was surprised to find that she loved being a Wife. She'd thought it would feel demeaning. She'd thought it would be like being a wife to Joshua except without the perks. Truth be told, after their few honeymoon years, Sophie didn't get many perks from her marriage. Joshua never earned money so he didn't bring her financial stability. He hadn't been a reliable source of childcare. He hadn't even kept her feet warm at night! When Sophie burrowed into bed with icy toes, Joshua would wriggle his legs away.

These days, whenever Sophie had free hours—late nights, weekends that the boys were with Joshua and Beatrice—she loaded her schedule with so much Mental Load that Lauren called one Friday evening and said, "I've reviewed the job chart on the app and I'm worried. Are you sure you can handle everything?"

As Sophie surveyed the to-do lists for her Spouses and her stack of student assessments on the table, Edna wove figure eights around her ankles. Tomorrow morning, Sophie had agreed to pick up an SUV for a Spouse and drive it to Westchester County for a New York State inspection. In the afternoon, she'd committed to checking out party venues in Lower Manhattan for someone's kid's Bar Mitzvah. Sunday she would do lesson prep for work, buy groceries for her family, and grab a Wife job for a woman who needed help screening social media apps for her preadolescent daughters and setting up a system to monitor their online activity.

"I can definitely handle it," Sophie said.

No, Sophie wasn't overwhelmed. In fact, she was relieved. After tomorrow, she could pay off the entire balance on her credit card.

"Remember college?" Sophie asked Lauren. "Remember how I used to register for extra classes for the heck of it? I'm happiest when I'm busy."

Lauren sounded like she was typing in the background. Often she peed while they were on the phone or washed dishes or walked her dog. "Promise you'll reach out if you need help. Willow is doing great as Madeline. She says she can take on more if you need to share your Load."

"I promise," Sophie reassured Lauren. Edna jumped on the kitchen table and walked across her keyboard. Sophie picked up the cat and dropped her back on the floor.

Now, a week later, Sophie sat on her couch on a subzero Saturday morning in January. She wrapped her fingers around a mug of hot tea and choreographed how to tell her children about the Wife App. It was time. Their lives were changing, and they deserved to know.

For once in Sophie's life, she didn't feel the choke of financial stress that had always squeezed the life out of her. For once in Sophie's life, she had extra. Send Noah to that pricey soccer camp that his best buddies were going to? She'd inform him today that she could put down a deposit. Get Charlie cognitive behavioral therapy? That was the first thing Sophie did when she had enough Wife App money. Two weeks ago, Charlie began weekly sessions with a CBT therapist at Mount Sinai.

"Boys!" Sophie called in the direction of their bedroom. She could hear *Phineas and Ferb* finish on the iPad and she wanted to intercept them before the next episode began. "Time to come into the living room like we talked about. Family meeting."

"What is it, Mommy?" Charlie galloped in and plunked onto the couch.

Noah slunk in behind him. "Yeah, is this going to take long? I have homework."

Sophie smiled back at her older son. She wouldn't let Noah rattle her. Not today. "I have big news that I want to share with you both."

"Are you having a baby?" Charlie bounced up and down on the cushion. "That's what Daddy and Beatrice said when they told us Baby Clementine was coming. They said *big news*."

"No!" Sophie shook her hair from side to side. "Oh . . . no. No. No. No."

Noah leaned forward and checked the time on the microwave. He did it in an exaggerated way like, *I'm done here.* Sophie tried to overlook how much he reminded her of Joshua. She still had years to steer him in the right direction.

"Good." Charlie bobbed his chin. "Because babies are hard and what Beatrice talks about is that Daddy doesn't do enough. She's always mad at Daddy."

Sophie's breath caught. Her last few interactions with the boys' stepmom had been so positive. When Sophie emailed Joshua and informed him that she'd put Charlie in therapy, it was Beatrice who emailed back and said they were glad she'd sought help for his anxiety. Within minutes, Beatrice Venmoed their half of Charlie's monthly therapy bill to Sophie. Sophie wasn't sure what changed Joshua's mind, but she decided not to question it.

"Beatrice says this to you?" Sophie plunged the tea bag up and down in the hot water. "That she's mad at Daddy?"

Noah raked his fingers through his spiky hair and shifted uncomfortably.

"No," Charlie said. "On the phone. I don't know who she talks to.

Sometimes she cries. I was on the couch reading and she didn't know I was there. That's when I heard—"

Noah turned fast on his brother. "Shut up, okay? I don't think this is Mom's business."

Charlie's mouth opened in a worried *ooohhh* and he began to pick at his thumbnail.

"No biggie," Sophie said as she moved Charlie's hand. She played it cool but, *of course*, she'd turn all this over in her head later. "Every new mom has her moments, Charlie. And we don't say *shut up*, Noah. We are kind to each other."

Noah rolled his eyes. Charlie kicked his feet back and forth. He wore his Thomas the Tank Engine pajama bottoms that he'd had since kindergarten. They were several sizes too small. Sophie made a mental note to sort through his drawers and assemble a bag of hand-me-downs.

"The news I want to share is that I've gone into business with Lauren and Madeline. We've started an app. I may be busier than usual in the coming months so I wanted to give you a heads-up."

"I didn't know that you knew how to build apps," Noah said.

Sophie explained that Lauren oversaw the technical aspects. She and Madeline were cofounders. To preempt questions, she told them it was called the Wife App and she described some things the Wives did.

"Hold on." Noah scowled. *"Holdonholdonholdon.* You do *what?"*

Sophie had seen that coming. Noah was in middle school and he was at the height of being a jerk, which actually meant he was at the height of insecurity. Well, Sophie was ready. She was ready because she wasn't embarrassed about the Wife App. Even a few weeks ago, she wouldn't have said that. But something essential in her had shifted— she no longer wanted to apologize.

Sophie sipped from her tea and calmly explained that Wives got paid to do things that women—that *people*—should get paid for. She said that people should never take advantage of anyone doing free labor for them.

Noah nodded. "I guess that makes sense."

Once Sophie was certain she had her sons on board for the right reasons, she played her final card: soccer camp. Noah sprang from the couch and wrapped his arms around his mom.

"For real?" he asked. "In New Hampshire?"

Sophie breathed in her son. A little body odor. Some lingering sleep. A waft of yesterday's deodorant. But beneath all that she still smelled that fresh-bread scent he'd had since he was a baby.

"For real," she said. She smiled so hard her face hurt. Noah wanted this camp very badly. "Go text your friends and let them know. I've already made sure the camp has availability. We can put down the deposit today."

Noah skipped into his bedroom for his phone. He skipped! He hadn't skipped in years. At least not since the divorce. And Sophie had made it happen. The Wife App had made it happen.

That afternoon, Sophie got a sequence of texts from Lauren. The last she heard, Lauren was flying some kid to Seattle to visit his dad.

> **Lauren:** Hey Madeline and Soph! You were right. I was wrong. Effective immediately, the Wife App no longer has direct contact with children. My flight to Seattle was every single nail in that coffin.

> **Lauren:** Also, guess who was on my plane?

> **Lauren:** Think high school boyfriend. Think first love. Think cowboy.

Sophie sucked in her breath. Obviously Lauren was talking about Gideon Crane. His name had come up a few months ago when they talked about googling exes and, later, quietly, Sophie had looked up his little sister.

Now Lauren saw Gideon! Was he married? Or single as well? When Lauren arrived at Vassar, first year, she'd been heartbroken about their breakup. Even though there had been other boyfriends, culminating in her marriage to Eric, Sophie had the sense that Gideon gripped a chamber in Lauren's heart. When Sophie thought of Lauren and Gideon, she was reminded of the famous Joan Didion line: *I mean that I was in love with the city, the way you love the first person who ever touches you and you never love anyone quite that way again.*

Sophie sighed heavily and then gave a thumbs-up to Lauren's child-care comment. She didn't want to text "I told you so," but she'd said from the beginning that the Wife App shouldn't have direct contact with children.

> **Sophie:** Gideon??? Do tell!

> **Sophie:** Are you okay?

> **Madeline:** Is he hot? Or old and washed up?

> **Madeline:** Laur????

When Lauren didn't text back, Sophie called her but it went straight to voicemail. She was probably already on the flight home.

lauren

IN THE CAR HOME FROM the airport, after her hellish flight with Matthias, Lauren wriggled Gideon's number out of her jeans pocket. He still had the same handwriting—thin letters tilted forward. Lauren took a picture of the number in case she lost it, but she didn't enter his contact into her phone. It felt like too much to be able to tap an icon and reach Gideon.

She thought back to their last lunch, fifteen years ago, soon after she and Eric had gotten married. Gideon looked scruffy and sipped from a dented metal water bottle. The whole *Hitchhiker's Guide to the Galaxy* image felt out of place in a Manhattan restaurant. Or maybe Lauren was being a snob.

"So you're really married," Gideon had said. He needed a haircut and had deep circles under his eyes.

"I really am. Last June." She thrust out her white-gold wedding band, then quickly withdrew her fingers, embarrassed by the Bridezilla moment. When she and Gideon celebrated six months, they stayed up all night to watch the sunrise. At nine months, they skinny-dipped in his backyard pool, then lay down towels and had sex under the stars. Lauren still remembered how she crawled on top of him, how they moved together until their naked bodies were sweaty and limp.

"I always wondered. . . ." He picked at a potato chip next to his sandwich. "I was trying to be so practical back then, when I was headed to Berkeley and you were staying on the East Coast. You know, the whole long-distance thing."

Lauren chewed on the inside of her cheeks. Was Gideon honestly doing this now? Five years ago, if he'd swung through town on a wondering mission, she would have said, *Hell yes! I've never stopped wondering!* But now? She was married to Eric Turner, a handsome young lawyer. They wanted kids. They were stashing away a down payment for a prewar two-bedroom.

"Didn't you ever wonder?" Gideon stared at Lauren so intently her heart twisted.

"I'm glad we had what we had," she said quickly. "It set my bar high for all future relationships."

Gideon took a bite of his sandwich. "Eric is a good guy?"

"He's great."

"Good. I'm glad you're happy."

At some point, maybe ten years ago, Lauren heard through high school friends that Gideon had gotten married. She emailed him, *Congrats, I'm happy for you,* but his old Yahoo address bounced back. Maybe that was for the best. She wasn't *actually* happy for him. She and Eric were deep in the trenches of toddler twins. She was run ragged from work and parenting and being a wife. She craved that passion she felt at eighteen. She craved sex under the stars.

Lauren slid Gideon's number back in her pocket and watched as the car drew closer to the glittering Manhattan skyline.

Lauren woke up on January 20, hit "start" on the coffee maker, and realized with a jolt that it had been exactly a year since she discovered the texts on Eric's phone. A year ago, she never imagined that in twelve months she'd have built her own app. A year ago, she never imagined that her ex-husband would be having sex with someone almost half his age and that fact didn't kill her every second. Lauren hadn't slept with anyone since Eric. She hadn't sought it out and it hadn't come knocking. Sometimes she was so lonely her skin hurt.

A few weeks ago, Lauren ordered a purple vibrator with a long battery life. Sometimes she came and fell asleep. Sometimes she came and then sobbed. Sometimes there was no orgasm, just tears. She wasn't going to lie and say the post-divorce year was a picnic.

Two hours later, Lauren tapped the brass knocker at the front door of a stately brownstone on the Upper East Side.

"Good morning, Lauren," Theo said, greeting her with a slight bow. "Thanks for coming."

"Of course," Lauren said. "Good to see you again."

Theo Robinson was her favorite Spouse, and actually her first. He was the one who hired her last December to organize his tropical golf vacation. A retired anesthesiologist, he was widowed, and generous with praise and money. Their first connection was about death; Lauren lost her mom to the same type of cancer that had taken Theo's wife. Other Spouses, such as Conrad with the horse, had that entitled arrogance. Theo, by contrast, was grateful for Lauren's effort. For today's Mental Load, he wanted Lauren to create decades of family photo albums, something his wife had not been able to do before she died. He'd added a note that there was something else he wanted to discuss in person.

"I just put on coffee," Theo said. "Would you like some?"

"That would be great," Lauren said.

As Theo retreated to the kitchen, Lauren checked the Wife App to make sure the new "On the Job" feature worked. At first, she, Sophie, and Madeline texted each other whenever they entered someone's apartment. But with all these new Wives on the app, this added a measure of protection and addressed liability concerns.

"Would you like milk?" Theo called out.

"Do you have soy or almond?"

"Almond," Theo said. "My wife, my late wife, she also . . ."

"Almond milk is delicious." Lauren glanced out the doors of the living room, which looked onto a private backyard. The patio furniture was heaped in snow.

A few minutes later, Lauren sat with Theo at his long dining room table as they leafed through photographs. Real printed pictures from when he and Mari were first married, then the arrival of kids. A chocolate Lab showed up at some point. By the time grandchildren burst on the scene, Lauren and Theo had shifted to laptops—his current computer and Mari's old one—and Lauren took furious notes. Chronology of family history, vacations, in-laws, friends, boyfriends, girlfriends, weddings, retirement parties.

"Mari always wanted to do this," Theo explained several hours later. Their half-finished coffees were cold. They sipped seltzer and snacked on cheese and crackers. "She would put photos in shoeboxes or download pictures from her phone and say, 'As soon as I retire, I'm going to make photo books.'"

"Mari worked part time, right?" Lauren asked.

Theo tipped his head forward. "But even with part time she said there was never enough time."

Lauren glanced around the living room. If these walls could talk, they would tell Mari's story. They would tell all wives' stories. It's not just work, full time or part time. It's laundry if you have to do it yourself. If you have enough money, it's coordinating someone else to clean your clothes. It's groceries—no matter what income level, the family has to eat. It's home repairs—whether you do it yourself, harass your spouse to do it, or hire it out. It's school projects, sneakers that don't fit, brackets that pop off braces.

"Mari retired and then we took trips to visit our children." Theo rubbed his fingers back and forth across his forehead. "Then, of course, she got sick."

Lauren studied Theo's dark eyes, lids hooded like a basset hound. She tried to imagine what he was like when he was younger. She'd seen the pictures, of course. But what did he smell like? How did he move? She tried to picture him as a doctor, a husband, a naked man who slipped into bed beside his wife. Did he wake his wife with an erection in the night the way Eric did? She hoped he was kinder than her ex-husband.

"So what's this new thing you wanted to discuss?" Lauren asked. "You mentioned something on the app."

Theo grimaced as he capped one palm over each knee.

"We don't have to do this," Lauren said.

"No, no." Theo shifted uncomfortably. "I want to. It's just . . . the issue is . . . I'm lonely. I hadn't realized how much effort Mari put into keeping in touch with our friends. We had a social life. They all visited when she was sick and after she was gone."

Lauren nodded. She'd seen the same thing with her father—the parade of misery tourists who disappeared within weeks of her mom's death.

Theo looked into his lap. "I want to bring them back. Friends. Dinners. Plans. I organized that golf trip—well, you did that—but those friends and I haven't seen each other since. My kids say social media is the way to go. I know that's good for *finding* friends, but I want to maintain the relationships. Or whatever it is that Mari used to do."

Lauren nodded. "Do you ever send cards to any of these people?"

He shot her a blank expression. "Cards? Like birthday cards?"

"Theo," Lauren said, "get your coat and boots."

"Where are we going?"

"A post office for stamps." Lauren clicked onto Google Maps. She knew this neighborhood for dentist appointments and museums but not errands. "Then I'm going to find a stationery store to buy cards."

When Theo didn't budge, Lauren set her phone back down. "I imagine you've read the research," she said, "that male widowers are more socially disconnected than their female counterparts."

Theo nodded at the word *research*. Men liked research. Statistics. She was speaking his language.

She continued, "It's because when men don't do the work of maintaining social connections, and they don't have a wife to do it for them, those connections begin to evaporate. Which has adverse health effects on the surviving spouse." Lauren cleared her throat. "So I'm going to teach you how to make those social connections. And one tactic is the greeting card. It's not the only tactic, of course. We'll set up a schedule for you to text friends. Call them. Arrange to meet for coffee. For lunch. It's work to maintain friendships. But cards are on the first page of the Wife Handbook."

As Theo walked to the hall closet, he still looked skeptical.

Lauren called after him, "When your kids were younger, did Mari harass them to write thank-you notes?"

"Yes . . . my son put up the worst fights."

"And your daughter?" Lauren asked.

"She's the one who still mails me cards."

A smile spread over Theo's face. Lauren clicked *leaving residence* on the app, and then slid her arms into her jacket.

madeline

MADELINE WAS IN THE KITCHEN talking to Willow and cutting up organic kale when her mother called.

"Oh shit," she said as *Bianca* appeared on the screen. Her mom rarely called. If she did, Madeline rarely answered. Text was invented for relationships like theirs. Live conversations had become doubly agonizing since Madeline discovered that her stepdad fucked around. Every time her mom gloated about something "wonderful" that Ron did, Madeline bit her tongue. What would it accomplish to tell her about Bumble? It would make her mom hate *her*, the bearer of bad news, and not the actual person she should hate.

"Do you need to grab it?" Willow had been recounting her latest Wife App job. As Wife3, she'd gone to Surefoot to get customized ski boots for a wealthy lesbian couple who had no time to do it themselves.

"I'll let the call go to voicemail," Madeline said. She spread the kale across a large cookie sheet. "It's just my mom."

Willow widened her eyes. Her own mom—or "mum," as she called her—lived outside of Dublin. Madeline often heard Willow laughing with her on the phone while she cleaned the apartment. Madeline ached for a mom who doubled as her best friend. But then she reminded herself that she was that to Arabella. Well, she tried to be. These days, she wasn't sure *where* she stood.

The phone kept ringing.

"I guess I should grab it." Madeline dried her hands on a dish towel. "Make sure everything's okay."

As she walked into the living room, she tapped on the screen.

"Hi, Mom."

"I keep looking at this picture you texted me from when you and Arabella visited us last year," Bianca said. "I wonder if you could get it framed for me? It's the most beautiful photo I've ever seen of Arabella."

"Sure . . . okay," Madeline said. Her mom's sixty-seventh birthday was coming up in March. At least now Madeline knew what they could get her. Bianca's birthday was a perennial stumper. No food baskets, obviously, since they didn't eat. And who needed a gift card when you had millions?

"But you're making a funny face in the picture," Bianca said. "And your highlights are too light. Did you switch stylists?"

Madeline didn't respond. What was there to say?

"When you get it framed," Bianca asked, "can you ask the printer to crop you out? It's such a lovely photo of . . ."

Madeline held the phone away from her ear. It was classic Bianca. She was not in the mood for it.

When Bianca's voice finally went quiet, Madeline drew the phone back to her cheek. "Is this what you called to talk about? Cropping me out of the picture?"

Bianca coughed lightly. "You don't need to be so sensitive."

Madeline ran her hand across the top of Arabella's music stand. Arabella rarely used this one in the living room anymore. Now she practiced almost exclusively in her bedroom.

"Actually," Bianca said, "I wanted to talk to you about Arabella and London next year."

Madeline's stomach plummeted. She lowered herself onto the

couch. How the hell did her mom find out about London? Not Colin. Back when they were married, he considered Madeline's mom toxic. But it couldn't be Arabella, right? Madeline had specifically warned her daughter against this. Arabella saw firsthand how manipulative Bianca was. As much as Arabella wanted space, she would never cross enemy lines.

"Madeline, are you there?" Bianca asked.

"I'm here."

"I'm sure, as usual, your mind is made up about not letting Arabella live with her father but I want to present a different viewpoint. For one—"

"How did you even . . . ?" Madeline's voice felt far away from her body. "How do you know that . . . ?"

"Arabella, of course," Bianca said.

Madeline walked into her room and closed the door behind her. She sat gingerly on the edge of her bed.

"Arabella and I have our own relationship," Bianca said. "Anyway, when I called her the other day, we had a long conversation about next year. She wants you to be more supportive."

"Mom," Madeline managed to say. "Stop."

"I realize this might be hard for you—"

Madeline lay back on her pillow and closed her eyes.

"If you can't see the writing on the wall," Bianca said, "then I think you're being—"

"Stop!" Madeline shouted, sitting up. Her arms pulsed with energy. "Anyway, if you want to go around fixing lives, look at your own."

"What's that supposed to mean?" Bianca asked coldly.

"Talk to Ron," Madeline said. "Ask him about his Bumble account."

Without waiting for her mom to respond, Madeline stabbed "end" on the call.

sophie

"I'M GOING TO MAKE IT all the way across the park without checking my sneakers for dog poop," Charlie said. He laced his gloved hand in hers as they crossed Fifth Avenue and stepped into Central Park.

It was a cold afternoon, the first day of February, but at least the sky was blue. Charlie had just finished his cognitive behavioral therapy appointment, which was at Mount Sinai Hospital on the east side. If it wasn't raining, Sophie liked to walk home so Charlie could have a chance to process his session.

"Good plan," Sophie said. "Is that what you talked about with Jeffrey?"

"Yeah," Charlie said. "Jeffrey and I made this goal about the park. He said, *What's the worst thing that can happen? Even if you see dog poop on your sneaker you can't do anything about it in the middle of the park.*"

"I like that goal," Sophie said. She reached into her purse and pulled out a salted caramel Kind bar. Since Charlie's fingers were in gloves, she tore off the wrapper before handing it to him.

Charlie nibbled carefully at the snack. His front teeth were fully in now, but he had a few loose ones on the bottom. That was always a flurry of drama as the tooth was falling out—the freaky threads of skin keeping the baby tooth attached, that initial gush of blood. But then, joyously, cash from the Tooth Fairy the following morning.

"Jeffrey also said that I'm in control of my choices," Charlie said after a moment. "Do you think so . . . like for you?"

"Do I think so *what*?" Sophie asked. Why wasn't there a Tooth Fairy for adults, that mythical woman who waved her amnesiac wand and made yesterday's pain disappear?

"Do you think you're in control of your choices? Like what Jeffrey said."

"Hmmmm," Sophie said, stalling for time. It was a heavy conversation for an eight-year-old, but Charlie had always run deep. When he was four, he asked Sophie where lightning went in when it hit people. At five, he wanted to know how many years the sun had left to burn.

The path led them alongside a sports field that was dusted with snow. All of a sudden, Charlie paused, about to check his sneakers, but then shook his head back and forth.

"Did you see that, Mommy?" Charlie asked. "Did you see I didn't check?"

"Yes." Sophie squeezed her son's hand. "I did see. Nice job."

"So . . . do you?"

Sophie turned the question around in her brain. *Do I think I'm in control of my choices?* Sophie's choices had always been an uphill slog. In her heart of hearts, she wished she could have stayed home with her babies, toted them to soccer practice and swim lessons, delivered cookies and new books to them in a fantasy backyard tree house. It felt anti-feminist to admit this—and it wasn't like Sophie married rich or inherited generational wealth, so it was never an option not to work. But also, Sophie couldn't imagine living a life like her mother and sister, career wives and stay-at-home moms on steroids. Sophie set out, at eighteen, to do everything in polar opposition to them.

"I think I'm in control of my choices," Sophie finally said to Charlie. "It's not always easy."

"Jeffrey told me that too," Charlie said. "Is it always like that? Like, forever?"

Sophie tilted her head from side to side as she mulled this over. *Maybe it gets easier? Or maybe, as we get older, we let go of who we think we should be.* After years of resisting the traditional wife role, here was the Wife App. Here was Sophie, in her own version of career Wife. She felt pride in her work. Also, this was her *choice.* Maybe that was the most important part.

"It gets easier," Sophie said. "And we're brave, you and me. We can do things even if they're hard."

Charlie smiled at her with his new adult teeth on the top and his loose baby teeth on the bottom.

lauren

"I NEVER WANT TO BE a wife. Ever. It's boring."

"Maybe you could be a husband," Lauren suggested. She'd broached the topic of pronouns and gender identity with Amelia after that evening walk with Sophie back in December. Amelia had responded with something vague like, *A lot of kids at school are they/them . . . I don't know . . . I mean, how should I know?* Lauren told Amelia that she didn't *have* to know anything, that everyone realizes things about themselves at different times. Then she lifted from Sophie's language and added that there were no closets in their home, and that if Amelia ever did question her gender, she didn't need to hide it. At that point, Amelia got teary, and Lauren wrapped her arms around her daughter and kissed her forehead. Just as she began to rock her from side to side, Amelia wriggled away and said, *Okay, Mom! Back off! I'm not a baby.* Even so, it felt like the conversation had started. It felt like progress.

Or maybe not. Because when Lauren said that just now about being a husband instead of a wife, Amelia rolled her eyes to indicate that her mom was as annoying as humanly possible.

"This is so stupid." Amelia stared sourly at the screen. "And I'm only into year two of Theo and Mari's marriage. How many pictures can they possibly take of themselves on vacation? With their dog? I get what they look like. *We all do.*"

"You can quit the photo albums anytime," Lauren told her daughter. She sat next to her at the table, posting items in the Wife App Slack channel that she needed the engineers to tweak. On her other tab, she was menu-planning for a married couple and arranging for Wi-Fi to get installed at their remote country house. "I'll outsource the photo albums to another Wife."

"No, I like the money," Amelia said. "I'll stop complaining."

"That would be excellent."

As Amelia got back to work, Lauren studied her daughter. Maybe she shouldn't have hired her as a Wife, but Amelia had been a constant source of whining for weeks. She was bored since Ultimate Frisbee was over, bored since she completed her binge of *The Office*. It had gotten worse after Cady landed a lead in the middle-school play. Now, in addition to being bored, she was jealous.

"The Baker's *Wife*," Amelia ranted when Cady texted from school that she was cast as a lead. "The Baker's Wife doesn't even have a name. Her entire character is defined by who she is married to."

"The Baker doesn't have a name either," Lauren pointed out.

"Yeah, but he's defined by his career, not his marriage. See what I mean?"

Lauren made Amelia promise not to ruin it for her sister. This role in *Into the Woods* was a huge score for Cady.

Whenever Amelia's moods felt unbearable, Lauren thought about Matthias, about that flight to Seattle and his meltdown over the iPad. Interestingly, after texting Claudia from the airplane that "even a Wife has her limits," Lauren thought she'd alienated the wealthy cosmetics executive forever. But then, a day later—back in the middle of January—she'd received a series of texts on her phone.

ClaudiaSpouse: I've been thinking about what you said about Wives' limits and I realize I've let my husband push too many of mine.

ClaudiaSpouse: No need for the School Concierge Package anymore. I'm done trying to look like I can do it all.

ClaudiaSpouse: And no need to reimburse me for the plane tickets. I hope your flight wasn't too awful.

Lauren texted Claudia a gracious response and wished her the best. Maybe Claudia would make changes in her life. Maybe she'd go to bat for equality.

As far as the flight to Seattle, well, Lauren had nothing to say about that. Whenever she thought about it, she remembered Gideon. And right now, it was best not to go there.

madeline

MADELINE COULD NOT, UNDER ANY circumstance, tell Arabella what her grandma said. Maybe in the past, they were a team united against Bianca. But now Madeline had no idea where Arabella's loyalties lay. Evening meals were a choreographed dance of all that was not being said. And there was so much not being said.

At least she had a PTA meeting on Thursday. Bryan was on the fundraising committee too. After meetings, he generally walked her back to her apartment and they had no-strings-attached sex.

On Thursday morning, in anticipation of Bryan's visit, she made her bed and placed a vase of tulips on her dresser. But then, as they strolled out of Fryer Prep, he gestured in the opposite direction.

"I can't today," he said. He rubbed his large hands together and then blew air on them.

"Got it . . . okay." Madeline tried to disguise the hurt in her voice. Under her coat, she wore dark jeans, a sheer blouse, and a beige camisole. She looked hot, goddamn it.

"Maybe next week?" he asked.

Madeline stiffened her shoulders. There was a deep freeze last night that lingered in this morning's bitter air. "Sounds good."

"Cool," he said. A small drip pooled around his left nostril.

They stood outside a deli, nothing left to say. Strange how one week he was thrusting into you, and the next week he was a stranger on the corner of Columbus Avenue, someone you didn't know well enough to point out that his nose was running.

"I better go." Madeline gestured in the vague direction of her yoga studio. "I'll catch a yoga class. It's starting soon."

"Cool," he said again. "I'll text you."

Madeline kept a locker with spare exercise clothes at the studio. It was expensive but thoroughly worth it when she wanted to drop by last minute. She changed into her yoga pants and a strappy tank top. She grabbed two purple blocks and a neatly folded Mexican-style blanket, arranged them on the edge of her mat, then popped into the candlelit bathroom for a pee. As she sat on the toilet, she scrolled through her phone. An email instantly caught her eye.

The subject line was *Arabella Smith*.

The email was from *Remy Harris, Attorney-at-Law*.

With her yoga pants bunched around her knees, Madeline anxiously read on.

Via email
Re: Custody Arrangements for Arabella Smith
Index number: 365821

Dear Ms. Wallace:

I have been retained to represent your former husband, Colin Smith, concerning your failure to come to an agreement regarding where your daughter, Arabella, should reside for the next school year. Pursuant to paragraph III in your original custody agreement, you and Mr. Smith share decision-making related to your daughter.

*Your refusal to allow Arabella to live in London for a year is
adversely impacting her well-being and hindering her chance to
build a relationship with her father. In an effort to co-parent with
you, Mr. Smith reached out to you repeatedly over the past three
months. Unfortunately, you continually rebuked him and refused to
discuss Arabella's temporary move to London.*

*Should you stand in the way of a satisfying arrangement, Mr. Smith
will have no choice but to pursue an enforcement action in court,
pursuant to paragraph V of your settlement agreement. Please
confirm, or have your counsel confirm, receipt of this email by
February 8.*

Regards,
Remy Francesca Harris, Attorney at Law

Madeline barely remembered flushing the toilet. She barely remembered returning to her mat. The teacher, a young Swiss woman with
huge breasts, led the class through their *ohms* and into the Tadasana
Mountain Pose. Madeline tried to be present. She tried to be calm
and centered. But then, midway through the Three-Legged Downward
Dog, she let out a sharp sob. Avoiding the stares of the other yogis in
the class, Madeline grabbed her phone, hurried back to the bathroom,
and locked the door. As she leaned against the wall, she tried to forward
Colin's lawyer's memorandum to Serena but she kept fumbling and en-
tering the wrong email address. Madeline glanced angrily around the
bathroom. She hated the stupid sandalwood candle flickering on the
shelf. She hated the bamboo plant twisting out of a clear vase next to
the sink. She hated that she couldn't avoid it any longer; her worst-case
scenario was coming true.

sophie

"Soph?"

"Yep," Sophie said to her mom.

"Eva?" her mom asked.

"I'm here," Sophie's sister, Eva, said.

"Great," her mom purred. "Both girls on the line. Thanks for doing this call. TGIF, ladies!"

"I'll drink to that," Eva said.

Sophie pictured her sister on the sectional sofa in her cavernous living room outside of Carmel, Indiana, the stem of a fruity drink pinched between her manicured fingers. Then she imagined her mom, two suburbs away from Eva, in a slightly smaller living room. They went for manicures together on their weekly spa jaunt. Her mom probably sipped a glass of boxed merlot.

"So," her mom asked. "What do we think?"

"I think we like it," Eva said. "I'm opening it on my laptop so I can see it really big. Give me a second."

"I'll do that too," her mom said.

Sophie adjusted her earbuds and waited for the light to change. Once it did, she tipped her cart off the curb and pushed it across

Broadway. Her mom had texted earlier to see if she and Eva could have a three-way chat tonight. Sophie decided to take the call while doing Wife errands. Let it be a reminder to herself that she had a life outside of the vacuum her mom and sister created on their calls with her. Even if they weren't aware of the Wife App yet, Sophie stood taller knowing that she had this thing she loved. That she'd helped invent!

On this particular Friday night, Sophie had agreed to take on a quick Wife job. It was an older woman, someone Sophie had worked with several times before. She had scoliosis and couldn't walk well, but that wasn't why she hired Sophie. She could have easily hired someone more affordable on TaskRabbit or another odd-job platform to mail her packages and the like. But as she told Sophie when she first messaged her, *I was a wife for forty-one years. Even though my wonderful husband passed a decade ago, once a wife, always a wife. NO LONGER. Goodbye good girl (old lady?). I want to be footloose and mental-load free.*

Sophie laughed when she read that; she knew she would love this woman. They met at the woman's apartment on West End Avenue one weekend and hashed out exactly what she wanted. She gave Sophie a list of key children and grandchildren events, addresses, a budget for gifts. She gave Sophie contact info for her doctors and access to her calendar to book follow-up appointments. This evening, it was a fairly simple job. The woman had photographed a bunch of blouses and socks and texted, *Log onto my Amazon and return them. Then pick them up from my doorman at six to bring to UPS. Grab me a treat on the way home. Surprise me! I like caramel. Hate chocolate.*

"Okay," Eva said. "I'm zooming in. . . ."

"Me too," her mom said. "Soph, what shade are you wearing?"

"What shade of what?" Sophie wiped at her nose. It was a bitter night, so cold that her skin burned. She honestly had no idea what they were talking about.

"What shade of gloss, honey," her mom said. "What shade are you wearing in this photo you sent to Eva last week?"

Ah. Sophie should have guessed as much. Last week, Eva texted her that her husband, Matt, had a rich fraternity brother who was moving from Texas to New York City in April. He was divorced and, hey, why not give it a try? Eva asked Sophie to send her a photo so she could make the setup happen. Sophie, in the middle of a million things, texted her a picture from last summer when she and the boys went to Coney Island. Did she have gloss on? Maybe. Or maybe it was ChapStick with SPF.

"It's a cute shot . . . but . . ." Eva paused. "Maybe a little casual."

"I hadn't realized you wanted a red-carpet pose," Sophie said. She considered adding, *I hadn't realized you were going to share my picture with Mom,* but of course Eva forwarded it to their mom. Sophie doubted they had a secret between them.

"You realize this man is very well off," Sophie's mom said. "He made his money in the oil business."

Sophie stood on the corner of Broadway even though the light had changed. She watched a couple walk out of a sushi restaurant, hats pulled snug over their foreheads. She watched another couple hail a cab.

"Texas oil money, Eva?" Sophie asked. "Greek life? I'm not sure this guy and I will have a lot in common."

"Wow," Eva said coldly. "Wow."

Her mom cleared her throat. "Are you forgetting Eva's husband? Matt was in a fraternity."

"And I was in a sorority," Eva said. "You know I loved it. Those girls are like my own sisters."

Sophie long suspected that Eva had been a sorority girl from hell who wielded a Sharpie and circled her naked sisters' body fat. One of the reasons Sophie picked Vassar was because they didn't have a Greek system.

"Back to the topic at hand," Sophie's mom said. "How about another photo for Eva to send to this Texas man? You can get a makeover and have one of your girlfriends take a photo."

Girlfriends. In her mom's world, girlfriends were the people you gathered with for chick flicks, salads with dressing on the side. Girlfriends were never romantic, except maybe sometimes on Netflix.

"Think *sexy casual,*" Eva said. "Think *sexy glam casual.*"

Sophie tipped her cart up and pushed through the jingling door of the UPS Store. "Listen, I'm in a store. Hang on a second." To the guy at the counter, she said, "I'm here to drop off several packages." She held up her screen to show him her Spouse's QR codes.

As the man scanned the codes, Sophie's mom said, "What are you mailing?"

"It's for a friend," Sophie said vaguely. In the pause that followed, Sophie considered what caramel treat she should get for her Spouse. Her boys loved Ben and Jerry's Salted Caramel Core. Then again, there was nothing like reading a good book and sucking through a bag of Werther's Originals. . . .

"A boyfriend?" her mom asked, ever hopeful.

"Just a friend." Sophie waved at the UPS guy and wheeled her cart out of the store.

"You really should give Matt's friend a chance," Eva said. "If he'll give you a chance, of course. I'm not sure what type of woman he dates."

"Valentine's Day is coming up," her mom added. "A *friend* doesn't take you out to dinner on Valentine's Day."

Sophie rolled her eyes. "I'm sorry . . . I can't hear you. Is it the connection? Mom? Eva?"

"I can hear you just fine," her mom said. "It's probably on your end. You would think, in the middle of New York City—"

"We're breaking up. . . ." Sophie said, interrupting her. "Talk soon!"

Sophie smiled to herself as she hit "end" on the crystal clear connection.

lauren

On Sunday evening, when the twins arrived home from Eric's place, Cady danced giddily through the door.

"I love romance," she said as they sat at the table. She twirled her spaghetti around her fork. "I can't believe Valentine's Day is this week!"

Lauren sighed. This week before Valentine's Day was the busiest ever for the Wife App. Male Spouses hit up Wives to take care of their honey-do lists and shop for incredibly personal Valentine's Day gifts.

Amelia reached for the garlic bread. "You're obsessed with romance because you watched all the *Kissing Booth* movies this weekend. Hours and hours of them."

"Those movies are classics," Cady said.

Lauren forked up a leaf of arugula. "I hope you also got your homework done because—"

"That's not the only way you got ready for Valentine's Day," Amelia interrupted. Clearly, she was on a warpath to bust her sister. "You also went shopping with Trish."

Lauren's hand froze, the fork halfway descended to the table.

Cady turned to Lauren, her face red. "I was going to tell you after dinner. Dad needed to work on Saturday afternoon so he had Trish hang out with us. She took me to Thirty-Fourth Street and got me a dress to wear for the Valentine's party at school. Well, technically Dad got it because it was his credit card. You're not hurt, Mom, are you? Trish isn't as bad as I thought. Remember she wants to go into fashion?" Cady was rambling the way she did when she was nervous.

"Cady," Amelia said. "Shut up."

Cady glanced nervously at her mom, then her sister.

"That's great." Lauren picked at the crust of the garlic bread. "It's nice that Trish took you shopping. Amelia, did you go too?"

Amelia crossed her arms over her chest. "I hate shopping. I stayed at Dad's apartment."

Cady's face went loose with relief. "Mom, can I show you my dress? You're going to love it. I'm going to wear it to school on Friday. All the girls from *Into the Woods* are wearing dresses on Friday."

"After dinner," Lauren told her.

Cady gobbled up two more bites, flung her plate onto the counter, and ran into her bedroom. Two minutes later, she skipped into the living room, her eyes bright.

"Do you like it?" she asked.

Lauren stared in shock at her twelve-year-old daughter. Cady wore a skintight silver dress that barely grazed her thighs. There was an oval cutout at her chest that revealed fleshy cleavage. The back had torn strips holding it together.

Holy shit, Trish bought her daughter a prostitute dress! Was it a sick joke? Or was Trish really that dumb?

"Mom?" Cady asked.

"You look beautiful, lovie," Lauren said. "It's too mature, though. I'm sorry. We'll exchange it for something more age appropriate."

Cady glared at her. "You think I look fat, don't you?"

"That's not what I said."

"Trish said I look amazing," Cady told her.

"It's the dress . . . not you. Conversation over. Go change."

Cady slammed her bedroom door. Lauren quickly washed the dishes and then retreated to her room to call Eric and chew him out. What the hell was Trish thinking? And Eric must have seen the dress too, right?

Her finger hovered over her ex-husband's name, but something made her stop. What if she reached Eric when he was at a restaurant with Trish? Or in bed? The last thing Lauren wanted was to rage into their romantic bliss.

As Lauren stared at her phone, she remembered that she still had Eric's phone in her Life360 app. It started as a joke two years ago when they first bought phones for Cady and Amelia. Naturally Lauren was the one saddled with tracking their walks to school. Around that time, Eric frequently forgot to text when his plane landed on business trips.

"I should add you to Life360 because you're worse than the girls!" she joked to him.

"Go for it if it means I don't have to remember to text you every five minutes," he said as he swatted her tush. Lauren set it up but then Eric immediately forgot about the whole phone-tracking thing, and they'd never talked about it again.

When Lauren first added him, she'd watch the Eric dot commute to the office or board a plane to Denver and she'd feel a sense of security that, in retrospect, was false. After the divorce, Lauren almost deleted Eric from Life360 but something made her decide to keep him there. It was raw power that she could locate her ex-husband *and he had no idea.*

Lauren stabbed her finger on Life360 and stared at the Eric dot.
Office!
She closed the app and called him.

"It's about the dress, isn't it?" he answered, before she could say anything. "Lauren, I'm sorry. It's a terrible dress. The worst."

Lauren had been so prepared to lecture him that she was flummoxed. She let out a long breath. "Eric . . . what were you thinking letting her keep it? What was *she* thinking buying it for Cady?"

"I know," Eric said. "You don't even need to go there."

"Go where?" Lauren shocked herself by laughing. "Say that Cady looks like a twelve-year-old hooker?"

Eric laughed too. "It's that bad. I know."

There was a bittersweet silence. It was like neither of them had expected to laugh together again. But why wouldn't they? Humor had bonded them for years. Laughter at movies. Laughter at each other's stories. It hurt to laugh with Eric, but it also felt good. It reminded Lauren that she didn't hate *everything* about the man she'd spent almost two decades with.

"I'll handle Cady, okay?" Eric said. "Top priority. I've been slammed at work. Equity is throwing four million into a tech start-up and I'm mired in the legal. But the dress was a mistake. She . . . Trish . . . knew it too. She tried to suggest others but—"

"Okay . . . *okay*," Lauren said. No need to ruin this conversation by talking about the babysitter.

"I'll call Cady and tell her that we need to exchange the dress this week," Eric said. "I'll tell her it's my decision, not yours."

When they hung up, Lauren wiped her eyes. Maybe there was hope for conscious uncoupling. If Eric put in the effort, Lauren was willing to work hard at being a kick-ass divorced wife.

madeline

"You should be glad I'm not Chauncey Goldblatt," Arabella blurted out over dinner. "I'm just saying you should be glad I'm me."

"Of course I'm glad you're you." Madeline folded and unfolded her napkin. She was surprised by her daughter's sudden attempt at conversation. She and Arabella had been in a don't-ask-don't-tell standstill for weeks. Madeline knew that Arabella knew that Colin had hired a lawyer. Arabella dropped that over breakfast one morning. After nearly gagging on her hard-boiled egg, Madeline said as casually as she could muster, *I know . . . I have a lawyer too. It's not a big deal.* Of course it was a major fucking deal but Madeline didn't want to alarm her daughter. Anyway, all that had happened so far was that the lawyers had a phone call to see if things could be settled out of court. When Madeline asked Serena how the call went, she replied with an ominous, *I wasn't expecting a miracle.* To make matters worse, Colin had texted her a brief *checking in* a few days ago. It was the first she'd heard from him since January. She was too mad to write back to his latest text. Or maybe too confused. But she didn't want to be mad at Colin. She didn't want to hate him.

"Why Chauncey?" Madeline asked, lifting her glass to her mouth. "What does she have to do with you?"

Arabella took a bite of spinach quiche and chewed thoughtfully. "Nothing, thank god. I have nothing to do with the Penis Girls, of which Chauncey is the leader."

Madeline coughed into her seltzer. As she pressed her palm over her mouth, she tried not to look shocked. *The Penis Girls?* Chauncey was in ninth grade with Arabella. Like most kids at Fryer Prep, Madeline had known her since pre-K. It was an incredible vantage point, to see children progress from four to fourteen, to watch the strands that defined them as toddlers evolve into the teenagers they were now. Chauncey stood out in Madeline's memory as a bossy kindergartener, plump around the middle, with lopsided pigtails. Over the years, Chauncey and Arabella had overlapped at birthday parties but the two girls never hit it off.

"What's this Penis Girls thing?" Madeline asked.

"Maybe I shouldn't say anything." Arabella twisted her hair into a loose knot. "Promise you won't call school and get involved? I hate when you get so involved. You wouldn't do that, right?"

Madeline exhaled. On one hand, she wanted to grab Arabella's shoulders and tell her to show respect. On the other hand, that would push her further away. Another hand? If she didn't promise to keep Arabella's secret, she would lose her trust. Yet one more hand: if Arabella revealed something reckless, Madeline might have to get involved. The juggling act of motherhood required so many hands, like a human octopus.

Without waiting for a response, Arabella plunged ahead. "Okay. I'll tell you. *Whatever.* Chauncey and her friends are saying they're the Penis Girls because they service penises."

"O-*kay*," Madeline spoke slowly to buy herself time. She had given her first blow job in eighth grade. By fifteen, she was having sex in various apartments after school. But it's different when you're the adult. You want your kids to behave better. "It's young but sexuality is still normal. We've talked all about—"

"It's not normal, Mom." Arabella rolled her eyes. "They're *charging* for it. Chauncey and Thelma and Yasmine and others. Like, five or six of them. Hand jobs. Blow jobs. They're charging for penile services!"

Madeline ate a small bite of quiche just so she had something to do. Thelma, who had thick purple glasses in kindergarten and body odor by third grade? Yasmine with two daddies and an overbite?

"Gross," Arabella said as she searched her mom's face. "Right?"

Madeline swallowed too soon. The quiche nudged painfully down her throat.

"They don't even need the money, Mom! All the Penis Girls come from wealthy families." Arabella shook her head to emphasize how dumb the whole thing was. "They're trading sexual favors for bubble-tea gift cards or, like, Bar Mitzvah cash."

Stay calm, Madeline told herself.

"So why do you think they do it?" she asked.

Arabella reached into the tangerine bowl, picked out the largest one, and jabbed her thumbnail into the bright orange skin. "Chauncey told Ria and me that it's a feminist pursuit. Like, high school boys have always gotten their penises serviced without giving anything back. She says that time is over . . . boys taking girls for granted. It's time for them to pay."

Madeline folded her napkin again. How did little Chauncey Gold-blatt put all this together? Madeline did *not* advocate for baby prostitution. But other than the sexual element, the Penis Girls business wasn't so different from the Wife App. Not that she was going to say this to her daughter. Of course not.

"Wow," Madeline offered instead.

Arabella tore off the tangerine peels and stacked them on her plate. "Ria and I think it's disgusting. Chauncey and them but especially the guys. Anyway, I'm done talking about this. I have to practice."

Madeline picked up a stray peel and dropped it onto her plate. "I just want you to know that I think you have your head on right about this. I think that—"

"I said I'm done talking about it." Arabella shoved a section of tangerine in her mouth and then carried her plate to the sink. She had on hip-hugging sweatpants and a half shirt that showed off her taut belly. Her skin was tan even in February, an enviable trait she'd inherited from Colin.

Madeline suddenly felt like crying. She covered her mouth with her hand and looked down at the table.

On the way out of the kitchen, Arabella spun on her bare heel. "Oh, Mom. I want to go to acupuncture . . . see if it'll help my back. You know how my shoulders and back always hurt? Grandma says I hunch."

"Don't listen to Grandma."

Arabella tensed, her fists tight at her sides. "Well, I want to go to acupuncture. Every cellist I know has a messed-up back."

"Sure . . . okay," Madeline said. "I'll ask around at my yoga studio and see if anyone has recommendations."

"Ria's mom knows someone. Supposedly she's, like, the best. I've already done the intake form. I just need your credit card to hold my appointment. She has a long waitlist."

Madeline pressed her thumbs into her tight neck.

"Her first opening for new clients is March," Arabella said. "If I register, can you bring me? It says I need a guardian."

"Of course," Madeline managed. When had she tumbled down the status ladder from *mom* to *guardian*? "Of course I can."

Madeline listened as Arabella closed her door. Soon there were the familiar sounds of her tuning the cello, warming up with scales. Madeline loaded the plates into the dishwasher, wiped down the table, and reached for her phone to return Colin's text.

Madeline: Parenting a teenager is brutal.

Madeline: I'm feeling very alone in this.

Madeline: Oh god, it's midnight in London. I hope I'm not waking you up.

Colin: No, no. I'm awake.

Madeline: You sure?

Colin: Yes.

Colin: Are we talking now? Or do you hate me?

Colin: After the lawyer and all that.

Madeline: Yes we're talking.

Colin: I'm sorry. About the legal stuff. I know this isn't what you want.

Madeline: I'm pretty mad at you about that.

Colin: I know.

Madeline: I don't hate you.

Colin: And you're not alone.

sophie

THIS NEW SPOUSE CHECKED OFF that he was single when he joined the Wife App so Sophie hadn't asked him to fill out the Spouse Consent. Plus, it was a quick job. One and done. He wrote in his Mental Load that he'd fractured his ankle and needed a Wife to grab a case of Oktoberfest beer, pick up organic dog food from a specialty pet store, and get clothes from his tailor. No biggie. It was in a twenty-block radius from her apartment and the weather was mild. Sophie bumped her old-lady cart down the stairs, started an audiobook on her phone, and trekked south.

As she crossed Eighty-Sixth Street, a text dinged on her phone. It was from Dan, the dad who hired her to fill out his son's preschool applications.

> **Dan:** Amazing news! Finnian got into eight of the ten schools you applied him to!

Sophie paused her book and wrote him back.

> **Sophie:** Wonderful! Congrats!

> **Dan:** Since you are a superstar, can we hire you to read with Finnian and help him with early phonics?

Sophie: Sorry but the Wife App no longer has direct contact with kids. I'm happy to recommend tutors.

Dan: Would love that, thanks.

After they finished their conversation, Sophie didn't start her audiobook again. Her brain was in a hundred other places. It was weird, after a lifetime of being broke, to turn down this job. But she remained firm that the Wife App needed boundaries. It wasn't right to drag children into it, to have them form relationships with people whom they may never see again.

Sophie was also thinking about Beatrice. They'd likely heard from preschools today too. Where had Clementine gotten in? Ever since Sophie stopped following Beatrice, she was much more in the dark about Joshua's Family 2.0. But then Charlie said that thing about Beatrice crying. . . .

Sophie tapped open Instagram. Maybe it wouldn't hurt to follow Beatrice just for a bit. . . .

No!

She slid her phone into her bag. She was trying hard not to press the bruises in her life. She steadied her breathing and pushed her cart into the store that sold Oktoberfest beer. Next, Sophie picked up the dog food. She texted the receipts to this new Spouse. Within moments, he paid her back over Venmo.

Now she needed to hit the tailor, and then she would haul everything to this guy's apartment. He lived in an elevator building near the Museum of Natural History. Sophie figured she'd unload everything outside his front door or, if he seemed harmless, in the foyer of his apartment.

"I'm picking up order number three-three-six," she told the woman at the tailor's counter. She showed her a photo of the ticket that the Spouse had uploaded into his Mental Load.

The woman disappeared for a moment and then returned with three men's blazers and a skimpy green dress.

Sophie shook her head. "I think this might be the wrong order. The person from order three-three-six is a man. Mr. Grant? He said three blazers. He didn't mention a dress. Or a wife."

The woman gestured at the number on the paper stapled to the plastic sheath that covered the garments. "They come in all the time. Skinny lady. Too skinny."

Sophie's heart raced as she eyed the emerald dress. It was a sleeveless gown, dotted with sequins, the kind someone might wear to a gala dinner. *So maybe he has a girlfriend, not a wife.* But if he was in a committed relationship, then Sophie didn't want to run around behind anyone's back. No cheating. No lying. Essential principles of the Wife App.

Sophie folded the clothing in her cart and stepped outside. As she started uptown, she considered her options. If this Spouse was a liar about not being married, he could also be a liar about not being a rapist. Maybe she should dump everything in his lobby? But he didn't have a doorman and he specifically said he had a fractured ankle. Also, if she didn't haul his cargo upstairs, then she couldn't collect her Wife fees and it would be a wasted night.

Going in, Sophie clicked on the app. *Out in 5.*

She glanced at the vertical rows of buzzers in his building's foyer, scanning for 14E. Sure enough, the names listed next to 14E were *Nick & Ayala Grant*. This guy wasn't even attempting to conceal the fact that he had an actual wife! Sophie stabbed her finger into the button for his apartment and then rode the elevator to his floor. As she rang the front door, she gripped hard to her cart, listening as uneven footsteps approached the door.

"Heyyyyy!" Nick Grant was in his midforties, clean-cut with a button-up shirt and brown hair. And he was clearly buzzed. He leaned sideways and held on to the doorframe. Beads of sweat dotted his forehead. A medical boot encompassed his left leg. On his right foot, he wore a caramel-colored loafer.

"I've got everything," Sophie said coldly.

"Excellent," he said. "That's great. What a great service. My own hired Wife! Want to come in?"

"No, I'll just unload it here."

"Bring it in," he insisted. "No one's home. It's so dull. I've barely been able to get around since my ski accident. And you're the Wife tonight, right? I'll pay extra for you to come in."

"No one's home, like, your actual wife?" Sophie asked, her heart racing.

"What's that?"

"Those intake forms on the Wife App. You put down that you were single."

"I didn't think that was a big deal." He offered a sheepish grin and waved his hand dismissively.

"We actually need the Spouse Consent to work with you." Sophie handed him the dry cleaning and then turned to unload the heavy items. "I'll take out everything here and then I'll remove you from the app."

As Sophie leaned over, she could feel his eyes lingering on her butt.

"You're really fit," he said. "I can tell you—"

"Stop," Sophie cut in. "The Wife App does not entitle you to comment on my body. You've been charged for your Mental Load. You're done."

Without another word, Sophie walked to the elevator. On the ride down, she logged into her cofounder account, searched up Nick Grant, and clicked Vegas Divorce Clause. That had been Sophie's idea, as a joke. If a Spouse is truly terrible, you pull the plug. No questions asked. No begging for alimony and child support. No year of forced sex even though you hate the sight and smell of him. One click and you never had to see this Spouse again.

lauren

THE WOMEN IN TECH CONFERENCE finally arrived. Lauren went to sessions on fundraising and pitching your ideas. She took notes to share with her engineers about possible upgrades even though additional build-outs would cost more than she had in her rainy-day fund.

God, she needed seed funding. She needed an angel investor.

That came up a lot at the Becoming Financially Fabulous session. Attendees drilled the breakout leader on investors, Series A funding, Series B funding. Just as Lauren walked out, a woman wearing a yellow hijab approached her.

"Hey," she said. "I'm sorry . . . I'm blanking on your name."

Lauren studied her face. Large brown eyes, long lashes . . . it was that woman from the meeting in Union Square where those guys told her that the Wife App wasn't worth their time.

Lauren smiled. "You work at Mega, right? And it's Lauren. Lauren Zuckerman."

"Of course. And I'm Chloe Younis. I was nervous you wouldn't talk to me after my colleagues were so awful."

"No, of course I would. You were wonderful that day. So you're still at Mega?"

Chloe rolled her eyes. "Yep, still with Brick and Magnus. For now. They've dangled all these huge stock options in front of me. I have to stay another year for them to vest." She gestured her thumb over her shoulder and cracked up. "Hence Becoming Financially Fabulous. Once my stock options vest, I'm done being their bitch."

"I get it," Lauren said.

"Speaking of, I saw you built the Wife App! A friend texted it to me. It looks amazing. I'm totally going to hire a Wife when I get enough money."

Lauren nodded. "And if we ever get money, I'd love you to join our team. Once your stock options are in place, of course."

As they said goodbye, Chloe touched Lauren's arm. "Oh! Remember my friend Lila? She dumped Brick."

"Really?" Lauren asked.

Chloe nodded. "He keeps asking me what went wrong and when I explain it to him, he doesn't get it. He's a real—"

"Brickhead? Sorry. That was low."

Chloe smiled. "Believe me. I go there all the time."

As the evening cocktail party began, Lauren weaved through the crowd in search of Anika Kim. She *had* to be here by this point, right? Her closing keynote was at six-thirty. Lauren overheard a woman say that Anika Kim traveled with bodyguards. That made sense because, according to Google, she was worth $1.2 billion. But after several laps through the party with no glimpse of Anika Kim or any bodyguards, Lauren ordered a glass of Pinot and joined a conversation about using analytics to understand what features are most valuable.

Finally, it was time for the keynote.

Lauren arrived early but the first rows were packed. She could see Chloe in the fourth or fifth row, tapping at her phone. The air felt stale. Lauren touched her hand to her cheek. Or maybe it wasn't the air. Maybe it was the rows of women with hopeful expressions nearly identical to hers. Everyone gazed hungrily at the empty stage.

A few minutes later, the director of the conference approached the podium, welcomed the people in the audience, and rattled off all the Anika Kim accolades that everyone here already knew by heart.

And then, finally, it was time. Anika Kim strode onto the stage.

She was tall in real life, maybe five nine, and glamorous in her tailored pantsuit, silver scarf, and her black and silver hair perfectly blown out. Every bit the legend, she raised her hand to halt the applause. Instant silence! Anika Kim talked about her parents' journey from Korea to America, the racism her family encountered, how she was the only woman in computer science classes. Male classmates gave her hell and, in exchange, it made her want to beat them all.

The clapping was thunderous.

Lauren clapped along with everyone. She was twenty years younger than Anika Kim so she hadn't been the *only* woman in computer science. But she'd been one of a handful. Even at Vassar, a college that had deep roots in feminism, computer science was more of a male domain. Women flocked to sociology, art history, theater. The lucrative career paths. Ha.

Anika Kim nodded. "In so many ways, these early experiences were the blueprint for my career. As a woman in tech, I had to prove myself again and again. As a woman of color, I had to fight even harder to overcome bias. People called me aggressive. They called me bossy. They called me a lot worse. And maybe I had to be some of those things to get ahead. Many men say that women use parenting as an excuse to drop out of the workforce, so I called bullshit on that. I had two young children when my career was growing. I said women could do it all . . . and I did. Even if it was challenging. Even if it was lonely."

Listening to this, Lauren decided with a sinking feeling that she'd made the wrong choice to do the Mommy Freelance Thing while Eric built a lucrative career. Anika Kim never would have succumbed. Anika Kim was a fighter. Lauren wanted to become a fighter too.

"Unlike other female CEOs, I intentionally did *not* create a culture of women breastfeeding at work," she said. "Or women going part time when their babies arrived. I didn't want men to sling that mud at women as an excuse for not promoting them. For not promoting me. As I rose up in my companies, I created a culture where it was clear that women have the same abilities as men. We deserve the same opportunities. The same open doors. The same money."

As Anika Kim paused to sip water, women clapped and cheered. But then Anika Kim leaned dramatically into the mike and said, "I was wrong."

Lauren lowered her hands onto her knees. All around, women went silent.

After a long pause, Anika continued, "I have a twenty-eight-year-old daughter who doesn't talk to me and a thirty-year-old son who only calls me when his wife makes him. I have as much net worth as you've likely seen on Google. Probably more. But for what? My kids say they hated their childhood so much that they don't want children. Dozens of people invite me to lunch or dinner or breakfast every day to beg for funding for their start-ups. *Please, Ms. Kim, I have the next Uber. I have the next Instagram. Get on this train or it's leaving the station.* Sometimes I get on the train and sometimes I don't. But do you know what I really want?"

No one in the audience moved or coughed or even scratched their nostrils. Lauren couldn't believe she was talking like this. She'd watched several Anika Kim speeches and they were nothing but professional. She'd never talked about her family before. She'd never spoken this candidly.

"I want to have lunch with my daughter. I want to have dinner with my son. I want grandchildren . . . and a career. I wish I could go back in time and figure out how to change the rules. I wish I'd said, *Sure, women are smart and capable, but we shouldn't be forced to choose.*" Anika Kim stretched out her arms to the audience. "So that's your problem to solve, how women can truly *have it all*. If you can solve it, come to me. We'll have lunch. That's the challenge I give you."

At the end of the speech, Anika Kim was escorted off the stage by a man in a gray suit. Lauren sat in her chair and googled her investment firm. No contact info. The best she could find was a Reddit post with an admin's LinkedIn and someone complaining that solicitations always got ignored. Lauren put away her phone in defeat. Anyway, she had to pee.

The line at the bathroom was long. Lauren's toes hurt in her new heels. Why had she even worn heels? Half the women here were in sneakers. Her lower back ached. She was ready to go home. But she really had to use the bathroom before getting on the subway. She shifted her weight from one sore foot to another and suddenly remembered a small bathroom by where the cocktail party had been held. Lauren limped there as quickly as possible and slipped into a stall. She'd just approached the sink when a stall door swung open. She was staring at none other than Anika Kim.

"Oh!" Lauren said as she waved her hands under the faucet to start the water.

Anika Kim smiled tentatively. It was a what-do-you-want-from-me smile. Pretty but tense. She had freckles on her nose.

"Your speech," Lauren said as she squirted pink soap onto her palms. "It was amazing."

"I went out on a limb," Anika Kim said. "I hope it didn't break."

Lauren shook her head. "It gave people a lot to think about. Every woman who has children struggles with whether she's made the right choices. It's never easy, especially if you've been told you can have it all."

Anika Kim dried her hands, crumpled the paper towel, and tossed it in the trash. As she strode toward the door, Lauren thought, *Now or never.*

"I have the solution you're looking for," she said.

Anika Kim came to an abrupt halt.

"I recently built an app because . . ." Lauren swallowed the saliva pooled under her tongue. She'd arranged this pitch in her head, and she'd even practiced it in her mirror. But it was very different to recite it when a tech billionaire legend stared at her across an empty bathroom.

Lauren's hands trembled as she said, "I have a background in software engineering and product management, specifically in app development. Once I got married and had children, my career was pushed aside. After my divorce last year, I realized I'd been exploited as a wife. All the free labor. The mental load. And not just the endless dishes but—"

"Dishes!" Anika Kim surprised Lauren by laughing in recognition. "Early in my marriage, I remember spending hours at the sink. I would call out to my husband as he lounged on the couch . . . well, now he's my ex-husband . . . I would shout, 'I saw the best minds of my generation destroyed by dishes.'"

"Allen Ginsberg," Lauren said. "*Howl.*"

"With a twist."

"What would he say when you said that?" Lauren asked.

"He'd think he was savvy and he'd riff on *Howl*. He'd say, 'Are you *starving*, Anika? Are you *hysterical*? You don't look *naked* to me but . . .'"

Lauren rolled her eyes. "I'm Lauren Zuckerman. It's really nice to talk to you."

Just like in her fantasies, Anika Kim shot out her hand. It was a firm, no-nonsense shake. "So what's your solution?"

"It's called the Wife App," Lauren said. "People—we call them Spouses—join the app and hand over their mental load, their to-do lists, their annoying chores. The Wives—capital W—on the Wife App manage everything that people expect actual wives to juggle for free while also balancing careers and kids. Bottom line, for a fee, we perform the services of a wife."

Anika Kim's face hardened. "You have women working as prostitutes?"

"No . . . not sex." Lauren touched the edge of the sink to steady herself. For someone as kick-ass as Anika Kim, Lauren noted a certain horror as she said the word *prostitutes*. Maybe she, like Lauren, had been burned. Or maybe she was from a different generation where sex workers were Bad People and not women who maybe didn't have another choice, or who maybe—gasp!—actually opted for this line of work. "And it's not just *women* on the Wife App. We have men working as Wives too. Making sure medical forms are transferred between doctors. Taking in cars to get tuned up. Buying season tickets to sporting events. Overseeing contractors. Planning menus. Ordering groceries. Vacation logistics. The list is endless. You'll be relieved to know that our Wives don't do dishes. But we hire and manage housekeepers. That's one of our top requests."

"You said you've already launched?" Anika Kim asked. "Do you have seed investors? Angels?"

Lauren shook her head. "Not yet. I've put in my own money, but our budget is tiny. My cofounders and I . . . It's three of us. We're still—"

"How many users do you have?"

Lauren's underarms were slick. As of yesterday, they had one thousand nine hundred registered Spouses, which felt like a lot, since they were only in portions of Manhattan. But that was miniscule to someone in Anika Kim's league.

"We have about two thousand," Lauren said in her best attempt at confidence. "We're nascent . . . but growing."

"Do you have a business plan?" Anika Kim pressed. "Have you defined your competition?"

"No," Lauren admitted. *Crap.* Why didn't she have a business plan? Because she was trying to launch an app and be a single mom and make her freelance money. And because, despite her fantasies, she hadn't actually expected to meet her hero right here in the bathroom. "But I can assure you that there is nothing like this in the market. Sure, there are odd-job apps, but there's nothing that will take over your entire mental load. Like a wife does! We have concierge services where a Wife will manage your family calendar. And we do camp forms and school forms and we set up driver's ed for your teen. Do you remember how much time all that took? So it's not just the running-around grunt work. Wives take over the behind-the-scenes invisible work that, let's be honest, eats up hours. Even if it's just the mental acrobatics. What's truly revolutionary about the Wife App—and I hope this will change marriage dynamics forever—is that by charging for emotional labor, by showing that *this* is work just like work is work, spouses in actual marriages will no longer expect it for free."

Anika Kim shook her head. "What about a financial model? Have you determined the level of investment you're seeking and how and where you would use the funds?"

"Not exactly."

"Have you pitched advertisers? Taken their temperature on this?"

Before Lauren could respond, Anika Kim frowned. Clearly this was a waste of her time.

"Laurel—"

"Lauren," Lauren said quietly.

"You are light-years away from soliciting funding. And until you have more answers, I see this Wife App as a prostitution service without the sex. Good luck. You'll definitely need it."

Anika Kim's heels clicked as she exited the bathroom. Once the door swung shut, Lauren hurried into a stall, leaned against a wall, and lowered her head into her hands. She was too exhausted to cry.

madeline

ARABELLA'S ACUPUNCTURIST, LUCY JOHNSON, TURNED out to be a social media influencer. Hundreds of thousands of followers, celebrity clients, companies paying her to drink their flavored seltzers as she posed in her swank studio. Yet another thing about the world that Madeline didn't understand. How could someone who stuck needles into people be an influencer? Then again, why was anyone a social media influencer? Didn't people have their own internal compasses?

But did Madeline say anything? No. She shut up. She gave Arabella her credit card to hold the appointment. She didn't complain that Lucy Johnson charged a fortune to turn people into pincushions. If Ria's mom loved Lucy Johnson, then Arabella's mom would love her too.

On a balmy afternoon in March, Madeline met her daughter outside school. Packs of kids poured out of Fryer Prep. Madeline scanned the crowd for Chauncey Goldblatt or any of the Penis Girls crew. Not that she would say anything, of course. She waved at a mom she knew from PTA. She glimpsed the back of Bryan's head as he walked down the street with his little daughter. They hadn't had a sex date in two weeks, but they'd texted that morning and compared schedules for next Tuesday.

"Come on!" Arabella said as she approached her mom. Her backpack was slung over one shoulder. "Let's go."

"Hey, hon. How was your day?"

"Fine. We can talk about it in the car. I don't want to stand around here."

They hopped in an Uber to the midtown-based Integrated Healing Center. Arabella buckled herself in behind the driver, as far from her mom as possible, and pulled out her phone.

"Everything okay?" Madeline asked.

"Yep," Arabella said without looking up.

Madeline reached into her purse and pulled out a package of Arabella's favorite cookies, Ghirardelli dark chocolate melting wafers.

Arabella glanced at the cookies, then back to her phone. "Not hungry."

"Did something happen today?"

"I'm texting friends, Mom. Is that okay or did you need to talk?"

Madeline bristled. But did she say anything? No.

The Uber dropped them outside and they took the elevator to the fifteenth floor. Madeline braced herself for the cheesiness of Americans co-opting Eastern medicine. She was fully prepared to dislike this celebrity-influencer acupuncturist.

Lucy Johnson turned out to be tiny with curly dark hair and a silver nose ring. Her voice was calm yet confident. But not bullshit confident. She ushered them into a private treatment room and asked questions about Arabella's cello regimen, her shoulder and back issues, basic health history. After she got Arabella situated on a treatment table, Madeline stepped into the waiting room. Tea bags were stacked in rows on a bamboo tray, next to an earthenware kettle of hot water. Madeline helped herself to a steaming mug of oolong.

"I see you found the tea," Lucy said as she closed the door to the treatment room.

"I hope that's okay." Madeline had settled into a chair and was idly thumbing through a coffee-table book.

"Of course. Arabella will be about a half hour. You can just hang."

Lucy settled in behind the wooden counter and opened her computer. Madeline switched her phone to silent and sipped her tea. When she attempted a breath, she was surprised to feel her lungs fill with oxygen. She breathed again. There was the faint smell of essential oils in the air. Peppermint? Eucalyptus? Whatever it was, Madeline was overcome with a sense of peace.

"Oh frig," Lucy grumbled. "You've got to be kidding me."

Madeline glanced over at her.

"Sorry." Lucy shook her curls back and forth. "Just dealing with a thing. Sorry about the bitching."

Madeline laughed. "You never have to apologize to me for spontaneous bitching."

"Good to know." Lucy smiled at Madeline. A genuine smile. She had on a flowy blouse and an amethyst necklace. Madeline considered asking where she got the blouse.

"So what's the thing?" Madeline asked.

Lucy lowered the lid on her laptop. "A kid thing," she said. "Of course it's completely fallen on me."

"Are you a single mom too?" Madeline asked.

"Actually . . . no," Lucy said. "That's the irony. I have a husband. I have full-time childcare. And yet—"

"Believe me, I get it."

"I love my husband but at this point I would trade him for a wife. I work six days a week—my husband is part time—but it's my job to plan my son's fourth birthday party next month. I had all the details set but the venue just emailed to say they had a scheduling mishap and have to cancel. But invitations have been sent! The magician is booked and only works at this one place!" Lucy dragged her fingers across her forehead. "I don't mean to complain. These are first-world problems."

Madeline paused to unlock her phone and open the app. "You have to see this."

"What is it?" Lucy looked confused as Madeline walked to the counter and offered her screen.

"Just look."

As Lucy scrolled up and down, she asked, "Is this for real?"

"My friends and I started it," Madeline told her. "We're the cofounders."

"But this . . . Wife App? Could they really . . . ?"

"Yes," Madeline confirmed. "Register as a Spouse. Upload your Mental Load. Rank the birthday party as your top priority. You'll be assigned a Wife who will get started on that task. For a fee, of course."

Lucy nodded. "I'm just so . . . wow. I'm going to create an account right now."

"Enjoy having a Wife take care of things. Goodness knows, men have enjoyed that luxury for thousands of years."

"Amen." Lucy spritzed minty oil on her wrists and rubbed them together.

That evening, Lauren called Madeline.

"Did you see?" Lauren asked. Her voice was high-pitched, bordering on hysterical.

"See what?" Madeline was stripped naked and about to step into the tub. She'd bought several vials of essential oil from Lucy and was eager for a hot lavender soak.

"Your celebrity acupuncturist! She's on the Wife App!"

"I told her about it today," Madeline said. "I know she was planning to sign up."

"No, it's not that. She *did* sign up. That's not what I'm trying to say." Lauren was talking so quickly that Madeline put her on speakerphone and pumped the volume. "Madeline, she posted about us! That's what

I'm trying to say. This woman, Lucy, gave us rave reviews on all her channels."

Madeline tapped the icon to open the Wife App.

"We've exploded, Madeline," Lauren said. "We're blowing up."

Madeline used a dry washcloth to wipe the moisture off the screen and then squinted at her phone. Was she seeing this correctly?

"Is this for real?" Madeline asked. "We have more than five thousand users, Lauren."

"I'm refreshing right now," Lauren said. "Oh my god . . . another hundred."

"But what do we . . . I mean, do we have enough Wives to cover all the jobs?"

"No!" Lauren shrieked. "I've just posted on every job board in New York City. Luckily, Wives can onboard themselves. But there are always glitches, you know? Crap. Or this is good, right? But still. I'm going to be up all night. Can you help? I'll enlist Sophie as well." Lauren sucked in her breath. "Hang on! Another hundred. Holy shit . . . holy shit. I'm getting light-headed, Madeline. Should we cut off downloads?"

Madeline reached for her robe, slid her arms in, and tapped the drain with her heel to empty the tub. No bath tonight. They had to get their asses in gear to rise up and meet this moment.

"Six thousand!" Lauren shouted. "This is insane! Social media influencers are no joke."

"Buckle your seat belt, Lauren," Madeline said as she cinched the belt on her robe, "and let's enjoy the ride."

sophie

Sophie knew as soon as she saw the VIP request that she had struck Wife gold. Ever since the shout-out from the celebrity influencer a few weeks ago, usership had gone through the roof. They were written about in *Digital Trends*, *Tech Crunch*, and *Wired* as the "hottest new app this spring." Venture capital companies were sniffing around. Nothing formal yet but Lauren told them she'd received multiple inquiries about outside funding.

Sophie tried to keep a level head about the whole thing. *Midwestern humility. Smart Sophie Smart.* When things first went crazy, she, Lauren, and Madeline gathered at Le Pain Q. Over breakfast, Madeline offered to invest two hundred thousand in the Wife App. Lauren balked until Madeline reassured her that she would be an actual angel investor with a contract drafted by the lawyer. Sophie had barely recognized this version of Madeline. Gone were the lewd jokes, the braggy tales of talented Arabella. This was what Sophie imagined Madeline had been like in B-school—smart, savvy, confident. Madeline wanted to take on a strategic role with the app, work with analysts, figure out the steps they needed to get to Series A funding.

As Sophie nibbled her avocado toast that morning, she couldn't believe they were having this conversation. But, truly, it was necessary. Lauren needed Madeline's investment to hire people who specialized in product development. And salary! It was time for Lauren to draw an income because she'd put her freelance work on pause to focus full time on the Wife App.

They left that breakfast with a game plan and a division of labor. Madeline took on a business leadership role. Lauren oversaw the technology. And Sophie, who loved the Wife work, handled the VIP clients. She had been the one to reconfigure the birthday-party details for the celebrity acupuncturist, who then referred all her high-profile friends to Sophie as well.

Perhaps that's how this massive new Mental Load arrived on her portal. The Spouse's profile described him as an airline executive. When Sophie read his request, oh my god, she had to grip the back of the couch.

Holy moly.

Was it ethical?

Holy moly.

He offered more money than Sophie's annual salary.

But back to ethics. Ethics were what separated the Wife App from bad marriage situations like Eric sneaking around with sex workers, like Joshua withholding money, like Colin snatching Arabella. The Wife App was revolutionary, yes. It was lucrative, yes. But doing the right thing was its guiding light.

Sophie copied this Mental Load, including the financials, and pasted it into a text to Lauren.

Sophie: Does this sound ethical?

Two seconds later, her phone rang.

"Holy freakin' shit," Lauren shouted. "You're grabbing this one, right?"

"But doesn't it break the rules of the Wife App?"

"As long as it's not more than what he's asking . . . it's fine," Lauren said. "Go for it, Soph."

"Are you really sure?"

Lauren laughed. "If you don't click *accept* in the next ten seconds, I'm hacking into your account and taking this job for myself."

lauren

LAUREN HAD COME SO FAR since that March evening when she sobbed in the bathroom stall after being told by Anika Kim that she was a failure of a tech innovator who shouldn't bother trying. Okay, those weren't her exact words, but still.

She gave herself that one night to cry. The next day, she walked across Central Park to the Guggenheim to visit the Chagalls. As she gazed at the flowing reds, blues, and yellows of *The Flying Carriage*, she thought of her mom, of how much she had longed to visit the Musée National Marc Chagall. Why hadn't her mom gone on that pilgrimage to Southern France that she'd always talked about? What happens when you don't live to see a dream come true? Is the onus on the people you left behind to fulfill those dreams, or to pursue their own dreams even harder?

Lauren woke up one morning in April arguing with herself about Gideon. She'd had frequent internal debates since she saw him on the plane back in January.

You should text him, a voice in her head said.

But he's married! another voice yelled back.

What if he's not married anymore? He doesn't know I'm divorced, after all.

Yeah, so what if he's not married, Lauren? What are you going to do, leap into bed with a cowboy doctor high school ex who trots the globe, saving the world's sick?

What would be so wrong with that? After all, those toasty brown eyes. Those broad shoulders . . .

Finally, Lauren had had enough. She opened the photo she'd snapped of Gideon's number and typed him into her contacts.

Lauren: Hey, it's Lauren Zuckerman. Hope you're well.

Lauren sent the text and then tossed down her phone. After two seconds, she picked it up again. *Ellipsis. Ellipsis. Ellipsis.* Her mouth twitched with anticipation.

Gideon: Lauren! Hi from northern Uzbekistan.

Gideon: So good seeing you on that plane. Glad you wrote. How are you?

Lauren pressed her lips together. She wanted to be honest. Even when they were seventeen, she and Gideon had always been honest.

Lauren: Yeah, it took me a minute. Lots going on. I'll start with the big one. Eric and I got divorced last fall.

Gideon: Wow. Divorce.

Lauren: Yep.

Gideon: Me too. Sonia and I called it quits three years ago.

Lauren: I'm so sorry.

Gideon: It's been hard.

Gideon: Life definitely hasn't turned out how I thought it would.

Just then, Cady walked into Lauren's room—this girl never knocked!—and flopped onto the bed. Lauren quickly set her phone facedown on the nightstand.

"What's up with you?" Cady asked. "You're smiling really weird."

"Just texting with an old friend," Lauren said.

"Anyone I know?"

"Nope," Lauren said. "Now come here and give me a hug."

As Cady snuggled into her arms, Lauren realized that life hadn't turned out how she thought either but maybe that wasn't the worst thing.

The Wife App now had eighteen thousand registered users, with five thousand active accounts. They had hundreds of Wives working on the app. That, in itself, was insane! They had their designer and their developers on call. They still only had Wives working in Manhattan but they'd added seven zip codes, and they were about to scale up to Brooklyn. In addition to her Wife jobs, Willow—who'd stepped down as Madeline's housekeeper and was now on payroll for the Wife App—had taken charge of the geographic expansion. Willow was also the one who scored those write-ups in *Digital Trends*, *Tech Crunch*, and *Wired*.

Over the past few months, the Wife App had become a lucrative, well-oiled machine. And yet Lauren wanted more. She was tired of pretending like she wasn't ambitious. She was fucking ambitious!

Same with Madeline. She stopped by Lauren's apartment one morning to show her the pitch deck she was working on.

"This looks amazing." Lauren scanned the Wife App's mission, their competition, and their long-term vision. One of the last slides displayed the revenue projections and, holy shit, Madeline went big.

"These numbers—" Lauren started. "There's no actual way, right?"

"These are projections. But if we want to pitch this as an investment opportunity, I'm not going to shortchange ourselves. I've been going back and forth on this with my former B-school professor. . . . Remember I told you about her?"

Lauren nodded, her eyes on the screen. Madeline had mentioned a lunch at Stern Business School a few weeks ago.

"She said that women are notoriously worse at getting funding than men," Madeline said, "and it's because they won't bullshit. Men spin numbers, and investors clamor to hop on their train. You know what happens when female tech innovators meet with potential investors? Investors ask them, *Why don't you have a male cofounder? Are you sure you've checked these numbers?* And you know what I say to that?"

As Madeline talked, Lauren glanced across the living room at the portrait of Coco that she did that night at Paint and Sip. It sat on the floor, propped against the wall. It was insane to think how far the Wife App had come since then.

"I say, we won't lie about our numbers," Madeline concluded, "but we also won't sell ourselves short."

Lauren pulled Madeline into a hug. She swore she could feel her friend's heart beating against her own chest.

A few minutes later, as Lauren walked Madeline to the elevator, she said, "I texted with Gideon the other day."

"Gideon, your high school boyfriend? From the plane?"

Lauren nodded. "He's divorced too. Three years ago."

"And?"

"Nothing so far," Lauren said. "It's just a few texts but, of course, I'm terrified."

"That's being alive," Madeline said as she stepped into the elevator.

That evening, on her nightly dog walk with Coco, Lauren got a text.

Eric: Do you have a minute?

Lauren contemplated his question and then decided, *Nah, I've given him too many minutes. I'll keep this minute to myself.* She'd just slid her phone in her pocket when it dinged again.

Eric: Calling right now.

Lauren considered not answering. But then her mind flashed to those morning cups of coffee that Eric used to deliver to her in bed. She imagined him in the kitchen as he poured in almond milk, stirred in a spoonful of sugar.

"Hey, what's up?" Lauren asked.

"Hey to you," Eric said.

"I'm walking Coco."

"You're a busy woman these days. It's been hard to get hold of you with everything going on."

Eric was referring, of course, to the Wife App. After the app went viral and the press started pouring in, Eric texted her congratulations. It was slightly awkward, because the Wife App was borne of her frustrations as his actual wife, but they avoided any conversation regarding the idea's origins.

"Yeah," Lauren said as she stepped over a scattering of crushed pretzels. "It's been insane."

"I'll cut to the chase," Eric said. "I wanted to give you a heads-up that Equity is talking about your app."

Lauren paused on the sidewalk. Eric was a lawyer in charge of acquisition and investment contracts at Equity. It was a hugely success-ful firm, and very sought after in the tech world.

Eric continued, "They want our analysts to run the numbers, assess the possible value, and then they'd like to put money in. They're throw-ing around numbers up to a million."

Hang on. . . . What? A million-dollar investment?

This was major news that they were running the numbers on the Wife App. Then again, Lauren had just spent the past fifteen months disentangling herself from Eric. She did not want to dive back in again. Lauren gripped the dog's leash and tugged her away from the pretzel bits.

"Our lead investor will be in touch about a meeting. A new guy. He's excited. He even said to me this afternoon that we would love to make you our Wives." Eric laughed as he said this.

"I . . . uh . . ." Lauren managed to say.

"This is big money, Lauren. I thought you'd be—"

"I have to go," she said abruptly.

"But—"

Lauren hung up. *We would love to make you our Wives?* She *had* been Eric's wife! And then he'd paid someone else to do what she did for free. Lauren tapped Madeline's number.

"No fucking way," Madeline said after Lauren filled her in. "Eric and his cronies do not get to make us their wives."

"Are you sure?" Lauren asked. "What if they offer big money? Madeline, a million-dollar investment could change everything."

Madeline cleared her throat. "Give me more time. You saw that pitch deck. I'm still working out our numbers and then I'll get funding meetings set up. But, really, you don't have to worry about that. You keep the app running and growing. Eric can hire his own damn Wife, but it won't be us."

madeline

WHEN WILLOW CALLED ON WEDNESDAY, Madeline quickly added a column about cash flow to a spreadsheet she'd been working on, then looked out the window at the cherry blossoms in Central Park.

"Hey, Willow," she said. Even though Willow no longer worked as Madeline's housekeeper, they were in frequent contact about the Wife App, and also Willow was generously on standby whenever her replacement had questions. Anytime Willow stepped in to guide the new housekeeper, Madeline Venmoed her some money. No one should work for free. Madeline felt more certain about this than ever.

"Goddamn Wife stuff," Willow said.

Madeline smiled. "Now you sound like me. What's up?"

"I usually don't mind the Wifing. It's just . . . my boyfriend got this insane last-minute invitation to a free place in the Bahamas. I've never seen the tropics! I can bring all the administrative Wife App work and do it there . . . but I promised a bunch of things to a Spouse this week. I don't want to bug Lauren because she's busy enough as it is."

Madeline glanced at her laptop, at all the statistical information for the Wife App. She'd had several lunches with her former business school professor, who steadily guided her through the process of securing funding. In the years since Madeline's stint at B-school, new ways to evaluate a start-up had developed. These days, everyone placed value on a company's EBITDA, which were earnings before interest, taxes, depreciation, and amortization. Madeline had been scrambling to learn these metrics of performance.

It wasn't awful, though. She liked using this part of her brain. It kept her distracted from everything going on with Arabella. Serena emailed last week to alert her that Colin's lawyer had filed a legal motion for a custody change, and it looked like the court date would be in June.

"What's the Wife job?" Madeline asked. "I could probably bail you out. As long as it doesn't involve taking a dog for a butt shave."

Willow laughed. "No dogs. It's a rich guy from Texas. He made, like, millions in the oil business. So American, right? Anyway, he moved to the city a few weeks ago and he needs help furnishing his apartment and buying nice stuff for the kitchen and getting fancy linens and all that. I don't think he brought anything with him. He even needed me to get him a toilet plunger!"

Madeline nodded to herself. She could do linens. She could do high-end kitchen. "Is there a wife in the picture?"

"No," Willow said. "He and his wife divorced last year. He said that all his frat brothers are trying to set him up with New York women. But they don't know that he's gay, so it's been awkward. I guess that's why he got a divorce. He's not publicly out yet."

"A semi-closeted gay millionaire frat boy from Texas?" Madeline asked. "Sure. I can do it."

"Oh my god, thank you!" Willow gushed. "You're saving my ass. I'll let you have all the money. I can share the job on the Wife App portal with you. Of course, I'll make sure he's okay with you taking over. But I'm sure he'll be fine. You have better taste than I do."

"You can keep the money," Madeline said. This would be one more thing to take her mind off Arabella and London, even for a few hours. "You've saved my ass a thousand times."

"Nope," Willow said. "As you've been telling me, work is work and we shouldn't call it by any other name."

Madeline watched as the wind rustled the cherry trees. Their flowers were so bright they looked like pink puffs of cotton candy. "You're on," she said after a moment. "You're completely right."

sophie

"I REALIZE IT'S NOT A typical assignment, which is why I came to you," the new Spouse said to Sophie. They were meeting for a drink at a winery near Central Park South. "The Wife App has gotten rave reviews and I like to work with the best."

"I'm glad you asked," Sophie said. *Glad* being the understatement of the year. This Spouse had been vague with the job description but clear on the money. A hundred grand. Sophie felt dizzy just thinking about that.

His name was Samuel Bliss. He was on the diminutive side, only a few inches taller than Sophie, with wooly gray hair and hazel eyes. Sophie had googled him, as she did with all her Spouses. She learned that he owned a lucrative charter airline, the kind that flies rich people on private jets to Barbados or to London for a weekend shopping trip. His net worth was in the hundreds of millions, and he was a major donor to Central Park and the High Line. But that was about it. Sophie couldn't find any details about his personal life.

"Let me explain more about the job," Samuel Bliss said. "But before I do, could I please ask you to sign a nondisclosure agreement? I know that feels like a cold way to start our conversation but I've been burned before, and I like to keep my private life private."

As he handed a piece of paper across the table and then reached into his breast pocket for a pen, Sophie eyed him carefully. Did she trust him enough to sign? Or was this a creepy move? Like, was she about to relinquish her ability to tell anyone if he cut her to pieces and stuffed her down a trash chute?

"I should make it clear that I don't have negative motives," Samuel Bliss added as if reading her mind. "As I said, I'm a private person. I have two daughters, now in college, and I've tried hard to keep them out of the spotlight. I completely understand if you don't want to sign, though. We can enjoy a glass of wine and call it a night."

It was the *daughters* that got her. Or maybe it was his eyes, which were kind and genuine. Sophie felt it instinctively—she trusted this person.

"No, it's fine." Sophie reached into her purse for her own pen. "Let me take a look."

Sophie scanned the NDA. Not seeing any red flags, she signed at the bottom, dated it, and slid the paper back to him. With the privacy factor taken care of, Samuel Bliss crossed his arms over his chest and began to explain the nature of the job.

Sophie had to admit—it was intriguing. Samuel Bliss had international executives coming to the city in two weeks to finalize a merger between several charter airlines. These people were from Brazil, South Korea, and Germany. All of them were men, and they were all bringing their wives. Along with the business meetings, they wanted to go out on the town, make the trip social and fun. Samuel Bliss stood to make millions if the deal came together. Part of the negotiations involved mingling with the couples—a few Michelin-starred restaurants, a gourmet sunset dinner cruise in the New York Harbor. The problem was Samuel Bliss and his wife had been estranged for the past five months. Sure, he could be the single guy in the mix—he'd flown solo in business negotiations for years. But in his experience, when couples come to town, they want to socialize with other couples. If one person shows up without a spouse, it throws off the dynamic. Samuel Bliss didn't want to do anything to weaken this deal, so he needed to immediately summon a significant other.

"Can't you just ask a female friend?" Sophie asked.

"I've been married for twenty-seven years," he said. "All my female friends are my wife's friends. Halves of couples. I have colleagues at work but . . . no. That would be awkward. I like to keep my work life separate. Of course, I sound like a hypocrite saying I need a spouse for these events. No, not a spouse. I'm thinking . . . fiancée."

"Why fiancée?" Sophie asked. "Why not a wife?"

"For one, I'm still legally married. Not that these people know about my personal life, but it doesn't feel right." He swirled his wine in his glass and took a sip. "Girlfriend sounds too adolescent. Fiancée has the right formality without overly stretching the truth."

Sophie didn't agree that this wasn't stretching the truth. Fiancée was still pretty darn official. They'd have to come up with a story about how they met, what they liked to do together, whether they'd set a wedding date.

Sophie sipped her wine and placed the glass carefully on the table. She understood what he was saying about couple friends. After her divorce, she'd gotten together with a few couples whom she and Joshua had socialized with during their marriage. It was always awkward—lots of "*we* love cilantro" and "*we* hate oat milk" from the couple, as if they were two people with one set of taste buds, and way too much brainstorming about potential setups for Sophie.

"I don't want to sound like an ass, but you seem like you're right for the job." Samuel Bliss rubbed his hands over his eyes as if he were considering how to phrase something. "Okay . . . I'll put it out there. I want someone educated, which you are, and able to make conversation. I'm, uhh, vertically challenged so I'm hoping for someone who doesn't tower over me."

Sophie had to laugh. "I'm definitely not going to do that."

Samuel Bliss nodded. "I realize this all sounds so traditional. My daughters would kill me if they found out I was hiring someone to pretend to be my fiancée. But business is business, and I'd like to give this my best shot."

Sophie considered it all for a moment. Samuel Bliss seemed fine. Again, no red flags. And Sophie couldn't get over the money. He'd explained that the hundred thousand dollars would be paid in four sums over the next several weeks.

"I'm in," she said.

"Wonderful," he said. "Let's do this."

Sophie pushed her wineglass toward the center of the table. If she was going to do this, she would do it right. No buzz clouding her brain. "We need to be on the same page about absolutely everything," she told him. "Every detail. Every story. We need to have it all covered. You need to tell me who you want me to be, what you want me to talk about with these wives. Everything."

"I agree completely," Samuel Bliss said. "I've scheduled three sessions for us to talk through our story prior to the event, and to get to know each other so we're not strangers."

Sophie tilted away from him in her chair. "I need to clarify . . . please don't take offense here . . . but this is going to be a purely platonic arrangement. We need to have that out in the open from the start."

"Of course." Samuel Bliss's face remained impassive but a tiny muscle in his jaw twitched.

Old Sophie would have pretended she didn't see that twitch. Old Sophie would have avoided uncomfortable truths. But this new Sophie? No way.

"I get the sense something else is going on?" she asked.

He shook his head. "No. I mean, well, yes. I was thinking about my wife. It's a tough situation. No need to elaborate. But I'll be clear. You seem wonderful. You work with children and literacy, which the international wives will appreciate." He held up his hands, then shook them back and forth like windshield wipers. "I didn't mean to say anything that made you uncomfortable. Yes, this is purely platonic."

Sophie's fingers itched. She spread her hands across the tabletop and resisted the urge to scratch them. The fiancée of a multimillionaire doesn't have rough patches of eczema. She has delicate, silky hands. The hands of someone who hires out her dishwashing and gets regular manicures. Sophie would douse her fingers in prescription cream tonight. She'd been too busy to tend to her hands these past few weeks.

"The next time we meet we can go over personal details and make sure our stories are aligned," Sophie said. "But I should find out now if there are certain things you want me to wear to the events. If you can tell me the names of the venues, I'll do research and figure out dress codes."

"As far as attire," Samuel Bliss said, "I'll save you time and let you know right now that it will be formal. High-end designer."

Sophie tried not to grimace. The highest-end designer she owned was J.Crew. Maybe a formal dress or two from Banana Republic. Because she was a legit *public school teacher*, and not actually engaged to an airplane tycoon! Sure, she could pull together a little black dress and heels, but it wasn't going to be Prada.

"I will take care of wardrobe," he said. "My admin will be in touch with you tomorrow to arrange appointments with personal shoppers. You'll need footwear too. We'll cover it all."

Personal shoppers? High-end designers? This was Madeline's world but certainly not Sophie's.

"You can keep it all when we're done," he added. "Except the jewelry. We'll have someone from Harry Winston contact you about a necklace and a diamond ring but those will be loaners. The rest is yours. Does that work for you?"

Does that work for you?

"It sounds wonderful," Sophie said as calmly as possible. "I'm looking forward to it."

"As far as payment, I'll transfer one-fourth to you now, as a deposit. The other fourths will be paid after each of the three events. It's a large sum so I'm assuming bank transfer is best. That'll happen at the start of the business day tomorrow. My admin will call you to set it up."

Tomorrow's amount would catapult Sophie's bank account to the highest it had ever been. When she got the full sum, it was enough for a down payment on a home. It was enough to take Joshua back to court for more child support. It was enough to dream!

"If you're not a fan of Harry Winston," Samuel Bliss said as he drained his carafe of wine, "I can contact Tiffany. My wife loves Harry Winston so that's where I've done most of my business."

"Harry Winston will work out fine," Sophie said, not quite believing the sentence that had just come out of her mouth.

The next morning, Sophie woke to a call from her ex-husband. On mornings that the boys were at Joshua and Beatrice's, her alarm didn't ring until six-thirty. But today, at seventeen minutes after six, her phone startled her awake.

"Where have you been?" Joshua barked. "I've been texting for the past fifteen minutes."

"Is everything okay?" Sophie pressed her phone against her ear. "Are the boys okay?"

"Yes. No. It's Charlie. He wants some Yankees shirt that he says is at your place. He needs it for this fucking 'dress like your favorite baseball team' day and he's hysterical that he doesn't have it."

Oh god. Sophie meant to tuck his Yankees shirt into his backpack when he went to his dad's on Sunday but it had been in the laundry, and then it slipped her mind.

"Can I bring it to school today?" Sophie's arms felt weak. That was what happened whenever Joshua yelled at her. "Tell him I can meet him at Jessi's class a few minutes early."

"No!" Joshua snapped. "That's what's pissing me off. He's whining and carrying on and he says he needs it right now."

Sophie knew exactly the mode that Joshua was in. His fuse was blown, and he was about to curse someone out. Please don't let it be her sweet Charlie, who'd come so far in cognitive behavioral therapy. The last thing he needed was to have his dad berate him.

"Let's meet and I'll hand it off to you," she said as she climbed out of bed. "I can be out the door in five minutes. I'll walk up Columbus and you walk down."

"Okay. Dammit. This is the last thing I need this morning."

Sophie didn't even respond. She just hit "end" on the call, hurried into the bathroom to pee, and then tugged on some clothes from a pile on the floor.

Ten minutes later, Sophie passed the shirt to Joshua, who received it with a frown. Sophie knew that sooner or later his good looks were going to be eclipsed by his bad personality. What was it that Lincoln said? *Every man over forty is responsible for his own face.* Joshua would be forty in September. His time was coming.

"How's Charlie?" Sophie asked as Joshua twisted the small navy shirt in his hand.

"Annoying the hell out of me," he said.

"Please don't be hard on him," Sophie said. "We don't need any setbacks."

Joshua snorted. "Someone has to be. Between you and Beatrice, that kid will never be able to cope with the world. It's pathetic."

Sophie opened her mouth to respond but then, thinking better of it, she walked into a nearby deli without saying goodbye. She would buy a cup of tea. She would go home and shower and wash Joshua off her skin. In the past, when he said something was pathetic, she took it as *you are pathetic.*

No longer. Sophie would no longer allow Joshua to take one ounce of self-respect away from her.

Over the next few weeks, Sophie learned that Samuel Bliss had two daughters, one premed at Grinnell out in Iowa, one studying literature at Oxford. He never again mentioned his estranged wife, and Sophie didn't ask. She learned that he loved to run in Central Park, so they could say they ran together. They were both big readers. He played golf in Westchester County. Of course he did. Sophie had never partaken in anything but mini-golf with the boys. They agreed to say that golf was something he did with male friends.

She told him about Noah and Charlie. Her work. Her childhood in the Midwest. Her time at Vassar. He listened somewhat, though always with one eye on his phone. *Whatever*. Sophie wasn't on the hunt for an actual fiancé.

With the help of the personal shopper—and with an unlimited budget—Sophie chose three dresses, three pairs of strappy heels, wraps, matching purses. She splurged and got a manicure, an eyebrow wax, some blond highlights for her hair. She justified all this as a professional expense. For the first dinner, she wore Oscar de la Renta. The second dinner, her personal shopper selected a Carolina Herrera gown. Both evenings, Samuel Bliss picked her up in his chauffeured Mercedes sedan so they could arrive together. As they sped through the streets of Manhattan, he fastened a stunning jewel around her neck and passed her the four-carat diamond ring to slip on her finger. Instant fiancée.

At the dinners, Samuel Bliss talked business with the men. Sophie plied the wives with questions about their countries, their kids, their travels. As much as she and Samuel Bliss had prepared a legit "couple story," no one asked her any personal questions. They were satisfied by her appearance and her outfits—she checked all the boxes. She looked the part. After they stepped into the Mercedes at the end of both dinners, Sophie handed back the jewelry and Samuel Bliss tucked it away for next time.

The last event was the sunset cruise in the New York Harbor. That seemed like a risky choice for late April. Some years, April in Manhattan means cherry blossoms. Other years, sidewalks are covered in dirty heaps of snow. To accommodate for various weather situations, the personal shopper helped Sophie select a long-sleeved Badgley Mischka gown. They went with blue to evoke a mariner feel.

After work on the day of the cruise, Sophie visited a salon on Amsterdam to get her hair blown out. She had to admit that she could get used to this pampering!

"You look lovely," Samuel Bliss told her on the ride to South Street Seaport. "And thank goodness the rain stopped. We are so close to finalizing this deal. We definitely don't want everyone to get caught in a downpour."

"I'm glad it's working out." Sophie traced her finger across the window, the outside damp with raindrops. Right before his car arrived, the sky opened up and doused the city in a heavy spring rain. Now the clouds parted, and the sun forced its way through.

"Oh! Do you see that?" Samuel Bliss gestured past Sophie to a hazy rainbow arching over the city. It ended in the New York Harbor. "Let's hope this bodes well for tonight."

In the car home, Samuel Bliss thanked Sophie.

"It's been nice getting to know you," he added. "I'll definitely recommend the Wife App, though of course I'll have to think of a story for what I used it for."

"No, thank *you*," Sophie said. "I've had a wonderful time as your fiancée. Thank you for hiring me, and also the new dresses are amazing."

Samuel Bliss frowned and turned to his window. Sophie had seen this before. He would smile pleasantly during conversations but as soon as things went quiet, his face slackened to reveal something sad underneath.

"I hope I'm not overstepping," Sophie said, "but I get the sense that you miss your wife. Is there any hope of reconciliation?"

Silence.

"Am I wrong?" Sophie asked.

Samuel Bliss shook his head. "I'm afraid that ship has sailed."

"What makes you so sure?"

"I'll be blunt here. Is it okay if I'm blunt?"

Oh man, did he cheat? After the fiasco with Lauren's ex-husband, Sophie had no patience for cheaters. Oh, and Madeline's stepdad. And that drunk Spouse who wanted the Oktoberfest beer and a home visit. Did all men cheat? Sophie braced herself for a guilty revelation.

"No . . . no, I didn't stray," Samuel Bliss said quickly, seeing Sophie's face. "It's more subtle than that. I was consumed by work. Forgot anniversaries. Late to birthday dinners. Several times, she asked me to go to couples therapy."

"Did you go?" Sophie asked. She assumed the answer was no. So many husbands were couples-therapy resisters. Joshua, for example, had said it would be a waste of time and money. Several colleagues complained about the same thing in the teachers' lounge. "I don't want to be too personal but—"

"No, I did go. We tried a few different counselors. But it never seemed to move the needle. She was always so mad at me." Samuel Bliss paused before saying, "One morning about five months ago, we got into a typical argument. I can't even remember how it started . . . something about who would contact our interior designer. When I arrived at the office, she texted me, I quote, 'I'm not your fucking maid.'"

"What did you say?"

"I wrote back that if she felt burdened, we could hire more help. We could hire a full-time maid."

"No, you didn't!"

"That bad?" he asked.

Sophie nodded to indicate that yes, it was that bad.

"When I got home that evening, she was gone. I found out through our daughters that she moved to our ski house in Telluride."

"Have you tried to talk to her?"

"She refuses. We text about logistics but whenever I call she won't answer. I sent her a letter apologizing for that maid comment. I had my admin pick out her favorite flowers. I even texted her suggesting we find another marriage counselor, but she wrote that she didn't think that was a good idea. I think she's had it. I'm waiting for divorce papers any day now."

Sophie turned it over in her head. There are moments in a marriage when you can walk through one door—or exit through another. But to chart a new marital course, you have to put in the work. Joshua hadn't been willing to do it. Maybe Samuel Bliss was.

"Can I be blunt back?" Sophie asked.

"Fire away," he said.

"Text her when you get home and suggest you go to couples therapy again. But tell her you want to try a new approach. You will go to your own counseling too, and you'll try to understand the ways that you undervalued her. If you're up for that. That's on you to decide. And if you truly have nothing to hide, then why not talk things out?"

He stroked his finger over his chin. "Should I say something about the maid comment again?"

"If you've already apologized for that, I don't think you need to. But if she lets you know what's making her mad, listen. Consider it. Don't get defensive and negate her frustrations. Also, make sure she understands that you want to examine your attitude toward her and the work she did. Because it's work to be a wife!"

The Mercedes pulled up to Sophie's building. She and Samuel Bliss said their goodbyes. Once she was through the front door, Sophie held her heels in her hands as she walked barefoot up the four narrow flights to her apartment.

Sophie was brushing her teeth when her phone buzzed with a text.

> **Samuel Bliss:** I took your advice and texted my wife. I said exactly what you told me to say.

> **Sophie:** And?

> **Samuel Bliss:** Nothing yet.

Sophie: She'll agree to talk. And when she does, be open.

Sophie: Don't get defensive.

Sophie: Stay off your phone the whole time.

Samuel Bliss: Keep that marital advice flowing. I'm happy to send you a bonus.

Sophie: Nah.

Sophie: This one is on me.

The following morning, on the walk to work, Sophie called Lauren.

"How's the airplane tycoon?" Lauren asked.

"Mission accomplished," Sophie said. "But I have something to run by you."

"Shoot," Lauren said.

"I'd like to add a feature to the Wife App," Sophie said. "We could call it 'Marital Guidance.' Not like marriage counseling where you have to get an actual certification. More like how wives are called on to be wise and grounded as the family's in-house therapist. The person to steer a marriage through rocky times. What do you think?"

"Oh my god, I love it," Lauren said. "Wife as Mental Health Expert. We should totally collect on that one. I'll ask the developers to add it."

"Send any inquiring Spouse to me," Sophie said. "I'll VIP the crap out of that one."

lauren

LAUREN PUT THE TWINS IN an Uber to Eric's place and walked down Broadway. It was the Friday of Memorial Day weekend, and the city was empty. She'd just texted with Gideon. They were in touch a few times a week now. His big news was that he was returning from Central Asia this summer. He told Lauren that he'd swing through the East Coast to visit friends and family, and then move into his apartment in Seattle while he worked out his next field assignment. Lauren wondered about the East Coast visit. Then she kicked herself for wondering, and the internal argument raged on.

Are you really considering sleeping with your high school boyfriend? What the fuck kind of stupid person tries to turn back the clock?

Don't swear at yourself. It's not turning back the clock. Let's just call it . . . another shot?

Another shot at what? At running around taking care of a man's mental load? Are you going to throw it all away again?

She'd just passed the Beacon Theatre when she heard someone call her name.

"Lauren! Hey . . . Lauren!"

It was Ayala Grant, mom of Daisy, leaser of horses, dental surgeon, wife of the perfect husband. Lauren hadn't seen her since the night before Thanksgiving. She should probably avoid walks down here on holiday weekends.

"Oh . . . Ayala. How are you?"

"I read about your app." Ayala plucked out her earbuds. She looked skinnier and her face was gaunt. "It sounds amazing. Congrats."

"Thanks," Lauren said.

"I'm guessing you heard the news," Ayala said.

"What news?"

"Nick and I . . . we recently split up."

"No!" Lauren said. The way Ayala talked about their marriage, you'd have thought they were Barbie and Ken. Well, if Ken had a penis.

"There were ongoing issues." Ayala squeezed her earbuds in her fist and then shook her head like she was willing herself not to cry. "Drinking. Infidelity. You know how it is."

Ayala certainly hadn't let on to this in her years of painting her family portrait. Definitely not last fall when she simultaneously gloated about married life and warned Lauren not to crack her teeth in the divorce process.

"I'm so sorry," Lauren said. She wouldn't hold it against Ayala. Lauren had learned, in marriages, that wives sustain large levels of denial just to make it through the day. "I didn't know things were rough with you guys."

"Yeah, well, Nick shows well." Ayala paused. "Can you believe he rented a penthouse in Battery Park? Three bedrooms and three bathrooms. But Daisy refuses to sleep over there. Nick is furious at me—he thinks I turned her against him."

As Ayala wiped her eyes, Lauren nodded sympathetically. Clearly this was all very new.

"It gets better," Lauren told her. "It doesn't hurt this badly forever."

Lauren gave her a hug and then started uptown.

So what were you saying? the voice in her head asked. *Another shot at what?*

I don't know, okay? Sex? Happiness? I'm willing to take that risk, so shut up and leave me alone.

madeline

On a Saturday morning in early June, Arabella went on the attack. She was headed to Juilliard soon. Her end-of-year recital was in three weeks. In addition to the Bach cello suites, Arabella would perform Dvořák. Her practice sessions consumed more than four hours each day. Tension was high. Every minute counted.

Madeline could hear Arabella getting ready in her bedroom. But really Madeline was only partly listening from her makeshift office at the kitchen table. For the past month, she'd been deep in the process of securing funding for the Wife App. It was so busy that she had to drop out of the PTA. Twice she canceled her highlights appointment, and she hadn't gotten a facial in over a month. Night and day, she corresponded with investors and met with analysts and went back and forth with her former B-school professor, who helped connect her with influential money people.

Several investors were interested but Madeline kept them at bay until she found exactly what she was looking for. Bottom line, she wanted it all—a massive infusion of cash and a platform to expand while still allowing the founders to retain control.

Who knew Madeline had such a knack for making money?

Maybe she was more like her dad than she thought.

She definitely wasn't anything like her mom, whom she hadn't spoken to since that phone call back in February. Another crazy thing. Madeline hadn't been on Bumble in three months. Her only sex was the occasional hookup with Bryan. At least she managed to squeeze in yoga classes, especially as her court date with Colin crept closer. In late May, Madeline got a letter, forwarded from Serena, that the custody hearing would be in Lower Manhattan the week that Colin came to town for Arabella's recital. Madeline asked Colin to keep the court date under wraps for now. Madeline would tell Arabella, privately, the day after her recital.

After more than seven months, Madeline had never been able to tease much information out of Arabella about why she wanted to spend a year with Colin. Whenever she brought it up, Arabella shut it down with some version of *it's complicated, it'll make you sad, can we please stop talking about this?* Even though Madeline reassured her daughter that she was a grown-up and she could handle it, Arabella refused to elaborate.

"Mom?"

Madeline looked up from her laptop. Arabella's damp hair was loose around her shoulders and she wore a black Juilliard T-shirt and leggings. For years, Madeline spent Saturdays at Juilliard with her. Parents weren't allowed into lessons but Madeline, along with a brigade of moms, populated the lobby benches. The moms plied their kids with high-protein snacks and fruit slices, did their hair and makeup on performance days, and swapped brags about what summer programs their child was auditioning for.

That all stopped last fall. At the beginning of the school year, Arabella insisted on going alone and grabbing lunch at Starbucks. Just like she insisted on going to her acupuncture appointments alone. Madeline would have loved to join her daughter at the Integrated Healing Center, to drink tea and chat with Lucy. But Arabella shut that down after the first visit.

"Yes?" Madeline asked Arabella now. "What's up?"

"You know how I'm sleeping over at Ria's tonight?" Arabella asked. She held her rock stop in one hand and then casually tossed it to her other palm. "Juilliard is supposed to let out at six. I figure I can drop off my cello at home and be there by seven."

No, Madeline did not know about this. But she wasn't surprised. Arabella slept over at her best friend's a few times a month.

"I guess that's fine," Madeline said. "You don't need to practice tonight so your evening is free. I just wish you'd run it by me first."

Arabella pursed her lips. "Well, that's the thing."

"What thing?"

"We're invited to a party and Ria's mom said she can go but she said I need to get your permission. She offered to text you, but I told her I would ask."

"Ah," Madeline said, stalling for time. It was the spring of ninth grade. Parties were beginning to happen. As far as Madeline knew, Arabella hadn't been to one yet. "Who's having the party?"

"Chauncey Goldblatt. Her parents are going out of town, but they said she can have people over."

"No," Madeline said immediately. The head of the Penis Girls? No way.

"Oh my god!" Arabella clenched her fists in anger. "Ria's mom said it was okay. You're seriously going to let Ria go and make me stay home?"

Ria's mom. So often, it was Ria's mom *this* and Ria's mom *that.* Clearly, Arabella wanted to ditch Madeline for Ria's mom. Just like she wanted to ditch Madeline for Colin.

All of a sudden, Madeline had a crystal clear revelation.

I don't care if Arabella likes me. Because I love her and I'm her mom and no one can take that away. Not Ria's mom. Not my mom. Not even Colin. And as her mom, I will not let her go to a party thrown by a girl who trades hand jobs for Starbucks gift cards.

"Sorry," Madeline said. "Ria's mom gets to set her limits and I get to set mine."

"Is it because of what I told you about Chauncey and her friends?"

Madeline closed her laptop. "It's because I said no."

Arabella stomped her foot like a petulant toddler. "I can't believe I ever told you that. I can't believe you're taking something I shared in confidence and using it against me! Do you really think that if you do that, I will *ever* tell you anything again?"

Arabella was smart. Maybe even a little manipulative. But Madeline would not budge. She would not let her daughter walk all over her.

"Sorry," she said. "No."

Arabella ran into her room and slammed the door.

sophie

On Saturday morning, Sophie lay in bed soaking. *Soaking* was a term she'd acquired from her ex-girlfriend, Cara. It referred to those moments when you first wake up and your body is frozen in post-sleep paralysis. Your mind wanders in, out, and around. Your bed is cozy. Your toes curl. The world feels slow and luxurious.

Sophie hadn't soaked in years. Probably not since she had children. Definitely not since her marriage plummeted. But on this sunny Saturday morning, she lay motionless under her sheets. She hadn't looked at social media in days. She hadn't worried about money in over a month. After the windfall from Samuel Bliss, Sophie consulted with a financial advisor. She set aside a bundle for Charlie's therapy and for taxes and transferred the remaining amount into long-term savings.

Sophie's life was changing.

Charlie hadn't picked his skin for so long that his fingers were beginning to heal. After his last therapy session, Jeffrey said they could wrap up by summer. And Noah, following a school year of preteen hostility, allowed his sweet self to reemerge when he didn't think anyone was looking.

Sophie finally got out of bed, put on tea, and glanced at the Wife

App. She had several Mental Loads tomorrow, but she'd reserved today for baking muffins and getting new running sneakers. Maybe a neck massage. Imagine that luxury! Never in Sophie's life had she been able to turn down the opportunity to make money. Never had she set aside an entire day for self-care.

There was a new Spouse with an urgent VIP request. Her name was Evelyn. Sophie was about to hit "decline" when she realized the request was filed under Marital Advice. On top of that, this Spouse specifically asked for Sophie.

Sophie turned off the kettle, leaned against the counter, and reviewed the Mental Load.

I'll be brutally honest here, Evelyn wrote. *I'm beginning to hate my husband or maybe I already hate him. I feel trapped in my marriage. I don't know whether to work to make it better or call it quits while I still have an ounce of self-esteem. Help!*

Sophie nodded in recognition. As much as she'd been looking forward to a wide-open day, she was overcome by a higher calling to help this Spouse understand that she was worth it. That you are never trapped.

Sophie clicked "accept" and messaged Evelyn possible times and places to meet and proposed a fee.

Within minutes, Evelyn responded. The money was fine. The Soldiers' and Sailors' Monument in Riverside Park was perfect. The sooner the better.

Sophie poured boiling water in her teacup. Her day of self-pampering would have to wait. Or perhaps this was another form of pampering—deeper and more meaningful—where she helped herself by helping others.

Sophie walked briskly across West End Avenue. Kids in Little League gear scurried into Riverside Park—tall socks, team shirts, backpacks loaded with baseball bats. Charlie and Noah had West Side Soccer ten blocks uptown. Maybe after meeting with Evelyn, she'd pop up and watch their games. That would mean cheering from the sidelines with Joshua and Beatrice. Ugh. Maybe not.

Sophie crossed Riverside Drive, walked up the steps to the Soldiers' and Sailors' Monument, and glanced at the people on the—

Oh no.

Please don't let it be.

But it is.

Right there on the stone bench.

Sophie took a few steps backward. She would send a message to Evelyn. She would apologize for bailing. Or . . . no. She would suggest a change of location.

Just as she was about to turn around and find a hidden spot to message Evelyn from, Beatrice looked up. "Hey there," she said. She seemed unfazed to see Sophie.

Sophie's phone nearly fell out of her hands. "Hi . . . uh . . . I'm actually meeting someone but—"

"It's me," Beatrice said. Her golden eyes flashed in the morning sun.

Sophie stared at Beatrice, then at Clementine sucking a pacifier in her stroller. The baby had Charlie's button nose, the fierce set of Noah's chin.

"My middle name is Evelyn," Beatrice told her.

Sophie's thighs felt wobbly. She thought back to the Wife App request. *I'm beginning to hate my husband or maybe I already hate him. I feel trapped in my marriage.*

"But I don't," Sophie said. "I can't . . ."

Instead of finishing her sentence, she leapt down the stone stairs and began to run away.

lauren

LAUREN STARED AT HER TO-DO list. It was Saturday around 11:00 a.m., which should have been the unwinding part of the week. Regardless, she had tons of Wife App business. Also, she had to figure out if she was going to accept a new product management assignment for her freelance job. She'd turned down the last offer, which was scary and also exhilarating. But as long as the Wife App generated income and she could draw a salary from it, she could take a pass on the Amazing Animalz app. There were also the end-of-school-year potlucks. Teacher gifts. And then there was the Goddamn Camp List.

Ever since Cady and Amelia started going to sleepaway camp, Lauren had been haunted by the grueling process of making sure her kids had twelve pairs of underwear, hiking boots, rain boots, water shoes. Duffel bags. Laundry bags. Toiletries bags. Envelopes and stamps. Flashlights and batteries. And then, of course, she had to label every item with *Cady Turner* or *Amelia Turner*; god forbid they switch cheap white washcloths with another child. Historically, the Goddamn Camp List consumed much of Lauren's June.

Not this year.

Lauren surfed the Wife App until she found one of her favorite

Wives. He was thirty with a handlebar mustache and vintage Hawaiian shirts. If a VIP Spouse needed something done and Sophie didn't have the bandwidth, he was your man. *Wife.* Whatever.

Lauren tapped his profile, uploaded the packing lists, and entered specific details about this Mental Load.

Within minutes, he texted her, *Consider it done!*

With those three words, Lauren wanted to tell him that she'd won the wife lottery. Ha! Instead, she sent him a deposit and put the Goddamn Camp List out of her mind forever.

madeline

An hour later, Arabella came out of her room. She still had her rock stop in her hand. Madeline was at the table, hard at work on a spreadsheet, trying to distract herself from Arabella's earlier outburst.

"I've been thinking about it and I want to tell you something," Arabella said. "The thing is, I hate being around you and I can't wait to go live with Dad next year."

Madeline wouldn't let herself get flustered. She was a top-notch mom. A self-aware, loving, thoughtful mom. She was no longer going to let Arabella rattle her like she'd been doing all year. No, Madeline was going to be rightfully pissed at Arabella for not showing her more respect.

Arabella stared hard at her mom. Madeline stared right back and said, "Well, you live with me now and you're not going to the party."

Arabella chucked her rock stop on the wood floor so hard it bounced up and hit the wall. Then she ran into her room, grabbed her cello and her bag, and stormed out of the apartment.

Once she was gone, Madeline leaned down to the spot where the rock stop struck. It had left a small dent in the cherry floor and a scuff on the wall.

sophie

SOPHIE GLANCED OVER HER SHOULDER. Beatrice was jogging after her. Clementine worked at her pacifier and twirled her hair with one finger. When Noah was a baby, he used to do the same thing.

"Please . . . Sophie," Beatrice called out. "Please wait. I'm sorry. Let me explain."

People in Riverside Park shot looks at Sophie. Running away from a woman with a baby? If the roles were reversed, she'd stare as well.

"Sophie. Please. I'm sorry I said I was Evelyn."

Sophie stumbled over an uprooted stone tile. Back when she was married to Joshua, she used to apologize about everything. Sometimes she would apologize before she even spoke, just to preempt his rage. Sophie paused and looked behind her again.

"I'm sorry I misled you," Beatrice said as she dabbed at her eyes. "I didn't—"

"You can stop saying you're sorry." Sophie dug around in her bag for a packet of tissues. Beatrice's mascara had leaked onto her cheeks. Sophie had never seen her so . . . not composed.

Beatrice swabbed at her eyes. "Thanks for the tissue."

"No problem," Sophie said. "I should have stopped sooner. I was freaked out. I guess I still am."

"I probably would have run away too. I should have just texted you. I shouldn't have done it over the Wife App. But I didn't think you'd want to talk to me."

"Why not?" Sophie asked, even though it was true. Sophie never would have agreed to get together with Beatrice. She tried hard to stay away from Joshua's shiny new life.

They faced each other in awkward silence. Tears began to run down Beatrice's face. She turned away so Clementine wouldn't see.

"Want to walk?" Sophie asked. "Let's walk, okay?"

She said it in a soothing voice so Clementine wouldn't worry. Kids don't deserve to grow up in bad marriages. No one does.

"A walk would be perfect," Beatrice said. "I really am sorry that—"

Sophie held up her hand. "We've covered that. Let's walk. Let's talk. Tell me what's going on."

Sophie provided tissues while Beatrice navigated the stroller down various ramps. Clementine snuggled deep into her stroller, her eyelids heavy with sleep. Once they reached the Hudson River, they headed south. While they walked, Beatrice told her that Joshua had begun to smoke weed again. He was back in rehearsals with Friend of the Sun. But it wasn't just that. It was his temper, his insults, the demeaning way he spoke to Beatrice and the boys. So far, Clementine was exempt, but it was just a matter of time until he turned on her too.

"It was a sudden shift." Beatrice released the stroller with one hand to snap her fingers. "Maybe nine months ago. Clementine was still little, and I was nursing so my hormones were all over the place. He used to be charming . . . and funny in that snarky Joshua way. Maybe this is going to sound terrible but it's almost like he used to worship me."

"What about other people?" Sophie asked even though she knew the answer.

"Definitely not as charming. Well, unless he needed something. Then he was super friendly. I always hated how he talked to you, but I figured you guys had water under the bridge. Even so, I could never reconcile his sharp edges with the effusive Joshua I interacted with on a daily basis."

Sophie nodded. Joshua was a master of the honeymoon period. He was the king of turning on charm, then turning it off like a faucet.

Beatrice continued. "When we first got together, he was always commenting about how impressed he was with my career and my ambition, that I was on the partner track at my firm. He was kind of in awe."

Sophie giggled despite herself. "My career definitely wasn't fancy enough for him."

"He loves that I make money," Beatrice added with a half smile. "He complains about a lot but never that. Sorry. That sounds tacky. But it's true."

Beatrice described how she bought their condo. She paid for those trips to Hawaii and California. It wasn't that Joshua didn't make money, because several high-profile clients came to his recording studio. But he hoarded his cash like a miser. He had the least generous spirit of anyone Beatrice had ever met.

"But why all your posts?" Sophie asked. "You seem so happy on Instagram."

Beatrice raised her eyebrows. "You really have to ask if social media is real?"

Sophie leaned over a water fountain. "It all looked so perfect I had to stop following you."

"I noticed."

Sophie's breath caught. "You did?"

Beatrice glanced down at her sleeping daughter. "I guess I was trying to create the life I wanted to have. The life I thought I had until it turned sour. Anyway, I haven't posted in months. I just . . . can't."

"How did you decide to reach out to me?"

Beatrice explained how, as soon as Noah told her about the Wife App, she'd followed its ascent. How cool to profit from a wife's invisible labor! But it was more than that. Sophie was the only person who truly knew how it was to be married to Joshua. Beatrice had parsed this with her friends, of course, but it felt like Sophie was the only one who could help her figure out how to walk away.

"You mean a divorce?" Sophie asked.

"I think so. My parents—they live in L.A.—they've been telling me for months that I should divorce him. My friends hate the way he treats me. They're telling me to get out. But I can't work up the nerve. We have a child together. I want Clementine to grow up with two parents. Maybe it'll get better."

As soon as those words were out of Beatrice's mouth, she laughed bitterly and rotated the diamond ring on her finger. "You're going to tell me it doesn't get better, right?"

"It doesn't," Sophie said.

They walked until they reached an outdoor café. They ordered chicken wraps to go and a plain bagel for Clementine, who was just rousing from her nap. After they ate and the baby gummed at the bagel, Beatrice lay Clementine across a bench to change her diaper. She squealed and kicked her feet in the air. Beatrice used one arm to keep her daughter from falling while Sophie handed over wipes. As she did, their fingers touched. Sophie quickly pulled away.

"It's just . . . uhhh." Sophie's cheeks flushed as she tried to summon what to say next.

"Diaper changing is a two-woman job." Beatrice smiled at her daughter's plump, naked belly. "Especially when you have a future gymnast in action."

Sophie laughed and, as she did, Beatrice caught her eye. They held each other's gaze for a few extra seconds. When Sophie passed Beatrice a clean diaper, they let their hands linger.

Beatrice smiled shyly. "This is . . ."

Sophie smiled back. "I know. . . ."

"But."

"I know."

Sophie had always steered clear of Beatrice. She'd told herself it was because she didn't want anything to do with Joshua's Family 2.0. But maybe, deep down, she sensed this connection. The more she saw of Beatrice, the more Sophie couldn't deny what she now knew was true—their connection went much deeper than having married the same man.

As Beatrice buckled her daughter back into the stroller, both women's phones chirped. They glanced at their screens and then, nervously, at each other.

"Joshua said the boys' soccer games are over," Beatrice said. "He wants to know where I am. I told him I was meeting a friend."

"He texted me too," Sophie said. "Well, Charlie texted from Joshua's phone. He said they won their game. Noah did too."

Beatrice smiled. "Charlie was so nervous about it at breakfast."

The women looked out at the sky, the boats on the river. Sophie didn't want to say goodbye. And, as she looked over at Beatrice, she could tell she wasn't the only one.

lauren

By mid-afternoon, Lauren had finished her Wife App business. She was about to step in the shower when she got a ping through the Wife911 feature on the app. They'd added it in case of emergencies. Lauren quickly tapped on the Wife's profile. Maria from Hoboken. They had so many Wives now she barely knew any of them.

> **MariaTWA:** Sorry! I'm not in danger but I'm having a crisis. I have to pack for a Spouse who leaves for a business trip to Japan in three hours and I DROPPED HIS KEYS DOWN THE ELEVATOR SHAFT. The Spouse isn't answering his phone. The Super doesn't work weekends. Help!

Lauren immediately sympathized. Before Eric's business trips, she used to dash around picking up his prescriptions, tracking down dry cleaning, making sure he had razors. It was always a traffic jam of stress until Eric got in the car to the airport. She quickly responded to Maria.

> **Wife911:** Glad you're safe. Send us the address where you are, including the apartment number. We'll get on it right away.

As soon as Lauren heard back, she texted Maria's information to Willow. Madeline's former housekeeper was the Wife App's secret weapon. As far as Lauren had seen, Willow could do it all. Since she was now a salaried employee, that meant she had to be available for Marital Crises and last-minute Wife no-shows—aka the Runaway Brides.

Lauren checked her phone. Nothing from Willow. Five minutes later, still nothing. She wriggled into her sneakers and hurried to the subway.

"I'm so sorry," Maria said when Lauren met her inside the lobby of the Spouse's building. She was a curvy woman, hair dyed green. Her eyes were bloodshot; she'd clearly been crying. "I still haven't heard back from the Spouse and I'm freaking out. And I can't leave the building because then I'll be locked out."

"We'll figure it out," Lauren said. "Let's try the Super again."

Just at that moment, Willow appeared at the glass front door. Her hair was in a ponytail and she looked relaxed and happy.

"Hey, Lauren . . . sorry I didn't get your texts," Willow said. "I was underground and didn't have mobile service. But it's all good. I've already called an elevator engineer that my boyfriend knows. They're on their way."

Lauren shook her head. Willow was truly incredible. "How do you know an elevator engineer?"

Before Willow could answer, Maria gaped at Lauren. "Hang on, are you Lauren Zuckerman? The founder of the Wife App? What are you doing here?"

"Let's just say the Wife App is an all-hands-on-deck operation," Lauren said, shrugging. "Like a marriage. A good marriage."

"Want to check the basement?" Willow pressed the down button on the elevator. "We can look for someone who has access to the elevator shaft. I'm Willow, by the way."

"I'm just so embarrassed," Maria said as they stepped into the elevator. "I can't believe I messed up and now I'm with Lauren Zuckerman! I can't believe I dropped the keys. I do so much gig work and I've never done anything this stupid."

Willow reassured her that it was okay. "Even Wives are human," she said.

Lauren nodded in agreement. The elevator was refreshingly cool and smelled like lemons.

"What gig work have you done?" Lauren asked as they walked around the empty basement.

"I've done it all," Maria said. "TaskRabbit, Fancy Hands. I even drove an Uber for a while. But that was in New Jersey. I like the Wife App best, and I'm not just saying that. I'm married, you know? And it's hard! I guess I hate how people expect the woman to take care of everything. But once I became a paid Wife, I felt like I had the choice."

"That's what we're about," Lauren said. "Calling work what it is."

Maria frowned. "The thing is—"

Willow's phone rang. "It's my elevator person." She stepped away from them and talked into the phone.

"What thing?" Lauren asked.

"I feel like I shouldn't say this," Maria said. "I'm the one who messed up and made you guys run over here."

"Tell me," Lauren said. "I really want to know."

"I'm just saying I've been a gig worker for a while, and it's great because I have freedom, you know? I like that. But gig work exploits people who don't have money and lets rich people keep having it easy. Does that make sense? I love that the Wife App has a sliding scale, but I was talking to my friend who is also a Wife about how rich people's stress is shifted to the gig workers, who have no sick days or worker protection." Maria shot Lauren an apologetic look. "Sorry . . . I hope I don't sound like a jerk."

Lauren nodded to buy herself a few seconds. She'd been so busy launching the app that, admittedly, she hadn't thought about the Wives' comp plans as much as she should have. But for the Wives on her app, this was also their life. Their livelihood.

Maria eyed her nervously.

"You don't sound like a jerk," Lauren said. She smiled and added, "Go on. I'm listening."

"It's real life that some people have money and some people don't. But I think you could figure out a payment method where Wives are paid fairly, and even get, like, sick leave. That's what my friend and I were talking about."

Just then, Willow walked over to where they were talking. "He's five minutes away," she said.

"Thank you so much." Maria bit her lip and then turned to Lauren. "And thank you for listening to my rant. I hope I didn't offend you."

Lauren nodded reassuringly at Maria. She could let herself off the hook for not having hashed out Wives' benefits from the get-go. But to hear it directly from a Wife now, she'd be negligent not to take the rant to heart. Of course, Lauren knew this would be extremely difficult, and she'd have to do some serious conferencing with Madeline and Sophie to determine how to increase worker benefits and sick pay, and to figure out how they could swing it all. But she would try her best because the Wife App put Wives first. Everything else followed.

"I'm glad you told me," Lauren said after a moment, "and I promise that we will do better."

madeline

ARABELLA GOT HOME FROM JUILLIARD a little after six. She didn't text Madeline for the entire day after their fight, and Madeline didn't text her either. Madeline tracked her and saw that she was at her music school so . . . fine. Let her be.

When Arabella walked in the door, she tossed her bag on the bench in the foyer and stomped into her room. Madeline sipped some water and knocked on her daughter's door.

No answer.

She knocked again. A small voice said, "Yeah?"

Madeline knew that voice. It was the voice of shame. Madeline had felt so much shame around her own mom, and she wouldn't allow her daughter to wallow in that rotten stew. Madeline knocked once more, turned the doorknob, and walked into Arabella's room.

"I'm not mad at you, okay?" she told her daughter. Arabella was sprawled across her bed. She quickly dropped her phone and rolled onto her side.

"I didn't like how you acted," Madeline added, "but I love you and I know you love me."

Arabella stared hard at her mom. She tried to look angry but that lasted about three seconds before she collapsed into sobs.

"Oh my god, Mom. I'm so sorry. I've been awful. You have every right to hate me."

"Sweetie," Madeline said. She sat on the bedspread next to her daughter and pulled her up into her arms. "I'm not mad at you. I would never hate you."

"But what about me wanting to live with Dad next year?" Arabella asked. Her head was buried so deep in her mom's shoulder that her voice was muffled. "I've been worried that you're mad at me about that. That you think I'm doing it because I don't love you. Because that's not true."

"I've been sad about it," Madeline said. "I'll miss you if you go. But we'll decide with the lawyers what's best for next year. We have a court date coming up in a few weeks. Dad and I were going to tell you later because we didn't want you to get stressed about it. But what I'm trying to say is that you don't bear the weight of this. The adults will figure it out."

Arabella slid down onto her pillow. As she did, Madeline glanced around her bedroom. A gang of stuffed animals resided in a canvas hamper against one wall. Across the room, a phone charger, containers of makeup, racks of necklaces.

Arabella pushed back her sweaty tangle of hair. "You know how you keep asking me about why I want to live in London? And I've never been able to tell you. The thing is . . . you really don't know? Like, what it's all about?"

Hang on . . . there's an actual reason? Madeline searched her brain for a fight they'd had last fall, some pivotal moment when her daughter decided she no longer wanted to live with her.

"Mom," Arabella said as she wiped her wet eyes. She had calloused fingers from her hundreds of hours of cello practice. "Think about how old you were when your dad died."

Oh my god.

"I'm fourteen," Arabella said. "And I barely know my dad. When I add up how much time I've spent with him in my entire life, it's barely a year."

Oh my god.

"I've always heard so much about how you loved your dad, and even that day when he had his heart attack and you were home alone with him—" Arabella paused. "Is this too hard to hear, Mom? I can tell you're about to cry. I'm so sorry, Mom. It's just—"

"No," Madeline said quietly. "It's okay."

"If Dad died now, like when your dad died, I'd have so many regrets that I never knew him more. I don't want to have regrets."

Madeline scooped her daughter back into her arms. How long had it been since Arabella let herself get hugged like this? Too long. Or maybe just-right long. Maybe they needed this time apart to figure out what they wanted independent of each other.

After a few minutes, Madeline stood up. "Why don't you change into something more comfortable? I'll order us dinner. Thai?"

Arabella nodded. "Can we watch a movie together?"

"I would love to. Yes."

In the living room, Madeline opened Seamless on her phone. She was about to place an order for Pad Thai and shrimp curry. Instead, she opened her email and wrote a note to Colin's lawyer, with Serena Kilgannon and Colin copied:

> *I've decided to accept Colin Smith's motion to have our daughter, Arabella, live with him in London for a year. We can cancel the court date. My lawyer, Serena Kilgannon (cc'd here) will draft a contract ensuring that Arabella will only live in London for twelve months, and that this is not a permanent change of residential custody. After careful consideration, I feel this is in the*

*best interests of Arabella and her father. I wholeheartedly
support it.*

Sincerely,
Madeline Wallace

Madeline hit "send" and then watched out the window as the evening sun shined down on Central Park.

sophie

FIVE DAYS LATER, ON A quiet Thursday morning, Sophie got another Wife request from "Evelyn." She wrote in her Mental Load:

> *Marital update. Can you swing a last-minute lunch? Also, I really*
> *liked our walk on Saturday. The Wife App is . . . just what I needed.*

Sophie glanced at the table in front of her, spread thick with forms and evaluations. There was no school today. Both boys were at a soccer clinic in Central Park. Sophie had spent the morning writing end-of-year student assessments. She had heaps of work left, all of it due to the principal this evening. If Sophie met Beatrice for lunch, she would almost certainly miss the deadline, which was completely out of character for her.

After a moment, she responded to Evelyn/Beatrice:
I really liked our walk too. And yes to lunch. I accept.

"I realized on the subway down here that your initials spell out the first three letters of your name." Sophie took a bite of the kale Caesar salad on her lap. "Beatrice Evelyn Allen. Does anyone ever call you Bea?"

Beatrice popped an olive in her mouth. "My mom calls me Bea. My name is her doing. She loves letter play."

Sophie raked through her salad with her clear plastic fork and looked out at the New York Harbor. They were on a bench in Battery Park, a few blocks from Beatrice's office, with a direct view of the Statue of Liberty. A few sailboats lagged in the harbor, searching for wind. The Staten Island Ferry slogged toward its terminal.

"I know it's weird that I hired you on the Wife App again," Beatrice said. "It's just . . . there's a lot going on. With Joshua. It didn't feel right to text you on the chain we use to discuss weeks with the boys and handoffs. I wanted this to be different."

"I get it," Sophie said. Then, despite herself, she added, "I'm glad you did."

Beatrice set down her fork. "You are?"

Sophie's stomach flipped. Maybe all these interactions with Beatrice weren't despite herself. Maybe they were *because* of herself. She wanted to be here. She wanted to be doing this.

"I've been thinking about you since Saturday, wondering how you're doing with Joshua. I know how hard it is." Sophie paused. "I've also just been thinking about you."

"I've been thinking about you too," Beatrice said. She sipped her lemon seltzer. "I wanted to tell you that I thought about everything we talked about. The truth is, my marriage has been over for a long time. Or maybe I should say I'm over it. Anyway, I talked to a lawyer on Monday. There's a partner in my firm who handles divorces. He's smart and calm and always gets what his clients want. I talked to him, confidentially, and he agreed to work with me."

"A lawyer?" Sophie asked. "Not just a mediator?"

"Do you really think Joshua will be civil about this?"

Sophie felt so nervous for Beatrice that she had to sit on her hands to keep from scratching them.

"I'm going to tell him this evening," Beatrice added. "A friend of mine has agreed to take Clem for an overnight so she's nowhere near this."

"Are you freaking out?" Sophie asked. She pressed her fingernails into the backs of her thighs. "I was freaking out when I gave Joshua the ultimatums that ended our marriage. It took me so long to get there."

Beatrice shook her head. "I guess that's it. It took me a long time to get here but when I came to this realization, I knew it was the right thing. So I guess I'm relieved. I'm not looking forward to tonight, of course."

"Nope."

"And then it'll be over. I already have a bunch of calls to Realtors for furnished apartments. Short-term rentals. I like to have all my ducks lined up."

Sophie nodded. "You can always call or text if you need to talk. And you don't need to hire me on the Wife App. In fact, there's no way you're paying me for today, and I'm going to Venmo you that money from Saturday."

They were both quiet as they stared out at the view.

"What does it say on the Statue of Liberty again?" Beatrice asked. "Like, on the pedestal? *Give me your tired, your poor, your huddled masses. . . .*"

Sophie squinted toward Liberty Island. It was a hot spring day and the sun was high in the sky. "It's a poem written by Emma Lazarus. It's ideologically beautiful but too bad it's not put into practice." Sophie coughed and then took a long sip of water. A bit of a crouton was lodged in her throat. "I just read a book about Emma Lazarus. She was an activist for Jewish refugees. She died young, like at thirty-eight. And yes, that was a total nerd moment."

Beatrice watched Sophie. "I like nerds."

Sophie's heart did a somersault. She closed her salad container.

"This is crazy, right?" Beatrice said. "I'm telling my husband tonight that we're over and then . . ."

"We have this." Sophie slid closer to Beatrice on the bench until their thighs touched and their hands rested inches from each other.

"You feel it too?" Beatrice asked.

"I think I've felt it for a while," Sophie said.

"Me too." Beatrice turned to look at Sophie. "I hope it's okay that I know this, but Joshua told me a long time ago that you've been with women. Like, you had a girlfriend in grad school? I didn't think much about it, other than the fact that I'm queer. But when I started feeling a connection to you, I just—"

"You're queer?" Sophie asked. Her stomach was turning to liquid.

Beatrice nodded. "I dated men and women before Joshua. To be honest, I never thought I'd end up married to a man."

"How weird that Joshua married two women who . . ."

"I know," Beatrice said. "But I've wasted too much time trying to figure out Joshua. I'm done."

They sat quietly on the bench, their fingers close, their heads pulling closer. Sophie's gaze drifted from Beatrice's golden eyes to her lips.

"Are we going to do this?" Beatrice asked. "You realize once we do this, there is no going back."

"I don't want to go back," Sophie whispered.

The two women smiled as they leaned close to each other. And then they stopped smiling because they were kissing.

lauren

A WEEK BEFORE THE TWINS left for camp, Lauren and Amelia walked across Central Park to deliver the photo albums to Theo. All through this Wife job, Amelia insisted she was only in it for the money. But when the albums arrived in the mail, Amelia thumbed through them on the couch with an uncharacteristic display of emotion.

"It tells the story of a family," she said as she wiped at her eyes. "A happy family who didn't break up."

"We're still a happy family," Lauren said. "Our path is just a little different."

Amelia closed an album—Theo and Mari on a cruise in Norway—and opened one from twenty years before. The birth of their second baby. "I hope Theo likes them. I think they came out really nice."

"He's going to love the albums. Do you want to join me when I deliver them?" Lauren asked. "It's not a paid Wife job."

"Yeah," Amelia said, surprising Lauren. "I'd like that."

So here they were, lugging the albums across Central Park in two heavy canvas bags. Lauren had suggested they take a cab but Amelia surprised Lauren again by suggesting they walk to Theo's brownstone.

"The park is so pretty this time of year," Amelia said.

They had just passed the Great Lawn when Amelia said, "You know what we talked about? I've been thinking a lot about it."

Lauren had no idea what Amelia was referring to, so she shifted a bag on her shoulder and offered a vague, "Okay."

"The gender stuff," Amelia said. "I wanted to tell you that I've been thinking about it. Don't tell Cady. Definitely don't tell Dad."

"Of course not," Lauren said. "I'm with you whatever you decide. You even have the right to change your mind as many times as you want."

"Really?"

"We all do," Lauren said.

They walked in silence for several minutes, both in their own thoughts. Lauren had recently gotten a text from Gideon that he'd be back in the States in July and was renting a house on Cape Cod, hosting various East Coast friends throughout the week. Did Lauren want to join for any part? It was a big house, lots of room. No pressure. Lauren thought about it for a few days and then said yes, sure, she'd love to. The kids would be at camp. Madeline and Sophie could deal with the app. Thinking about it now, Lauren reminded herself that what she told Amelia also applied to herself. She was free to back out, to get cold feet. She gave herself permission to change her mind as much as she wanted.

When they got to Theo's house, Amelia sat next to him on the couch.

"I love it when you got your dog," Amelia said, pointing at a photo. "It's so cute. We have a dog too. Coco."

Theo's eyes twinkled. "Ah . . . Joleen."

"I wondered what its name was. I tried to read the tag."

"Joleen was a dog's dog. Everyone loved her. When she really got going wagging her tail, she'd involuntarily tweak her back leg."

"My dog does that too!" Amelia said, giggling.

As Lauren watched them talking, she glanced at the flowers on the patio. She and Theo had worked closely on his social life over the months. With Lauren's guidance, he'd sent out greeting cards, re-kindled fading relationships, had frequent lunches and dinners. He seemed much better than he was in January.

Amelia touched another picture. "I noticed on your cruise in Norway, Mari was wearing that blue bracelet. But then—" Amelia fished an album out of the bag on the floor. "Way back here, like twenty or thirty years ago, she had on the same bracelet."

Theo smiled. "I gave Mari that opal bracelet on our first wedding anniversary. There's this whole list of what a husband is supposed to give his wife on various anniversaries, but I never listened to that. Mari loved opals."

"I don't listen to a lot of the rules about what people are supposed to do," Amelia responded.

Lauren smiled at her child. She had never felt so proud.

madeline

ON THE MORNING OF ARABELLA'S recital, Bianca sent two bouquets. One was for Arabella, white roses. The card read:

> *Sweet Arabella,*
> *Break a leg at your recital!*
> *Love,*
> *Grandma*

The other bouquet, to Madeline, was orchids. The card simply read: *I'm sorry.*

"Why is Grandma sorry?" Arabella asked as she glanced over her mom's shoulder.

Madeline tucked the card in her pocket. Of course her mother would know that orchids—fragile, expensive—were the official flower of apologies. Her mom knew all the right things to do, the right traditions to follow.

"Why is Grandma sorry?" Arabella asked again. She sat down at the kitchen table and dug into her omelet. Soon she had to head to Juilliard. Even recital days had the regular Pre-College programming.

Arabella got an hour off to dress up, and a little time after the concert to mingle with guests. Colin had flown in, and Lauren would be there. Sophie was coming too, and Ria, and several of Arabella's friends from Juilliard.

"Long story," Madeline said vaguely.

"Was it about me?"

Madeline shook her head because, really, it wasn't about Arabella. It was about Madeline and Bianca, and the different choices they'd made in their lives.

Madeline set the roses in the middle of the kitchen table. She stared at the orchids. Part of her wanted to carry them to the trash chute and hurl them in. Instead she brought them into the dining room and placed them on the table.

"So I'll see you at one?" Madeline asked a few minutes later as her daughter gathered her things.

"Yep. You'll bring the gown and my makeup?"

"Definitely," Madeline said. "And you really want me to help with your hair and makeup?"

"Of course I do, Mom!" Arabella told her. She shouted it with such certainty it was as if this past year hadn't happened. "I can't imagine a recital without you doing my hair and makeup."

Madeline was relieved. But she also wouldn't have been crushed if Arabella said no. Three months ago, that kind of rejection would have toppled her. But she was working hard on letting Arabella go. In doing so, she'd found within herself a certain peace. Maybe that was why she decided to end the sex dates with Bryan. She did it over text and he immediately texted back: *cool*. That emotionless response, after months of sex, affirmed to Madeline that she was done separating her body from her inner life.

Arabella hoisted her cello onto her back and walked to the elevator. Once Madeline could see that she was in the Uber, she called her mom.

"Thanks for the flowers," she said when Bianca answered.

"Oh, they arrived?" her mom asked. Her voice was high-pitched. This was how she sounded when she was nervous, or when she was in the presence of someone wealthier than she was.

"Yes, Arabella got to see the flowers before she left for Juilliard." Madeline paused to collect her thoughts. "Listen, I'm sorry too. About what I said about Ron. About Bumble."

Crickets.

When her mom didn't say anything, Madeline added, "It's okay. We don't have to talk about it. It's okay if you—"

"No," Bianca said. "I have something to say. I was just trying to figure out how to put it."

Another silence. Madeline rotated the orchids on the table.

"The thing is," her mom said. "I knew."

Madeline swallowed hard. Surely she wasn't hearing this correctly.

"Was I happy about it?" her mom asked. "Of course not. But Ron and I . . . it's been a long time since we've had that kind of relationship. That kind of intimacy. This is where he gets it, and I'd rather it be with my blessing."

Hang on. *What?* Was her mom saying that since she and Ron no longer had sex, she looked away while he screwed around on hookup apps? Madeline was all for sexual agency—she was a poster child for it! But in open marriages, there was often the sad subtext that one spouse slept around while the other spouse felt cheated on.

"Successful marriages are all about compromise," Bianca concluded. "You have to make a million compromises in marriage, Madeline. This is one of mine."

Madeline shook her head *no.* You don't have to make compromises that hurt. Even while married, you are entitled to feel respected.

"It works for us," Bianca said. Her voice had shifted. She was done talking about this. "Listen, we'll be in the Hamptons after July fourth. Come for a visit, you and Arabella. Or come alone. Don't be a stranger."

"Uh-huh," Madeline said vaguely. Maybe she could take a day trip, or stay in a hotel on the beach and see Bianca in small doses. Or maybe she wouldn't go. She was, after all, still the person that Bianca asked to crop out of the photo.

"Really?" Bianca asked. "You really will visit?"

Madeline detected something in her mom's voice that she'd never heard before. *Was it . . . ? Could it be . . . ?* Madeline realized with a start that she heard a mom scared she was losing her only daughter. *Oh my god.* Madeline heard herself.

"I really will," Madeline said. This time she meant it.

Arabella had just finished a movement of Schumann's Cello Concerto in A Minor, op. 129 when Madeline caught Colin's eye. They sat side by side in the front row of Juilliard's Paul Recital Hall. When she smiled over at him, he smiled back at her.

Colin looked good. Tall and handsome in his tailored suit. Anderson & Sheppard, Madeline guessed, eyeing it. Colin had always been a sharp dresser, his suits custom-made by tailors on Savile Row. But it was his face that seemed different. More relaxed. For many years, Colin's face had been tight with tension from his eighty-hour work-weeks. He told Madeline on a recent call that he'd begun to scale back hours in preparation for Arabella's move. He said it was long overdue.

After Madeline sent that email earlier in the month, Colin called her within minutes. It was the middle of the night in London. *Is this for real?* he'd asked. *Are you sure?* Moments later, she received a call from her lawyer.

"You have the law on your side, Madeline," Serena Kilgannon told her. "You will likely win at the hearing."

"But what will I lose?" Madeline asked.

Colin had flown in late last night and was staying at the Soho Grand. On Monday, he would rent a car and the three of them would drive to Arabella's music camp in the Berkshires, where she would remain for five weeks. After that, Colin would return to England. When Arabella finished Greenwood in early August, she'd have a week with her mom in Manhattan, then she'd head to her dad's for the year. Madeline would visit—she'd already booked a trip to London in October—but she'd also be okay. She had her friends. She had the Wife App.

Arabella reached up to her stand, tidied the sheet music, and then nodded at her accompanist. It was a showpiece—brilliant, short, and virtuosic—the perfect way to wrap up her recital. Her teacher, Mei Chien, sat three seats down, nodding and smiling. Madeline could see in her peripheral vision that Colin had his phone up, filming. She'd ask him to text it to her later.

After the recital, after Arabella was congratulated by friends and family and pulled into a hug by her teacher, Colin and Madeline walked down the long steps of Juilliard and out onto Sixty-Fifth Street. Heat radiated from the sidewalk; sweat and trash and car fumes filled the air. Most New Yorkers who had the means fled the city in late June, but Madeline loved summer in Manhattan in all its feverish, stinky glory.

"Do you mind taking these for a moment?" Colin asked. He handed Madeline two of Arabella's bouquets so he could shrug off his suit jacket.

Madeline positioned these bouquets, along with the two she'd been holding, in the crooks of both arms. She wore an off-white Jonathan Simkhai dress and Christian Louboutin pumps that she'd bought for this occasion.

"Much better," he said as he draped his jacket over one arm. "So where to? Want to grab a bite? I'm still on U.K. time so I'm famished."

Madeline touched her new amethyst necklace. "I'd love to."

As they passed the Apple Store, Madeline glanced at the flowers in her arms. Lauren brought red roses. Sophie brought Gerbera daisies. Arabella's teacher presented her with tulips.

"Actually," Madeline said, "do you mind if we swing by my apartment first? I'd love to get these flowers into vases."

"Of course." Colin smiled at her and then, in his most British accent, said, "You mean *vases*."

Vases. *Vases*. Aluminum. *Aluminum*. Either. *Either*. This had been a running joke when they were married, the words that Americans and Brits pronounce differently.

Madeline grinned at him. They walked over to Central Park West, green and lush, Madeline's favorite avenue in the city. They passed the building where they lived when they were married, ten blocks downtown from Madeline's current apartment. There was a new doorman out front. Madeline glanced up at their old windows. They were so much younger then, so much more clueless. What if she'd insisted he not take the transfer to London? Or what if she and Arabella had moved with Colin? Who knows? It was so long ago. Ancient history.

They walked quietly through her lobby. Madeline pressed the button for the elevator. She adjusted the strap on her dress. She suddenly remembered how, when she was pregnant with Arabella, Colin encouraged her to stick it out in B-school. He said they could hire nannies around the clock. He said she was too talented to walk away. Back then, Madeline had been furious with him for not supporting her decision. She'd been raised by round-the-clock nannies. That was the last thing she wanted for her baby. But maybe she had read it wrong. Maybe Colin had been trying to help her have it all ways—wife, mom, successful finance person. Again, ancient history.

They stepped into the elevator. As the door closed, Colin leaned against the railing and blinked at her. Madeline watched her ex-husband watching her. When they entered the apartment, Madeline set the flowers on the bench. Colin flung down his jacket and wiped his hand across his forehead.

"I forgot how hot New York City gets in the summer," he said.

Madeline leaned over to wriggle off her pumps. "It's a good hot, though. An honest hot."

"An *honest* hot? Now that sounds interesting." Colin's voice was deeper, huskier.

Madeline tipped her head to one side. "Are you thinking what I'm thinking you're thinking?"

"Maybe," Colin said.

"Or maybe not?"

"I would say I am." Colin's lids were heavy as he grinned at her.

"I'm glad," Madeline said as she stepped slowly toward him, "that you still have those thoughts about me."

Colin dipped his hand under Madeline's dress, then dragged his fingers up the inside of her thigh. "I definitely do."

Madeline was getting wet. She held Colin's gaze as she rocked her body into his palm. "Are you seeing anyone now?"

"No." He moved closer to her. "What about you?"

Madeline shook her head. "I was . . . but it's over."

"Good," Colin whispered. "That's very good."

Madeline unzipped Colin's slacks and reached inside his boxers. His cock was smooth and thick and just as beautiful as she remembered. As she stroked him, he pressed her shoulders against the foyer wall and kissed her hard and deep. Oh my god, how long had it been since Madeline had been kissed like this? A decade? There had been many others, but no man kissed like Colin.

Somehow they made it to bed. As he separated her knees with his hands, he said, "I am so happy to be here with you."

She moaned in pleasure. "So am I."

They fucked fast and hard, like they were fucking toward something, like they were fucking their way back to each other. Madeline cried out when she came, and held on to Colin. A minute later, Colin winced and groaned and collapsed next to her.

They napped for a while. Who knows how long? They had nowhere to be. Madeline woke up first. A moment later, Colin reached over and stroked his hand along her cheek. There was a new warmth to him that Madeline hadn't remembered from when they were married.

"I didn't see that coming," he said. "I mean . . . I hoped."

"I'm glad it did."

They lay side by side in the sunlight, their hands laced together.

"Arabella," Madeline said after a minute. "I can't remember if I told you that she's allergic to pomegranates. She never really eats them. She knows to avoid them. But if she accidentally has even a seed or two, her lips will swell. You should have Benadryl at home, just in case."

Colin nodded. "Good to know."

"And you know she loves dark chocolate," Madeline said. "And citrus, like grapefruits and tangerines. She's insane about tangerines."

Colin squeezed Madeline's hand. "Thank you."

It was a "thanks for the info" but it was deeper than that. It was *Thank you for raising our daughter. Thank you for giving me a turn.*

Madeline rolled onto her side. Colin began to kiss her shoulders, caress her breasts. She could feel his erection between her legs. Colin reached into the nightstand for another condom, then straddled her as he put it on. This time they took it slow and tender, and they came at the exact same time.

sophie

SOPHIE AND BEATRICE WERE IN love. Deep, mad, shout-it-from-the-skyscrapers love. Of course they were terrified that they were rushing it. That it was nuts. Then again . . . when you know, you know.

Beatrice had told her friends and parents but no one in Sophie's world knew yet. It had only been six weeks. But that was the big question. When to tell Noah and Charlie that their stepmom would remain the same; she was just switching parents? When to tell Joshua, who was already livid that Beatrice had moved out and filed for divorce? He texted angry rants to Beatrice, and even called Sophie one evening to complain. Sophie answered the phone because Joshua was the father of her boys, but as soon as he unleashed a string of profanities about Beatrice, she hung up. When to tell him that his reviled first ex-wife and his reviled second almost-ex-wife were in love? When to tell her mom and sister that she was in a relationship with a woman? When to tell Lauren and Madeline?

That particular omission gnawed at Sophie whenever she talked to her friends—and they were in frequent communication about the Wife App. But how could Sophie tell Lauren, who was aggressively opposed to cheating, that she had hooked up with Beatrice while Beatrice was still with Joshua? To make matters worse, Sophie and Beatrice got together through the Wife App. One of the founding principles was that the app was not a purveyor of sexual connections.

Sophie worried. She ruminated. But she didn't scratch her hands. Ever since she and Beatrice got together, her eczema had magically disappeared. Generally, Sophie hated it when people described life happenings in terms of *magic* and *miracles*. But until a month ago, Sophie's hands had always been her itchy, raw enemy. Now they were calm. A miracle.

Which was exactly how she would describe Beatrice. Whenever Sophie panicked about how everyone would react to their relationship, Beatrice reassured her that it would be okay.

"But what if it isn't?" Sophie asked one morning in bed.

It was mid-July, a Sunday, and they'd gone back to sleep after some steaming-hot wake-up sex. Clementine was sleeping over at Joshua's place, and Noah and Charlie were at camp. Sophie and Beatrice had the rare luxury of spending the night together, their naked limbs wound around each other. With Beatrice in her bed, Sophie succumbed to one of the deepest sleeps she'd ever had.

"What do you mean, what if it isn't?" Beatrice asked.

"I mean, what if they all judge us and blame us and think we're horrible people?"

"For one, we are not horrible people." Beatrice traced her finger across Sophie's collarbone. "We are good, decent people who fell in love. We didn't plan it, but it happened. Maybe it was inevitable. If they judge us, that's their choice. Our choice is to not care."

Sophie's skin tingled where Beatrice's finger had been, and she felt pulsing between her legs. She reached over and slid her hand along the curve of Beatrice's waist from her hip up to her breasts. She cupped a breast, her hand trembling. *Can I really do this? Am I really allowed?* Yes, she was. After so many years of suppressing her desires, she was ready to fully give in.

And it wasn't anything like how it was with Cara, Sophie's ex-girlfriend from grad school, who was great in bed but a critical person the rest of the time. Beatrice was kind and generous. Interestingly, she had a similar sexuality story. Well, not totally. Sophie had never realized this before—how could she have?—but Beatrice realized she was queer as a teenager, and had been in as many relationships with women as with men.

Sophie rolled onto her back, shifting to loosen a twinge in her spine. "But the boys . . . It's not about them judging us. We're asking them to grapple with major stuff."

"That's what therapy is for," Beatrice said. "We keep Charlie in his CBT and we get Noah into talk therapy. They'll hash things out with someone who isn't us. They'll have to find a way to make this their story. And think on the bright side. They'll finally land in a happy household with two people who love and respect each other. Those are the roots that a kid needs."

Beatrice made so many good points. It was the lawyer in her. She thought like a lawyer, and she expressed herself like a lawyer, and when she made a decision she didn't constantly second-guess it the way Sophie did. Another benefit of being a lawyer was that Beatrice had financial autonomy. When Beatrice told Sophie what she earned, including the year-end bonus from the law firm where she was a junior partner, Sophie said, *Holy shit!* And it took a lot to make Sophie swear.

Financial autonomy was what allowed Beatrice to move out of the apartment she shared with Joshua and rent her own place a week after she and Sophie kissed. When Beatrice was done, she was done.

Sophie was blown away by Beatrice's boldness, by how she got her head around what she wanted and then demanded it. It was inspiring. Watching Beatrice in action, Sophie began to draft her own custody and child-support demands for when she took Joshua back to court. She had an appointment with a lawyer in August.

"The game plan is that I live here for a few months while we work through the divorce logistics," Beatrice explained to Sophie as she toured her around the apartment. It was sleek and modern, perched on the twenty-second story of a high-rise overlooking the Hudson River.

"Do you think Joshua will try to keep your condo?" Sophie asked. She knew Joshua. He was vengeful and petty, and that's when he was in a good mood. Balls to the wall, he was a monster.

"Ha," Beatrice said.

"Ha?"

"I'm an estate lawyer, babe." Beatrice opened the fridge and pulled out a bottle of chilled white wine. "I made sure he signed a prenup. The condo is mine. The money is mine. Joshua was just along for the ride."

Sophie stared at Beatrice in shock. Joshua would lose his wife, his home, and his bottomless supply of mooched money. And what Joshua was losing, Sophie would be gaining. Well, she wasn't a freeloader. She would continue to earn her own income. But still. Joshua's lifestyle was about to tank. He might even have to move in with his parents in Montclair. That would be a pain as far as the boys visiting him, and part of her felt sad that everything had gone south for Joshua. Then again, he'd made his bed. Now he had to sleep in it, even if it was on the other side of the Hudson River.

Beatrice pulled out two wineglasses, filled them with Sancerre, and offered one to Sophie.

"Shall we?" she asked, smiling at her.

"We shall," Sophie said.

They carried their glasses into the living room and settled on the slate-gray sofa. The sky burst into flames while the sun set over the river, over New Jersey. Sophie held Beatrice's hand, overcome with gratitude for this life unfolding. As it grew dark, they toasted new beginnings and then they stretched across the plush cushions and they made love.

Who knew sex could be so amazing?

That was why it was hard to get out of bed on the rare occasion that they spent the night together. Most times, it was quickies at one of their apartments before Beatrice picked up Clementine from the sitter or after she dropped her off at her morning preschool.

"I'll tell the boys after camp," Sophie said as she slid out of bed now and reached for the tank top she'd discarded on a chair the night before.

"They get home next Saturday, right?" Beatrice asked.

Sophie nodded. Noah and Charlie were taking the camp bus home from New Hampshire. She was impressed that Charlie had wanted to go to soccer camp with his brother, impressed that he felt so in control of his anxiety that he could sleep away from home for three weeks. But there it was. Sophie would go to the mat with anyone who didn't believe in cognitive behavioral therapy. Another miracle.

"We'll tell Joshua right after we tell the boys." Sophie pulled the tank top over her head and dug through her top drawer. She was naked from the waist down and she could feel Beatrice watching her, which turned her on. Everything about Beatrice turned her on. Sophie pulled a pair of black underwear from her drawer. "I don't want the boys to feel like they have to keep a secret from their dad."

"How about we tag-team?" Beatrice asked. "When you tell the boys after camp, I'll have the sitter take Clem to the playground and I'll break it to Joshua."

Sophie shuddered as she stepped into her underwear, one bare leg and then the other. "He's going to freak out."

"So he does."

"It's going to be ugly."

"So it is," Beatrice said. "But I can make the choice to walk away from that. The second his ugly starts, I'm out of there."

Sophie sighed. "And then there's my mom and Eva. The boys and I are supposed to go to Indiana in August. I definitely want to tell them before, give them a chance to get their heads around it."

"Get their heads around what? That you're finally happy? That you're in love?"

Sophie nodded glumly. There were times when she wished she could cut off contact with her family of origin, put that entire conservative world behind her. But her kids loved their cousins. They loved their grandparents. It wasn't Sophie's place to break that up.

"Do you want to come with me?" Sophie asked suddenly. She was inspired by Beatrice's lack of fear.

"Really?"

"Really," Sophie said. A happy feeling swelled inside her. Ever since the divorce, even *before* the divorce, Sophie dreaded those summer pilgrimages to Indiana. But with Beatrice, she would be okay. It might even be fun. "I'll tell them before we go out, get them prepared for the big shocker."

"I have a better idea," Beatrice said. "I can post about us after we tell Joshua and the boys. I happen to know that your sister follows my Instagram. She once commented that Clem is adorable. It'll be a gorgeous post. It'll be FOMO like they've never seen before. Let your family find out that way. Don't let them think it's a shocking secret."

This was what Sophie was talking about. Yet another reason she loved this woman. All her life, Sophie had suffered from Fear of Missing Out. She'd never told this to Beatrice. But here was Beatrice, bringing Sophie in, creating content that would leave other people feeling like *they* were the ones missing out.

"No," Sophie said.

"No?" Beatrice sat up in Sophie's bed and hugged the sheet around her breasts. A pillow crease dented her left cheek.

"Let's not post how you did with Joshua, or how most people do. All those shiny, happy family shots. Let's go real. Our life is wonderful but it's not perfect. Let's show that."

"You're totally right." Beatrice nodded thoughtfully. "We go out real. We don't evoke lifestyle jealousy."

"Exactly," Sophie said.

"Maybe just one?" Beatrice's golden eyes flashed mischievously. "One jealousy-inducing post proclaiming our love? And then I'm done?"

"One and done." Sophie held up her finger, and then stretched her hand toward Beatrice. "You sitting there naked is way too sexy for your own good."

Sophie climbed back in bed. As Beatrice wriggled Sophie's tank top over her head, Sophie moaned happily. All her worries about who and when to tell were quickly pushed aside.

The following Friday, the day before the boys returned from soccer camp, Sophie blocked off her Wife schedule, Beatrice took a personal day, and they drove up to the river towns to meet with a Realtor. Sophie had that large sum from Samuel Bliss. Beatrice would turn a profit as soon as she sold the condo. Maybe they were being crazy. Maybe it was nuts to imagine that they could move their blended family of five to the Hudson Valley, to a house with a yard and good schools and space to play and dream.

Yes, it was a dream.

But why not dream?

They realized, in their many conversations, that they were both fed up with gritty, noisy city life. They were sick of battling for a spot in a school or battling for a swing at the playground. Beatrice wanted to learn how to grill. Sophie wanted to go to farmers markets and fill up on local produce and load it into a car instead of straining her back to haul everything home. They could build a tree house for the kids. And sit on a deck and watch the stars. Have a fresh start.

They were firm that they wanted to find a town where a queer family wouldn't be some kind of unicorn. But all the complications could be talked out, figured out. This was what they discussed on the trip up Route 9 to Dobbs Ferry. Beatrice drove her silver SUV that she kept in a garage on the Upper West Side, and Sophie sat in the passenger seat as they mused over the logistics of a possible move.

"I'd stay at the law firm," Beatrice said, "and commute into the city on Metro-North. It would be easy."

"I could come in to the school," Sophie said. "But I was also thinking about applying to schools up here. Or shifting my attention more to the app. There must be a lot of needy small-town Spouses. I would love to spend more time with the kids." Sophie smiled, thinking of Clementine. Just yesterday, Clem let her do bath time. They sang "The Wheels on the Bus" and played peekaboo. "I was so stressed when the boys were little. I never got to enjoy it. I would love to be around them without constantly worrying about running off to work."

Beatrice glanced briefly to her right. "For real?"

"For real, what?"

"Like, you want to be a stay-at-home mom? Because I can totally picture that. You would be awesome."

Sophie turned Beatrice's words over in her head. Did she want to be a stay-at-home mom? It seemed sweet and tender. Then again, she didn't want to be like a Wife on the app, or like the wife she'd been in her previous relationship, making everyone else's life run smoothly and putting her own needs at the bottom of the list.

"I would," Sophie said after a moment. "But I'd want to do it differently. I would want backup childcare, and I'd work part time, earn some of my own money. And I'd want us to have regular check-ins, like maybe Saturday night dates? Where we could compare our mental loads and make sure neither of us is taking on too much."

Beatrice flicked her blinker. "Did Joshua ever tell you that he didn't believe in mental load? Sorry to bring him up."

"Only all the time," Sophie said. "It used to drive me crazy."

"I would love Saturday night dates. I love the idea of check-ins."

"I love the idea of driving Noah and Charlie to soccer games, and taking Clem to music class, and cooking family dinners that aren't fro-zen pizza."

"I love picturing you in a minivan with baggies of snacks," Beatrice said.

"Please no minivan!" Sophie shrieked. She swatted Beatrice's arm and then slid her hand down and let it rest on her thigh.

Beatrice pulled up to a yellow house with green trim. There was an oak tree looming over the driveway. Sophie grabbed her purse and hopped out of the car. As they walked to greet the Realtor, they held hands and didn't let go.

This yellow house was a dud, though. The bedrooms were small and musty. The kitchen was set apart from the rest of the living area. Not only that, the backyard was tiny—no room for a tree house or a place for the kids to kick soccer balls.

"How many kids do you have?" the Realtor asked. She was a short woman with a pronounced overbite that gave her a rabbit-y vibe.

Sophie held her breath. This Realtor, unbeknownst to her, was So-phie's trial run at coming out as a couple. But how much to explain? Their situation suddenly felt complicated.

"Three," Beatrice said. "Two boys and a little girl."

"How sweet," the Realtor said.

Sophie felt a fresh wave of love for Beatrice because she was so right. Why tell this woman anything? Why give her the opportunity to judge them? They were in love.

The Realtor described how she had the perfect house in mind. She hadn't sent it to them yesterday, in her listings, because it came on the market this morning. It was in New Rochelle, about twenty minutes away, and it fit their criteria.

"We could hop in our cars and meet there now," the Realtor said. "I just put on the lockbox before I came here."

Once they were back in the SUV, Sophie read the listing out loud to Beatrice. "It's a stone house, more than a hundred years old, but it's been gutted and remodeled. A farmhouse kitchen. A deck for grilling. And the backyard, babe. It's a full half acre."

Beatrice adjusted the air. The day had started out mild, low eighties, but the temperature was creeping up to ninety now.

"And their Municipal Equality Index earned a top score," Sophie added. "One of the best of the river towns. I have a good feeling about this one."

Beatrice let go of the wheel with one hand and laced her fingers around Sophie's. "I have a good feeling about it too," she said. "I feel like this is the house where we could build a life. Where we could be wives together."

Sophie sighed happily and glanced out the window. She would love to be a wife again. A wife on her own terms.

lauren

THE TWINS HAD BEEN AT camp for three weeks. Lauren loved her quiet evenings. Dog walked. Dishes done. Daily Wife App business taken care of. Lauren hadn't heard much from Sophie in the past month. Sophie did her Wife jobs but whenever Lauren reached out about a personal thing, all she got was a terse *So busy . . . talk soon!* Conversely, she and Madeline now talked five times a day about pitches and funding meetings.

In the evenings, Lauren watched shows and wrote letters to Cady and Amelia. She hired a Wife to mail them care packages but letters were easy enough. She never heard back from Amelia and only received one generic postcard from Cady. That was fine. The kids rarely wrote from camp.

But then, in the middle of July, Amelia sent a long letter informing Lauren that they were nonbinary and their pronouns were they/them. *I told Cady but please don't tell Dad,* Amelia added. *He'll be stupid and annoying. Or he'll say it's a phase.*

Lauren wrote back immediately that she was in full support. She'd seen this coming all year, or maybe even before. Maybe Amelia had never seemed comfortable, and this was the start of a new ease in their body.

The Eric thing was more fraught. He and Trish were flying to Maine to see Cady and Amelia for visiting weekend. Lauren got visiting weekend last summer, so it was only fair. But with Amelia's new pronouns, Lauren felt protective of her child. She considered calling Eric and prepping him for how to react if Amelia told him. In short, doing all the things she used to do as a wife.

Lauren googled articles with advice for parents of nonbinary children. She ran it by Madeline. She finally got Sophie on the phone. At Sophie's behest, Lauren wrote to Amelia and suggested that—if they're ready—they tell their dad with the help of a supportive camp counselor.

Amelia sent back a postcard that simply said, *Okay*.

That was two days before visiting weekend.

The day before visiting weekend, Lauren loaded the car and drove east toward Cape Cod. As she glanced at New York City in her rearview mirror, she inhaled through her nose and hoped for the best.

The first thing Lauren noticed as she stepped out of her car, after the six-hour drive from Manhattan to nearly the tip of Cape Cod, was that Gideon still had the scar under his right eye. She'd been so flustered on the flight to Seattle that she hadn't noticed it. Somehow the fact that the scar was there allowed a wave of reassurance to wash over her. It was still the same Gideon.

"Lauren," he said, pulling her into his arms.

Lauren wore orange shorts, a white tank top, and a baseball hat over her curls. She breathed in the briny air from the bay. She breathed in Gideon. He felt familiar and also so different. It had been more than two decades since they'd touched. A few times over breaks during college, when they were home visiting their parents, they fell into bed together. Hot sex in childhood rooms! But that ended the summer before Gideon started med school, before Lauren moved to Manhattan.

During that midtown lunch right after she got married, they hadn't touched other than a handshake. Maybe a loose hug.

"So," Gideon said as he stepped back. "It's you."

"I was thinking the same thing. It's good to see you."

"How was your drive? Come on into the house. The mosquitoes are biting."

Lauren tapped the button to open her trunk. Gideon pulled out her suitcase while Lauren stretched into the front seat and gathered her water bottle, her half-finished seltzer, her bag. She reached up to her throat with her pointer and middle finger and checked her pulse. It raced so hard she could feel it in her temples.

"So . . . here's the house," Gideon said as he led her into a sunny living room. There were framed prints of sailboats all over the walls. The curtains were fashioned from old sails. The sliding doors opened to the bay where people balanced on stand-up paddleboards. "Airbnb didn't quite do justice to its nautical theme. But it's fine. Four bedrooms. Lots of space."

"It's nice." Lauren shivered as she hugged her bare arms to her chest. "I like sailboats."

"Are you cold?" Gideon asked. "The AC is on. I can turn it down. Open the windows."

"No, it's okay. It's just . . ," Lauren paused. "It's . . . this. It's a lot."

"I know."

Lauren glanced out at the bay again. A man paddled by with a dog in his kayak. She and Eric had come to Cape Cod once, years ago, for an October wedding. Someone Eric worked with. The bride had gotten embarrassingly drunk. Lauren wondered if they were still married, if they were happy.

"My friends from D.C. get here on Tuesday," Gideon explained as he wheeled Lauren's bag into a bedroom. "I know them from MSF but they got out years ago. They're in private practice now. Another friend might come down from New Hampshire at the end of the week. I'm still waiting to hear from him."

Lauren glanced at the dresser, the chair, the decorative lifesaver ring mounted on the wall. A large bed with a comforter covered in anchors. Was she really in a room with Gideon, both of them divorced? Would anything happen? If it did, would their bodies remember each other? Lauren dropped her hand to her middle. She had her scar from her C-section, a little extra weight on her hips.

"You'll like them," Gideon said. "Their kids are at camp now too."

"Wonderful," Lauren said. *Stop,* she told her brain. *Stop going to these places. Be here. Be present.* "I'm looking forward to meeting them. Thanks for inviting me along."

"I'm glad you're here."

"You must have friends all over the world."

Gideon nodded and crossed his arms over his chest. "That's definitely how it goes. I've lived everywhere, and I've also sort of lived nowhere. I have an apartment in Seattle that I keep but barely use. Sonia and I bought it years ago. She lives in Los Angeles now. She left MSF too."

Out on the bay, there was a loud splash. The dog had leapt off the kayak and was swimming toward shore.

"So," Gideon said.

"So," Lauren said.

Another splash. The man had jumped into the water, laughing and kicking as he pushed his kayak after the dog.

"Do you want to go first?" Gideon asked. "Maybe we could take a walk? There are some beautiful dunes near here. Or we could go to the ocean?"

"Go first?" Lauren asked.

"Your divorce. Your kids. Your last twenty years. Your app. I looked it up. It looks incredible."

Lauren had to laugh. "I'll need more than a few dunes and an ocean."

Gideon smiled. "The ocean is pretty big. But if we need more, there's always the sky."

Back when they were together, they used to lay on the grass in his backyard and look for the shapes in the clouds. Lauren touched her pulse again. It had finally started to slow down.

Over the next few hours, Lauren and Gideon hiked through miles of sand dunes—undulating golden mountains coated in mint-green beach grass. As they walked, Lauren told him about her marriage to Eric, the good, the bad, and the way it ended. What did she have to lose? If anything moved forward with Gideon—even just a friendship—she didn't want secrets. Gideon told her about his field assignment in Uzbekistan, and before that Yemen, where he was laid up for months with cholera. That was when his marriage fell apart, when Sonia left Doctors Without Borders and moved to California.

"Sonia and I were both so focused on our work, on trying to help save the world," he said as he brushed sand off his calf. "I realize that sounds lofty and pretentious out loud. But what I'm saying is that I think, in a way, we sacrificed building something together. Planting deeper roots."

Lauren paused at the top of a dune. She could see the Atlantic Ocean in the distance. Around them, couples took selfies and kids squealed as they rolled down sandy slopes.

"All I did for the past few decades was plant deep roots," Lauren said. "That doesn't always work out either."

Gideon nodded. "We also had the issue of kids."

"What about kids?"

"I wanted them . . . Sonia didn't. We could never move beyond that."

As they started walking again, he asked about Cady and Amelia. Lauren found herself smiling as she described Cady, her drama queen, and Amelia, who was in the brave process of figuring out their gender. Gideon asked questions, true questions, like he was really listening.

They reached the ocean. Gideon pointed out that her shoulders were getting red. The sun was scorching even though it was after four.

"I have sunblock in my backpack," he said. "Want some?"

"Sure . . . thanks."

The shock of sunblock felt icy on her skin. As Gideon swirled his hand over her neck, Lauren soaked in his touch, his gesture of intimacy. Eric always grumbled when Lauren asked him to do her shoulders. Never mind that she was the sunburn police for the rest of the family.

"My friend told me that Doctors Without Borders doctors are cowboys," Lauren said as they sat on the sand. The waves rolled into the shore and gulls screeched in the sky. A few people splashed in the surf but other than that the beach was empty.

Gideon laughed. "It's definitely true at times. I hope I wasn't a cowboy . . . but there is this attitude of being a tough guy, pushing through pain and discomfort for the sake of adventure, of being a hero."

"That sounds exciting, I guess," Lauren said.

"And exhausting." Gideon dug his toes in the sand. "I'm ready for a break. Maybe to establish a life somewhere. I took the summer off and then I need to let MSF know where I want to be."

"Can you choose? I don't know a lot about this world."

"I have a certain amount of seniority. I may ask for an office role. Their office in the States is in New York City."

"Really?" she asked.

As Gideon nodded, Lauren's arms prickled with goosebumps. *New York City?*

"Everything is in flux. It's scary. But I guess it's also good. I've been long overdue for a life reboot."

Lauren cracked up. "I know exactly what you're talking about."

After they drove back from the dunes, they retreated to their own rooms, showered, and changed for dinner. Sophie had texted Lauren asking how it was going. Lauren sent her a yellow thumbs-up and a round face kissing a heart.

Around dusk, they settled at a candlelit table in the backyard of an elegant restaurant. They ordered salads, wine, lobster paella for him, vegetable risotto for her. Gideon asked about the Wife App. He had read the press on it and surfed around the app. She told him how it came to be, how she and her friends were trying to right marital inequities. Gideon said that if they had the Wife App during their marriage, maybe Sonia would have agreed to have kids. She was worried that domestic responsibilities would fall on her by default.

"I feel like I've talked so much," Lauren told him as the check came.

They both raced to put down their credit cards.

"How about I get it tonight?" Gideon asked. "And I like hearing about your life. It's good to catch up."

Lauren put away her Visa. "As long as I can get dinner tomorrow."

When they returned to the house, Lauren felt so happy inside, so full. They'd been talking for hours and yet it seemed like the conversation had just begun. Also, with his white linen shirt and shorts that hung low on his hips, the man was sexy. No denying it.

Before she could second-guess herself, she gestured to her bedroom. "Want to come in?"

"Is that okay?" Gideon asked.

Lauren's chest felt tight as she pushed open her door. "Let's just see."

They stretched out on top of the comforter. His shirt had come up a little, revealing a line of hair that spread from his belly button into his shorts. As Lauren looked at it, she felt warmth between her legs.

"You still have your scar," she said. "I remember when you got it."

"You do? Middle school?"

"I didn't know you then. But I remember when it happened."

It was an ice-skating field trip in seventh grade. Lauren had been in another homeroom but the whole grade was combined for the day. She remembered there was blood on the ice. Several girls cried. The EMTs loaded a small boy into an ambulance.

"And you still have your dimple," Gideon said.

Lauren smiled. "Remember how you told me, when we broke up, that I would always be your Princess Bride?"

"Did I really say that? We were obsessed with that movie."

"Cady went through a phase where she watched *The Princess Bride* nonstop," she said. "I always thought of you."

Gideon rolled onto his side, his fingers on Lauren's mouth. Lauren pressed her hips toward Gideon. She wanted to. Or maybe she didn't. Maybe it was too much.

"I can't," she said suddenly.

All those years of obligatory sex with Eric. Never again. Moving forward, Lauren would only do it when she was completely certain.

"I don't know," she added. "I guess I'm not ready."

"Should I leave?"

"I think so. For now."

Gideon kissed Lauren's cheek. "As you wish," he said, quoting *The Princess Bride*. Then he pushed up from the bed and walked out the door.

The following morning, Lauren and Gideon ate omelets at an airy café, then held hands as they took in the manicured rhododendron bushes and pristine Cape Cod–style houses. Lauren wasn't sure what it meant that they were holding hands. Their fingers just found each other as they walked out of breakfast, and they stayed that way.

At a tourist shop, Lauren bought a small Pride flag for Amelia. Eric and Trish would finish visiting weekend soon. They were probably leaving Maine in the next few hours. She'd mail the flag to Amelia at camp, along with a letter asking if they told their dad about their gender. Lauren hoped Eric handled it well. She hoped he was kind.

A little before eleven, Lauren and Gideon strolled toward the rental house. He had a plan to meet someone who lived in Truro and play tennis on his private court.

"It won't be long." Gideon swatted at a mosquito on his arm. "You're welcome to come."

"You playing tennis brings back so many memories," Lauren said.

She used to watch his varsity matches, clapping and cheering from the sidelines.

"I was probably a lot better back then," Gideon said. "But this court will be nicer than the one in high school. This guy is a big MSF donor."

As they turned into the driveway, two shirtless men in bathing suits cycled past them. One wore a bike helmet and one didn't. Lauren wondered how you decided to take risks, or how you chose to protect yourself. She'd always been in the helmet camp but now she craved letting her hair blow in the wind a little.

"He's a nice guy," Gideon added, "but to be honest you'll likely be stuck drinking iced tea and making small talk with his husband."

Back when Lauren was a wife, she would have come along, made the chitchat, played the role. "I think I'll just read here."

After Gideon left, Lauren checked her phone. Madeline had texted some financial questions about the app. Sophie texted about a VIP job. Lauren responded to the questions, plugged in her phone, and stepped into the shower. As the warm water ran over her naked body, she shaved her legs. It was exciting to imagine her legs tightening around Gideon, the two of them moving together. Lauren had a feeling their bodies would still fit.

Just as she wrapped herself in a towel, her phone rang. She hurried over to glance at the screen. It was a Maine area code.

"Hello?" Lauren asked quickly.

"Mom?" It was Cady. Her voice was barely a whisper.

"Where are you calling from? Aren't you with Dad?"

"About that," Cady said.

"Is Amelia okay?" Lauren asked. "Did they tell Dad?"

"They're in the car waiting for Dad to drive us back to camp. Since I don't have my phone here I'm calling from the hotel phone." Cady started crying. "And no they didn't tell Dad because . . . he . . . doesn't . . . deseeeeerve . . ."

Lauren rubbed her towel over her hair. "Lovie, can you calm down? I can't understand you when you're hysterical."

"I'll try . . . but, Mooooom . . ."

As Lauren pulled on a bra and underwear, Cady described how she and Amelia had just been swimming in the hotel pool when Eric and Trish got into a fight on the deck. Trish screamed at Eric that one of her friends had seen him coming out of a suite in Hell's Kitchen the other day. The friend did some research and just texted Trish something about sex workers.

Lauren's body went cold. She raked through a drawer, wriggled a sundress over her head, and sank onto a chair. The wet towel soaked through her dress and onto her back.

Cady continued crying. "I'm freaking out, Mom. Like, is a sex worker a prostitute?"

Lauren's mouth felt dry. She reached for the cranberry seltzer, but the bottle was empty. "I'm so sorry you heard that."

"Amelia and I heard something else too," Cady said. "Trish was screaming, and you know what else she said?"

Lauren tapped her phone onto speaker and lowered her chin into her hands.

"Trish said that she should have known better," Cady sobbed. "She said, *Once a cheater, always a cheater*."

Lauren closed her eyes. She couldn't even look at the bed where she and Gideon had lain. How could she have considered having sex with him? How could she be vulnerable to anyone ever again?

Cady hiccupped. "Trish stormed off and said she was taking a bus back to New York. She didn't even say goodbye to us. Is it true, Mom? Did Dad cheat on you too?"

Lauren hated imagining her twins treading water in a sad hotel pool, learning things they never needed to know.

"Cady," she said slowly. "What happened between Dad and me is our business. I'm okay. I'm strong. The rest of the stuff . . . We'll talk about it when you get home from camp."

"Are you sure?" Cady sounded small and scared. "You're really okay?"

"You don't have to worry about me," Lauren lied. "Tell Amelia that too. Also, I'll call the camp director and make sure there's someone who can help you two at camp. Give you support."

Once Lauren hung up, she ran her hands back and forth over her thighs. Her muscles were cold with adrenaline. She stood up abruptly and hurried around the room, scooping up clothes, her book, the phone charger. She yanked at the comforter in a crude attempt to make the bed. Over the past year, she'd convinced herself that Eric's penchant for prostitutes was a symptom of their decaying marriage. But it was clear: Eric probably went to sex workers for their entire marriage. The evenings out, drinks with colleagues, all those work trips. Their marriage had been a lie.

Lauren carried the empty seltzer bottle to the recycling bin and then gripped her phone in her hand. She tapped the messaging app and hit Gideon's name.

> **Lauren:** Something came up. I have to leave early. I'm really sorry. Please apologize to your friends for me as well.

She watched the screen for a moment. No ellipsis. He was likely playing tennis. He wouldn't get her text for another half hour. By then, she'd be long gone. As Lauren dragged her bag to the car, her phone chimed.

> **Madeline:** Sorry to break up your sexy getaway but you need to hustle your ass home right now. We have the meeting of our lives tomorrow morning!

Lauren got in the car and steered onto Route 6. She'd just pulled in to get gas when her phone chimed again.

> **Eric:** It wasn't what it looked like.

> **Eric:** Call as soon as you can.

Lauren peered at the gas pump. She struggled to remember how to select the fuel grade. Her brain felt fuzzy. Once again, Eric had decimated her.

Her phone rang.

Gideon.

Lauren switched it to "do not disturb" and slumped against the car door, her face wet with tears.

"It's anonymous investors," Madeline explained the next morning as they hurried through the Flatiron District. They had planned to meet at a café ahead of time to do a run-through of the pitch, but Lauren had been too distraught to get out of bed. She cried into her pillow, and texted Madeline and Sophie that she was running late. Her lids were swollen and she'd dusted on makeup to cover the bags under her eyes.

"I've talked on the phone with them several times but this isn't even their main office," Madeline added. "It's a satellite branch. They're being very discreet about their identity but they have an impressive portfolio, and lots of money."

"Why anonymous?" Sophie asked as she slid on lipstick.

They showed their licenses to a uniformed security guard in the lobby and collected their stick-on paper ID badges.

"This sometimes happens with high-profile investors," Madeline said. As they stepped onto the elevator, she turned her phone camera on herself to check her reflection. "They don't want other investors taking notice. These things get competitive fast. But the lead investor—he's a bit of a hotshot—he's offering a million or two. I may push for three."

"Three *million*?" Sophie asked, her voice high. She wore cream slacks, a lime-green top, and flats. It was hard for Lauren to see much beyond how awful she felt right now. But if she could appreciate Sophie for a moment, she'd say that her friend looked radiant.

"That's the range we're in," Madeline said.

"I'm so nervous," Sophie said.

"It's okay," Madeline said. "I'm ready. I'll do all the talking. You just be prepared to field questions."

Lauren sighed. Everything hurt so much—her heart, her brain, her eyeballs. All she could think about was Eric's deception, her lost decades, ditching Gideon in Cape Cod. She sighed again.

"Are you okay?" Madeline asked Lauren. The elevator passed twenty-two, twenty-three.

Lauren couldn't talk. If she spoke, she would cry.

"Is it something about Gideon?" Madeline asked. "I'm sorry we had to bust it up. Maybe you can get on a plane back to the Cape this afternoon? I'm happy to buy you a ticket."

"I thought it went well," Sophie said. "You texted me that thumbs-up."

Lauren stared up at the floors. *Twenty-seven, twenty-eight, twenty-nine.* They were going to thirty-two.

The elevator opened to a sweeping floor-through office—high ceilings, mounted graffiti, a large neon sign that read: *Adrenaline Is My Drug of Choice.* An extremely tall man and two thin women in black glasses approached them.

The tall man introduced himself as Archer, the lead investor. The women said they were analysts. Two more men appeared, not quite as tall but dressed in similar summer casual. Lauren, Sophie, and Madeline followed them into a conference room. The table was arranged with bottles of Pellegrino, trays of iced coffee. On the screen, there was a projection of the Wife App logo.

Madeline nodded approvingly as she settled into a chair. Lauren flanked her on one side, Sophie on the other.

"I'll start off by saying that we're big, big fans," Archer said. He sat at the head of the table. The other men and the two analysts sat down next. Both women opened their laptops.

"Good to hear," Madeline said.

Sophie reached for a glass bottle of sparkling water. Lauren held her hands in her lap, twisting the ID badge and then tearing it in half.

Archer kicked off the meeting with a speech about how he'd been following the Wife App for months, ever since the celebrity acupuncturist gave it props. He had his analysts run the numbers and they were blown away by the rapid expansion, the untapped potential. He spoke quickly and drummed his pen against the table. One of his male sidekicks jiggled his knee. The analysts barely looked up from their laptops.

"You clearly have all the numbers worked out," Archer added, "and you're in strong financial shape to court an investor."

One of the other guys said, "Of course, we have questions."

"Fire away," Madeline said.

"Your finances are airtight," the third guy said. "And the market analysis is fantastic. We're ready to infuse a bundle of money and take the Wife App to the next level. We're thinking L.A., Houston, Chicago."

Madeline clicked her pen in and out. "Is that your question?"

"Don't take this the wrong way," Archer said, "but people on our team were wondering about . . . well . . . about the *range* of your services. They want to make sure you're only meeting Spouses for platonic Wife jobs. So tell us your rules. Reassure us that you're legit."

Madeline laughed hoarsely. "Are you asking if we're a prostitution service? Because the answer is no. We don't set up sex work on this app."

Archer dragged his finger over his shiny forehead. "We didn't mean it that way. We just want to cover our asses."

"Reassure them, Lauren," Madeline said. She turned toward Lauren with a twinkle in her eyes. She was loving this. "Tell them, Sophie. They seem to think we have sex with the Spouses we meet on the app instead of managing all the boring aspects of their lives."

Sophie drained her water, then reached for another bottle. Ever since Lauren had known Sophie, she'd been uncomfortable talking about sex.

Lauren cleared her throat. "We would never engage in a physical relationship with someone we met over the Wife App."

Archer nodded, satisfied. "So it's more like nineteen-fifties throwback housewife stuff?"

"You think fifties housewives didn't have sex?" Madeline grinned. "I'm teasing you. It's the basic mental load from any decade."

Archer tilted back in his chair, arms crossed over his chest. "Well, we would love to make you our Wives. We are prepared to offer two point three million but—"

Lauren's heart surged. "What did you just say?"

"What's that?" Archer asked.

"About the financials?" one of the other guys asked. "He said we are prepared to offer—"

"No, the other thing," Lauren said. "You said 'we would love to make you our Wives.'"

"Yeah." Archer frowned. "That's what I said."

A hush fell over the conference room. The analysts peered up from their laptops. Sophie set down her water a little too loudly. Madeline touched Lauren's arm as if to say, *Everything okay?*

Lauren slid her phone out of her bag. Madeline turned to Archer, who cleared his throat awkwardly. *We'd love to make you our Wives.* Eric told her those same words back in April, when he called Lauren to say that his company was interested in investing. Could it be possible that this guy, Archer, worked with Eric? Could it be possible that they came in as anonymous investors because if Lauren realized the truth she would never consent to this?

Lauren opened Life360 and her eyes moved over the screen.

Sure enough, Eric's dot placed him in this building. Lauren hadn't realized that Equity had a satellite office but clearly they did and Eric was right here. Right now.

Lauren swiveled her chair toward the glass wall. There were several closed doors lining the hallway. Was Eric waiting behind one of them, ready to toast Archer as soon as she left?

Lauren tapped Eric's name, then held her phone to her ear. It rang once, twice.

"Laur?" Madeline's voice was tight, her smile tense.

Sophie began to itch her hand.

Lauren put her phone on speaker. "Listen to this."

"Lauren?" Eric's voice said. "What's going on?"

"Hey, Eric," she said to her ex-husband. "Why don't you come in here? We're in the conference room with the glass wall."

Madeline's eyes went big. Sophie's mouth dropped open. Archer glanced nervously at his associates. The two analysts closed their laptops, their mouths curved in amusement.

"Wait," Eric said. "Uh. Wait. We can—"

"Forget it." Lauren hung up. She nodded to her friends, who were already gathering their things. "Let's get out of here."

Archer unfolded to his full height. He was a big guy, maybe six five. "Eric Turner is really just in the background. He was helping secure this from the periphery."

Madeline snorted. "Yeah . . . no thanks."

Archer moved toward the door as if to intercept them. "We wanted to be discreet, given Eric and Lauren's marital history."

Lauren spotted Eric on the other side of the glass. He'd shaved his beard, cut his hair. As she glanced at him, she realized there was no love left. She no longer felt nostalgia over folding his boxers, buying his cookies, stroking the blond hair on his chest as they lay in bed. She was done. She owed him nothing.

"We can drop Eric in a second," Archer snapped his fingers loudly, bone on bone. "Eric is disposable."

"I agree," Lauren said. "But no. Keep him. You guys deserve each other."

Lauren, Sophie, and Madeline walked past Archer, past Eric, past the neon sign. Lauren forced herself to hold it together until she got to the elevator.

"Oh. My. God!" Madeline said as the doors closed. She wrapped her arms around Lauren and pulled her in. "Oh, Lauren. I had no idea. If I had any idea, I never would have taken this meeting."

As the elevator descended, Lauren tried to explain about Archer's "Wife" comment but the tears were coming so fast. They stepped into the lobby, off to one side, near a waxy fern.

"We are walking away from more than two million in funding because of me," Lauren said, suppressing a hiccup. "I should have asked you to go outside and discuss it."

"Don't be ridiculous," Madeline said. "It's one for all and all for one. Right, Soph?"

They both looked over at Sophie and realized that she was crying too.

"Sophie." Lauren rested her hands on her friend's shoulders. They were so narrow, as small as when she was eighteen. "I'm sorry I let us walk away from—"

"That's not it," Sophie said. She wiped her hands across her wet face. "I broke the Wife App rules. When he said that before about our rules . . . I've broken them and it could ruin us."

Lauren and Madeline glanced at each other, then back to Sophie.

"I'm having sex with someone I connected with through the Wife App." Sophie hugged her arms to her blouse and stared at the floor. "You should get rid of me because I broke the Wife App's code of conduct."

"The airplane tycoon?" Lauren asked.

Sophie stared at Lauren, then laughed through her tears. "Samuel Bliss? No! He and his wife are finally talking again. He's so happy he's offered me a free chartered flight anywhere in the world. Didn't I tell you that? I was thinking—"

"Sophie," Lauren said. "What's going on?"

Sophie rubbed her hands on her slacks. "I'm in love with Beatrice. We're in love with each other."

"Beatrice, Joshua's wife?" Madeline asked.

"Ex-wife," Sophie said. "Remember I told you that she left him?"

"She left him for you?" Lauren asked.

Sophie bobbed her head. "She contacted me through the Wife App . . . for advice. We met up twice through the app. So even though I knew her before, the Wife App brought us together. I totally messed up and I should step down."

"Sophie," Lauren said. "Of course you're still on the app."

Sophie's eyes began to stream again.

"For one, you didn't meet Beatrice through the app," Madeline said. "And, yes, we want to hear everything . . . but as your friends. Because we're excited for you! But we're not letting you leave. For two—"

"Who the fuck cares if people think we're a prostitution service?" Lauren asked suddenly. "Sex workers should get paid for what they do. I'm over being shocked about that. I just don't want my husband paying for sex. That's my line."

"What's the second thing?" Sophie asked. "Madeline, you said, *for two?*"

Madeline grinned. "How's the sex?"

"Really fucking amazing," Sophie said.

"Let's not worry about those dickwads upstairs." Madeline linked arms with Lauren and then Sophie. "I'll find something better."

The three of them walked across the lobby and into the sunlight. It had only been forty-five minutes. Maybe an hour. But it felt like a lifetime.

That afternoon, Lauren walked along the Hudson. She walked thirty, forty blocks. When she got home, she drank a glass of water, stuck Band-Aids on her blisters, and went right back out and headed to Central Park. As she walked, she tried not to think about the look on Eric's face as he realized he no longer wielded power over her. She tried not to think about how they'd turned down Archer's millions. She tried not to think about that phone call from Cady. She tried not to think about Gideon.

On Tuesday, Wednesday, Thursday, and Friday, Lauren blew past all previous walking data on her phone.

On Saturday evening, she took Coco for a walk down West End Avenue even though it was pouring rain. When she got back to her lobby her raincoat was drenched and her shorts stuck to her legs. As soon as she saw him, she pulled in a sharp breath.

"Gideon."

"Hey." He gave her a half-wave, then lowered his hand to his side.

"How long have you been here?"

"About fifteen minutes," he said. "Your doorman said you were walking the dog."

Lauren wrapped the leash around her wrist once, then twice. "How did you get my address?"

"My little sister messaged your friend Sophie," he said. "I asked them to keep it quiet because I wanted to . . . It's just . . . I left Cape Cod this morning."

"I'm sorry I took off like that. That totally wasn't cool." Lauren bit her bottom lip. "Some stuff came up with my kids. With my ex. More of what I told you about. I freaked out."

"I'm so sorry. I know that's not easy."

"It is what it is."

Gideon ran his hands through his hair. "I talked to my friends a lot about you. About us. I realize we don't have a clear path. But they encouraged me to come, even just to say goodbye in person."

Beside Lauren, Coco shook her fur, spraying wet dots onto the lobby floor.

"Want to come upstairs?" Lauren said. "I should dry the dog."

"If that's okay . . . I don't want to . . ."

"Yes," Lauren said. "I'd like that."

In the apartment, Gideon went to the bathroom while Lauren rubbed the dog with a towel and changed into dry clothes. A few minutes later, they sat on the couch and Lauren poured them both a glass of wine.

"What did you tell your friends?" She thought she'd be nervous having Gideon in her space, but she was glad he was here. It felt natural.

Gideon shrugged. "I told them how good it was to reconnect. It's been an intense few years, with getting cholera and also splitting up with Sonia. And then, since the divorce, I buried myself in work without taking time to consider having a life. But then I saw you on that plane and it brought back so much. I was trying to be practical about long distance when we went to college. It's crazy to even talk about that time. We were kids, you know? I guess I wish we could do it over. . . ."

Lauren took his hand and clasped it between both of hers. Gideon was saying a lot of what she'd thought over the past several months—the desire to do it over. Except maybe that's not how it works. Maybe life is about muddling through the hard stuff, trying to do a little better every time.

"I'm glad we're here now," she said as she rubbed her thumb across his knuckles.

Gideon sipped his wine. "I still have no idea where I'll be next year."

"Me neither," Lauren said. "I mean, yes. In this apartment. But the big picture. I have no idea too."

Gideon touched her cheek with his hand. "Is it okay if I kiss you? I've been wanting to kiss you since last Saturday, or maybe since I saw you on the plane with that crazy kid."

"Matthias." Lauren groaned.

Gideon's brown eyes were trained on her.

After a moment, Lauren nodded. "As you wish."

TWO MONTHS LATER

lauren

"I'VE GOT A COMPELLING INVESTMENT possibility," Madeline told Lauren on the phone. "It's coming together quickly. We need to act fast."

It was a late September afternoon, and the school year was in full swing. Manhattan, after two lazy months, was filled to capacity. People hurried to work while moms and nannies stared at their phones on playground benches. Cady and Amelia had started eighth grade this month. They were handling the academic stress with more maturity than Lauren expected. As far as their dad, it was a mixed bag. Amelia had refused to see Eric since they got back from camp. Cady met him for a few dinners but no longer wanted to sleep over. Both kids were set up with good therapists now, and they often all laughed through the tears. They were muddling through.

"Who's this meeting with?" Lauren asked. She was at an outdoor café on Broadway, sipping an Americano with almond milk and pinching up bits of a pumpkin muffin. She was partially paying attention to Madeline but also scrolling through Mental Loads. The Wife App had been quiet in August but after Labor Day weekend they had an explosion of new users.

"It's a tech investment firm from Seattle," Madeline said. "It could be big. I've mostly spoken with the junior acquisition team but the boss wants to meet us. They said they can do tomorrow, four-thirty, at an office on Columbus Circle. Can you swing it?"

Lauren nodded to herself. Madeline had lined up several meetings over the eight weeks since they'd walked away from Eric and Archer. Unfortunately, none had worked out. The investors either didn't get the mission of the Wife App or they wanted more control than Madeline was willing to relinquish.

"Let me talk to Sophie," Lauren said. "Hopefully she can come into the city. I'll get back to you."

As soon as Lauren hung up, she texted to see if Sophie could join tomorrow. It made things more complicated that Sophie and Beatrice lived in the Hudson Valley. They'd rented a cottage up there so the boys could start the school year in the district where they were buying. When Sophie showed Lauren photos of the stone house in New Rochelle—they were closing in November—she looked like she was about to explode. Lauren had known Sophie for more than half her life and this was the happiest she'd ever seen her.

Lauren texted Sophie again. When she didn't hear back, she called her.

"Hey, you're on speakerphone!" Sophie shouted. "Was that you texting just now?"

"Yeah . . . Where are you?"

Sophie explained that she was carpooling Noah and Charlie to soccer, then driving Clementine to her swim lesson. Lauren took a bite of muffin and conjured an image of Sophie as a soccer mom. With her blond bob, leggings, and sneakers, she fit the bill. Thankfully, Sophie had reassured Lauren that she and Beatrice were determined to do it differently, to never let anyone feel exploited.

"Can you come into the city for a meeting tomorrow?" Lauren asked. "Madeline has investors lined up."

"What time?"

"Four-thirty. Though we should meet before to review the pitch."

"Bah bah bah," Clementine said from the background.

"Mom?" Charlie's voice asked. "Can Clem have a banana? She keeps reaching for mine."

"That's fine," Sophie said. "Just peel it for her and let her gnaw on it. Let me see if I can get a sitter for Clementine and the boys, and I'll get back to you. Give me a few minutes."

As Lauren waited for Sophie to respond, she texted hi to Gideon and he texted back a heart. He was living in Seattle for the fall as he negotiated his contract with MSF. It looked like New York City could happen. Either way, they planned to meet somewhere in between their two cities next month. Maybe Austin or Chicago. Lauren wasn't making any commitments but she also wasn't closing doors.

A new text appeared on the screen.

> **Sophie:** I got a sitter for Clem and the boys. I'm in.

> **Sophie:** And Beatrice is coming home early so I can stay as long as we need!

Lauren sent Sophie a thumbs-up and then texted Madeline that they were on.

The next afternoon, Lauren, Sophie, and Madeline walked across the lobby of a steel-and-glass skyscraper. Madeline smiled on the elevator ride up. She wouldn't tell them anything about these potential investors, but her excitement was palpable.

"I'm so nervous," Sophie said.

"We'll be fine," Madeline said breezily. "I've got this."

Lauren watched Madeline for a moment. Her friend had always been confident about her beauty, her sex appeal, her financial stability. But this take-charge Madeline was something new. A month ago, she'd put Arabella on a plane to London and then worked twelve-hour days on the Wife App finances. She told Lauren that she missed her daughter but she was okay. She was happy Arabella could have this year with her dad.

As the elevator doors opened, a young man led them down a hallway to a sunny office with a sweeping view of midtown. Outside the office door, two men in gray suits kept watch, their expressions fixed straight ahead.

There was a woman at the broad desk, her back to them. Her silver hair was perfectly styled. Her high heels were crossed in front of her. When the man walked out, she spun around.

Lauren sucked in her breath. It was Anika Kim, the tech giant! Anika Kim, who devastated Lauren by telling her that the Wife App was nothing more than a prostitution service without the sex.

"Madeline Wallace," Anika Kim said. She extended her hand. "Lauren Zuckerman. Sophie Smart. Sit down. Please."

As Lauren sat in one of the empty chairs, she glanced at Madeline, who winked at her. Sophie stared in awe at Anika Kim, then reached up and tucked a strand of hair behind her ear.

"I'll cut to the chase," Anika Kim told them. "I've been watching the Wife App since you and I met in March, Lauren. You've done everything I wanted you to do. You've exceeded all my expectations."

Lauren allowed herself to soak in those words. *You've done everything I wanted you to do. You've exceeded all my expectations.* Seriously, if she didn't accomplish one more thing in her entire professional life she would always have this moment.

Anika Kim pressed both hands on her desk, smiled, and then said, "I'm prepared to offer you ten million in funding to take the Wife App to the next level."

For a second, nobody said anything. Lauren and Sophie were too stunned to speak. Finally, Madeline whistled under her breath. It was the first time Lauren had ever seen Madeline shocked about money.

Anika Kim laughed. "Unless that's too much."

"No, no . . . not at all," Madeline said. "Tell us your terms."

"The terms are that the three of you retain fifty percent control. My company will have the other fifty percent, and with that I will serve in an advisor capacity. I've got plans to grow the Wife App beyond your wildest dreams. My lawyer has the paperwork drafted and ready to go. I can have her send it to your lawyer to review. I'm flying back to Seattle tomorrow morning but I'm sure we'll be in close touch. How does that sound?"

"It sounds amazing," Lauren said, "but—"

"There's a 'but'?" Anika Kim asked, her voice fast.

Lauren felt her friends' eyes on her, staring hard. She wouldn't let herself look back at them or she'd lose her nerve.

"When you said you'd grow the Wife App beyond our wildest dreams," Lauren said, "what do you mean by that?"

"Good question," Anika Kim said. "Of course we'll add more regional markets, scale up until we're nationwide. By February of next year, I plan to take out a Super Bowl ad. I like to go big. It'll be toward the end of the game, when the rates come down, but we'd still reach more than a hundred million viewers."

Lauren nodded calmly even though her heart pounded. *A Super Bowl ad?* Jesus.

"But you realize," Lauren said, still refusing to catch her friends' eyes, "that the Super Bowl attracts more male viewers than female? I think it's about fifty percent of American men versus twenty-five or thirty percent of women."

Anika Kim's lips tightened. "I've run a dozen Super Bowl ads over the years, Lauren. And that's the point. We want to reach men with the Wife App. We want to own the entire male experience. You need a Wife to make your days easier? Here is a solution flashed right in front of your face."

Was Anika Kim getting pissed? Well, Lauren wasn't afraid of a little anger. It wouldn't kill her.

"It's a perfect goal to own the male experience," Lauren said, "but we also want to present women with solutions. We want to meet women where they are too. Football-viewing women but also women who watch chick flicks or true-crime dramas. If we sign with you, I want a commitment that for every Super Bowl ad, we reach the same number of women."

"You want that in the contract?"

"I realize we didn't discuss this part on the phone." Madeline smiled stiffly. "If you need time to think it over, we can—"

"No," Anika Kim said sharply.

"No?" Lauren asked. Underneath her blouse, she was sweating bullets.

"No, I don't need time. You made a solid point." Anika Kim sighed. "You drive a hard bargain, Lauren Zuckerman. But I'm not going to hold that against you."

"So it's a yes?" Lauren asked. Her stomach churned and her head grew light with excitement.

"It's a yes from me," Anika Kim said. "What about you three?"

Lauren glanced at Madeline, then Sophie, and they all nodded.

"Yes from us!" Lauren said.

"Welcome aboard," Anika Kim said. "Here's to dismantling the marriage institution one user at a time."

Once the meeting was over, they headed uptown to the Lincoln. After they settled into a booth—two booths over from where they celebrated Lauren's divorce—they went back and forth with the waiter over which champagne to order. It was the same blond surfer guy from a year ago. His hair was longer and streaked with late summer sunshine.

A few minutes later, he brought over the Cristal, three flutes, and a bottle of sparkling water.

"Thanks," Lauren told him.

He grinned. "No worries!"

Lauren watched him walk away. He suddenly didn't seem like such a dreamy hunk anymore, nor did Lauren envy his freedom. Anyway, worry wasn't the worst thing. Worry pushes you to get shit done.

"I still can't believe it," Sophie said.

"How come you didn't tell us it was Anika Kim?" Lauren asked.

"I once read a *New Yorker* profile on her," Sophie said. "There was this famous meeting, like with Microsoft or Apple, where she literally dismissed several top male executives from the room because they wouldn't stop talking over a female colleague. And it's not like she was easy on women! In the profile alone, two different women said Anika Kim routinely left them in tears, but they also admired her more than anyone on the planet. I can't believe you got her to accept that request, Lauren. I was so nervous I almost wet my pants."

"Truth?" Madeline asked. "Me too."

Lauren raised one hand in the air. "That makes three of us."

"It all happened quickly," Madeline said. "Her people contacted me, looked over our finances, and we set up this meeting. It felt too good to be true. I didn't want to jinx it."

The three women raised their glasses but before they could clink, Sophie declared, "Here's to new beginnings and happy endings!"

Lauren and Madeline burst out laughing.

"What?" Sophie asked. She raised her eyebrows as she looked back and forth between her friends. "What did I say?"

"'Happy endings,' Soph," Madeline said. She pantomimed sliding her free hand in and out from her crotch. "As in hand jobs."

Lauren doubled over laughing. "Probably not the best toast. Given how the Wife App started."

"Well, I didn't mean *those* happy endings," Sophie said.

"It's okay," Lauren said. "I'll toast to any kind of happy ending that got us to this one."

"To happy endings!" they all cried out as they clinked their glasses together.

acknowledgments

I am beyond lucky to have the best and fiercest agent in the business. Jodi Reamer and I have been together longer than I've known my husband, and I'm eternally grateful for this publishing marriage. Thank you to my editor, Carina Guiterman, who is smart, funny, insightful, and somehow convinces me that I can do this. Also at Simon & Schuster, thanks to Lashanda Anakwah, Hannah Bishop, Danielle Prielipp, Kgabo Mametja, Natalia Olbinski, Jackie Seow, Lara Robbins, and Morgan Hart. At Writers House, thanks to Kate Boggs, Cecilia de la Campa, and Maja Nikolic. At William Morris Endeavor, thank you to Anna DeRoy, Nicole Weinroth, Lara Bahr, and Stephanie Shipman. Thanks to Daniel Berkowitz for the web design. And a massive thanks to Marysue Rucci, who said yes.

Thank you to my friends—my writer friends, my mom friends, my wife friends—for the walks, laughs, lunches, gossip, phone calls, hugs, and advice; for reading drafts of *The Wife App*; for answering my endless questions about emotional labor and marital roles. You help carry my mental load, and I hope I do the same. Thanks and love to: Dina Abderhalden, Jenny Falcon, Sarah Banerjee, Jaclyn Okin Barney, Caroline Baron, Judy Blume, Sara Leeder Bonin, Wendy Brawer,

Dianne Choie, Betsy Codding, Juliet Eastland, Gayle Forman, E. R. Frank, Mariah Fredericks, Ashley Goodwin, Jenny Greenberg, Amy Harmon, Louise Klebanoff, Sarah Klock, Runa Øyehaug Lundqvist, Cary McLaughlin, Abbey Nova, Stephanie Rath, Jennifer Roloff, Sara Sanders, Melissa van Twest, Krista Wathney, Melissa Weiner, Ismée Williams, Jacqueline Woodson, and Gabrielle Zevin.

Thanks to everyone who helped me seem knowledgeable about tech, start-ups, Juilliard Pre-College, B-school, and custody battles: Leah Amory, Joanna Catalano, Hsin-Yun Huang, Kelly Levy, Brandon McCoy, Viola Pirri, and Noreen Wu.

I am indebted to the Wages for Housework movement, which issued brave demands for financial compensation for domestic work. Much of this is documented in *Wages for Housework: A History of an International Feminist Movement, 1972–77* by Louise Toupin and *Revolution at Point Zero: Housework, Reproduction, and Feminist Struggle* by Silvia Federici. Thanks to Claire Cain Miller for her coverage on gender, work, and family in the *New York Times*, and Charles Duhigg and Anna Wiener for their eloquent articles on Silicon Valley in the *New Yorker*. The stories in Emotional Thread: The MetaFilter Thread Condensed edited by Olivia K. Lima, Josh Millard, and Timid Robot Zehta were hilarious, heartbreaking, and fully relatable. Thanks to the StartUp podcast for giving me a peek into what it's like to launch a start-up.

Thanks to my family. Without the steady support of my parents, stepparents, parents-in-law, aunts, uncles, and cousins, I wouldn't be able to do what I love to do. My deepest gratitude to my husband, Jonas Rideout, and my boys, Miles Rideout and Leif Rideout. You are my people and I love you forever.

about the author

Carolyn Mackler is the acclaimed author of the YA novels *The Earth, My Butt, and Other Big Round Things; Infinite in Between;* and *The Future of Us* (cowritten with Jay Asher), among others. Her novels have been translated into more than twenty-five languages. Carolyn lives in New York City with her husband and two sons. *The Wife App* is her first novel for adults. Visit her online at **carolynmackler.com**.